A NIGHT TO REMEMBER

Honoria opened the door. Scanning the room, she gave a silent gasp, too awed to speak. Burning tapers lined the nightstands and mantel, casting everything in muted, undulating shadows. The candle-filled table, set with sparkling crystal and snowy white linen, held domed warming dishes, an elegant floral arrangement, and a variety of silverware. Classical music played softly in the background, completing the romantic setting. The only thing missing was fairy dust or some other magical element that might prove the scene was a dream.

Holding a glass of champagne, Alex stood in front of the fireplace. Staring into the flames, he seemed so lost in thought it took every bit of self-control for Honoria to hold her curiosity in check and not ask what he was thinking. She cleared her throat and he started, then quickly turned. His robe gaped open, and she tried not to ogle.

"I thought I'd change into something more—" She worried her lower lip as warmth flooded her face. Well, duh! How corny did that sound?

Alex eased into a lazy grin, which brought her heated cheeks to the flash point. "Comfortable?" he said, finishing the sentence. "I wondered if I was ever going to see you in one of those gowns."

"You did?"

He ambled around the sofa. Stopping at the table, his jaw clenched as his gaze raked her from head to toe. "How about if you wear the red one?"

Dumbly, she nodded and bent to take it out of the drawer. Clutching it to her chest, she said, "I'll just be a second."

"Take all the time you need." He folded his arms, blocking the heady view of his finely muscled chest covered in curling, golden hair. "But hurry."

Other Kensington books by Judi McCoy

I DREAM OF YOU
(Waldenbook's Best-Selling
Debut Romance of 2001)

YOU'RE THE ONE

SAY YOU'RE MINE

HEAVEN IN YOUR EYES
(Fallen Angel Review's Best
Kensington book of 2003)

HEAVEN SENT

MATCH MADE IN HEAVEN

Judi McCoy

ZEBRA BOOKS
KENSINGTON PUBLISHING CORP.
http://www.kensingtonbooks.com

Prologue

"Sit down, Junior. We need to talk."

Junior gave an earnest grin and dropped into the chair-shaped cloud across from Milton's pristine white marble desk. He'd been waiting forever for this promotion to full-fledged guiding angel with his own roster of souls. He shifted to the edge of his seat. Better not look too comfortable, he thought. Or too cocky. This was Milton, after all. The Special-Angel-in-Charge.

"I've been reviewing your work," Milton began. Steepling his fingers, he tapped them on his dimpled chin. "You've done an acceptable job."

Acceptable! That was it? Not stellar or outstanding, or even excellent? Merely acceptable?

Junior hid his disappointment behind another eager grin. No need to get upset. Coming from Milton, acceptable was fine praise. It was just that he'd hoped for so much more.

"Thank you," he responded, showing plenty of teeth. It was said the Doughboy loved a cheerful angel.

"Have you looked in on Eloise and Nathan lately? Can you give me a report?"

Puffing out his chest, Junior tucked his thumbs under

his suspenders. On that topic, at least, he was an expert. "Head over heels in love and happily married for almost a year now. Nathan decided to take that desk job after all. Eloise is expecting their first child—a girl, by the way, just as little Phoebe ordered—with two sons to follow in rapid succession. Things are looking A-OK, if I do say so myself."

Milton's blue eyes twinkled at the job well done. "Good, good." He sat back and folded his hands on the desk. "So tell me, how do you think *you're* doing?"

Junior smoothed a hand over his crew cut. Could be this was a trick question. You just never knew with the Special-Angel-in-Charge. "I think I'm doing okay, too," he hedged. "I kind of like seeing to it that people are happy, you know?"

"Ah, yes." Milton's cherubic cheeks rounded in a grin. "That I do. I surely do." He raised a plump hand, and a large book embossed with gold lettering appeared. The leaves fluttered and turned of their own accord until they remained open on a page. Running a finger down one margin, he muttered to himself. As if satisfied he'd found what he was looking for, he raised his blue eyes and gave Junior a penetrating stare.

"You should know that, so far, you've been given tasks We consider to be mundane. This next test is going to be a bit more daunting. We need to make certain you're capable of working under pressure when there are, shall we say, tougher nuts to crack." Milton sat back in his chair. "Do you think you're up to it, my boy?"

Junior swallowed down his hesitation. Better not say no, or he could blow his chance at the big promotion. "Yeah, sure. Why not? Lay it on me."

"I must warn you, it won't be easy. You'll be dealing with two humans who are worlds apart on the outside, but soul mates within. Both are stubborn and set in their ways, each positive true love will never find them."

"So was Nathan, and I managed to get him to see the light," Junior pointed out. "How bad can these two be?"

"Ah, but you weren't Nathan's guiding angel, and Eloise was the one who did most of the work." Milton closed his eyes. "I'm so pleased she made the correct choice. I always knew she had the potential to be an excellent human being."

"Right, right. Eloise is a saint." Junior moved to the edge of his chair and tried to read upside down.

The heavenly tome snapped closed, and he jumped. Waggling a finger, Milton chuckled. "Honoria Hewitt and Alexander Vandencort. Are you familiar with either of them?"

"Honoria is that prissy woman at El's school, if I remember right." Junior wrinkled his brow. "But I don't know anyone named Alexander Vanden-whosits."

Milton's chuckle turned to outright laughter. "Oh, you will, my boy. Believe me, you will."

"So, uh, which one of them is mine?"

Milton crossed his arms over his plentiful middle. "Alex will be yours permanently. His angel hasn't exactly turned the boy in, but he is frustrated. And since Honoria's angel is embroiled in a bit of a crisis at the moment, you're in charge of her, as well. It's your final test, Junior. Fail and you'll be shopping for a new winter coat, because it's back to the polar ice cap for you." Milton raised a bushy white brow. "Still think you can handle it?"

"You mean all I have to do is get them together and I've passed? I'll get my own list of souls to care for permanently?"

"That's right. Just see to it that Honoria and Alexander fall in love and make a total commitment to cherish one another until death do them part. It's the only thing We want to see up here, remember?"

"Yes, sir." He stood. "Are there any special instructions? Do I have a time frame?"

"You do. Unfortunately, it's a short one. Just nine earthly days, ten at the outside. I'm going to expect regular updates via the Heavenly Net—if the pesky thing is up and running." He frowned. "I detest modern technology. It's so—so—technical. And the programmers up here are rather full of themselves." He sighed. "But back to the matter at hand. Alex and Honoria—still think you can do it?"

Rocking back on his heels, Junior thumbed his suspenders again. Before he'd been given the chance to be a guiding angel, he'd seriously considered applying for a transfer to one of the new HeavenNet positions. But now that he'd had a chance to work with humans, he felt the same as Milton. Humans were so much more personal than technology.

"Piece of cake."

"So you say. Now remember, daily reports listing your progress—nothing less. Is that clear?"

Junior opened his mouth to speak, and Milton waved a dismissive hand, sending the angel-in-training from view. "Oh, my boy, if only you knew what you were getting yourself into," he said with a smile. "If only you knew."

Chapter One

"Hold still, Honoria. How do you expect me to zip up this dress if you keep wriggling?"

Honoria Hewitt tugged at the bodice of the strapless, fire-engine-red dress and for the first time in her life thanked her Maker for giving her a figure that would do Mae West proud. Without her ample bosom, the top of this scandalous evening gown would have slipped to her waist with her first indrawn breath.

"I wouldn't be wriggling if the darned thing wasn't cutting off my circulation. I still don't understand why you didn't buy a bigger size or let me wear a—a—foundation garment."

"Trust me, Honoria, it is the proper size," snapped Ruth Roberts. "And modern women no longer blush when they use words like bra or lingerie, no matter what your mother told you. Besides, the dress has a built-in underwire, so you needn't worry." She walked around to Honoria's backside. "You are wearing those thong panties we bought, aren't you?"

Honoria's face burned with embarrassment. "I am, and they are the most insubstantial and uncomfortable underpants I have ever worn. I simply can't imagine a sensible woman going about her business with little more than a string up her you-know-where all day."

"Women don't buy lingerie to be sensible—they buy it to have fun. Something you could use a bit more of in your life," teased Ruth, who had circled back to Honoria's front. She tossed out a blinding smile. "Today's women do not wear underpants, at least none of the ones under sixty. They wear thongs or bikinis or G-strings in lace, satin, spandex, and sometimes even leather, and it wouldn't hurt you to do the same. It's about time everybody learns what a fantastic body you've been hiding under all that scratchy gray wool."

Honoria wanted to tell Ruth she needed to have her eyes examined, that women who were five-feet-nine and weighed one-sixty on a slim day were not considered to have fantastic bodies, but she just couldn't spit out the words. In the past year, she'd found her first true female friends and she didn't want to lose them, even if Faith Hewitt would disapprove because they were mothers of her students.

When they'd gotten wind of her financial difficulties, her friends had gone on a crusade to hold this charity auction, and nothing she'd said could dissuade them.

"If Mother were here, she'd be positively—" Before she finished the sentence, someone swiped the glasses from her nose, setting her adrift in a haze of throaty feminine laughter and diamond-like sparkles. "Hey! Wait! I can't see without those!"

One of her self-appointed guards snickered, but Honoria couldn't identify the traitor, especially since everything around her looked fuzzy and out of focus. The faces surrounding her blurred into a single mass of perfectly made-up women. Tonight's bachelor-bachelorette auction for the Hewitt Academy had given the mothers a reason to dress as if they were attending the inaugural ball, which she knew several actually had.

"You don't need to see. You just have to stand there and look glamorous. Nathan will do the rest."

Honoria recognized the voice of Eloise Baxter, the academy's kindergarten teacher and stepmother to one of its first graders, but she had to squint in order to make out the woman's hairdo of platinum curls. "I can't look glamorous. I don't know how."

"Stop being so down on yourself," Karen Chin said with a *tsk*. "When we get through with you, you're going to look as good as any of the bachelorettes who've already gone on the block. Better, in fact, if we have anything to say about it. Right, ladies?"

"Damn straight," said Ruth.

"I second that," agreed Claire Taylor. "Just wait until Phillip sees—"

"Ahem!" Ruth grabbed Honoria by the elbow and led her to a table at the rear of the dressing room, then called to the circle of tittering women, "Eloise, come over here and see what you can do about getting Honoria's eye shadow and liner on straight. Claire, Karen, we need to talk."

Honoria stared at her blurry toenails, tipped a decadent red and encased in matching color straps. She should have known something unholy was going to happen the second Eloise had asked her shoe size. The torturous strips of leather made it feel as if her feet were wrapped in straitjackets. Between trying to figure out how to keep her school afloat and worrying about the outcome of this gala, the last thing she had expected was to find herself as the evening's grand finale.

"Eloise, please," she began when her friend appeared beside her. "Make them understand this just isn't me."

"Stop complaining. I can't guarantee where this eyeliner is going to end up if I'm distracted."

Honoria remembered a time about a year ago when Eloise could barely do her own hair, never mind put on cosmetics. Now she came to school every day perfectly made up, with clothes to match. Of course, it helped that she was positively glowing with her pregnancy.

"I can't do this. I can't let complete strangers see me looking like a—a—"

"A what?" asked Eloise. "A lovely young woman who's dressed like a cover model instead of a drudge?"

"A drudge?" Honoria's chest tightened. "Is that what you think I look like?"

Eloise stepped back to appraise her handiwork. Frowning, she leaned in and chewed on her lower lip. When Honoria spotted the daunting bit of plastic heading her way, she sat rigidly at attention.

"I'm sorry if the truth hurts, but yes," Eloise finally murmured, daubing at Honoria's left eyelid. "You do dress like a woman twice your age. Even my mother-in-law wears younger looking clothes, and she's over fifty."

"The dress I'd planned to wear tonight was my mother's," Honoria countered when Eloise straightened. "She always used to say a Chanel never went out of style."

"I don't mean to sound harsh, but your mother has passed away. And though I respect what she had to say about your Chanel original, I don't agree. As far as I can tell, a dress that old ought to be in the Smithsonian, alongside the Jackie Kennedy collection. Now, make a pout with your lips."

Voices from across the room made Honoria frown instead.

"I said a pout, not a pucker," Eloise commanded. "Try to exude just the tiniest bit of sex appeal."

I can't be something I'm not, Honoria wanted to snap. But she tried, truly tried, to pout.

"That's better." Taking a step back, Eloise nodded. "I'm glad I decided against using foundation. You have lovely skin. Probably because you stay cooped up in your office all day and never go out in the sun."

"Listening to you, one would think I was a vampire," Honoria grumbled good-naturedly, trying to lighten the pain swelling deep in her chest. These women were all close to her in age, yet she felt years older, like the unattractive spinster sister they'd finally convinced to attend the ball.

"Just let me touch up your nose with a bit of powder . . . and add a little blush . . . now close your eyes halfway—you know, like you do when you chew out one of the students."

"I do not *chew out* my students, I merely—"

"Just do it," Eloise said with a sigh.

The other women broke from their huddle and sauntered over. "You ready for the crowning touch?" asked Ruth. "I know just what I'm going to do with your hair."

Honoria blinked. Between her missing glasses and mascara'd eyelashes, the trio looked faint and out of focus. She patted at her impossible-to-handle hair. The thought of anyone touching the straight, shoulder-length mop made her nervous as a mouse in a room full of hungry cats. "Couldn't I just put it in a bun?"

The women broke out in giggles. "No way. Now let Ruth do her thing," said Eloise. "Claire, I need to speak with you for a minute."

Eloise left Honoria in Ruth and Karen's capable hands and led Claire to a corner of the room. "Whew, for a second there I thought you were going to blow it."

Claire rolled her big blue eyes. "Me too. I can't believe I almost slipped up about Phillip."

"You're sure he's out there?" asked Eloise.

"I saw him earlier. He looks very nice."

"Yes, but is he the right man for Honoria? She's going to be madder than you-know-where if she finds out we rigged her part of the auction. And I still don't see what makes Phillip Cummings so perfect for her."

Claire smiled as if she had it all figured out. "Because he's exactly like her. They have so much in common they can't not hit it off. Phillip is reserved and he doesn't smoke or drink. He took care of his ailing father until the man passed away last year, just like Honoria did with her mother. And he teaches accounting, so he can help her with those financial ledgers she's been complaining about. Who could be better for her than someone who knows where she's coming from?"

Eloise folded her arms over her burgeoning belly. "How about a man who can bring her out of her shell and show her how to live? Someone who can put a little spring in her step and teach her about passion? Opposites attract, remember?"

"And like calls to like. Just because you and Nathan caught the sheets on fire the moment you—"

"Claire! That isn't funny."

"Maybe not, but it's true. You two had the entire school talking, getting married just a month after you arrived here. The cop and the ex-nun." She fluttered her eyelashes in exaggeration. "It's the stuff Hollywood movies are made of. I've never been to a more touching wedding."

"It was, wasn't it?" Eloise cupped her stomach in a loving gesture. "But the honeymoon was better. And that's my point. You couldn't have invented two people more opposite than Nathan and myself, and we're happy as clams. Just because you've found a man who shares some of Honoria's better qualities doesn't mean they'll be a perfect match."

"It's a start, isn't it? And she deserves a vacation. I don't think she's had a day off since she graduated college and came back to help her mother. Phillip's already caught a glimpse of her and likes her looks, and he's ready to tackle the job of untangling thirty years of shoddy bookkeeping in the bargain. Even if they don't hit it off romantically, she'll have six glorious days at Club Paradise."

Claire peeked around Eloise's shoulder to check on

the hair detail. "When did you pack her suitcase and what did you buy?"

"I lifted her keys and sneaked into her apartment during lunch break. And I had to buy the works. She didn't have one thing in her closet fit to wear in the tropics," said Eloise. "Luckily, we're almost the same size."

"What about her passport and the contacts?"

"I gave Karen the passport for the tote bag. Found the lenses and an unopened eye care kit in her medicine cabinet and threw them into the suitcase. Do you know why she doesn't wear them?"

"I suspect it's because those Tweetie-bird glasses give her another wall to hide behind. Darn her mother for being such an unyielding stick in the mud."

Eloise had to agree. She'd never met Faith Hewitt, but she'd heard all about the woman's rigid ethics and beliefs. In the year she'd known Honoria, the principal had done nothing but work. Eloise had to practically beg her to be the maid of honor at her and Nathan's wedding. After she'd returned from her honeymoon, she'd invited Honoria to several get-togethers in hopes of introducing her to a nice guy, but the woman always claimed she was too busy.

She'd almost given up hope of finding the headmistress the right man when some of the wealthier parents in the school decided to hold this auction. Word had leaked out that after years of service to the community, the Hewitt Academy was going under. It was time for the alumni to give something back to the family that had educated so many of the area's wealthy citizens while being secretly charitable to a raft of less fortunate children.

Karen and Ruth had come up with the idea of auctioning Honoria as the grand finale of the evening. Claire had happened upon Phillip and decided he was the perfect man for her, then made him an offer he couldn't refuse. They'd taken up a collection to ensure

Phillip would have the funds to win Honoria as his date. They'd also booked and paid for a six-day stay for two at the exclusive Club Paradise. It was the date of a lifetime.

Eloise only hoped the headmistress would agree.

Honoria wiped her sweaty palms down her waist and over her hips, smoothing the fabric of her skintight dress and calming her nerves at the same time. She'd been plucked, pummeled, prodded, poked, and perfumed all in the space of three hours, and instead of giving her a feeling of confidence, as she imagined it would most women, she felt like a plow horse someone had decided to run in the Kentucky Derby.

Worse, her mother was probably spinning in her grave at this very moment, along with her grandmother Charity and her great grandmother Hope. Never in a million years would they have condoned the idea of a Hewitt being put on the block like a steer at auction.

She shuddered at her second unintentional reference to animal flesh, while at the same time thinking of another: beefcake. Earlier, when she'd still worn her glasses, she'd been able to sneak a few peeks at the bachelors, most of whom had arrived in tuxedos. As the bidding escalated, many had suavely slipped out of their jackets to strut and flex muscles she'd forgotten existed.

And speaking of shameful, the women who'd done the bidding while egging them on had been worse. Eloise and Karen had told her it was all in good fun, but to have supposed *ladies* catcalling to men they didn't know in such a boisterous manner was downright embarrassing. It was probably for the best that her mother wasn't here to witness such a distasteful display.

Stepping to the curtain, Honoria felt her hair swing from side to side as it brushed her bare shoulders. Ruth had brought a tote bag full of products in the hopes of coaxing a bend in her thick, broomstick-straight hair.

When she'd finally realized it was impossible, the woman had used something to make it soft and swingy. Running her fingers through the strands, she had to admit her hair felt silky, not coarse as it usually did. The style was so different from her normal tucked-up bun she almost felt as if she were wearing a wig.

"Hey, Honoria, you look fantastic. How're you holding up?"

She jumped at the deep, mellow voice. Turning, she smiled at a blurry version of Nathan Baxter, Eloise's husband and the master of ceremonies for tonight's gala.

"I'm a little nervous," she confessed, squinting to see his facial expression. With her three-inch heels, she was practically eye to eye with the man, and that was no small feat. "Has the crowd settled down any?"

"Not so you'd notice. The orchestra is setting up in the gym, where my mother and Joe will lead off the dancing while the caterers lay out the buffet. That's going to be as soon as you're handed to the highest bidder, by the way."

Honoria frowned. "How much did the last bachelor raise for the school?"

"Five thousand dollars. But that's not the best part."

"You mean someone earned more?"

"Yep—a man."

"A man? Really? Who was it?"

Nathan's mouth quirked up at a corner. "Remember that dapper old guy who owns the deli down the street? The one who was robbed the night Eloise and I got shot? Apparently there are a few wealthy ladies out there who go for septuagenarians parading around in orthopedic shoes."

"Mr. Belgradian is a very nice man," Honoria informed him, secretly pleased to learn who it was. "He's become a great supporter of the school, even gives the children a discount when they come in the store."

"Well, he brought in five thousand dollars and one cent all on his own tonight," said Nathan.

"Five thousand and—one cent?"

"That's right. Some woman in Rita Mae's yoga class topped the last bid of five big ones by a penny. I had to close the auction before she and Rosemary Moffet got in a catfight over the old guy."

"Oh, Lord." Then Honoria heard the piped-in music and realized she didn't have much time. "Nathan, please get me out of here. There's a back exit behind the scenery drop on the left side of the stage. If we wend our way through the curtains, no one will see us leave."

He shook his head. "No way. Eloise would have my head. Besides, what are you afraid of? You look great, and this is all in fun. Relax."

What was she afraid of? She didn't have enough fingers to add it all up. The laughter of the crowd, the embarrassment of flaunting herself in a dress no self-respecting stripper would wear, the thought that no one—absolutely not one single man—would have the urge to bid on her—

"I think I'm going to be sick," she said, hoping Nathan would take pity on her and lead her to the restroom. Even half blind, she could find her way out of the building from there, hail a cab, and be home before the dancing started.

A bone-rattling fanfare sounded through the curtain and Honoria bolted, but she got only a few feet away before Nathan grabbed her elbow. "There's our cue. They're playing your song, Honoria. Now take my arm and hang on tight. You're going to be the hit of the evening. Guaranteed."

Alexander Vandencort was bored. He had no idea what had possessed him to come to this stupid black tie event. He'd tossed the first invitation he'd received straight in the trash the day he opened it. The five others that had found their way into his mailbox over the following week had gone that route as well, and ticked him off in the process. The last thing he needed was a computer glitch that burped out his address label like a dinner of bad Chinese food.

When his manipulative baby sister, Claire, had tried to convince him to attend as one of the bachelors, he'd choked out a laugh and told her to take a hike. He may have gone to the academy from kindergarten through high school, but that didn't mean he owed his alma mater another moment of his time.

Still, when Rick Bethune had phoned and asked him to join a group of their classmates at the auction, the words *all right* had slipped from between his lips as if he was a ventriloquist's dummy. He still didn't know what had made him agree.

Except for Rick and Steve, he was sitting at a table with men he'd seen only at the racquetball club or on the golf course or tennis court for the last twelve years. Though he could call a few of them friends, he'd never really felt comfortable in their presence, even though they'd been considered the boys most likely to succeed when they'd graduated from this place.

He gazed around the room and spotted most of his former classmates, including Cissy Westfall. Newly divorced, she waggled her fingers at him in a totally come-and-get-me manner, and he cringed inside. The woman had chased him throughout high school and between her two marriages. School policy had dictated that he escort her to homecoming and he'd done his duty, but there had never been any real chemistry between them, mostly because, and it pained Alex to admit it, Cissy was too much like him—too wealthy and too self-absorbed to care about anyone but herself.

Nevertheless, she was persistent.

She might have received more attention if she'd consented to be auctioned, but that was probably beneath her, just as he'd thought it was too lowbrow for him. When a woman was working on wealthy husband number three as hard as she seemed to be, she had to think being sold at auction was akin to taking a step down in the world.

"So, Alex," the man on his left said, loud enough to be heard above the racket. "See anything you like?"

Bill Ellsworth had bid on and won a date with Laura Wembly, another newly divorced woman who made the social rounds in D.C. He was an up-and-coming lobbyist for two environmental groups, and Laura's father was a senator. Bill had been trying to find a way into Senator Wembly's pocket for two years. Now that the senator's only daughter was single he had, at the very least, a leg up on his goal.

"Alex doesn't have to bid on a woman to go out with her," Rick announced to the table. "Besides, he's already dated half the ladies in this room."

"No kidding? So what can you tell me about that little blonde sitting over by the door?" This from Larry Brenner, a junior partner in Baily, Fitch and Klein, a huge, old-guard law firm in the District.

Alex zeroed in on the woman the lawyer had just referred to. Andrea Vogel deserved better than a guy like Larry, infamous for his inability to be discreet. Alex and Andrea had gone out a time or two, and he knew her to be sensitive and sweet, too sweet for the likes of a shark attorney.

"She's not your type," he said, giving a serious smile. "She's a Democrat."

Swallowing as if he'd just been rescued from drowning, Larry tugged at his bow tie. "Thanks for clueing me in. I'll cross her off my list."

Another man at the table, new to town and a friend of Larry's, raised his glass in salute. "Is it true what Rick just said? Have you dated half the women in the room?"

Alex knew what the guy was implying and he didn't like it, but masculine pride and his vow to never kiss and tell kept him silent. Instead, he sipped his Scotch.

"Alex had the girls fawning all over him in high school," offered Rick. "We roomed together in college, and I don't think he ever wrote a paper. Always managed to find some babe on the tennis team to do it for him."

Alex groaned at his best friend's schoolboy prattle. Years ago, their fathers had merged already successful advertising firms to start Bethune and Vandencort. Along with product representation, they were also one of the hottest image consulting companies on the east coast. Besides the fact that the two of them had grown up close as cousins, Rick was one of the few people who knew Alex's secret. Ever since Rick had married, he'd been trying to get Alex to take the plunge, too.

"Come on, buddy, name names. Who's hot and who's not?" egged Larry. "Surely there must be one woman in this place who turned down your offer to take her to bed."

Cissy Westfall took that moment to approach their table. "Well, well, well, if it isn't the toothsome threesome," she purred, referring to the high school nickname the girls had given to Alex, Rick, and Steve. She tossed a waterfall of long blond hair over an alabaster shoulder. "See anything you like?"

The new man sat at attention and offered his hand. "The name's Kevin Lewiston. I gather you went to school with these gentlemen?"

"I sure did." She let go of Kevin and batted her eyelashes at Alex. "Hi, Alex. Long time no see."

"Cissy." He ground his back molars. "How are you?"

"Fine, now that I'm on this side of the room. I only came tonight because Mother insisted, seeing as this place was her alma mater, too." She continued her blatant perusal. "What about you? Have you bid on anyone tonight? Or have you already dated every woman who's appeared on stage?"

"Pull back your claws, Cissy. You know better."

She threw Rick a cutting glare. "Alone already, Rick? What happened to Elaine?"

"She's at a conference in San Francisco. Now get off Alex's back."

Ignoring his comment, she craned her swanlike neck. "There must be at least one woman in this room he'd have to pay to get a date with. How about Suzette Holden?"

"Alex took her to the black and white cotillion last spring," said Rick.

"Lisa Jordan?"

"AIDS fund-raiser this past fall," said Steve.

Tired of the game, Alex fisted his hands on the table. "My social life is no one's business but my own. Now if you'll excuse me—"

"Care to bet on that?" dared Cissy.

"What the hell is wrong with you people? I said I'm not interested in anyone here," he growled.

"Oh, come on, it could be fun. It's going to be a while before we get together for our fifteen-year class reunion. We ought to let it all hang out." She tapped a manicured finger to her chin. "I say we make a wager."

"Wager?" egged Bill. "Like what?"

Cissy smiled, showing a mouth full of perfectly capped teeth. "Alex has to woo and win a woman in this room— someone he's never dated—and bed her in a week."

"Sounds like fun to me," said Kevin. "And since I'm new in town, how about I choose the woman? Just tell me if I pick someone Alex has already taken out. Now what do we bet?"

"Hmm." Cissy spotted the Save the Academy envelopes displayed prominently in the center of the table. "Well, since we're here to help our alma mater, how about a donation to the Hewitt Academy?"

Alex pushed back his chair. "This has gone far enough."

All of a sudden the music rose to a crescendo. The curtain parted and out stepped the gung ho master of ceremonies and a woman in a body-hugging tube of bright red spandex.

"Oh. My. God." Cissy's hot pink mouth dropped open. "I don't believe it."

"Who in the heck is that?" asked Kevin.

"Is that who I think it is?" added Rick.

Cissy plopped into a vacant chair. "Honoria Hewitt."

"Who's Honoria Hewitt?" Kevin prodded.

"She was our classmate for thirteen long years," said Steve. "Now she runs the school."

"This place must need the money worse than I thought," said Cissy. "Otherwise she never would have put herself in such an embarrassing position."

"Does she always wear clothes that tight? It looks like she was sewed into that dress," said Kevin, the admiration in his voice clear.

"You have got to be kidding," said Cissy, her tone snide. "She won't do it."

"What the heck are you babbling about?" asked Bill.

"Honoria Hewitt, she won't do it," said Cissy. "That was the rhyme we made up about her in high school. She was such a Miss Priss, always gawking through those big round glasses. When the girls were smoking under the bleachers or putting on makeup in the washroom, she'd just stare and walk away. Got to be downright spooky. Thanks to her, Shelly, Amber, and I spent a lot of time in detention."

"She wasn't like that, Cissy," said Steve. "The way I remember it, Honoria tried hard to fit in, but you girls never let her. None of the guys thought she was her mother's stool pigeon."

"Hey, Alex, didn't she tutor you in math that last year in school?" Larry prompted.

Alex heard the disparaging comments as if he were standing in a tunnel. Every nasty remark about Honoria echoed in his brain, and he didn't like it one bit. Honoria may not have approved of him, but she didn't deserve the trashy talk.

A sudden urge to protect her rose up from the pit of his stomach and surged to his throat. "Knock it off," he almost shouted. "Can't you see she's upset?"

"Oh-oh," Cissy said with a sneer. "Alex is on his white charger again."

The music stopped and the master of ceremonies quieted the crowd. The room became still as a tomb. Honoria seemed to shrink into herself, even though she was standing almost eye-to-eye with the emcee.

"Who'll open the bidding at five hundred?" the emcee asked. "Five hundred dollars for a date with the lovely owner of the Hewitt Academy, and a fun time that I personally guarantee will knock your socks off."

"This is too rich," hissed Cissy after ten seconds of silence. "Not a man in the place is going to bid on her. If you ask me, it's just what Miss Priss deserves."

"Five hundred dollars," came a male voice from somewhere in the back of the room.

"One thousand," said another near the front.

Cissy *tsked* when she heard the bids. "So, Alex, we always wondered if you and Miss Priss got together when she tutored you. All the girls knew she had a huge crush on you."

Alex trained his gaze on the stage. A crush? Let them think so, but he knew the truth. Still, he couldn't halt the longing to reach out and stroke Honoria's sleek fall of mahogany colored hair, just to reassure her that everything was going to be all right.

"Do I hear two thousand?"

"Two thousand," shouted the first voice.

"Twenty-five hundred," called the second.

Thanks to the emcee, the verbal sparring continued to escalate.

"Who the heck is bidding on her?" asked Larry. "Maybe we should have Cissy go over and warn them she won't put out."

"Eight thousand dollars," one of the two voices shouted.

The audience gasped as one.

Alex inhaled a breath. Damn if Honoria wasn't going to end up the top bid of the night, even if she looked scared to death. She flinched with every call, as if each word cut like a whip. He felt her pain with every rousing shout and round of applause. Someone had to stop the bidding and put her out of her misery, fast.

"Ladies and gentlemen," whispered Kevin, "I think we've just found Alex's date. Now what are we going to bet?"

"Ten thousand dollars," said one of the bidders, his voice breaking with the effort to be heard.

The room settled into hushed expectancy, waiting to cheer the victor. The emcee grinned like a man who knew he'd done an excellent job, and Alex heard a roaring in his brain.

"Ten thousand once."

"How does this sound? If Alex manages to get her in bed, each of us will donate twenty thousand to the Hewitt Academy bailout fund," suggested Cissy. "If he doesn't, then Alex has to pay out for us." She began to count heads at the table. "Rick, Bill, Steve, Larry—I'll even include Kevin if he doesn't mind. With Alex, that makes one hundred forty thousand if he doesn't sleep with her in a week."

"Count me out," said Rick, his expression one of disgust. "And if Alex agrees to this fiasco and he does get her into bed, he's only out the twenty grand. The rest of you will send a donation to the school in his name."

"Ten thousand twice—"

"Sounds good to me." Cissy turned her smug gaze on Alex. "But he can't tell her or the bet is off, and when he's through we expect a detailed account." She flicked a finger against the satiny lapel of Alex's tux. "So what do you say, Alex? Depending on your prowess, the bet will cost you either one hundred twenty thousand or twenty thousand. Are you up for it?"

The roaring exploded into a thunderous rush of disbelief. Alex swallowed, but his mouth took on a life of its own as the words bubbled up from deep inside of him.

"Twenty thousand dollars!"

Chapter Two

Rick slapped Alex on the back so hard he thought his teeth might fall out. But he needed it. If nothing else, it brought him back to reality. What the hell had he just done? The room rang with applause and a general buzz of goodwill. How fitting that the woman they were here to rescue was the top prize of the evening—and he'd ended up the hero.

Suddenly, Claire was at his side, her sisterly hiss reminiscent of a punctured tire. "Take that bid back this instant, Alex." She poked a finger in his chest. "You're ruining everything."

He glanced at Rick and Steve, who were whistling as well as clapping along with the crowd, then at Bill, Larry, and Cissy. Mr. New-Guy-Call-Me-Kevin whispered in Cissy's ear. Laughing, she turned to the stage and Alex followed her malicious glare. Peeking out from between splayed fingers, Honoria looked aghast as wild applause echoed through the auditorium.

"This is the dumbest thing you have ever done," said his sister, punctuating every syllable with a jab.

For a fleeting second, Alex thought about reneging

on the bid. Then he realized what it would do to Honoria. The last thing she needed was further humiliation. He tossed Claire one of his most charming smiles. "What are you so upset about, sis? I'm good for the money."

"It isn't the money, you dope, but you have screwed up everything. We gave Phillip enough cash to bid to ten thousand, which was more than he needed to win the date. Then that second guy entered the mix. When he stopped bidding, we figured Phillip was home free. You called out that ridiculous number and blew our hard work to pieces. Now take it back."

Alex frowned. The auction had been rigged? "You set up the bidding? Did Honoria know?"

Claire rolled her eyes. "Of course not. She never would have agreed to anything like that."

"So why did you do it?" he asked, but he already knew the answer. His sister was a woman, and just like most women she couldn't stand to see an unmated adult, especially if said adult was male. God knows she'd tried to fix him up more times than he could count. It had to be a female thing, like matching salt and pepper shakers or napkins and tablecloths or champagne and caviar. The urge to pair off males and females as if they were marching to the ark had to be ingrained in a woman's DNA chain, just like the urge to bolt was fused to a man's. Honoria was the next challenge in his sister's crusade to make things match.

"Because we like Honoria and we want her to be happy," chattered Claire, confirming his suspicions. "Beneath that reserved exterior, she's a warm, giving woman who deserves a nice guy, someone who'll treat her right. We decided to fix her up with the perfect man, so she'd have a good time on the vacation."

"Who's we? And what vacation?"

The emcee took that moment to quiet the crowd. "Okay, okay, thank you. Now would the generous gentleman who made the winning bid please come up here so I can tell him exactly what he's won?"

Steve grabbed Alex's arm and dragged him to the stairs at the side of the stage, but not before Cissy and Kevin managed to remind him of their ridiculous bet. Alex figured he was already two rungs up the ladder to a fool—he might as well climb all the way to the top. Straightening his bow tie, he sauntered up the steps and walked to the announcer, who seemed to be hiding Honoria from view.

The two men shook hands. "Nathan Baxter. And you are?"

"Alex Vandencort," Alex answered through gritted teeth.

"Alex?" Baxter raised a brow. "You're sure your name is Alex?"

Alex folded his arms. "It was, the last time I looked at my driver's license."

"Well, Alex." Nathan gave him a tight-lipped smile. "Let me be the first to offer my congratulations. You're a very lucky man."

"Yeah, sure." He tried to peer at Honoria over the emcee's shoulder, but Baxter blocked his view.

"All right, ladies and gentlemen, it's my pleasure to reveal the grand prize of the evening, and I can assure you it runs a poor second to the lovely Ms. Hewitt."

The crowd grew quiet.

"Honoria and, uh . . . Alex, your prize has been donated by a generous group of patrons who wish to remain anonymous, but want you to have a wonderful time. Your five-star date begins immediately with a limo ride to Reagan National Airport, where you'll catch a flight on a chartered jet for a seven-day stay with deluxe accommodations at the ultimate luxury resort, Club Paradise."

The crowd roared its approval. Again Alex tried to see around the guy, but was blocked.

Turning away from the mike, the emcee whispered, "Show some teeth, buddy, or I'll knock a few lose."

"Excuse me?" said Alex, not quite sure he'd heard correctly.

Though pale in the stage lights, Baxter was taller and a bit bulkier than Alex, and he was totally in control. "I said smile. Act like this was your idea and you're loving every second of it, because if I hear you gave Honoria one moment of grief or embarrassment, you'll answer to me." Subtly, he shifted his jacket to reveal a gun. "Do I make myself clear?"

Holy shit! Alex swallowed a smart-assed comment. What the hell had he gotten himself into?

Honoria felt faint. She was still in shock over the bidding. Not one, not two, but three bachelors had vied for her hand. And the winner was a man on whom she'd once had a major crush. Alexander Vandencort had bid twenty thousand dollars to go on a date—no, a vacation—with her. They were supposed to spend a week together in a virtual paradise and—oh, Lord, she didn't want to think about that part of it. She had so much work to do at the school she couldn't afford even a morning off to get her car serviced. No way could she take a vacation.

She craned her neck, but all she could see was the back of Nathan's head. He mumbled something to Alex and Alex responded, but the sound of applause muffled his answer.

Nathan returned to the microphone. "Okay, folks, it's time to say bon voyage to the lucky couple and head for the gym to celebrate. This auction is officially over, but the party's just beginning."

He grabbed her by an elbow and did the same to Alex. Shuffling them to the rear of the stage, he pushed through the curtain and hauled them to a fuzzy cluster of well-dressed women Honoria assumed were her friends.

"This guy says he's Alex somebody-or-other," Nathan muttered to Eloise. "I thought he was supposed to be named Phillip."

Alex was supposed to be Phillip? Why would Alex change his name? And how could she take a vacation when her school was in the middle of a crisis? A knot formed in the middle of Honoria's forehead. Her feet felt as if they were wrapped in piano wire and her dress was cutting off her circulation. She was having a hard time following the conversation, so she decided to concentrate on the one thing she deemed most urgent.

"Eloise, I can't go away for seven days. Who's going to look after the academy?"

"We will, Honoria. I've already lined up Rita Mae to take care of the office, and Karen and Ruth promised to help." She turned to Nathan. "What do you mean, his name is Alex? What happened to Phillip?"

"If you'll give me a minute, I can explain—" Claire began, only to be interrupted by Ruth.

"Hmm-hmm-hmm. So this is Phillip. He sure doesn't look like an accountant to me."

Honoria shuddered at the thought of anyone other than family meddling in the inner workings of her school. Thanks to her mother's inept accounting, she'd been left with a mess that had to be untangled by the end of the year or she would have the IRS on her tail. And she couldn't very well run a private school from Leavenworth.

Hoping to get her point across, she raised her voice in protest. "Rita Mae is a wonderful woman, but the Hewitt Academy requires—"

"Common sense and a clear head, both of which my mother-in-law possesses in abundance. You need some time off. Trust me, things will be fine." Eloise turned to Claire. "Not to belabor the point, but where is Phillip?"

"I need a scorecard. Will someone please clue me in on who's who?" Nathan demanded.

"But I haven't packed," Honoria reminded them. "I don't have the proper clothes or—or—"

"We took care of it, sweetie. Eloise saw to your luggage and I packed what you'll need for the flight." Karen handed her a huge white canvas bag, then turned to Claire. "If this isn't Phillip, who is he?"

Claire heaved a breath. "My soon-to-be-dead brother."

"Your brother?" chirped Ruth. "What's he doing here?"

Squinting, Honoria clutched the bag to her chest. "But—"

"Would someone please tell me what's going on?" bellowed Nathan, clearly frustrated.

"Explaining won't help," moaned Claire. "The two of them will just have to make the best of it."

"Claire's right." Eloise gave Alex a head-to-toe going over. Smiling like Mona Lisa, she glanced at Claire. "He isn't insane or anything, is he?"

"I didn't think so until a few minutes ago."

"Then we'll just have to live with it," she decreed with a touch of amusement. "Mr. Vandencort's very generous bid won the auction, so he's going on the date. And if they want to catch their flight, they have to leave now. Nathan, maybe you could see to it?"

The mass confusion made Honoria's head swim, but she was fairly certain things hadn't gone the way anyone planned. She tried to get a better view of Alex, who was supposed to be someone named Phillip, but everything was a blur. First Karen, then Ruth kissed her cheek and told her to have a good time. Claire mumbled something about patience and gave her a hug. Eloise whispered *have a great time* in her ear and before Honoria could say a word, Nathan grabbed her by the elbow and propelled them out of the building. The trio stumbled through the clutter behind stage, down the back stairs, and into the limo, with Alex sliding in last.

Nathan patted her knee. "Don't worry about a thing,

Honoria. According to Eloise, everything is going to turn out just fine."

"You ready back there?" called the driver.

"Give the man your address, Vandencort," said Nathan. "You have to go home and pack a bag."

"I have no intention of going to Club Paradise."

Honoria wanted to crawl under the seat. She could tell from his tone that Alex hadn't expected he'd be taking a trip. It didn't even sound as if he wanted a date with her. But if that was the case, why had he bid?

"It's all right, Nathan. If Mr. Vandencort—"

Shifting in his seat, Nathan turned his back to her. "Give the driver your address. Now."

Alex grumpily rattled off a toney address in the heart of Georgetown, not far from the school. A few minutes later the chauffeur double-parked the limo in front of what seemed to be a huge house made of white brick. Honoria wished she could see more than a foot in front of her so she could get a better view of the home.

"You stay here with the driver while I go inside with your *date*, just to make sure he packs everything he needs," said Nathan. He slid toward the door, shoving Alex out in front of him. "We'll be back in a minute."

The door slammed and Honoria breathed a sigh. In the space of a heartbeat, she'd been sold like a mare at auction and sent on a vacation with a man who, from the sound of it, didn't even like her. Sitting upright, she reached out and placed her hand on the chauffeur's shoulder. "Maybe you should just take me home. I live about six blocks from here."

The man hitched around in his seat. "Sorry, miss, no can do. I have a schedule to follow. But if you don't mind my asking, why would you want to miss out on such a wonderful holiday?"

"You don't understand. It would only be wonderful if the two people going wanted to be together."

"And you don't want to be with a good-lookin' rich guy like him?"

"I'm afraid it's the other way around," she said sourly. She could barely see the driver's face, but from the sound of his voice she thought he might be on the far side of sixty. "Alex doesn't want to go anywhere with me. I'm still trying to figure out why he entered the auction in the first place."

"Maybe because you're a fine-lookin' lady. Any man with a pulse would be happy to go on a romantic getaway with you."

"That's very nice of you to say," she answered, thinking he had to be as blind as she was. "But I'm not much fun."

"Really? Well, you'd never know it from lookin' at you."

"Trust me. Alex would have a better time with his goldfish—if he had a goldfish, that is—than he would with me."

"I hear there's lotsa things to do on those islands. Swimming, snorkeling, dancing in the moonlight . . ."

"I can't swim or dance—and I definitely don't snorkel. Like I said, I don't do anything that most people consider fun."

"So change."

"I beg your pardon?"

"Start being fun. You can take lessons for most anything these days."

"Oh, no, I couldn't be—fun, that is. It's not in my genes."

"The way I look at it, a nice tight pair of jeans on a figure like yours would definitely be fun, if you'll excuse my saying so."

"You're excused. And I meant my genetic makeup. You know, the stuff that makes us who we are. My mother never allowed me to do any of the things you just mentioned. I did have lessons in ballroom dancing, but I haven't been on a dance floor since college. You see, I come from a long line of educators whose only goal in life has been molding youngsters into intelligent and upstanding adults."

"That sounds like a noble profession."

"I used to think so when Mother was around. Lately, it's been nothing but hard work. It's taken years of practice to emulate her moral fiber and strength of character."

"So where is she now, this mother of yours?"

"Faith passed away eighteen months ago. Why do you ask?"

"Because you sound like a sensible woman. If you're so full of moral fiber, I doubt you'll do anything stupid, so why not trust your own judgment and do what you want? It isn't like your mother is going to stop you."

Honoria nibbled on a newly manicured cuticle. The driver had a point. When her mother had been diagnosed with cancer, she'd worked around the clock nursing her through her illness and putting in sixty hours a week trying to keep the Hewitt Academy afloat. The school was hers now, to do with as she saw fit. She was still thinking about what the driver suggested when the trunk popped open and she heard a thump. Then Nathan and Alex climbed back inside. Nathan tapped the front seat and the car shot down the street.

"You doing okay?" he asked.

"A little shell-shocked, but I'll survive. What about Alex?" She peered across Nathan's lap and saw her date hunched in the far corner, gazing out the window. While inside, he'd changed into a light-colored jacket and slacks.

"I'm guessing he's overwhelmed, but he'll be fine once you're in the air."

In the air! Honoria swallowed. She'd forgotten all about

having to fly. Still worrying her cuticle, she wondered if she should warn Alex, then decided against it. He'd find out soon enough what being on a plane did to her.

Alex stowed their luggage in the overhead compartment, then settled into the first class seat and took stock of his surroundings. Thanks to their directionally impaired chauffeur, who had taken a half dozen wrong turns before he'd found the airport, they'd barely made it to the boarding ramp. Baxter had been with them the entire time they'd rushed through the check-in line and security, right up to their arrival at the gate. It dawned on him that the emcee was some kind of law enforcement officer when a security guard waved them through after Baxter flashed a badge. At least that explained the gun.

Honoria hadn't said more than a few words since they'd arrived on airport property, and she'd hit the restroom the second they boarded, so the seat beside him was empty. She'd seemed genuinely surprised to hear she was going on a vacation, and it was clear from the overlapping conversations she hadn't known anything about that Phillip character, either. Was she upset that he'd won the bid, or did she have another problem?

He drummed his fingers on the armrest. How in the hell had he landed in this predicament? He hadn't planned to attend the auction in the first place, and now he was on his way to Club Paradise with the prize package of the night . . . and into the Hewitt Academy for upward of a hundred thousand dollars, because he had no intention of collecting on that wager. Good thing he had the money and the time, or the problem would be huge.

Unlike Honoria, there wasn't anyone who depended on him. His father never seemed to care whether or not he was in the office, as long as he wined and dined the customers before turning them over to one of the company's golden boys. He pulled out a PDA from his jacket and looked over his coded shorthand, checking his schedule for the coming week. The elections were over and most of the candidates they consulted for had won. He had a dinner meeting with Barrow and Stone and a follow-up lunch with the reps of a major drug company. Both appointments could be postponed or handled by someone else. Other than that, his week was empty.

"Can I get you something to drink before takeoff? A Paradise Punch or mixed drink?" The flight attendant batted her baby blue eyes. "We'll be serving a midnight supper once we're in the air."

"I'll have a glass of red wine, thanks."

"And your seatmate?"

"I have absolutely no idea what the lady wants, but she's in the restroom. You should probably warn her to get out of there before liftoff."

The attendant nodded. Gliding by the washroom, she rapped on the door. "Five minutes, miss. You need to finish up and find your seat. Would you like a Paradise Punch?"

Honoria gave a mumbled response and he leaned back. The washroom door opened and he heard her voice a second time. An older woman waiting to use the facility began to dig in her handbag. Smiling, she pulled a pill bottle from her purse and passed it through the door. Half a minute later, a manicured hand returned the container. Then his traveling companion stepped from the restroom and headed down the aisle, the reason for her long absence clear.

She'd rid herself of the slinky tube of red satin and changed into a pair of tailored white slacks and a clingy yellow sweater set. Though it resembled an outfit his sister owned, the supple fabric had never molded to Claire the way it did to this woman's impressive curves. Then again, his sister wasn't built like a Viking princess.

He stood and Honoria slipped past him. After stuffing her huge canvas tote under the seat in front of her, she snapped on her seat belt and he did the same. The flight attendant handed him a glass of red wine and placed what looked like a glass of fruit juice decorated with a paper umbrella on the console.

Honoria squinted at the drink. "What's this?"

"A Paradise Punch. Remember, I asked if you wanted one when I knocked on the restroom door."

"Oh, sure. I couldn't hear you very well with the plane noise and all." She fidgeted in her seat. "I guess a little juice won't hurt."

She downed the punch in one swallow while Alex sipped at his wine. The urge to say something, anything to make it clear why he'd shouted out his bid scratched at his throat, but he couldn't think of a polite way to explain that stupid bet. Passengers continued to traipse past them, some dressed in comfortable island wear, others in brightly patterned shirts, slacks, and straw hats. At least he'd been able to change into something lightweight and tasteful while Baxter had packed his bag. He just hoped the guy had found his resort wear in the guest bedroom closet, as instructed.

The stewardess handed Honoria a second drink. "There you go. I'll be back after takeoff to get your dinner order."

The engines revved and Honoria gulped down her fresh drink, then set the empty glass on the cocktail napkin. "I . . . um . . . I think you need to know that flying makes me a little . . . nervous."

"The rum should help with that."

Pointing at the drink, she gasped. "Rum! But it tasted just like fruit juice."

"It may have started out as fruit juice, but when you

mix it with champagne and a little rum it's called a Paradise Punch. Is there a problem?"

"No . . . at least I hope not. That lady in the first row was kind enough to give me a Dramamine."

"So you'll sleep until we get there."

The plane began to back out of the jet way, and she knotted her fingers to her middle. "Do you think there's a problem with the plane? Those engines sound awfully loud and rumbly."

"This is a big jet. They're supposed to sound that way."

The plane jerked onto the runway and Honoria lurched with it. "What was that?"

Hoping to put her at ease, he gazed out the window. "Just a bump. Relax."

She fisted her hands in her lap. "I don't fly very often."

"Well, I do." Feeling protective again, he patted one of her hands, and she grabbed at his fingers. "These babies are safe as a cradle."

Still clutching his hand, Honoria bit at her lower lip, and Alex realized she was probably confused as hell. Not only was she terrified of flying, she'd been forced to leave her job so she could spend the next seven days with someone she hadn't seen in a dozen years.

He owed her an explanation, but he didn't have a clue what to say, so he decided to punt. "I guess you're wondering why I called out that bid?"

Owl-like, she blinked her honey-colored eyes. "Now that you mention it, the thought did cross my mind." The jet throttled to full force and she turned her head. "Those engines sound like they're going to fall off. Are you sure they're supposed to be that loud?"

The flight attendant came by and removed their glasses. "Just a few more seconds and we'll be in the air."

Honoria clamped his hand like a vise. Her face flushed and her breathing took on the cadence of someone in the middle of an aerobics class. When the pilot announced they'd been cleared for takeoff, she gurgled out a few unintelligible words, and Alex thought the bones in his fingers might break. Not only had the night been expensive, it was becoming damned hazardous to his health.

The plane rolled down the runway, picking up speed. Honoria closed her eyes and moved her lips as if in silent prayer. If the situation wasn't so ludicrous, Alex thought he might be able to have a good time on this vacation. Without her oversized glasses and schoolteacher frown, Honoria was actually pretty. She had a small, straight nose and a wide, kissable mouth he'd never noticed while they were in school. Since most of the women he knew had been married at least once by the time they turned thirty, he figured she had to be one of those females whose careers came first. The kind who didn't need a man in her life to complicate things or make her feel complete. He'd been on a few leisurely weekends with that type of woman, and it had suited him just fine. Between his mother, father, and Claire, there'd been nine marriages and seven divorces in his family. He wasn't about to add to the number.

Honoria turned to face him, and he marveled at the color of her skin. He'd never seen anyone that green before. Roaring, the jet rose into the air. Her shoulders heaved and she trembled. He grimaced when she fumbled for the seat pocket in front of her, whipped out a barf bag, and used it.

Damn, but he hated to see good liquor go to waste.

Junior wedged himself between the top of the television console and the ceiling of the plane and heaved a sigh. Throwing his voice during the auction had been tricky, but he'd managed to stay hidden in the shadows of the auditorium while he'd bid. Driving that enormous limousine was the thing that had almost done him in. This was the perfect place to catch a little nap before they arrived at their destination.

He'd never been on a jumbo jet before, but so far it was the easiest part of the evening. Too bad Honoria didn't feel the same. Right now, the poor girl's complexion rivaled the color of a cocktail olive.

Milton had been right. Alex was stubborn and set in his ways. But from the moment Junior had first dropped in on his new charge, he'd sensed a wave of vulnerability hidden deep in the man's soul. Alex wasn't the confirmed bachelor he portrayed, nor was he the charming playboy everyone thought him. Along with his disability, he was simply frightened of making a commitment to a woman. And who could blame him? The Vandencort family's marital track record was dismal at best.

Arranging for him to receive those multiple invitations had been clever, but they wouldn't have swayed him into attending the gala without Rick's help. Even after Alex's long-buried feelings for Honoria had risen to the surface, he had ignored them and refused to join the auction. Luckily, those so-called friends of his had an evil streak a mile wide. Otherwise Phillip Cummings would be occupying the seat next to Honoria right now instead of Alex.

As far as Junior could tell, Honoria had been in love with Alex in high school and secretly harbored feelings for him still. Alex thought Honoria was attractive, but he also carried an ache inside that radiated outward toward her and most everyone else in his life. He'd been hurt by someone he cared about a long time ago, and was now fearful of being hurt again. Once Alex learned that Honoria would never cause him pain, he would be free to love her in return.

The only problem was that darned bet. Honoria had been taught to live up to her name. Junior doubted she would take kindly to knowing she was part of such a dastardly scheme, even if his charge hadn't *actually* agreed to it.

If she ever got wind of that stupid wager, Junior had no doubt he'd be shopping for a new winter coat, because Alex Vandencort wouldn't stand a chance.

Chapter Three

Honoria walked openmouthed to the check-in desk while Alex saw to their luggage. Even without her glasses, she could tell the hotel was magnificent. Accessible to the sea breeze on all sides and done in marble and tile, it resembled a palace. She'd never been in a place so lovely, or one that smelled so good. The idea of a vacation was beginning to grow on her, especially since she was here and everything was arranged. After she checked in and relaxed a bit, she might actually be able to do what the chauffeur had suggested—try to have a little fun.

Unfortunately, she'd probably have that fun without Alex. After her humiliating display on the plane, she'd fallen asleep and hadn't awakened until landing. She'd stumbled off the jet and onto the tarmac, fished her passport out of her bag and gone through customs like a zombie, then boarded the shuttle to the resort. The fresh island air flowing through the van's windows had left her feeling one hundred percent better, but from the expression on Alex's face, she'd either drooled, snored, or done both while sleeping on the flight.

So much for impressing a man with whom she'd

once been enamored. If there was even the slightest chance of having a romantic moment with him during their stay, she'd blown it. Not that something personal could ever happen between them, of course. Alex had barely glanced her way on the ride over, and she was still trying to figure out why he'd made that bid.

"Good morning," she said to the clerk, a young man with a nut-brown complexion and toothy smile. Leaning forward, she squinted at his name tag: Junior, Assistant Front Desk Manager. "I'm Honoria Hewitt. I believe you have a reservation in my name."

"Let me be the first to welcome you to Club Paradise, Miss Hewitt." He thumbed through a bank of files and pulled out an index card. "Ah, yes. You and your companion have the Tropical Breeze suite, a lovely set of rooms with balconies facing the ocean from both bedrooms and the center parlor."

"I'd like to change the reservation, please," Honoria said with a firm inflection in her voice. "We'll be needing two single rooms."

The clerk kept on grinning. "Separate rooms? I'm afraid that's not possible. We are booked to capacity. Besides, we don't have any single rooms at Club Paradise, unless you count the cottages located directly on the beach. Unfortunately, none of those are free, either. I'm sorry, but your original request is all we can honor."

"This is a huge place. Surely there's an empty room I can occupy? Maybe one of the maid's chambers or—"

Oozing charm, Alex stepped to the desk and rested an elbow on the counter. "Is there a problem?"

"Are you Ms. Hewitt's guest companion?"

"I am, and the name is Vandencort, Alexander Vandencort." Alex pulled out his passport and set it down.

Junior copied Alex's name onto the card and returned his passport. "Welcome to Club Paradise, Mr. Vandencort. We hope you have a pleasant stay." The clerk straightened his pristine white jacket. "I was just informing Ms. Hewitt that we have no single rooms, nor any accommodation other than what was originally booked. The resort is filled to capacity."

"What sort of room do we have?" Alex asked.

"The Tropical Breeze is one of our finest suites, two identical bedrooms joined by a single parlor with balconies facing the ocean." The clerk raised a brow. "I could call the other resort on the island to see if they have what you request, but I must warn you it is the busy season."

"Maybe I can find a room in the village—" Honoria continued.

"Give us a second to talk it over, okay?" Alex shuttled her aside before she could argue. Folding his arms, he kept his voice low. "The suite has separate bedrooms, Honoria, and I'm sure there's plenty to do here. I can amuse myself and you can do . . . whatever to keep busy. I got the impression from my sister that your friends already paid the bill. It would be rude to ignore their gift, especially when they went to so much trouble to arrange this surprise."

A soft morning breeze wafted through the spacious lobby. Rife with the scent of sea, sun, and tropical flowers, it ruffled Alex's dark blond hair and teased at the neckline of his shirt. Despite the cooling wind, Honoria felt her face warm. She'd kept track of his wealthy lifestyle through the semiannual alumni newsletter written by a member of their class. Reports of Alex's globetrotting and his appearance at various charity events with assorted social butterflies were legion. No wonder he sounded like a sensible, well-traveled sophisticate while she was acting like an illogical prude.

If one of the other bachelors bidding on her had won this date, would she be so hesitant or so contrary? Of course she would, she told herself. She was in a strange place with a man she barely knew, and he seemed to be just as unhappy about the situation as she was. Sadly, she had no choice but to make the best of it.

"Well, when you put it that way, I suppose I could find something to occupy my time. What exactly do you plan on doing—to keep busy, I mean?"

His sexy lips turned up at the corners. "Besides playing tennis and lazing on the beach, I like to scuba dive and windsurf. What about you?"

She swallowed at the thought of Alex's muscular body, tan face, and navy eyes set off perfectly by tennis whites. Her one attempt at the taxing game had left her with a turned ankle and a minor case of heatstroke. But the idea of sitting on a lounge chair at the ocean shore did hold a certain appeal. She could read or catch up on her sleep, something she definitely needed more of.

"The beach thing sounds nice, but I've never really had much time to do any of the other things you just said."

His smile seemed to brighten. "Maybe I could play tutor to thank you for coaching me through algebra senior year. Tennis is good for your cardiovascular system. It can be an easy game once you get the hang of it."

Not without my glasses, she thought, rubbing the bridge of her nose. She didn't recall much of the time she and Alex had spent studying together. She'd had such a huge crush on him, most afternoons she could barely speak. But she did remember his easy laugh and popularity with the rest of the students—especially the girls. He'd been charming and clever, convincing her to finish enough of his assignments to earn him a passing grade. When her mother had found out how Alex had manipulated her into doing his work, Faith had shuffled her off to another project and found someone else to take over as his tutor.

"Speaking of those lessons, I always meant to tell you it wasn't my idea to stop," she said, squinting to see his face. "My mother just thought I could be of more use elsewhere, and she did run the school."

Alex's gaze turned distant, but his smile never wavered. "Sure, Bob Dooley explained it to me when he took over. You had better things to do; you were a brain and I was . . . well, to put it politely, I was an underachiever, at best. Now, how about it? Shall we share the suite and try to have a good time?"

Honoria nodded in agreement. She didn't like the flippant way he said *you had better things to do,* as if she'd been the one to dismiss him, but this wasn't the time to get into what had happened twelve years ago.

Alex returned to the front desk. "The suite will be fine. Is there anything else we need to know?"

Junior handed them each a room key and a thin plastic card. "This is your guest pass. You're booked on the ultimate luxury plan, which means breakfast, lunch, and dinner are included as well as virtually everything the club has to offer. The only things you'll be billed for at the end of your stay are alcoholic beverages, spa treatments, and any tour you might want to take off the resort." He gave them each a pamphlet. "This is a list of events that need to be booked separately. You can order room service or dine on the terrace at our sumptuous breakfast buffet from six A.M. to eleven; lunch runs from eleven to three at any of our four award winning restaurants. All you have to do is show your card and sign your name."

He reached under the desk and pulled out a large, official-looking book. "Dinner is served in the main dining room, and you need to choose a seating. We have a six-thirty, an eight o'clock, and a nine-thirty. Which would you prefer?"

"Six-thirty," said Honoria.

"Eight," said Alex.

Junior threw them a teasing frown. "I'm sorry, but you need to choose one time for the both of you."

Honoria licked at her lips. "But—"

"All the tables are for two. We don't book separate seatings. This is a place for romance, not a meet and greet." He winked at Alex. "Maybe the lady would be willing to alternate dinners, so she didn't have to face you across the table."

Honoria's already frayed nerves began to unravel. She was having a hard enough time coming to grips with the way she'd been maneuvered here. She didn't need a desk clerk making her sound foolish or difficult. And she didn't look forward to being a third wheel at a table for two.

"Eight is fine," she said, trying to be reasonable. If Alex continued to act distant, she'd just skip dinner. She might actually be able to lose a few pounds if she ate healthy, relaxing meals instead of the fast food she normally gulped down at her desk every day.

"You heard the lady," said Alex, his mouth set in a straight line. "Now, how do we get to our room?"

"Eight it is, and you'll be sitting at table twenty-three." The clerk handed him a map of the resort and gave directions, then snapped his fingers. A bellman appeared at their side with a luggage cart in tow.

"I am your personal contact at the hotel," Junior confided. "Feel free to call on me at any time during your stay—just dial ninety-nine on a house phone." He turned to the bellman. "See our guests to the Tropical Breeze suite."

Alex held his temper in check as they trailed behind the bellman. They walked down a long marble corridor decorated in tasteful island statuary and antique sideboards holding vases of fresh flowers. Rattan chairs with brightly patterned cushions clustered around matching tables set under rotating paddle fans. Colorful pottery filled with fragrant tropical plants lined the walkway, exotic pictures graced the walls. The entire lobby was open to the sunlight and sea air, giving a comfortable yet elegant flair to the resort.

The trio rode the elevator to the top floor in silence. Alex could feel Honoria giving off waves of keep-your-distance energy. Just as she'd done in their tutoring sessions, she was acting reserved and untouchable. And why wouldn't she? She was still the same highly intelligent, prim and proper lady she'd been in high school, and he was still the same stup—

Scratch that, he ordered himself, glowering at his reflection in the mirrored wall. He'd come a long way from needing her or anyone else to do his homework and write his papers. Even his father no longer called him a dunce, now that dear old dad had seen how well his son charmed their clients. Too bad his father never let him write a contract or close a deal. Then again, who was he kidding? He wouldn't be able to make heads or tails out of a contract anyway, so why bother?

They reached the room and the bellman opened the door. Honoria walked in first and Alex followed. He almost ran smack into her backside when she stopped short in the middle of the suite.

Zigzagging around her, he crossed the parlor and went to the bedroom on the left. The desk clerk hadn't lied. The suite was as impressive as the lobby. A king-size bed with a wicker headboard and two nightstands dominated the room. One wall housed an entertainment center, the other a huge walk-in closet that held a chest of drawers and a safe. The balcony sat directly across from the foot of the bed, its sheer curtains fluttering in the breeze.

The bellman set his bag on the bed and Alex handed the guy a ten-dollar bill. "Take the lady's belongings to the other room and see yourself out."

He waited a few seconds, then returned to the parlor. Honoria was nowhere in sight, so he checked out that area as well. A pair of love seats covered in a floral print flanked a gas fireplace. Tables decorated with bric-a-brac, assorted chairs, and a wet bar filled out the room.

An archway on the opposite side of the entry led to a large bathroom. Terra-cotta tiles covered the floor, dual pedestal sinks stood in front of full-length mirrors, and matching white terry cloth bathrobes hung on brass pegs jutting from the wall. He inspected the private commode hidden behind a door, then checked out the far corner with its triple-sized, glass-enclosed shower and multiple water jets.

A sunken tub big enough to bathe an elephant rested in the center of the room, its porcelain ledge stacked with pastel-colored towels and facecloths. Jars of sea salt scrub, scented soaps and—he removed the top of a container—exotic-smelling lotions sat on one end of the tub. Baskets filled with an assortment of sponges and bath brushes lined the other.

Estimating on the conservative side, Alex guessed three people could drown in the tub and six could hold a serious orgy in the shower. Grinning, he shook his head. If ever there had been a bathroom designed for two adventurous lovers, this was it.

Honoria sat at the foot of the bed and contemplated her surroundings. She sincerely hoped that Eloise had remembered to pack her glasses, or she was going to have a difficult time appreciating this place. Her town home, a valuable piece of property that had been in the family for almost a hundred years, was woefully shabby and filled with furniture from her grandmother's day. All the rooms were dark and gloomy, nothing like this luxurious suite.

Faith hadn't believed in wasting money on appearances when the Hewitt Academy demanded her attention.

Over the years, she had insisted on numerous improvements to the school. First, there'd been the auditorium addition. Then the outdoor fields had needed resurfacing and new bleachers. Then they'd installed central air-conditioning. Honoria had attended college on a full scholarship, but her mother had been forced to hire an administrative assistant during that time, which had evened out the savings. A few years ago, she and her mother had agreed to add the computer science wing, considered essential if they were to keep up with advancing technology. After her mother died, Honoria raised the salaries of the staff in order to retain her most competent teachers and draw others with the proper credentials.

No doubt about it, the academy was a money pit, but it had been in her family for as long as the house. She could never remember a time for frivolity or vacations. There'd been only the school, with its reputation and its future to think of. As the last of the Hewitt women, she was honor bound to keep it running.

"So what do you think?"

Alex's deep voice startled her and she jumped from the bed.

"It's beautiful . . . from what I can see of it."

"Have you taken a look at the view?" Walking to the French doors, he threw them open, letting in a waft of fresh air and sunshine. When he disappeared through the billowing apricot-colored curtains, Honoria followed.

Standing next to Alex, she rested her palms on the wide balcony railing. Even without glasses, she could see the ocean stretching before them, its color so brilliant a blue she couldn't tell where the water ended and the sky began. The white sand beach glistened like a luminous pearl, beckoning her to come relax and enjoy all the shore had to offer.

"Wow," she managed on a whisper. "It's like a picture postcard, isn't it?"

"It's nice, smaller than a private hotel I once stayed at in Antigua, but not cramped. Actually, it reminds me of a beach I was on in Maui a few years back."

His casual comment only reinforced what she already suspected. Alex had traveled the world, while the farthest she'd ever been was a yearly meeting in Indianapolis held especially for owners of private schools.

The sound of Latin music, loud and rousing, filled the air. "What is that?" she asked, peering into the courtyard below.

Alex smiled. "A band of some sort. Looks like they've stopped right under our balcony." He turned to her, raising his voice. "You ready for some lunch, or is your stomach still queasy from the flight?"

Honoria was starving. She hadn't eaten since yesterday, and what little she'd managed to nibble on backstage had gone the way of her punch. Her mouth tasted sour and her clothes, the ones she'd found in the tote bag Karen had packed, were wrinkled and grimy. She glanced down at her feet, still encased in red leather straps. Along with her glasses, she prayed Eloise had packed her worn sneakers and a pair of sweats, her favorite lounging attire. She'd always preferred comfort to fashion, mostly because she never spent time anywhere but at home or the school. Once Alex saw her in her own clothes, she doubted he'd want to be seen in public with her.

"Um . . . I need to unpack and freshen up first. Can I have about an hour?"

"No problem. It's still early. I'll just put away my clothes and take a look at the brochures the desk clerk gave us."

He left and Honoria closed the door. A wave of sound blasted through the room and she shook her head. Music pounded, practically vibrating the walls. She could barely hear herself think and she was five floors up; there was no need to worry about lunch conversation, because neither she nor Alex would be able to hear one another through the din.

She opened her suitcase and her eyes narrowed when she lifted the first item from the bag, a sheer and very feminine ice blue nightgown and matching robe, then a rather risqué gown and robe in bright red satin. After that came a half dozen pairs of lacy bikini panties in assorted colors and three bras, two a sheer creamy white and one a shimmery black.

Suspicious, she fisted her hands on her hips and bent forward to read the name tag on the suitcase. It was definitely her luggage, but this was not her clothing. At least, not the stuff she stored in her closet back home.

She plucked out a stack of cotton T-shirts in bright, primary colors, white short shorts and a pair of black, then a pair of khaki pants and another of diaphanous white that draped her legs like a skirt. Three low-cut, thin-strapped sundresses in soft flowery prints followed. Then came two bathing suits, one a black maillot with a plunging neckline and an even plungier back, the other a two piece in hot pink. Attached to the bikini was a jungle print sarong-style garment she supposed was meant to be used as a cover-up. On the bottom were two pairs of flat-heeled sandals, one white and one black, a pair of brand new sneakers; a bag of makeup, toiletries, and hair care products; and a plastic case holding her one foray into self-improvement: contact lenses and solutions.

Plopping down next to the suitcase, she sighed. A bit of paper peeked out from the front flap and she unzipped the inside lining. Two full length dresses tumbled from the rustling tissue, one a buttery yellow and the other a gauzy black.

Desperate, Honoria upended the large travel tote Karen had thrust into her hands before she'd left. Out dropped the torturous hooker dress, a large round brush and a smaller one, the bottle of goo Ruth had used to tame her hair, a lipstick labeled Kiss Me Red, a bottle of sunblock, a pair of sunglasses, and an assortment of hair bands.

No ratty sneakers or comfy sweats—and worse, no glasses.

Not only had she been shanghaied, her *good friends* had stolen her clothes and replaced them with expensive and too revealing substitutes. It looked as if they'd thought of everything, right down to her underwear. *Lingerie,* she amended, remembering what Ruth had told her.

Tears sprang to her eyes, and she brushed them away with an angry swipe. In their subtle way, Eloise, Claire, and the rest were letting her know what they really thought of her: dumpy, frumpy, and boring.

Alex opened his suitcase and took out a pair of swim trunks, then a couple pairs of silk boxers, two pairs of wrinkled linen slacks and three rumpled shirts in assorted colors. Crumpled in the bottom like so much used packing paper were a pair of leather sandals, his rattiest tennis shoes, and a dressing gown that he'd meant to give to the used clothing drive the next time Claire pestered him for a donation.

He tipped the suitcase forward and checked the side zippers and pockets. That was it. No toiletries or shaving gear, no evening wear, no tennis racket, no socks or shorts. Not even a toothbrush. Damn Nathan Baxter. The jerk probably thought he was being funny when he'd dumped this assortment of crap into Alex's luggage. So what if the guy carried a gun? When he got back to D.C., he had a good mind to find the jackass and ram this bag up his ass.

There was nothing Alex hated more than being less than well-dressed. Besides going with his image, wearing expensive clothes gave him a self-confidence all the IQ points in the world couldn't. Whenever he thought about not being able to hold his own with words, he could always count on the fact that he was the one being admired when he entered a room, the man the other men envied. He might not have the brains, but he had the looks, the money, and the charm—everything that counted in today's money-equals-success oriented world.

Claire liked to accuse him of being shallow, usually when they were having a friendly brother-sister spat. She was too kind to mention that he didn't measure up in the smarts department, but he knew she'd heard their father's disparaging remarks when they'd been children. When he bothered to show up at dinner or the occasional family gathering, Samuel Vandencort seemed to delight in degrading his only son. By the time his mother had found the good sense to divorce the man, Alex had started high school. Because his sister had been ten and young enough to change schools, Alice had taken Claire with her and Alex had stayed with his father.

Only when he'd been a senior had Claire and Alice returned to the District. By that time, his sister was in high school and their reunion had been bearable. He and Claire had made it a point to relate as brother and sister and regain their sibling bond. He didn't blame her for leaving him alone with their father. He'd even learned to stop blaming his mother. Alice Reynolds Vandencort Havers McBride had taken a shitload of verbal abuse throughout her entire first marriage. His mother never said so, but Alex knew he reminded her of the man she'd left. Now married to a prominent D.C. attorney, it had taken her fifteen years and a laundry list of shrinks to finally find someone who appreciated her and made her feel worthy.

He and Alice had an okay relationship, even if it was

Claire who saw to it they got together once a month. And that was fine by him. He was a grown-up. He didn't need a mother.

He didn't need anyone.

Surveying his pathetically inadequate wardrobe, he raked his fingers through his hair. The best he could do was send out the tropical blend suit he was wearing to be cleaned, along with the wrinkled shirts and crumpled slacks. He'd shop the men's resort wear store in the hotel after lunch for whatever else he needed.

Culling through the clothing, he chose the least crushed of the pants and shirts and stuffed the rest into a laundry bag, called housekeeping for a pickup, and set the bag in the hall. Then he gathered his clothes and headed for the bathroom. A warm shower would go a long way toward calming his temper.

Stomping to the parlor, he grimaced at the blaring music. Honoria's door was shut, and he figured she had closed it to drown out the racket as well as sequester herself from his prying. She was probably folding her things and getting settled in her room. His musings turned to shock when he opened the bathroom door and was greeted by a blast of warm steamy air. Rooted in the doorway, his gaze was automatically drawn to the car-wash-size shower in the far corner of the bathroom.

Staring through the steam, he could barely see the person indulging in the luxury of pulsating jets and frothy bubbles. But what he did see made his mouth go dry and his groin snap to attention.

Honoria, her back to the door, covered in a lather of foam and running water, stood like a goddess caged in glass. With her arms raised toward the heavens, her curvy body seemed cast in the finest marble. Long, shapely legs that went on forever led to flaring hips and a nicely rounded bottom that flowed into an indented waist and up farther to a lightly muscled back and broad-but-well-formed shoulders.

She turned a quarter circle to the left and the air hissed from his lips. Soapsuds slid down one bountiful breast, stopped at a turgid pink nipple, and dripped onto the shower floor. Stepping backward, Alex blotted at the perspiration dotting his brow. All through grade school and high school, Honoria had worn baggy, out-of-date clothes, some a replica of her mother's. After last night, the entire alumni knew that she'd been hiding an impressive figure, but who would believe she was every man's fantasy centerfold?

At the sound of the shower spray dribbling to a halt, he inched the bathroom door closed and retreated to his room. With the racket from the strolling orchestra echoing in the background, he should have had the common sense to put his ear to the door, or at the very least have knocked before entering. But if he'd been that smart, he would have lost the chance to see Honoria in all her glory.

He inhaled a breath. It was going to take a lot of tennis and windsurfing to forget about her spectacular breasts, flaring hips, and model-perfect legs.

It had been one hell of a twelve hours. He'd gone to a function he'd sworn to avoid, then been tricked into a wager he wouldn't have taken for any amount of money. Now he was on a vacation, sharing a suite with one of the two women who had walked out on him when he needed them most.

He wandered to the balcony and gazed down at the musicians, who'd finally decided to take a break. Raising his sights, he took in the sun worshipers, half of them female and most wearing little more than a few strips of spandex on their toned and terrific bodies. Honoria's dynamite figure could put all of theirs to shame, he thought, and he did have a reputation to uphold.

Suddenly, he began to rethink his decision to sleep alone on this trip. He and Honoria were consenting adults who'd been thrown together by accident. Why shouldn't they enjoy what was being offered? If he used caution and kept things light, he could send her a thank-you trinket and ease from her life as soon as they returned to the District, exactly as he did with all the women he slept with. They'd both have a week of fun and sexual pleasure, he'd shut up Cissy once and for all, and Honoria would earn a hefty amount of money for her precious Hewitt Academy.

How could she complain?

Chapter Four

Honoria turned in the mirror, trying to get a better view of herself in the gauzy white slacks. Alex had suggested they have lunch together, which sounded promising, and she wanted to look her best. It would be difficult for him to ignore her if they sat across from one another at a table, and maybe she'd find a way to bring up the auction and ask why he'd bid on her.

She'd tried on most of the casual clothes and thought both pairs of shorts too revealing and the khakis too tight. Well, not exactly tight, because they'd buttoned and zipped just fine, but they conformed to her like pantyhose, outlining her bottom and showing every bump and curve. These pants fit the same, but their flowing legs weren't constricting and they made her feel less exposed.

She chose a bright yellow T-shirt, also tighter than she was used to, which, with the new underwire bra, made her look even more full-breasted than before. Big breasts were the curse of the Hewitt women, she reminded herself. Faith hadn't inherited the trait, but she'd never failed to point it out to her only child on a daily basis, especially after she would insist that Honoria stand up straight and stop slouching.

It had been difficult trying to exhibit good posture while slumping, but whenever Honoria asked her mother how she was supposed to do both at the same time, she'd been met with a disapproving glower. Finally, she'd stopped arguing and learned to alternately slouch and keep her shoulders straight, knowing that when Faith got an idea in her brain, even a sledgehammer couldn't pound it out. The machinations made Honoria's neck crick and her head ache at odd hours, but she'd learned to live with the discomfort.

Staring into the mirror, she sighed. The contacts made her eyes water, but at least she could see. Wearing makeup was out of the question, but maybe if she tried the product Ruth had used she could do something with the pile of hair now sitting like damp straw on the top of her head. Working with the big round brush, she blew her hair dry, then put a little of the thick, gel-like substance in her palms and patted it over her hair, rubbing it in and down with her fingers. After that, she used the smaller brush to smooth out the strands.

Smiling, she turned her head from side to side. Amazing. Her hair was shiny and swingy, just like last night. If her eyes stopped itching, she might actually be able to get through the next six days.

She slid her feet into the white sandals, which felt like bedroom slippers after those uncomfortable three-inch heels, and picked through the items still scattered across her bed. Discarding the lipstick, she dropped her room key and the card she'd been given at the front desk into the canvas tote, put on the sunglasses, hoisted the bag over her shoulder, and took another look in the mirror. Satisfied this was the best she could do, she headed to the parlor to find Alex.

The room was empty, but the sound of slamming drawers convinced her to sit and wait. She scanned the living area, taking in the fresh flowers, cozy love seats, and the huge basket of fruit on the wet bar. The band had moved on, though she could still hear them playing in the distance.

Eloise and the rest of her friends had gone to a great deal of trouble to arrange this vacation. The hotel and her new clothes had probably cost a lot of money. How could she fault them, when it seemed they only had her best interest at heart? If she could break through Alex's standoffish demeanor, she might even be able to relax and have a good time.

Alex's bedroom door opened, and he strolled out, wearing a pair of wrinkled slacks and an equally rumpled dress shirt with the sleeves rolled up to reveal his muscular forearms. A day's growth of beard shadowed his square jaw, adding an aura of danger to his too handsome face.

"You ready?" he asked, his navy blue eyes not quite meeting her brown ones.

"Yes. Did you choose a restaurant from the brochure?"

He held out the pamphlet. "The Island Bistro sounds good. It's casual with a view of the ocean and a light menu. What do you think?"

After checking out the offerings, she raised her gaze to find him staring at her chest. Resisting the urge to slouch, she tucked the brochure in her tote and said brightly, "It sounds fine. Lead the way."

A corner of his mouth twitched as he turned and walked to the door, opened it, and gestured for her to go first. Shoving her embarrassment aside, Honoria held her tongue while they strode to the elevator. Like most men, Alex was fascinated by the female form, and she had *form* to spare. But from everything she'd read and seen on TV, men hated women who babbled. With all of Alex's worldly experience she was positive he would be a scintillating conversationalist, so her own words needed to be witty and concise or profound and thought provoking as well. If all else failed, talking about tennis would probably work, since he'd been on the team in high school. Unfortunately, the sport was something she knew little about, so she decided to skip that topic and find a common ground.

"What are your plans for the afternoon?" she asked, trying not to sound nosy.

"I need to go to the men's shop. That announcer fellow—"

"Nathan?"

"That's the one. Let's just say he did a bad packing job and leave it at that. Thanks to him, I'll need a new wardrobe to be comfortable here."

The elevator arrived and they rode it down to the lobby. "I'm sorry. I guess he was in a hurry."

"No need for you to be sorry. He's the one I'd like to—" He ran a hand through his tousled hair. "I'll just pick up what I need. It doesn't matter."

"Oh, but it does," she insisted. Honoria doubted she could afford so much as a blouse in the women's shop she'd spotted in the lobby. "The clothes here are going to be expensive."

"It's not a problem. I have a trip planned for Christmastime, and I could use a few new things." His gaze went from her head to her toes and back again. "It looks like you did some shopping yourself in preparation for this trip."

"Um, not exactly. You were right about all this being a surprise. Eloise and Karen shopped and packed for me. They bought things I wouldn't normally wear. I'm really more comfortable in less reveal—plainer—"

Honoria realized she was in danger of babbling and shut up. Following him out the elevator to the rear of the hotel, she found that she couldn't have said more if she wanted to. Now that she could finally see, her mouth dropped open at the three huge swimming pools, gaily decorated patios, magnificent gardens and lush flowering plants that made up the outside of the resort. They crossed one of the pool areas and walked over a wooden bridge to an open-sided, thatch-roofed hut sitting on a platform near the water. A lovely woman wearing a sarong led them to a table overlooking the ocean and handed them menus.

Alex watched Honoria through lowered eyes. He'd used a smile to bluff his way past the embarrassing moment when she'd caught him staring at her breasts. It was obvious she wasn't used to flaunting her figure, even though she had nothing to feel inadequate about. He would have to tread with caution if he planned on getting her into bed. If he remembered correctly, she wasn't the type to giggle or act coy, so he doubted flattery would work. There had to be a chink in her prudish armor, one thing that would soften her up and allow him to get close.

He set the menu down and waited to speak until she did the same. "Have you decided on something?"

"Everything sounds good."

She gazed at the water, then the other diners, almost as if she were afraid to look him in the eye. When they finally connected, he smiled. "Is something wrong?"

Her expression grew more serious. "I know you're used to places like this, but I've never been to a resort."

He almost said *no kidding*, then thought better of it. Making a joke of her modest lifestyle was probably not the best way to proceed. Instead he said, "And why was that?"

She moved the flatware from side to side, then opened her napkin. "Mother—that is—we never had the time. The school always needed a new addition or repair, and that had to come first." The waitress returned to take their order. "The coconut shrimp salad, please, and iced tea."

"Would you like a Long Island ice tea or a Paradise Punch?" the woman asked.

"Um . . . no, thank you." She gave a feeble smile. "I found out in college that alcohol and my system don't get along. I'm mortified about what happened on the plane and I—"

"No problem. Nerves get to everybody once in a while," he answered, putting aside the incident. His own nerves had frayed a little when she'd asked him to choose a place for lunch. Good thing the front desk clerk he'd called had been willing to describe each of the restaurants and their offerings.

"I'll have the same as the lady, and a glass of white wine. Thanks." He set his napkin on his lap. "I'm not much of a drinker either. Red or white wine, the occasional beer or glass of champagne is about it." He leaned back in his chair. "Where did you go to college?"

"Princeton. It was close, so I could come home on weekends to help Mother. I was surprised when I heard you went to an Ivy League school."

"Really? How come?"

"Because you didn't take the SATs. At the time, I didn't think you could get into one without them."

Her comment sounded innocent enough, but he couldn't help wonder if she was fishing for a way to bring up his only insecurity. "It was my father's alma mater, and his father's before him. All it took was a few calls to the proper authorities and a small endowment, and I was in." Two million spread over four years was chump change to his dad, cheap enough to guarantee the family tradition and avoid the humiliation of a son who couldn't get out of the triple digits on the entrance exam. "I have a degree in business. What about you?"

"Education," Honoria said. "I went to George Washington for a masters in educational administration and planning. Mother wanted to make sure the school would be in good hands."

It was the second or third time she'd mentioned her mother. Maybe talking about Faith Hewitt was the key to gaining her trust. "I was sad to hear that she'd passed away," he lied. "She always seemed so . . . concerned." In truth, Old Lady Hewitt, as she'd been called by the students, had been a harridan and a harpy. They'd all sworn she kept a pointy hat and broomstick in her office, just to stay in character. "I liked your mother."

"You did?"

The surprise in her voice had him grinning. "Sure. We all knew she was strict because she cared."

"Funny," Honoria said with a straight face. "I thought everyone disliked her. That's one of the reasons I decided to change the family strategy toward the goals of the school. The Hewitt Academy needs to attract students, and to do so we need to project a sharper, more modern image. I'm trying to be less judgmental and more hands-on with the children. I want them to know we understand what they're going through and can help, even when it seems their parents and the other authority figures in their life can't."

Alex doubted Honoria ever had an outbreak of acne or a second of teenage angst. He remembered her as a brain with a cool way of standing back and observing, mostly at dances and sporting events or anywhere there were crowds. Cissy had said she and her friends thought Honoria a snob, but their male classmates had simply thought her untouchable.

"Sounds like you enjoy your job. That's a plus in today's world."

"It's interesting how we both ended up taking after our parents," she said with a happy lilt. "You're still working at your father's firm, correct?"

Alex thought he might shoot himself if anyone ever accused him of taking after his father. And work was too strong a word to use where his duties were concerned. Samuel Vandencort didn't give a toot whether or not his only son showed his face in the office, just as long as he charmed the necessary clients. But it sounded as if

Honoria liked the idea of them having something in common, which worked well with his plans.

"I do. Maybe we could compare notes on what it was like having to live up to our parents' expectations."

The waitress brought their drinks and food to the table, and Honoria picked up her fork. "This looks wonderful."

She speared a shrimp and bit daintily with her flawless white teeth, causing Alex's groin to clench. When she raised her gaze and found him watching, color brightened her cheeks.

Smiling internally, Alex dug into his salad, his automatic reaction to her simple gesture proof positive that the sexual chemistry he felt pulsing between them was real.

Assuming she felt it, too, he guessed his road to seduction would be a smooth one. If his luck held, they'd be together in bed by the end of the night.

Honoria stood in awe of Alex and his fashion acumen. When he'd first walked into the men's store, his mere presence had set the clerk to groveling. He'd placed an order for a half dozen pairs of silk boxers in assorted colors, six Egyptian cotton shirts with silk ties to match, two pairs of linen blend slacks, six pairs of tennis shorts and complimentary shirts, a variety of dress and casual socks and a few accessories. Then he'd thumbed through the sport jackets and chosen one in navy blue. After taking stock of the Italian leather shoe selection, he tried on two different styles and bought both pairs.

Now at the counter, Alex pulled out his PDA and asked for the use of a phone. He then called a man she assumed was his personal tailor, and instructed him to immediately express mail an Armani suit in a specific style and color to the hotel.

She'd tried to hide her shock when she got a peek at the price of the shirts. The cost of the slacks had so astounded her she forgot to check the price of the shoes, but the total bill had rung up in the thousands. She doubted her entire closet of clothes back home was worth a tenth of his order or the amount he was paying for that Armani suit.

Staring down at her simple T-shirt and stylish pants, she shuddered at the thought of what Eloise and her friends must have spent to outfit her for this trip. She'd recognized a few of the designer names when she'd read the tags, but she had no idea how expensive even the most casual of clothing could be when there was a name tacked to it. If there was any way she could pay them back, she vowed then and there to find it.

"Have everything delivered to my suite by seven this evening," Alex said to the clerk, an older man with a wizened face and serious attitude.

"But I need to measure the slacks while you wear them in order to be sure of the length," the clerk insisted. "And they'll need to be hemmed, so it's impossible to do as you ask. Our tailor has gone home for the day."

"Then call him and see if he's willing to return and work overtime," Alex said in a pleasant tone. "I'll be happy to pay for the service." He glanced at her. "Do you mind waiting? It should only take a minute."

"Uh . . . sure. I'll just stop by the women's department and have a look around."

Alex walked to the dressing room with the eager clerk in tow, his tape measure fluttering behind him. She went through the connecting door that led to the women's store, hoping to find a bathing suit she could afford, since she had no intention of wearing either of the suits Eloise had packed for her. Disappointed when she realized that none of the swimwear was on sale, she forged ahead. Holding her breath, she turned over the tag on the least revealing suit on the rack, a sedate, dark purple number with a modest neckline and boy cut legs. The price made her eyes water worse than the contacts.

"May I help you?"

Honoria jumped at the sound of the saleswoman's voice. "Oh, no, thank you. I'm just waiting for my . . . um . . ." What the heck was she supposed to call Alex, anyway? They weren't dating, so he wasn't her boyfriend, and they certainly weren't engaged. Significant other would be a lie and companion sounded so . . . so sleazy and lowbrow.

Ignoring the woman's questioning look, she finally decided to call Alex exactly what he was. "I'm waiting for my friend."

She dabbed at the moisture on her cheeks, and the clerk raised a finely penciled brow. Digging in her pocket, she handed Honoria a fresh tissue. "That's quite a reaction you're having. I hope you're not allergic to anything in the hotel or on the island."

"I don't think so," said Honoria. After wiping her eyes, she blew her nose.

"Flowers, mold, paint, pets? Do any of those things make your eyes itch and water?"

"I think it's just these contacts."

The woman nodded. "I had the same problem, but it's an easy fix. I'll bet you're allergic to the preservatives in the saline." She walked to the cash register, set a handbag on the counter and pulled out a small plastic bottle. "Here, this is what you need to buy. They sell it next door. It's on the shelf near the sunglasses."

Honoria read the name on the container and noted the product description, marked clearly as hypoallergenic and guaranteed not to irritate. "Thank you. I'll go there as soon as I meet up with my—"

"Find anything you like?"

Coming from over her shoulder, the sound of Alex's deep voice sent a shockwave pulsing through her system.

Almost as if calculating Alex's net worth, the sales-woman sized him up through appraising eyes. "I have some lovely evening wear that just came in. There's a dress or two that would look divine with your friend's hair and eye color."

"That's not necessary." Honoria shook her head. "I have everything I need up in my room."

Without saying a word, Alex overrode her protest and nodded at the clerk.

The woman scurried to a far wall and began sifting through the racks. Striving to hold her temper, Honoria spun on her heel. "I don't need a new gown."

"It will be my treat," he said lightly. "It's the least I can do for letting me tag along on this vacation."

"I didn't *let you tag along*," she said with a frown. "You paid twenty thousand dollars to accompany me, and you didn't even know it was a vacation." Folding her arms, she jutted her chin. "I've been meaning to ask. Why did you shout out that—"

"Here we are." The clerk slipped between them, two dresses draped over her arm, and gave an encouraging smile. "I took the liberty of approximating your size. Both of these would be spectacular with your coloring."

Honoria blinked as she gazed at the dresses. The first, a blushing apricot with white piping, had a plunging neckline held up by little more than skinny straps and a promise. The second, a beautiful, shimmering turquoise blue, looked more modest but equally stylish.

"I couldn't possibly—"

Alex placed his hand firmly on her back and guided her to a dressing room. "Try them on. Then we'll talk."

Still sputtering, she dug in her heels, but he wouldn't be deterred. "Come on, Honoria, be a sport. Who knows, you might like them."

She glanced around the store. Several women had come in and were now watching with avid curiosity. Short of embarrassing herself and Alex by marching out, she really didn't have a choice.

The clerk opened the dressing room door and hung the gowns on an inside hook. "Call me if you need help."

Gazing at her reflection a minute later, Honoria bit at her lower lip. The apricot-colored dress molded to her figure like the hooker dress she'd worn at the auction, but it didn't look quite so scandalous. The only problem was the bustline. In order for the dress to fit properly, she would have to forego wearing a bra.

She slipped out of the gown and hung it on the hanger, with a good mind to not try on the second one. She thought about the dresses waiting for her in their suite. If memory served her, both of them were as daring but not as pretty as these two, and she owed it to her friends to wear them.

She leaned against the changing room wall and banged her head, hoping to knock loose some common sense. Why was she even thinking about owning the dresses, when she couldn't afford either one? She certainly had no intention of letting Alex foot the bill.

"Is everything all right in there?" came the clerk's singsong voice.

"Everything's fine," warbled Honoria, still glaring at the gowns. The blue one reminded her of the ocean the first time she'd seen it from her balcony. Could trying it on be that dumb a thing to do?

She slipped the dress over her head. Inanely, the rustle of fabric sounded expensive as it slid down her body. She raised her gaze and stared in wonder, immobilized by the woman in the mirror. Slim, sensuous, and sultry were the first words that came to mind. Her hair played off the fabric's vibrant color, shining like a wave of mahogany satin, while her mud brown eyes lightened to gold. Turning, she admired the way the silky folds caressed her bottom, not too tight but just right. Turning in the opposite direction, she found that her left leg, all the way to mid-thigh, was exposed.

Heat flared in her cheeks. The dress could be hers; all she had to do was take it to the counter and say yes. Giving herself a final once-over in the mirror, she rubbed at her nose. If she were prone to temper tantrums, she'd stomp her foot at the unfairness of it all. She'd never been this taken with a piece of clothing in her life. She undressed and hung the garment carefully on its hanger, then gave it a quick inspection. Finding no price tag, she checked the apricot dress, but it, too, was devoid of tags. The scenario could only spell a disaster of gigantic proportions.

If she allowed Alex to buy her this gown, every virtue her mother had instilled in her would be compromised.

After changing back into her T-shirt and slacks, she returned to the counter to find Alex holding court in front of the salesclerk and several female customers. Looking completely at ease while he joked with the strange women, he smiled that lazy smile of his and made room for her by his side.

"How did the dresses fit?" asked the saleswoman.

"They didn't," said Honoria, refusing to be swept into the circle.

"Oh, what a pity. I was certain I'd sized them properly. Would you like me to look further?"

"No, thank you," Honoria replied. "Alex, I'm going to the shop next door. Maybe I'll see you later?"

"Are you sure you want to leave him at our mercy?" teased one of the giggling customers, a petite redhead wearing little more than short shorts, a bandeau top, and a smile.

"I think he can handle it," Honoria muttered. The woman tittered and she strode out the door, determined to buy nothing more than saline for her contacts.

If she could afford it.

*　*　*

Standing in front of the book display, Honoria fumed in silence. What in the world had made her think she'd be witty or interesting enough to hold Alex's attention for more than a single lunch? Every woman in that store had been attractive and slim, glittering in a way she imagined the society debs he dated on a regular basis did. And any one of them would have more in common with Alex than she did.

Thinking a good book would take her mind off of her suite mate and help her to relax, she chose a novel from the top shelf and tucked it into the crook of her arm. She didn't know the author, but the cover seemed restful and the back jacket sounded interesting. She could sit on her balcony and read or nap, or gaze out at the ocean and think about the dress she *didn't* buy.

Better yet, she could watch the sunset and forget the financial difficulties waiting for her at the school. If she fell asleep and missed dinner, she'd take a walk on the beach and plan out the rest of her stay—alone.

Walking to the sunglasses case, she found the contact lens solution the saleswoman had recommended and grabbed a bottle.

"Did you find what you were looking for?" a deep voice said from close behind her.

Freezing in place, Honoria held her hand to her heart. Would she ever get used to Alex sneaking up on her? Turning, she tossed him what she hoped was an imperious smile. "I did."

He inspected the next shelf and removed a package of disposable razors and a can of shaving cream, then sidled over to the deodorant display. After choosing a brand, he moved to face her and saw what she had in her hand. "You're wearing contacts. I wondered what happened to your glasses."

"Someone forgot to pack them," she said archly. An image of Alex standing in front of a mirror with shaving foam dotting his square jaw popped into Honoria's mind and she ducked her head, fearful he could tell simply by looking at her what she was thinking. Just her luck, the errant vision had him bare-chested with only a towel slung around his narrow hips. Next, she'd be imagining him in a pair of swim trunks—or, worse, in the shower.

Pushing the scene from her mind, she headed for the checkout, where she paid for the contact solution and book. Just as she was about to leave, Alex stepped beside her and placed his purchases on the counter.

"Do you have plans for the rest of the afternoon?"

She held up the book. "I thought I might take a nap or read on the balcony."

"I'm going to the pro shop to reserve a tennis court for tomorrow. How about if I sign us both up?"

She shook her head. "Trust me, if I tagged along you wouldn't have any fun. I don't know a thing about the game," Honoria reminded him, hiding her regret at not being more athletic. Since she'd fired one of the janitors in order to pay teacher's salaries, she was forced to do much of the grunt work at the school herself. The only exercise she'd managed lately was lugging boxes of books or moving classroom furniture around.

"I'm sure you're exaggerating. Besides, I don't mind giving a few lessons."

"It's good to hear you still play," said Honoria, avoiding his offer. "I remember how much you enjoyed the game in school. Didn't I read somewhere that you'd broken into the top-one hundred ranking in college?"

Alex thought briefly about his foray into professional tennis, another of his failures. Then again, his father had warned him he'd never make it as a world-class player, and dear old dad was always right.

"Sophomore year in college. Sparred with the pros for a few years after that, but I never got higher than ninety-two, so there wasn't much point in going on. Besides, when I graduated I was expected to join the firm, so I almost had to quit."

"Don't diminish your accomplishment. Millions of people play, and you were good enough to beat the ones who counted to earn a ranking. The odds are similar in the field I'd thought about breaking into."

"And what might that be?" Alex asked, unwilling to accept her compliment. Hadn't she just admitted she knew nothing about the sport?

"I always wanted to write a novel, but Mother said it was an unrealistic dream. Hewitt women were educators, not authors of fiction. I've heard only three percent of all manuscripts submitted for publication are accepted, which sounds rather daunting."

"I don't find much time to read," he hedged. "But if you agreed to join me tomorrow, I wouldn't have to play with a stranger." He took out his hotel guest card and handed it to the clerk. "I promise to make it fun."

She smiled. "I guess I could at least think about it. I have to have a few stories to tell when I return, or Eloise and the others will think I wasted their money."

"And don't forget, we're supposed to have dinner together." The clerk finished ringing him up. Alex slid his guest card back in his wallet and collected his purchase. "It's early. I'm going to run up to the room and change into my swimsuit. Then I'm going to make the reservation. Why don't you drop off your package and do the same? I'll meet you poolside in, say . . . thirty minutes."

"I don't think that's such a good i—"

"Sure it is. You could just as easily read your book or take a nap in a lounge chair by the pool as on the balcony."

Pretending he didn't hear her sputter, Alex headed for the elevators. If he expected to get Honoria in bed anytime soon, he had to step up his plan for seduction. The more time they spent together, the easier it would be.

Chapter Five

Alex glanced one more time at his watch. Damn if he hadn't scored a zero with his reluctant roommate. It had been over an hour since he'd left Honoria in the gift shop, and she was nowhere to be seen. He hadn't meant to bully her, but thinking back, he might have come on too strong. He shook his head. As if he could manipulate a woman like her.

They hadn't hung out together in high school, but the way he remembered it, Honoria always had a mind of her own. When the girls in their class were streaking their hair and peppering themselves with tattoos, she'd ignored the trend. She'd taken charge of the school's crusade against drugs and led the student body in sponsoring a program to clean up a section of Rock Creek Park. Despite the smear efforts of Cissy and her friends, she'd even been elected senior class president. Yes, she'd been a bit aloof and avoided the party scene; being the principal's daughter had left her little choice. But she had never snubbed anyone. She'd been just as polite to the kids on scholarship as she'd been to the children of diplomats, ignoring all the boundaries money automatically placed on peer groups.

It stood to reason that if she wasn't someone who could be easily intimidated and she wasn't a snob, at least not where money was concerned, there could be only one problem—him. Honoria had figured out his secret years ago, and still didn't want to be around him—even for a few days of fun in the sun. She didn't want to spend time with someone she perceived as less than intelligent, not for dinner conversation or tennis lessons, and certainly not as a friend.

Standing, Alex raked his fingers through his hair. He'd taken a chance doing what he'd done in the women's shop, but hey, it was only money. He'd seen Honoria's expression when she'd left the dressing room, the one that said she was abandoning a best friend. When he'd taken a good look at the dresses, he'd sensed immediately which of the two gowns would be spectacular on her. He just hoped Honoria would take it the right way. The women he knew would be thrilled with his magnanimous gesture. He'd gone the gift route plenty of times in the past, sometimes when he began a relationship and always when he ended one. It was amazing how far a diamond bracelet or other costly trinket could got toward softening the blow of saying good-bye.

He scanned the pool area and saw that it was sparsely populated, which told him most couples were taking a siesta or engaging in a little horizontal recreation before dinner. He enjoyed the water almost as much as he enjoyed playing tennis. If Honoria had decided she didn't want to meet him here, he'd act like it was no big deal and swim out his frustration. He'd just have to come up with another plan to get her into bed. His reputation depended on it.

Walking to the diving board, he inhaled a breath. With a nearly empty pool, there wouldn't be a problem swimming laps. Taking a few running steps, he snapped off the end of the board and jackknifed neatly into the water.

* * *

Honoria rifled through her dresser drawers looking for something to wear. She'd dragged her feet on the walk from the gift shop because she didn't want to run into Alex. After she arrived at the room, she'd removed her contacts and left them to soak in the new saline solution while she sat in a lounge chair on the balcony. With the book held about six inches from her nose, she hadn't been able to see into the pool area below and check out any of the sunbathers. She wasn't even sure Alex was down there. He'd probably forgotten about his invitation and stayed at the tennis courts.

Unfortunately, she hadn't been able to read or even close her eyes to nap. The sounds of laughter and splashing water, coupled with the warmth of the sun, sang a siren's song to come and play.

At first, she'd ignored the persistent voices telling her to loosen up and have fun. *Live a little.* Then she recalled the advice given her by the limo driver and her friends. Even Alex seemed to be nudging her in a more congenial direction. He expected her to meet him poolside.

Poolside. It was the kind of word he'd probably used hundreds of times, just as easily as he said *put it on my account* or *I'll take the silk and the Egyptian cotton.* The phrases conjured exotic places and a world Honoria couldn't imagine herself slipping into, even for a few days.

Clutching the flowered cover-up in one hand, she slammed a drawer, ready to flop on the bed and pull the sarong over her head. Instead, her gaze was drawn to the black bathing suit she'd found in her luggage. She'd spied it in the dresser, but she hadn't taken it out . . . had she?

Of course she hadn't. She would have remembered removing it from the drawer and setting it on the coverlet.

Unless she was losing her mind.

No, that couldn't be. She hadn't been in the sun long enough to have heatstroke or anything else vaguely resembling a mental breakdown.

So how had the suit gotten there?

She took a tentative step and touched the stretchy fabric. She had yet to try it on, but she could tell from the cut it was not a garment she would feel comfortable wearing. Then she remembered the turquoise gown. She hadn't thought she would like that dress either, but once she'd slipped it over her head, it had fit like it was made especially for her.

Steeling her nerves, she blew out a breath. This was supposed to be the vacation of a lifetime, and though she was a mere thirty years old, she felt as if she had yet to live. Maybe it was time to break free from her mother's legacy, time to do something solely for herself. Even if Alex wasn't waiting for her *poolside*, she could go down and take a look around.

She tugged the T-shirt off and tossed it on the bed, then stepped out of the pants and hung them in the closet. After removing her panties and bra, she stood naked in front of the billowing curtains while the island breeze whispered across her skin and nudged her closer to the suit.

Trance-like, she stepped into it and eased the black fabric over her hips, stomach, and chest. The underwires cupped her breasts, raising them up and leaving little to the imagination, while the high leg showed more skin than she knew was proper. But who would care?

Hurriedly, she wrapped the sarong around her hips and tied the longer ends into a knot, then went to her dresser and inserted her contacts. Relief buoyed her confidence when she blinked and found herself tear free. Smiling, she grabbed the canvas tote and stuffed her book, sunglasses, Club Paradise card, and room key inside. After slipping her feet into sandals, she almost raced from the room.

The elevator seemed to take forever. She hit the lobby at a trot and stepped lively onto the terrace and down the rear stairs. Alex hadn't said at which of the three pools he'd be waiting, so she zeroed in on the one closest to the hotel. If he wasn't there, she'd find a cozy spot to sit back and admire the view, relax and read, or just people watch.

She strode into the pool area in time to see Alex walk onto the diving board. The thought that she'd been wrong, that he'd meant what he said and been waiting for her, made her warm all over. But seeing him arc gracefully from the board and plunge into the water lobbed a jolt of heat straight to her midsection. Honoria had imagined him tanned and toned from tennis, but she'd missed the mark by a mile. His body was a heart-stopping display of taut, sinewy muscle and tempting bronzed skin, more beautiful than any man had a right to be.

She stumbled to a group of lounge chairs arranged around small, glass-topped tables clustered under potted palms. She had no idea where Alex had been sitting, so she grabbed two towels from a stack and chose one of a pair of chairs partially shaded by the trees. After adjusting the chair back and making a pillow from the towels, she took out her book, intent on reading, but her gaze kept straying to Alex cutting a swift line through the crystalline blue water. It was apparent from his strong, smooth stokes that he swam as well as he played tennis. He was a natural athlete.

A waiter came by and asked if he could bring her a cool beverage. Honoria ordered a glass of club soda with a wedge of lime and refocused on the pool. Alex was still swimming, but at a more leisurely pace.

"Having a good time?" a cheery voice asked, breaking into her covert perusal.

Honoria turned to face a golden-skinned blonde wearing a miniscule white bikini. The woman had taken a seat in one of two lounge chairs to her right.

"Yes, I am," Honoria answered truthfully, drinking in the warm sun and scent of tropical flowers.

"Me too," the blonde confided. "I'm Gloria, by the way, and that's my other half over there." She nodded toward the far end of the pool where an older man was gingerly treading water. "My Leo is a real sweetie pie. I just love him to death."

Unless Gloria had taken advantage of thousands of dollars worth of plastic surgery or found the fountain of youth, Leo had to be a good thirty years her senior. Pudgy, pale, and balding, he didn't look the type to frequent romantic resorts or spend much time in the sun.

"I'm Honoria. I'm here with a friend," Honoria said, giving the woman a hesitant smile.

"Well, sure you are. Everybody knows Club Paradise is for couples only." Peeking over the top of her sunglasses, the woman threw her a wry grin. "So where is your guy?"

Honoria settled her gaze on Alex, who had downshifted to a slow crawl. How would he feel if he knew the other guests automatically assumed they were a couple? She pointed a finger. "The one doing laps in the pool."

"Honeymoon?" asked Gloria.

"Um . . . no."

"Anniversary trip?"

"No."

"Significant other?"

"Hardly."

"Oh, then you two are like Leo and me."

Honoria's cheeks turned hot as her sensibilities cooled. "Not knowing exactly how you and Leo are, I really couldn't say." The waiter set her drink on the table along with a ticket. She pulled out her guest card and showed it to him, then signed the slip.

"I'd like a Paradise Punch," said Gloria, "and you can bring a vodka Collins, heavy on the vodka, for my fella."

The waiter strode away and she swiveled to her left. "I didn't mean it as an insult. This is the new millennium. Lots of men and women who aren't married or engaged or even involved go on vacation together. It's nothing to be ashamed of."

Ashamed? The distasteful word called up lectures from her mother on not sullying the family name or making a public display of herself. Honoria had done only one thing in her life that she'd been ashamed of, and more for being foolish than tarnishing the Hewitt reputation. She'd managed to hide the mistake from Faith, but every so often the imprudent transgression crept into her brain, reminding her of her bad judgment and the dangers of losing her heart. There was no reason to take out her frustration on a stranger.

"It's difficult to explain. My . . . um . . . friend and I are here under what you could call unusual circumstances. We've never even been on a date."

Gloria stretched out on the chaise and clasped her hands over her stomach, covering the gold belly ring piercing her navel. "You came to a place like this to have a platonic vacation? What's wrong? Is your companion gay?"

Honoria fought the bubble of laughter rising in her chest. "I don't think so, but the situation is a little awkward. Some women friends gave me this trip as a gift—sort of—and Alex kind of came along with it."

"He's part of a present?" Gloria shaded her eyes with a neatly manicured hand. "Which one is he again?"

Like a bronzed god, Alex took that moment to rise from the water. "The man climbing out of the pool—in the black trunks," she said with a tremor of pride.

Gloria's pointy chin dropped to her collarbone. "Oh. My. God. Someone *gave* you *him* as part of a gift?" She sat up straight in the lounge chair. Pushing her sunglasses to the tip of her nose, she stared at Honoria. "I need to find a better group of friends."

Alex grabbed a towel from a waiting attendant and rubbed at his tawny hair. Sunlight bounced off the gilded strands and played about his broad shoulders while droplets of water dotted the golden hair on his finely muscled chest. When he raised his head and caught Honoria ogling, he flashed a blinding smile and ambled toward her.

"Are you telling me you're here with a heterosexual man who looks like that and you haven't slept with him yet?" Gloria made the statement sound more like an observation of criminal behavior than a question.

"We only arrived this morning. There hasn't been— I mean I don't—we don't—"

The waiter brought her drinks and Gloria signed the slip. Rolling her eyes, she watched Alex stroll their way. "Well, I certainly hope you're planning to. Otherwise I have to think you're a few fries short of a Happy Meal."

Before Honoria could answer, Alex stood at the foot of her lounge chair, grinning as if he'd just scored the winning run. "Hey, you made it."

Her heart stuttered in her chest. He was even more beautiful up close than he was from a distance. "I had a hard time deciding what to wear." At least that was the truth.

He ran his navy blue gaze from the tips of her toes to her face. "The suit looks great. Your friends have good taste."

"You can say that again," interjected Gloria. She held out a hand dripping with gold bracelets and jewel-studded rings. "I'm Gloria, by the way. Honey, here—you don't mind if I call you Honey, do you? Honoria is simply too big a mouthful—Honey was just telling me about how she won this vacation."

"I'm Alex. Nice to meet you." He smiled as he shook Gloria's hand. "Glad you decided to join me, *Honey.*"

Honoria nodded mutely. Alex's teasing endearment

and Gloria's run-on sentences made her dizzy, almost as if she were backstage after the auction. He settled into the lounge chair on her other side, and she picked at a thread on the knot of her sarong. "Did you make the tennis reservations?"

"Ten A.M. We have the court for an hour."

"You play tennis?" Gloria asked after taking a sip of her drink. "That's wonderful. Leo and I don't, but we're great supporters of the game. Last year he took me to the Open, you know, in Flushing Meadows. This July we're going to Wimbledon—that's in England. Do you mind if we watch the two of you play tomorrow?"

Alex peeked around Honoria. "That's up to my partner. It's going to be her first time on a court and I don't want her to be nervous."

Gloria's expression turned pleading. "How about it, Honey? Can Leo and I catch your game?"

Honoria forced out a grin. The courts were open to all guests. Even if she and Alex wanted to, they couldn't stop anyone from watching. But if Gloria and Leo were hoping for Wimbledon, they were in for a huge disappointment.

"I guess it would be okay."

"Great. I can't wait to tell my fella. See you in the morning." The woman finished the rest of her drink in one long swallow, then stood and gathered her things. Picking up the vodka Collins, she headed toward Leo, who was climbing from the pool with more than a bit of difficulty.

At Alex's insistence, Honoria showered first. Women, he'd told her, always seemed to need more time to get ready than men. In the hour it would take her to do her hair and makeup, he could shower, shave, dress, and watch a tennis match. He'd used Claire as his example, but Honoria had a suspicion Alex had plenty of experience waiting for women to make themselves presentable before tonight.

Finished with her shower, she wrapped herself in one of the big, fluffy robes hanging on the bathroom wall and checked herself in the mirror. After smoothing on a bit more of Ruth's hair gel, she scooped up her toiletries and walked into the parlor. To be courteous, she knocked on Alex's bedroom door to inform him the shower was free, but when he opened the door and propped himself against the frame, Honoria felt her color rise.

Still wearing his swimsuit, his gaze raked over her hair and face, down to the gap in her robe. "Thanks, and take your time dressing. We have almost an hour."

She pulled the robe's lapels tighter. "It will only take me a few more minutes."

He quirked up a corner of his sexy mouth. "If you say so."

Flustered, Honoria hurried to her room. Alex acted as if she needed major assembly, like some kind of Barbie doll primping for a date. She'd never primped a day in her life. Of course, the fact that she'd had precious few dates might have been the reason. Still, all she had to do was slip into one of the dresses Eloise had packed and put on her shoes. What else was there?

She set her toiletries on the dresser top and paced to her closet. She hadn't tried on either dress, and prayed she would look presentable in at least one of them. Reaching into the closet, her hand froze in midair. She blinked, thinking the new lens solution was causing her to see double, or in this case triple, because there were three dresses hanging side by side: the yellow one, the black one . . . and the turquoise gown she'd fallen in love with in the women's shop.

Afraid this might be an incident similar to the one she'd experienced with the black bathing suit, she reached out and touched the dress. The silky fabric soothed her trembling fingers, just as it had in the dressing room. She distinctly remembered telling the saleswoman the gown didn't fit. How had it gotten in her closet?

The answer hit her like a ton of bricks. *Alex.* After she'd left the store, he must have asked the saleswoman to talk to the men's wear clerk and have the gown added to his purchases. It was the only logical answer.

She sat on the edge of the bed and swallowed down a tremor of frustration. This entire trip had been one long, emotional roller coaster ride, and she was ready to get off. First she'd found out her best friends were planning a fund-raiser the likes of which would have sent her mother screaming. Then they'd informed her she was going on the auction block like so much prized beef, and there wasn't a thing she could do to stop it. She'd been handed to the highest bidder, a man she hadn't seen in a dozen years, who had offered such a ridiculous amount of money for her she'd thought he might actually want to be with her. Then he'd acted as if she had the plague.

So far, they'd disagreed on just about everything: the time they were supposed to eat dinner, the kind of activities they were interested in pursuing, even how long it should take them to get ready to go out. To make things more confusing, after they'd arrived, Alex seemed to change his tune, inviting her to lunch and offering her private tennis lessons.

Now this.

She'd made it clear she hadn't been able afford so much as a pair of sunglasses for the trip, so Alex knew she couldn't buy the dress. What gave him the right to give her such an extravagant gift?

Still in her robe, she stomped to the parlor. The sound of the shower reminded her of where he was. Closing her eyes to dispel the vision of Alex standing under running water, his gorgeous body slick with soap suds, she sucked in a gulp of air. Good Lord, what had come over her? It had to be Gloria and her suggestive thoughts. The woman had practically admitted she and Leo were here on an illicit tryst. She'd put the idea out there, intimating Honoria and Alex were doing the same.

The bathroom door opened and she stood.

Wearing the twin of her white terry robe, Alex strolled into the room. Freshly shaved, with every hair in place, he was walking eye candy. She could almost taste him on her tongue.

He stopped in his tracks and met her stare, his serene expression flattening to one of concern. "I see you found my little surprise," he said, taking a step closer.

Honoria swallowed the harsh words she'd been prepared to throw at him. He'd probably bought the dress to be nice, nothing more. "I did, and though it's a generous gesture, I'm afraid I can't accept it."

His golden brows rose into question marks. "Care to tell me why?"

She licked at her lips. "The dress didn't have a price tag."

He smiled. "Okay."

"That means it's way too expensive. Kind of like that old saying—if you have to ask how much you can't afford it."

"Ah, but that's the point." He grinned as if he'd just scored an ace. "I *can* afford it."

"You don't understand. I can't let you."

His smile grew wider as he folded his arms. "Because—?"

"It wouldn't be right."

"Says who?"

"Says my moth—says everyone. People talk. If they knew I'd accepted such an expensive gift—"

"Then you're saying you wouldn't be averse to accepting something on a lesser scale? Say a box of candy or flowers?"

She shook her head at his logic. "Well, yes. I mean probably."

"Probably?"

"Okay, yes, I guess I could accept candy or flowers."

"So it's the amount of money the gifter—that's me, by the way—spends that determines whether or not the giftee, which is you, can accept or decline a present?"

"No, of course not. People give gifts because they want to, not because of the—" She fisted her hands on her hips. "You're doing that on purpose."

"Sorry, I'm not sure what you mean by that remark."

"You know very well what I mean. You're deliberately twisting my words so I sound unreasonable."

Alex inched closer, but Honoria stood her ground. "You're the one who's not being logical. What's the difference whether I give you a present worth one dollar or a thousand?"

"For one thing, I can't reciprocate."

His eyes glowed with a humorous light. "So it's a pride thing? People can only accept gifts if they can give a present of equal value in return?"

"Yes."

"I don't mean to be nosy, but how do you intend on paying back your friends? You did tell me they gave you this vacation as a gift, right?"

"Well, yes. But—"

"And you accepted clothes from them."

"Yes. But they're—"

"Ah." He raised a finger in the air. "Let me see if I've got this straight. It's all right to accept a gift if it comes from a good friend and *if* you can reciprocate with one of equal value. And even if you can't, you'll still accept certain gifts because they're from women."

"I never said that."

"Honey, you didn't have to. It's written all over your face. Gifts from women are okay. Gifts from men are not. It's the old double standard, and to tell the truth, I'm flattered."

He was making no sense. "Flattered?"

"That you would think me so dastardly." He waggled his golden brows. "I can't remember the last time anyone thought of me as a lech."

"I don't think of you that way." *At least, I didn't until this moment.* "You're not like that."

He gave a little bow. "Thank you. I think."

"You're welcome. But I still can't accept the dress."

"Then consider the amount I spent as a loan and figure a way to pay me back. Take as long as you like. I'll still be able to buy groceries and take care of my electric bill."

Honoria wanted to stomp her feet and scream. What with his slick answer to her every objection, Alex should have been on the debating team instead of the tennis team. She sighed. The dress of her dreams was waiting for her. All she had to do was say yes to his offer. Maybe once the school started turning a profit again, she could pay him back.

"All right."

"All right what?"

"I accept the gown, but you have to let me repay you."

"Great." Turning, he headed for his bedroom.

"Wait!"

Alex stopped in his tracks. "Yes?"

"How much was the dress?"

"I don't know. Like you said, it didn't have a price tag."

She watched him saunter into his room and close the door. The idea that he could buy a gift for her, for anyone, and not even know how much money he was spending had Honoria reeling. It would do no good to find out the cost of the gown, because from the sound of it there was no way she could ever repay him.

She remembered the years she'd spent in high school, a period her mother often referred to as the golden years. The school had turned a huge profit during that time, enabling the addition of tennis courts, a new running track, and refurbishing of the stadium. By the time she'd graduated from college and come home as assistant principal, the academy was on a downward spiral and had just kept on spinning. Honoria was about to tackle the books Faith had insisted were in good working order, but then her mother had taken ill. After she died and Honoria had been able to delve into the accounting, it was too late. The Hewitt Academy was headed for bankruptcy at an alarming rate of speed.

Lost in thought, she walked slowly back to her room. Eloise and the others had assured her the auction would bring in big bucks, not only from the people who were bidding, but from the charitable donations of the alumni. Alex was an alumnus, as were so many others. If he had the cash to buy her an expensive dress, maybe he'd be amenable to making a donation. He was already into the school for twenty thousand dollars. From the sound of it, he could give more.

Honoria went to the closet. If memory served her, besides being in the advertising business, Alex's company was known for re-creating people and altering the way they were viewed by the world. Maybe she could talk him into donating his services as a consultant so they could revamp the public's perception of the Hewitt Academy, which in turn would lead to a higher enrollment and more endowments. His company could take the donation as a tax write-off, something she knew businesses did all the time, and her school would be saved.

After removing the gown from its hanger, she slipped

it over her head. The silk poured over her skin like warm cream, coating every curve. Glancing at her reflection in the full length mirror standing in the corner, she realized it didn't seem to matter that she wasn't wearing a bra or much of anything else under the dress. Here in this tropical paradise, she was free of her mother, free of the constraints of running a prestigious institution of higher learning. No one would care whether or not she wore undergarments or danced until dawn or walked naked on the beach. She was with a man she'd once dreamed about on a daily basis, and he'd bought her a gift.

Ever a practical woman, Honoria was smart enough to know that when they returned to Washington she would go back to her job as a school principal, while Alex returned to his glamorous lifestyle. But for the next six days, she could be and do anything she wanted.

And tonight, she wanted to have a good time. With Alex.

Chapter Six

The evening sky reminded Alex of a jeweler's cloth littered with diamonds. Even with the almost full moon, an amateur astronomer, as he liked to call himself, could spot the scattering of constellations filling the universe. He had a top of the line telescope on the roof of his town home, and when the weather was agreeable he spent hours on the rooftop terrace. Never had he seen the sky as it appeared tonight, so luminous with natural wonder.

Unwilling to believe a part of it was the companion on his arm, Alex tried not to stare at Honoria as they made their way to the dining room. He'd dated enough women to know she hadn't applied much in the way of cosmetics, yet dark lashes fringed her eyes and a faint blush tinted her cheeks. Besides the turquoise dress and white sandals, she wore a thin gold hoop in each ear and carried a small white evening bag. The gleam in her honey-colored eyes matched the brilliance of her expression, as if her megawatt smile was all the jewelry she needed.

Relieved that he'd been one hundred percent on the money about the gown, he hadn't done more than toss her a simple compliment, just in case she started lecturing him again on how she planned to pay him back. He'd given gifts to dozens of women and never once been accused of being anything other than generous, yet Honoria acted as if he had some nefarious scheme up his sleeve. Which was sort of true.

His plan was going to benefit both of them, Alex reminded himself. His reputation would remain intact, Honoria would receive a generous donation for her school, and they would both enjoy a satisfying week of fun in bed.

In silence, they followed the stream of elegantly dressed couples into the dining room. Alex had memorized the numbers two and three, had seen them in his mind so many times he felt certain he wouldn't screw it up and lead them astray. But before he had a chance to find his way, a photographer slipped in front of them and held up his hand.

"Hang on a second," the young man said, looking through the viewfinder. "Happy faces, please. I don't want you to miss out on winning the contest."

Honoria stiffened beside him. The flash went off and Alex was momentarily blinded. Not pleased with the ambush, he took a step toward the too cheerful man. "Care to explain what's going on?"

The photographer cocked his thumb. "Take a look and tell me if you like what you see."

Alex swiveled his head to find his and Honoria's bigger-than-life likeness smiling down from an enormous screen mounted on the wall at the front of the dining room.

"Wow," muttered Honoria, blinking her eyes. "We're huge."

"So what's the contest?" Alex asked, trying to sound disinterested. "Better yet, what do we get if we win?"

"You'll find out," the man said, grinning. "I'm supposed to pick the best of the best as they walk through the door and make sure they get seen. You guys are dynamite. What's your table number, by the way?"

"Twenty-three," said Alex. "Can we go now?"

The photographer scribbled on a piece of paper. "Sure, yeah. Have a great dinner, and don't forget to vote."

"Vote?" Honoria sputtered as Alex led her along behind him. Sometimes, he thought, it was better not to know.

He led her through the crush of diners all trying to find their places. He assumed from the number they'd been assigned that they were near the front, so he kept his gaze straight ahead. Spotting what he hoped was the number twenty mounted on a white card in the center of a floral arrangement, he confidently tugged her to their table. If this wasn't twenty-three . . .

When he pulled out Honoria's chair and she sat down, he breathed a silent sigh of relief. So far, so good. His only possible stumbling block was the menu. After taking his seat, he made a show of scouring the offerings while his tablemate read, her eyes wide.

Finally, he said, "So, what looks good to you?"

"Everything." Honoria didn't glance up, just continued to study the menu. "They have three lobster dishes and filet mignon, and some fish I've never heard of. I haven't had lobster in ages."

"Then lobster it is," he said jovially, tagging the filet for his entree. "What else?"

"Asparagus, for sure, and maybe the potatoes." She turned a page. "There are too many desserts listed to even to think about."

A busboy filled their water glasses, and a waiter came by to take their order. Alex figured he was approaching safe territory. All he had to do was request the side dishes she'd just mentioned and his meal was complete.

The waiter snapped open Honoria's napkin and placed

it on her lap, then threw him a curve. "And as an appetizer?"

"Ladies first," said Alex. He drummed his fingers on the table while she checked the menu again.

"Um . . ." Honoria nibbled on her lower lip. "What do you recommend? The chilled mango soup or the broiled prawns?"

"All of our cuisine is of the highest quality, but I prefer the prawns," the waiter offered, his pen poised to write.

"Then I'll try them," she said. "Alex?"

"I guess I'll be daring and go with the soup." Placing his napkin on his thighs, he leaned back in his chair. "Do you serve French wine or American?"

"We have both. All of our wines are listed."

Alex eyed the thick, leather-bound booklet, then met Honoria's gaze. "Interested in sharing a bottle?"

She shook her head. "I really shouldn't, but I would like a glass of club soda."

"That book's a bit much to wade through. Bring the lady her soda, and check to see if you carry—" Alex named two fairly popular but pricey reds whose vintages he'd memorized. When he took prospective customers out to dine in the District, he frequented the same three or four upscale restaurants, secure in the knowledge they carried the wine and food he enjoyed. If neither vintage was available tonight, he'd simply pretend nothing else suited his discerning palate and go without.

Instead of making idle conversation, he joined Honoria in taking stock of their surroundings. Centered in the front of the room was a dance floor, and behind it a stage. A trio wearing tuxedos played tepid dinner music, which led Alex to suspect they were merely fillers for the fun to come. The life-sized pictures of entering guests had been removed from the walls and the room lights dimmed. All of the tables were set with fresh flowers and a single lighted candle. The linens, a colorful mix of peach, beige, and umber, perfectly complemented the heavily embossed silver, delicate crystal, and fine china.

"I haven't been out to eat at a fancy restaurant in a while," Honoria said, fiddling with her dinner fork. "At home, it's mostly fast food or takeout from Mr. Belgradian's deli while I work on keeping the school afloat. Forgive me if I'm acting like a kid at her first circus."

He raised a brow. He'd set his goal this morning and gained ground this afternoon. Now was the perfect time to move toward the finish line in his quest to get her in his bed. What was it his sister always said? *Women love a domesticated man.*

"I get tired of the restaurant scene, so I've learned to cook for myself," he said smoothly. Honoria didn't need to know his entire repertoire of kitchen skills consisted of opening the carton on a frozen dinner and sticking it in the microwave.

"You? Cook?"

"Me. Cook," he deadpanned, aiming a thumb to his chest.

"I didn't mean to make it sound that way," she said, her smile bright. "I just assumed wealthy people had servants who did that kind of thing for them. If I remember correctly, your parents had a staff of six when you were in school."

"They did, but my dad and his current wife are alone in the house now, so they've cut back to three. I grew up with a nanny, maid, and butler at my beck and call twenty-four-seven. Believe me, it's not all it's cracked up to be."

"You didn't like being waited on?"

"I despised it," he bit out, then realized he sounded harsh. "It was my father's world, not mine."

The waiter returned with Honoria's soda and offered

Alex a bottle bearing a label he recognized. Alex sat patiently while the man went through the usual show of opening the wine, giving him the cork, pouring a dribble in the glass and waiting for the verdict. Alex realized he was home free. Expecting the heady rush that usually accompanied a game well played, he took a sip of wine, but the exhilaration never arrived. Instead, it felt as if he'd been cheating. It had taken him years to learn this sport. Why should playing it in front of Honoria somehow change the outcome?

A wine glass was set in front of each of them. "Sure you won't have a little?"

She chewed on her lower lip. "Well, maybe just a half glass?"

He nodded and the waiter poured a bit into her goblet, then filled his. Alex raised his glass to her and she accepted the toast, then sipped at the ruby red liquid. He smiled inwardly and concentrated on the activity around them. He and Honoria began the first course and spent time commenting on the food. Suddenly, he realized he was feeling more like himself than he had in a while. People who were looking to reinvent themselves usually opted for the rich and famous persona which, his father had drilled into Alex's head, was the image the company and its employees had to project, as well.

Honoria knew he came from money and didn't seem to have a problem with it. Since every little detail about this vacation seemed to impress her, he didn't have to try. She'd been standoffish because she'd been in awe of their surroundings, not because of him. There was just one thing that puzzled him. It was no secret the Hewitt Academy was having financial difficulties, but he'd always thought her family had money. Surely her mother had been smart enough to use a competent accountant to advise her properly? What kind of owner would put their own finances at risk when there were tax shelters, annuities, trusts—dozens of ways to protect personal income while running a business?

Honoria eyed the three-tiered dessert cart with a shudder. She loved chocolate and she loved raspberries, especially when they were mixed with whipped cream. She also enjoyed desserts made from lemons, oranges and strawberries, all of which the cart had in abundance. Each outrageous confection looked as if it had come straight from the pages of an upscale food magazine. The cart was so deadly, someone should have set an engraved placard on it that read *Diet Slayer,* just to warn people away.

"Maybe I should skip dessert." She rested her chin on her palm. "I really don't need the calories."

"You're on vacation," Alex reminded her. "Nothing you eat on vacation has calories. According to Claire, all women follow that rule."

"That's because your sister is model thin. She can afford to eat like every meal is her last."

"If you ask me, she's too skinny. I like the way a woman with curves fills out a dress or a bathing suit. Give me nicely rounded over stick thin any day."

Honoria couldn't believe her ears. If *nicely rounded* was his idea of the perfect woman, Alex had to think she was his dream girl times ten, an idea that tickled her from the inside out. "I'm serious. If I eat a bite of anything on that cart, this dress is going to split at the seams."

"I think I'd like to see that." Grinning, he pointed to a dessert that looked as if it was made of solid chocolate, and said to the waiter, "We'll have one of those." Inspecting the tiers carefully, he pointed to a second and finally a third choice.

"Alex, three?" she said with a little squeak. And how had he known to pick the very ones she'd been coveting? "Who's going to eat it all?"

"We are. Do you want coffee?"

"No, thank you. Drinking coffee at this hour will keep me awake all night."

"Really? Then maybe you should have a cup . . . or two."

She refused to comment on his suggestion. The half glass of wine had gone straight to her head, but she didn't feel sick, just relaxed. It sounded like Alex was flirting—a totally absurd idea. The waiter served their desserts and Alex waited for her to take the first bite. Instead of picking up her fork, she folded her arms and shook her head.

Alex cut into the chocolate dessert, raised his fork and held it close to her mouth, his grin tempting. "Come on, I can't take a bite until you do. I'm a gentleman, remember?"

Honoria was powerless to resist. Was this how he'd coerced her into doing his assignments in high school? She couldn't remember, but that had to be the case, because her stomach was jittery and she felt itchy all over, just as she had during their tutoring sessions.

Gamely, she opened her mouth and he slipped the fork inside. "Good?"

She nodded as she chewed. It was the best dessert she'd ever tasted.

He scooped into the raspberries and whipped cream and helped himself. Their eyes met and Honoria swallowed. Reaching for her water, she took a cooling gulp and switched her gaze to the front of the room. While they'd bickered over the dessert cart, the musical trio had been replaced by a full-sized orchestra. She concentrated on the master of ceremonies, a middle-aged man with a peppy attitude and mischievous grin.

"Ladies and gentlemen, I'd like to thank you for choosing Club Paradise as your romantic rendezvous. As some of you already know, our sole goal here is to help you have fun. If you don't want to join in, just say so. Better yet, order room service—" The audience broke out in applause. "But for those of you who don't want to be thought of as a stick-in-the-mud, each night we try to come up with a way to make the evening special. Tonight, we're holding one of our *best looking couple* nights."

The crowd cheered. Honoria remembered a comment the photographer had made to Alex. Since it took two to make a couple, that meant he thought she looked great too. Suddenly, the wall behind and above the orchestra exploded with light and a lineup of photos. There in the center was the one of her and Alex as they'd walked into the dining room.

"On your way in, our house photographer took the liberty of snapping a few pictures. Would the couples seated at tables seven, fifteen, sixteen, twenty-three, thirty, and fifty-six please come to the front of the stage?"

Alex set down his fork and pushed back his chair. "Come on, they're calling us up," he coaxed with a smile. "It's all in fun, Honoria. You don't want to be branded a stick-in-the-mud, do you?"

She smoothed her hair, adjusted the straps on her dress, sucked in a breath, and let it out slowly.

"Honoria. Honey, come on," he said, calling her by the nickname Gloria had given her at the pool. "It's just for fun."

And so not me, thought Honoria as she stood and clasped the hand he offered. "What do you think they'll make us do?" she hissed, still refusing to budge.

"I've seen shows like this before. They make you eat Cheezwhiz on a cracker, then they put a party hat on your head and force you to lip-synch to *Feelings.*"

She opened and closed her mouth.

Alex broke into a face-splitting grin. "I'm joking. Come on, let's go."

You did say you wanted to have fun, she reminded herself. And how could she resist such a sincere sounding plea? Alex moved so fast, she had to trot to keep up. They arrived in front of the stage and the announcer lined them up by table number. Beginning with couple seven, he asked each person to state their name. When their last names didn't match, the audience gave a chorus of teasing cheers. Then he asked each couple to tell the room why they were at the resort.

By the time the emcee reached her and Alex, Honoria's face felt as if it were on fire.

"Hello, table twenty-three." He held the microphone to her face. "And you are?"

"Honor—um—Honey. My name is Honey."

The announcer waggled his eyebrows suggestively, and the crowd erupted in giggles. "I see. Well, *Honey,* is this your first visit to Club Paradise?"

Honoria could tell they were in trouble by the naughty gleam in his warm brown eyes. "Y-yes."

"Great. And you, sir, are?"

"Mr. Honey," said Alex, barely hiding a grin.

The emcee turned to the cheering audience. "Aren't they cute? So, Mr. and Mrs. *Honey,* are you here on your *honey*moon?"

"No!" Honoria practically shouted.

"Yes," said Alex at the same time.

The diners applauded through their laughter.

"I see." The announcer winked at the crowd. "Well, Mr. and Mrs. *Honey,* who either are or are not on your *honey*moon, tell us a little bit about yourselves. Where did the two of you meet?"

"Um . . . in school. We met in school," mumbled Honoria. That, at least, was the truth.

"I see. And tell us, *Mr. Honey,* was it love at first sight or did she make you suffer?"

If the floor had taken that moment to open up and swallow her whole, Honoria would have cried with joy. Alex still looked jovial, but his smile didn't quite reach his eyes. She held her breath, waiting for his answer. What kind of lie was he going to tell next?

"Love at first sight, of course." Alex gave her a laser-like stare. "What else could it have been?"

The audience cheered, while the emcee thanked them both and moved down the line. Had Alex just used the words *love at first sight* in reference to her? Shocked, she kept her gaze on the floor.

"All right, everybody. Here's how we play the game." The announcer climbed back onto the platform. "Our couples are going to dance, and while they become one with the music, you, the audience, will vote on who you think is the best matched pair. Use any criteria you like—the way they're dressed, the way they dance together, or simply how well you thought they answered my questions. We don't care how you come up with a favorite couple, but at the end of the song we want you to vote. There are paper and pencils at each table. The waiters will come around to collect your votes, and the winning couple will be announced at the luau tomorrow night."

One by one, he walked behind each couple and gave out their numbers again. "Okay, contestants, here comes the music."

The orchestra began a slow song, something Honoria thought might have been sung by Whitney Houston. Alex took her in his arms and held her close. "You ready?"

She rolled her eyes. "I guess so, but please don't yell if I step on your feet. I'm not very good at this."

"Just follow my lead," he assured her, twirling them in place. "This contest is in the bag."

Honoria walked beside Alex, too content to speak. She'd never eaten such wonderful food or had so much fun as she'd had tonight. Alex was a fabulous dancer, which she attributed to his athleticism. He'd been easy to follow on the dance floor, even when the music had changed tempo and segued into a Latin beat. When they took their final bow, the audience had roared in approval.

Right now, they were casually strolling the walkway like the rest of the guests, and instead of tucking her hand in his elbow as would a gentleman, Alex was holding it as if they were on a date. The evening was warm, her dress was perfect and she was with a man she'd secretly admired for years. If the world were to end at this moment, she'd go to heaven a happy woman. Why had it taken her so long to loosen up and have some fun?

She glanced up at Alex, so tall and gorgeous and elegant in the moonlight. They entered the hotel, but instead of going to the elevators he steered her to a terrace on the opposite side of the lobby. Standing at the edge of the balcony, he let go of her hand and placed his palms on the railing.

Gazing skyward, he exhaled. "Have you ever stopped and looked at the stars, Honoria?" he asked her. "I mean really looked."

She settled against the railing and imitated his pose. Craning her neck, she focused on the sky with its amazing glitter of lights each twinkling in its own secret rhythm.

"Sometimes. But I have to confess I know next to nothing about astronomy."

Turning, Alex rested a hip against the balustrade and folded his arms. "There's a whole world out there we can't even imagine. The scope of it dwarfs mankind's insecurities and accomplishments, humbling me in a way I can't begin to express."

Honoria kept her eyes trained on the heavens, trying to envision what he'd just described. "I didn't know you were such a poet. Tell me, why didn't you major in astronomy instead of business in college?"

He shrugged and stepped closer to her side. "For the same reason you didn't major in English and start writing that book. It's hell living up to our parent's expectations."

Honoria's heart stuttered. Was Alex trying to tell her they had a connection, a bond that went further than being classmates?

"I learned to accept it. But what about you? I read about your firm all the time in the *Post*. It's said your company—"

"My father's company."

"Okay, it's said your *father's* company was responsible for electing a fifth of the senators now in office. And about a quarter of the House. That's an impressive record. Don't you think that's an important job, too?"

"If the senator or representative is worthy of the position, yes. Sometimes I wonder."

"I'd ask why you continue to work for the firm, but I guess it's for the same reason I'm running the school. Still, you're lucky—you can opt out anytime. It's not as if you're the only person who can do the job, the way I am at the academy." She didn't want to tell him that sometimes she felt like a prisoner, and wished she could chuck it all and leave. "If I walk away, the school would close and a hundred years of service to the community would end."

He peered at her through the darkness and she recognized the gleam in his eye. "You're going to make a joke, aren't you?"

"Who me? I wouldn't dare. Come on, let's go to the room."

Alex thought about kicking himself, and quickly tossed the idea aside. He'd gotten through life using charm and wit, and tonight was no different. He'd been clever enough to survive his father's disdain and hide his disability from the world. No way could he confess to Honoria that, short of living off his trust fund and becoming a tennis bum, there was little else he was fit to do with his life.

When Honoria gazed at him with those big golden eyes, he'd dived in with both feet, saying all the right words and sucking up her sympathy like a dry sponge. She had a comfortable way about her that made him forget about the secrets he'd kept hidden all this time. He hadn't meant to share so many of his feelings with her, but hey, if the ploy helped get her into his bed, why not?

Smoothly, he moved his hand from the small of her back to her upper arm and pulled her near. She melted into him and he smiled inside. She was so damned easy, it almost took away all the excitement of the chase.

They entered the elevator and he tilted up her chin with his thumb. "Honoria. Honey, look at me."

Trembling, she licked her lips with a delicate pink tongue, and he felt the quiver in his gut. The elevator lumbered upward and he bent his head, brushing his lips against hers in a practiced caress. She tasted like raspberries and chocolate and every other good thing they'd just shared.

Leaning into her, Alex moved his mouth, drinking in her sweetness. Then Honoria wrapped her arms around his neck and opened to his demand, molding her breasts to his chest, her hips to his groin. Her mouth reminded him of a summer peach, succulent and ripe under his lips, and he realized he'd been wrong. She was creating her own kind of excitement, sucking the air from his lungs and driving him crazy with need.

Pushing against her, he backed her into a corner and let his passion rise. His hands moved to her waist, and he lifted her up, nestling his knee between her legs. He'd known there would be sexual chemistry between them, but this white-hot desire was more than he'd imagined. If he played his cards right, they were going to have one hell of a week together.

The elevator doors opened and, reluctantly, he broke away. Back to reminding him of an innocent, Honoria blinked in surprise and fixed her golden gaze on his chest.

Alex nodded toward the door. "We're here."

She took his hand and followed him down the hall. After opening their door with the card key, he escorted her inside. Flicking on the lights, he thought about his next step. Should he bring her to his room or hers? Should he lead, or would it be better if she were the one to decide their first step? Would she appreciate being taken, or would she enjoy it more if he were subtle?

He reached out to pull her against his chest, but before he could touch her she gazed down at her feet.

"Oh my God! Alex!"

Honoria raced to the bathroom and he jogged behind her. *Great going, Vandencort,* he thought. *Get the woman alone and all she wants to do is hurl.* She opened the door and shrieked. He looked down at the soaked bathroom tiles and realized they were standing in an inch of water.

She fumbled with a stack of towels and turned toward the toilet. He followed her, but when she opened the door she jumped backward. Pushing her aside, Alex stared at the water bubbling up from the fixture.

The porcelain throne erupted like Mount Vesuvius, drowning them both.

Chapter Seven

TO: *Milton>Special-Angel-in-*
           Charge>@guidingangel.god
FROM: *Junior*
SUBJECT: *Hewitt-Vandencort assignment*
Via: *Heavenet*

All systems go. First twenty-four hours a rousing success. Working through a few personal issues, but not to worry. Will send further info tomorrow, same time. Over and out.

Junior stared at the message for a long while before hitting the SEND key. His ingenious plan had literally doused Alex's passion, something the bonehead sorely deserved. Too bad Honoria had gotten caught in the process, but there was nothing he could have done to avoid it.

Alex had actually regressed in his thinking, the stupid clod. He was going to take Honoria to bed for all the wrong reasons, which would have ruined everything. And Honoria, bless her innocent little heart, would have fallen for it.

Then again, sometimes a good healthy dose of mind-blowing passion did the trick. It was just too soon to tell if that was needed here. He would have to give it another day and see what developed.

Milton had insisted on updates every twenty-four hours, and Junior prided himself on being prompt. It was just about this time last night Alex had won that auction, setting the wheels of the rest of his life in motion. If he could get the stubborn human to think with his heart instead of the not-too-bright body part residing behind his zipper, things would be fine.

Crossing his mental fingers, he pushed the SEND key. A second later the screen went black and a small window popped up with the message: YOUR MAIL HAS BEEN DELIVERED. THANK YOU FOR USING THE HEAVENET. HAVE A NICE DAY.

Before he could leave the linen closet down the hall from Honoria and Alex's suite, his cell phone rang. Junior had a pretty good idea who it was, so he waited.

One ringy-dingy . . .

Two ringy-dingy . . .

"Hello. This is Junior. How may I assist you?"

"Junior? Come quick! For heaven's sake, you've got to do something!"

"Not to worry. Help is on the way," came Junior's cheery voice. She heard a click and the drone of a dial tone.

Help is on the way? Honoria knew most hotels could verify a room number from a phone call, but how could he identify the problem through the phone line? If he was still at the front desk at ten o'clock, it meant the poor man worked twenty-four hours a day. He had to be as exhausted as she felt. There was no way he could arrive prepared for the mess in their bathroom.

She set the receiver in its cradle and gaped at the encroaching water creeping like a lava flow across the living room floor. She'd noticed the wetness almost immediately after Alex unlocked their suite. First there'd been an odd squishy sensation under her feet. Then she'd heard a gurgle. The second she opened the bathroom door, water had inched over the soles of her sandals. When a quick scan of the shower, tub, and sinks told her they weren't the culprits, she'd headed for the commode.

Za-zoom! She'd never seen Old Faithful in action, but she imagined it looked very much like the toilet in the Tropical Breeze. When Alex had shoved her aside and shouted at her to call for help, all she could remember were Junior's last words after they'd checked in.

Call me anytime. Just dial ninety-nine and I'll be there.

Tiptoeing through the wet, Honoria listened at the bathroom door. She could hear Alex cursing as he stormed through the room. He'd already filled the bowl with towels and was probably stuffing the toilet with their robes at this very moment. She had no idea what had made the porcelain fixture erupt like a geyser, but they certainly couldn't stay here tonight.

Pounding rattled the door, and she rushed to answer it. Grinning from ear to ear, Junior trotted in followed by a bellman and two workmen wearing coveralls.

"I brought reinforcements," he warbled cheerfully, shooing the workmen toward the bathroom. He pointed to the bellman. "You. Go pack Ms. Hewitt's things. We have to get our guests out of here."

Alex stalked from the bathroom, his new suit drenched and his face on full scowl. "It's about time someone from the hotel arrived. I don't know what kind of place you're running here, but—"

Junior nodded effusively, his smile full of concern. "I know, I know, and you're absolutely right. Just to show how sorry we are for the inconvenience, we're moving you to our top of the line accommodation."

"I thought this *was* your top of the line accommodation," growled Alex, swiping at the lock of hair that snaked wetly onto his forehead.

"It is, if your room is *in* the hotel. We're moving you to a better place."

"What kind of *better place?*" demanded Alex. "I haven't seen any other buildings on the property."

"Not to worry," said Junior. "We're taking you to a cabana. They're totally modern, just a bit isolated. The only way to reach them is by golf cart or a nice long walk. Simply follow the path to the nude beach and make a left at the fork. We save them for our honeymooners, or those couples who wish to visit here while remaining—how shall I put this?—anonymous."

Honoria rolled her eyes. Great. It was bad enough she'd been sharing a suite with Alex, even if they had separate bedrooms. Now she was being moved to a . . . a love nest. And had Junior just said *nude beach?* If Eloise and the rest of them ever found out . . .

"What about single rooms . . . er . . . suites?" she pleaded. "Hasn't anyone checked out since this morning?"

Alex folded his arms and glared at Junior. "It doesn't matter, Honoria. Just let the man do his job."

The bellman entered the parlor with Honoria's suitcase in one hand and her hanging clothes in the other, and took them into the hall. Seconds later, he reappeared and dashed into Alex's bedroom. Alex marched after him, presumably to direct the transferal process, his new Italian loafers squishing with every step.

Junior turned to Honoria, his expression contrite. "As I said earlier, putting you in separate rooms is impossible."

"Impossible? But this wasn't our fault."

"Of course it wasn't. But we can't move you to a different suite if there aren't any available, now can we?"

Shouts and a strange kind of whooshing noise echoed from the bathroom. The workmen hurried through the parlor and into the hall. A second later they returned, brandishing huge wrenches and a device that resembled a roll of wire.

"Come on, let's get you out of here." Junior pushed gently at her back. "Who knows, the entire commode might blow at any moment. It wouldn't do to have you injured in the fallout, would it?"

Honoria moaned. If Faith wasn't still spinning in her grave over the entire auction thing, she'd take off like a top at the sight of her only daughter's obituary headline in *The Washington Post*:

HEADMISTRESS OF PRESTIGIOUS HEWITT ACADEMY FELLED BY EXPLODING COMMODE.

She followed Junior to the luggage trolley, still trying to figure out how he'd come prepared to tackle their problem. "Did I mention the toilet when I called you? I don't think I did."

Ignoring the question, Junior *tsked* as he inspected her from head to toe. "Oh, dear. Just look at that gown."

Shoving a hank of dripping hair from her face, Honoria swept her gaze downward and did her best to hold back tears. "My beautiful dress. Do you think we can find another one?"

"Just about anything material can be replaced," he said sagely. "It's matters of the heart that are sometimes lost forever."

She sniffed at his sensible words. The front desk clerk was quite the philosopher. He was also much better in a crisis than her roommate, who had bossed her around and ordered her out of the bathroom as if she were an idiot. And to think that only minutes earlier she'd been so lost is his kiss she'd been ready to follow Alex to a bed, any bed, and do whatever he asked.

Shaking the hem of her dress, Honoria stared at the

puddle it made on the hall carpet. No wonder men took cold showers to stem the flow of passion. It worked.

Alex walked into the hall carrying his suitcase, followed by the struggling bellman, who was overladen with hanging clothes. Without glancing her way, he jutted his chin toward Junior. "I assume the hotel will replace our ruined clothing?"

"Not a problem. I've already told Ms. Hewitt we'll be happy to take care of it."

Honoria wanted to smack Alex. He was acting like a jerk. Accidents happened, and this certainly had been a doozy. Junior and his rescue crew hadn't been at fault, so there was no need for him to snap off heads.

They rode the elevator in silence while she fumed. At the rear of the hotel, Junior led them to a golf cart while the bellman pushed the trolley along behind. Strains of a Latin band filled the night air. It was dark, but even at this late hour guests danced on the patio, swam in the pool, or huddled under towels on huge double-wide lounge chairs.

Shivering, Honoria climbed into the cart. Thanks to a strong island breeze, she was chilled from the inside out. Junior handed them both fresh towels, then levered himself into the driver's seat and started the engine. She blotted her face and hair and Alex did the same. Then she draped the towel over her shoulders like a shawl.

"You all right?" asked Alex.

"I'll be better after I take a warm shower and get some sleep."

"A shower?" He gave a snort. "Sure, why not?"

Alex knew Honoria was miffed, but he wasn't sure if she was upset with him, the situation, or both. Hell, it hadn't been his fault the toilet had blown. Okay, so maybe he'd been a little bossy, but someone had to try and shut down that bubbling commode. It made perfect sense that he did the grunt work while she called for help. He'd only made that crack about their clothes because he knew how much she liked her dress. And she hadn't even thanked him for saving her from a total drenching.

He caught her profile in the torches illuminating the path, and smiled to himself. She reminded him of a bedraggled kitten. Even with her pert nose raised in the air, she looked aloof and untouchable, just as she had in school, but he now knew it was only an act. Honoria really was a good sport. He hoped to coax her back to her old self. Then he could concentrate on replaying their scene in the elevator.

And he really wanted a reenactment. Soon.

Unfortunately, the sight of her tears and his stupid tirade gave him a sinking sensation. Once they arrived at the cabana, they wouldn't be sharing any more than a curt good night.

"You expect us to stay here?" Honoria gazed about the room as if she'd been escorted to a jail cell. The spacious cottage, decorated as elegantly as their suite, had a fireplace and sofa flanking a far wall and an efficiency kitchen with a wet bar tucked in the opposite corner.

"As I said earlier, it's all we have." Junior opened the door to a bathroom of the same size and layout as the one they'd just vacated. "These cabanas are completely private, yet only yards from the beach. In the morning you can take a leisurely stroll to the terrace buffet or call room service and they'll deliver breakfast to the porch." He scuttled about the room, opening closet doors and checking the amenities. "See? All the comforts of the Tropical Breeze."

"Not quite," muttered Honoria, staring at the single room's obvious focal point. The king-size bed, covered in colorful pillows and draped dramatically in mosquito netting, reminded her of a bed she'd once seen in a magazine layout for *A Thousand and One Arabian Nights.*

"Oh, that." Junior walked to what Honoria thought was another closet and opened the door. "Hmm. That's strange. There's supposed to be a rollaway in each cottage, on the off chance there's a problem."

"Looks like someone forgot to tell the bed," observed Alex, his tone dry as dust.

"Well, it's too late to do anything about it tonight." Junior opened the door for the bellman, then disappeared. A second later he popped back inside. "The hammock on the porch looks comfortable. Perhaps one of you could make use of it while I try to rustle up a cot for tomorrow."

"A hammock?" Alex stuffed his hands in his pockets. "Try again, buddy."

Tapping a finger to his chin, Junior hummed a tuneless ditty. Raising the same finger in the air, he opened a bottom dresser drawer, dragged out sheets, a blanket and pillow and set them on the couch. "There's always the sofa."

Honoria bit at her lower lip. Alex's hardened gaze ping-ponged from the bed to the sofa and back again, almost as if he was contemplating them sharing. Before she could beg Junior one more time to find them different rooms, he and the bellman slipped out the door.

"Remind me to talk to your friends once we get back to D.C." Alex tossed the pillow on the coffee table, picked up the linens and began to prepare the sofa. "I think they need to study up on the definition of *deluxe accommodations.*"

"That's not fair," argued Honoria. "No one could have predicted that—that—whatever you want to call what just happened would—happen, I mean." Annoyed she was babbling, she opened her suitcase and began to sort through her clothes and personal items. Then she realized the bellman had been the one to repack everything, including her underwear and nightgowns. Worse, without a bedroom of her own, Alex was going to see her unpacking the flimsy stuff.

Turning, she found him sitting on the sofa removing his shoes. "Are you sure you wouldn't be more comfortable in the hammock?"

He froze in the middle of peeling off a wet sock, one eyebrow raised in question. "The only place I'm willing to sleep outside of this couch is that bed, Honoria. Does that answer your question?"

"Oh."

Ruined shoes and socks in hand, he stood, a corner of his mouth lifting boyishly. "Why don't you collect your things and take that shower you were talking about? I'll put my own stuff away and stow the suitcases, then have my turn in the bathroom. By the time I finish brushing my teeth you'll be under the covers and I won't see a thing. Honest."

Too tired to fight, she retrieved her toiletries and the ice blue peignoir set and clutched everything to her chest. "I'll only be a minute."

"Take your time."

Honoria didn't say another word, just slipped into the bathroom and sagged against the door. Alex was back to being a gentleman, and she wasn't sure whether or not that pleased her. Granted, an exploding commode was a sure way to drown the flames of even the hottest romance, but now that they were alone he hadn't once stepped near her. Back in the elevator, she'd dived headlong into Alex's kiss. Her lack of experience had probably done more to cool his interest than the overflowing toilet. She knew her technique needed work, but not his.

Alex was a world-class kisser.

She turned the shower jets on warm. Not that she'd had a lot of kissing experience, but he'd certainly curled her toes—and a few other body parts she forgot existed. She sighed. This had been one of the longest days of her life, filled with so many ups and downs she thought she'd never get back on even ground. A good night's sleep would put her brain to rights. Maybe that would help her locate her common sense.

She and Alex were adults. If neither of them wanted to be intimate, they could still be civil to one another. They could still be friends.

Alex waited until Honoria shut the door and he heard water running before he took care of his own clothing. Good thing he'd added a pair of silk pajamas to his order before he'd left the men's shop, or she'd probably expect him to sleep fully dressed. Even then, he imagined Honoria's sensibilities would be wounded.

Glancing around the spacious cabana, he saw that the setup in this hideaway was better than in their old suite. If she balked at his advances, there were plenty of ruses he could use to finagle his way into bed. He was a tall guy and the sofa was little bigger than a love seat. He doubted he'd have to spend more than one night, two at the outside, on the couch once he started complaining about a bad back or his lack of a good night's rest.

The sound of the shower subsided and he stepped onto the porch. He'd promised Honoria she could slip under the covers in private, and he meant what he'd said. For now.

Gazing at the stars, he wished he was a smoker, because this was the perfect time for a cigarette. The kiss they'd shared in the elevator had been a hell of a beginning to a night of sexual fulfillment. Her red-hot reaction to his touch had fanned his desire, only hinting at the passion buried beneath her prim façade. He'd made love to his fair share of women, and few of them had been as responsive or felt so right in his arms as the usually oh-so-proper *Honey*.

His mind raced while his hands gripped the porch railing. Thanks to that kiss, it was going to be impossible to exorcise the memory of her in the shower with her arms raised and her generous body covered in soapy lather. Knowing what he did about Honoria, he suspected she slept in flannel granny gowns, buttoned from her chin to her toes. He could start at the top and undo the buttons one by one, revealing all of her charms inch by satiny inch, until the gown dropped to her feet and she was naked to his gaze.

Maybe he'd be able to convince her to wear the top half of his silk pajamas, with the buttons undone and the hem skimming her shapely thighs, or one of those eye-popping peignoir sets he'd seen her sneak out of her luggage. The ice blue one looked delicate as a butterfly's wing, but that red one . . . the fabric was sheer, so he'd be able to see every bit of her, from her swelling breasts with their aroused nipples to the dark thatch of hair at the juncture of her thighs.

He heard a door open and close and figured Honoria was finished. More than likely, she was sliding under the covers right now. If not for that damned exploding toilet, he'd be climbing in beside her, undoing buttons, and exploring at will. . . .

Vowing to be patient, Alex adjusted the fit of his slacks and headed for the door. He and Honoria had five more nights together at Club Paradise. Time enough to experience each of the scenarios he'd just imagined.

Some of them more than once.

Honoria stretched, luxuriating in the cool caress of satin sheets skimming her body. Birds sang gaily in the quiet morning air, while the scent of tropical flowers surrounded her. It had taken a long while to fall asleep last night, but once she had, she'd slept as if drugged.

She recalled that Alex, too, had had difficulty settling

down, and wondered if he'd been thinking about their kiss. She'd watched him through the shadows, admiring his nicely muscled back as he'd left the bathroom and strolled to the couch. She'd heard him moving around, mumbling to himself. She'd even heard a thud, as if he'd fallen off the sofa. Tonight was sure to be better. By then, Junior would have a cot delivered to the cabana and Alex would have a full-sized space in which to sleep.

Peeking from beneath the covers, she scanned the room. Sunlight streamed through the shutters over the wet bar, a sure sign it was morning, but Alex was nowhere to be seen. She heard a clatter in the distance, then a strange male voice and Alex's mingled in the morning quiet.

Honoria's stomach growled, reminding her of the time. Besides needing to eat, they had a date to play tennis. She had to get moving in order not to be late. Rising from the bed, she opened a drawer and retrieved fresh underwear, a pair of white shorts, and a lime green T-shirt and walked to the bathroom. Once inside, she took a quick shower, dressed and put in her contacts. Standing at the sink, she blew her hair dry and smoothed in some of Ruth's magic goo, then used the largest of her brushes to get the strands to behave.

Satisfied she'd done a decent job, she stepped back and inspected herself in the full-length mirror attached to the back of the door. Even though the T-shirt clung to her breasts like a second skin, it wasn't as bad as the shorts, which barely covered the tops of her thighs. Maybe it would be smarter to change into slacks. Then she remembered how every pair she had molded to her behind and left nothing to the imagination. Since Alex was going to all the trouble of giving her a lesson, she was determined to do her best—something that would be difficult in body-hugging slacks. She had no choice. She would have to play in the outfit she had on, because she doubted she could afford any of the tennis togs in the women's store, and she certainly didn't want Alex to buy her any more clothes.

Honoria jumped at the knock on the door. Opening it, she found Alex, still wearing his pajama bottoms, propped against the frame and looking as sexy as a male centerfold.

"Good morning." He appraised her through sleepy blue eyes. "I took the liberty of ordering breakfast. Nothing fancy, just a little fuel to get us through the workout. It's not a good idea to play tennis on an empty stomach, but you don't want to be stuffed. I figure we can make up for it at lunch."

"Oh, sure," she managed, concentrating on his smile. "Let me get out of the way, so you can shave—er—shower—er—" She stumbled past him, wishing the floor would sink beneath her feet. "I'll just go have a bite of breakfast."

"Have more than a bite," he called after her. "You're going to need it."

Warmed by the gleam of approval in Alex's eyes, Honoria scurried to the door and stepped onto the cabana's front porch to investigate her surroundings. Nestled in a tangle of flowering trees, the pale pink, vine-covered cottage was set back off the path. Baskets of cascading flowers hung from hooks anchored to the porch ceiling. Two chairs and a glass-topped wrought iron table set with more flowers, fine china, and an assortment of breakfast items took up one corner of the white painted, wide-planked floor. The infamous hammock—strung at an angle across the opposite side and wide enough to accommodate two—swung lazily in the early morning breeze.

Honoria sat and poured a cup of coffee from a delicately painted china pot, then added a drop of cream. Sipping slowly, she inhaled the bracing taste of the fresh morning brew as she inspected an oval platter overflowing with exotic looking fruit and pastries. Lifting her fork, she speared a rectangle of pineapple and bit into it, savoring the delicate sweetness. Then she tried a round of kiwi, a slice of mango and what she guessed was pomegranate. Everything tasted delicious.

Selecting a pastry, she turned at the sound of chirping and found she was being scrutinized by a brightly feathered bird about the size of a robin. "Well, hello. Where did you come from?"

Staring through flashing black eyes, the bird bobbed its orange-crested head.

"I agree. It is a wonderful morning."

The bird stilled, its bright ebony gaze concentrated on the triangle of flaky, sugared dough Honoria held in her hand.

"Oh, so you're hungry too? Well, how about you come join me?" Breaking off a corner of the pastry, she placed it on the edge of the table, then sat back and held her breath, willing the bird to venture near. "Come on," she encouraged. "If you want the treat, you need to get closer."

Just when she thought the bird was going to take up her offer, the front door opened and Alex stepped onto the porch, frightening her morning visitor back to the depths of the forest.

"Sorry, Dr. Dolittle," he said, his tone amused as he watched the bird fly away. "I didn't mean to interrupt your meaningful encounter with nature." He pulled out a chair and took a seat. "How's breakfast?"

It was difficult, but Honoria tried not to stare. She'd been correct when she'd envisioned Alex in tennis whites. His bronze skin played against the snowy, brushed cotton shirt and crisp linen shorts, while his dark eyes sparkled a blue that matched the color of the ocean. Even his sun-streaked hair shimmered with vitality.

"Is something wrong with the food?"

"Hmm?" She fumbled with her napkin. "Oh, no, everything is wonderful. The fruit tastes island fresh and the pastry is out of this world." Honoria caught movement from the corner of her eye and glanced at the railing. There sat her feathered pal, but this time he was accompanied by a smaller, less colorful bird. "Oh look, he's brought a friend."

Eyeing their visitors, Alex sipped at his coffee. "Judging by their plumage, I'd say they're a couple."

The female ruffled its pale gray feathers and quirked its head, looking from Honoria to Alex and back again, almost as if she knew what they were saying.

"Do you think I could get one of them to come closer?"

Laughing, he broke off a piece of his croissant and dropped it next to the crumb she'd set at the edge of the table. "I'm sure you can, with a little patience. These guys probably beg from all the tourists. It's just a matter of time before they get used to us."

No sooner had the words left his lips than the first bird fluttered near. Dipping gracefully to the table, it picked up Honoria's bit of pastry in its yellow beak and flew back to the railing, where it set the crumb down in front of its mate.

"He's sharing. Isn't that sweet?"

"Smart man. He knows the fastest way to her heart," Alex said, helping himself to a slice of fruit.

The female bird bobbed back and forth, deciding whether or not to accept the gift, which caused Honoria to smile. "If you ask me, she's thinking about her reputation. See how she's taking her time considering his offer? She doesn't want to be thought of as easy." Hoping to further impress her point, she added, "All women should be careful of males bearing gifts."

Alex eyed her over the rim of his coffee cup, silently reading her message. Finally, the bird scooped up the tidbit and gobbled it down. The male bird took that moment to go after the other crumb of pastry. Hopping onto the table, he pecked at the treat, then swallowed it in one gulp. Bobbing from foot to foot, he stood expectantly, eagerly waiting for more.

Alex finished his coffee, then checked his watch. "We have less than an hour before we're due on the court, and you still have to choose a racket. I think we need to get going."

In a flash, both birds disappeared into the trees. Honoria pushed her chair from the table and stared at her bare feet. "I don't have athletic shoes, just a pair of white sneakers. Will that be all right?"

"As long as they give you decent support, sure."

Since the sneakers had been purchased by Eloise and Honoria had yet to wear them, she had no idea if the shoes had support or not. She didn't even know if they would fit, though the sandals seemed fine. Crossing her fingers, she walked to the closet and found the sneakers. Tucked inside of each shoe were two pairs of white socks. Besides being an efficient packer, Eloise had thought of everything.

Chapter Eight

Honoria stared openmouthed at the tennis rackets, which took up one entire wall of the pro shop. She had no idea there would be so many to choose from. Oversized or regular and strung with nylon or horse gut—yeech!—all were composed of graphite or fiberglass, with several different grip sizes, weights, and strings per inch. The descriptions and brand choices were endless, the prices astronomical.

Alex immediately found the perfect racket—a twelve-ounce something or other with a specific number of strings, and decided to buy it as well as two cans of fluorescent yellow balls. Since they were only renting her equipment, he advised her to *try a few on for size*, as if he expected her to find the proper pair of snowshoes to wear on a trek through the wilds of Alaska.

She had no idea what she was supposed to look for. All the rackets were gray or black, and big. Very big. And they looked so heavy she couldn't imagine swinging one for the hour they were supposed to be on the court. Her arm would fall off before they finished a set or an inning, or whatever the term was for a round of tennis.

In the middle of her quandary, Alex walked over with the clerk in tow. Dumping an armload of rackets on top of a display of shirts, the salesman asked, "See anything you like? We have a rental for all but the most expensive models. One of them is sure to meet your needs."

Honoria had yet to touch a string or grip a handle. "Um . . . not yet." She glanced at Alex. "Sorry, I usually don't have this hard a time making up my mind, but all these choices make my head swim."

"No problem." He set his own racket down and chose one from the rental pile. Tossing it in the air, he caught it neatly and bounced the center against the heel of his hand. "This one has decent balance, but the strings might be a little tight. Here, try it out."

Curling her fingers around the handle, she held it like a sword, relieved it wasn't as heavy or uncomfortable as she'd expected. "It feels fine."

"Why don't you give it a swing?"

She looked from the salesclerk to the racket. Was the man deranged? "A swing?"

The clerk nodded encouragement. "Sure. Otherwise how can you tell if it's right for you?" The shop bell announced the arrival of more customers and he turned to Alex. "You know what you're doing, so I'll leave you to assist the lady. Just come to the register when you're ready and I'll sign you out."

Alex checked his watch. "We have five minutes before we're due on the court, but it's not a big deal if we're late. Like I said earlier, this is supposed to be fun."

Fun was relative, Honoria told herself, hefting the racket.

"Go ahead, give it a whirl. If it doesn't feel good, you can chose another."

She took a deep breath, swung the racket back and whacked a pile of hats off a table behind her and onto the tile floor. "Oh Lord." Dropping to her knees, she began gathering up the merchandise. Good thing she hadn't been standing in front of the pyramid of golf balls displayed a few tables over. "I knew this wasn't a smart idea."

"Hey, take it easy." Alex knelt beside her and stilled her hands. "By the way, you might want to wear one of these. There's no shade on the courts, so even at this early hour it's going to be hot." He sat a bright red hat on her head and tugged the brim down to protect her face. "And you should probably tie back your hair, so it doesn't get in the way."

Honoria stood, fumbled through her canvas tote and fished out her prize: a white elastic hair band. While Alex righted the tower of hats, she removed her cap and used the small brush to make a ponytail. When finished, she sat the hat back on her head and pulled her hair through the opening at the back.

"How's this?"

"Perfect." He picked up the racket and handed it to her. "Let's check you out so we can get started."

Honoria swiped at her damp forehead while Alex stood on the opposite side of the net and spoke to the young man who was gathering their used tennis balls. She felt warm all over and suspected it wasn't from the sun bathing the green-tinted court in morning light, or the mild exertion she'd just experienced. She'd been enveloped in Alex's arms for a while now, and the intimate contact turned her gooey from the inside out, like a bar of chocolate left too long in the sun.

After they'd arrived on the court, Alex had positioned her as if she was a mannequin, showing her the proper stance and arm action. Then he'd set up a machine that lobbed balls across the net one at a time in whatever rhythm the receiver wanted. Finally, he'd walked behind her and placed a hand on her waist while he wrapped his other palm around the hand in which she held her racket.

"We're going to take this nice and slow, Honoria. Just move with me and imitate my body language, and you'll do fine."

Instead of putting her at ease, his deep, hypnotic drawl caused her stomach to flip-flop and her heart rate to soar. When she turned her head and bumped her nose into his jaw, his warm breath fluttered against her mouth and she went hot and cold at the same time. She decided to fix her gaze on the yellow bullets shooting from the machine and pray that she didn't trip over her own two feet.

But she needn't have worried, because Alex made it easy, expertly guiding her in an erotic front-to-back tango on the pavement. As if one entity, they'd returned the never ending stream of balls across the net in long, sweeping strokes, until the machine had emptied itself and shuddered to a standstill. He'd left minutes ago to talk to the ball boy and she was still tied in knots, wondering why Alex had held her so close and been so solicitous.

Glancing around, she took stock of her surroundings, something she'd been too preoccupied to do until now. Their court was the last in a row of six, all occupied with players Honoria was certain were more proficient than she, and bent on having a good time. She suspected the couple next to them had been drinking all morning, because along with the empty glasses sitting in a row on the sideline, the man and woman laughed loudly at every misplaced shot. Though still serving, lobbing, and diving for the net, they seemed to miss more balls than they hit, but that didn't dampen their enthusiasm. Every time one of their cockeyed shots dropped into her and Alex's court, they would shout out a senseless warning.

Alex never said a word, just returned their balls with a well-placed *thwack* and went back to her lesson, but he had to be bored stiff. He'd been nothing but patient and well-mannered while he'd taken her through the steps. Now he was forced to fend off errant shots from strangers who had too much to drink before the day was half over.

She adjusted the brim of her hat, thankful he'd forced her to accept it, because he'd been right about the heat. Now if only she could hit the ball without his help . . .

"Hey, Honey! Woo-hoo, Honey, over here!"

Honoria winced at the shrill voice cutting through the air like a fire siren. She'd forgotten all about the woman she'd met yesterday at the pool. Pasting a smile on her face, she spun on her heel and found Gloria and Leo, each holding a drink, perched on a bench in the shade. Gloria waved, as did her companion, and she waggled her fingers politely, certain that once they realized there was no match they would leave.

Alex made his way around the net and walked to her side. "You ready to try returning a few?"

Honoria swallowed. "You want me to hit them back to you?"

A corner of his mouth hitched up in a grin. "That's the general idea, unless you'd feel more comfortable using the machine again. But I think you're ready."

"I don't know . . ."

"Come on. I promise to keep the ball low and slow. If you don't like it, we can stop."

"Go get him, Honey," yelled Gloria.

She sighed.

Alex waved his racket in Gloria and Leo's direction. "Your friends came to see us play. You don't want to let them down, do you?"

"They're not my friends," she hissed.

"That's not what it sounds like to me," he teased.

Folding his arms, he checked his watch. "Be a sport. We only have the court for about fifteen more minutes. How much trouble can you get into in that short a time?"

Plenty, she thought in silence, especially with an inebriated audience to cheer her on. "Okay, but no laughing if I make a fool of myself," she said half in jest.

Alex tossed a ball in the air and juggled it on his racket. "No laughing—got it." He glanced across her side of the court. "Stand in the middle about two thirds of the way from the net. I'll hit the ball right to you, and you hit it back, just the way we did with the machine."

Alex swaggered to his side and stood behind the boundary line. When he saw that she hadn't moved, he took a few practice swings. Honoria realized there was no way she could get out of it, so she walked to what she hoped was the appropriate spot and turned.

He bounced the ball on the pavement and she crouched, trying to remember what he'd told her about the importance of correct stance and swing. She was supposed to stay centered and anticipate his shots with a kind of balanced shift from foot to foot. Above all, she had to keep her eye on the ball.

Alex dropped the ball and stroked slowly, sending it straight to her right side.

Honoria waited for the bounce, then stepped into the shot. Hauling her racket back, she swung—and missed by a mile.

"That was a good try," yelled Alex. He took another ball from his pocket. "Here it comes again. Get ready."

Just then, one of the players to their left sent a ball zooming into Alex's side of the net. He deftly deflected the shot, but she could tell he wasn't pleased. Once again, he bounced a ball, setting up his serve.

Keep your eye on the ball, she reminded herself. *Keep your eye on the ball.*

Alex tapped his racket on the court. Honoria planted her feet, bent her knees and waited.

He hit the ball and it skimmed the net, low and slow just as he'd promised.

Throwing her racket back, she let go with a jerky forward stroke. The ball soared above his head, flew over the chain-link fence and sailed out of sight.

Honoria covered her face with a hand, peeking through splayed fingers. "I'm sorry," she finally called through her laughter. "Guess I don't know my own strength."

"Strength is good," called Alex in return. He gave her a moment to compose herself, then set up for the next serve. "Think about the contact," he reminded her. "Eye on the ball, control the stroke."

Eye on the ball—control the stroke. Honoria repeated the mantra in her head.

Once again the ball glided over the net in a long smooth arc. Racket back, she concentrated on her target. Her heart leaped when her strings made contact, and she returned his easy serve.

"That'a girl," called Alex, smacking the ball in her direction.

"Way to go, Honey," cried her personal cheerleader.

Honoria danced from foot to foot. Racket back, she stepped forward and connected a second time.

Alex didn't call out another word, but he did make the shot. Exhilarated, Honoria focused on the bright yellow missile, which seemed to come at her with a bit more speed and lift.

Thwack! She hit the ball over the net.

Thunk! It sailed back in her direction.

Wham! She set it flying toward Alex.

Alex raised his racket and eased another shot her way.

She shuffled to the left and whacked the ball, zapping it straight at him.

He stepped from side to side and returned the shot.

Filled with a sense of accomplishment, Honoria concentrated with each swing, totally engrossed in the fact that she was actually connecting with the object. Stretching back with her racket, she slammed the ball over the net.

Minutes passed while they volleyed in low-key yet determined silence. Somewhere in the back of her mind, she heard Gloria's encouraging comments, but everything paled at the pleasure she felt with her newfound ability to return a shot hit by a world-class player. She knew Alex was taking it easy and they weren't really engaged in competition, but hey, so what?

"Look out!"

Centered on the game, she ignored the shout. Between Gloria and their giddy neighbors she'd heard cheers and bogus warnings all morning. She wasn't about to let them ruin her good time.

"Honey, duck!" Gloria screamed.

Honoria raised her head and Alex's ball bounced past.

Whack!

Pain spiked into her brain, and her world turned black.

Alex jumped the net with his heart in his throat. If anything happened to her . . . Dropping to his knees, he gathered Honoria in his arms and brushed the cap dangling from her ponytail onto the ground. Though her breathing seemed normal, her left temple sported a mark the size and color of a tomato.

"Honoria. Honey, come on, open your eyes. Let me know that you're all right."

"Oh my God, look at that smackeroo." Still holding her drink, Gloria squatted next to him. "Maybe we should call the hotel doctor."

"I am so sorry. It was an accident, a complete accident." The woman from the next court hovered above them, wringing her hands. "What can I do to help?"

Alex glared, refusing to acknowledge the apology. "Just give us another minute." He ran his hands over Honoria's arms and legs, checking to make sure she hadn't broken or twisted anything in the fall. Then he shifted her in his arms so that she was propped securely against his bent knee and patted her cheek, willing her to come around. He'd heard that blows to the temple could be dangerous. If she was badly injured, he would never forgive himself.

Her eyelashes fluttered and he breathed a silent sigh of relief. When the ball boy handed him an open bottle of water, he accepted it gratefully. "Take a sip of this. Come on, you'll feel better if you do." He coaxed the bottle into her mouth and carefully tipped it, letting a few drops dribble through her open lips.

Honoria moaned. After swallowing the water, she coughed and blinked her eyes. Lifting a hand to the side of her head, she flinched. "What happened?"

"You got hit by a wild ball," Alex said sourly, still ignoring the culprits. "How do you feel?"

"Fine. I think."

She swiveled her head and her face filled with panic, as if she just realized she was on the ground in the middle of a crowd. Tucking her legs, she tried to stand, but Alex held her tight. "Take your time. There's no need to rush."

"I'm okay. Just help me up."

"It's too soon. Lie still and catch your breath," he admonished, hoping she would listen. He'd been beaned a few times himself and knew it wasn't the best of sensations. She'd been doing a good job, giving the lesson a no-holds-barred effort. The last thing she deserved was to end up ass over teakettle because of a whack on the head from an idiot court mate.

When she continued to struggle, he huffed out a breath. It figured that anyone who grew up with Faith Hewitt for a mother would be stubborn and used to holding her own. Gently, he wrapped one arm around her back and took her hand with the other while the ball boy grabbed her opposite elbow and eased her to her feet. She staggered and sank into his chest, but Alex kept her upright.

"Maybe we should get a stretcher," offered a voice from the crowd.

"No, no. I'm fine." Honoria clung to Alex's hand and opened her eyes again. "Really, I am."

He propped her against him and gave the victory signal. "How many fingers do you see?"

"Two," she said with a quiver. She blinked. "At least I think there are two."

"Good girl." Without making a big production, he checked her pupils and decided they were normal. Aside from the blotch on her temple and her unsteady footing, she seemed to be okay.

The middle-aged man from the next court stuffed his hands in the pockets of his tennis shorts. "I'm willing to take full responsibility for what happened. If she needs to see a doctor or you end up taking her to the hospital, we'll see to the expense. We're the Burnhams, by the way, and we're here for a few more days, so you can send the bill to our suite. Mitzi and I feel just terrible that this happened."

"Yeah, I'll bet," Alex grumbled.

"I don't need a doctor," Honoria said at the same time. "But I think I'd like to sit for a minute."

"You should probably go to your room. I'll get a golf cart." The ball boy trotted off, presumably to find one.

"Gee, Honey, that bump is gonna turn into a bruise the size of Pittsburgh if you don't get some ice on it." Gloria turned to her companion. "Leo, go find her some ice."

Like a friendly St. Bernard, Leo nodded and jogged toward the clubhouse. The crowd thinned, leaving only Gloria, the Burnhams, Alex, and Honoria on the court.

"Think you can walk?" Alex asked her.

She stiffened in his arms. "Of course I can walk." But her first step was shaky and unsure.

He guided her to a courtside bench and eased her down, then raised his gaze to the still hovering Burnhams. "We'll let you know if she needs anything. Right now, I think it's best if you just leave."

The subdued couple made another heartfelt apology and backed away. Gloria retrieved the fallen baseball cap and carried it to the bench. Sitting down, she handed it to Honoria while spouting words of comfort. "You'll feel better after you take a couple of aspirin and lie down. There's a luau tonight. You don't want to miss it, do you?"

"A luau?"

"You know, a party on the beach. Pig in a pit, roasted plantains, entertainment. The works. Wouldn't do for you to miss all the fun." Gloria drummed manicured fingers on the bench. "Where the hell did Leo go for that ice—Antarctica?"

Honoria hated being fussed over. As a child, she'd rarely cried, mostly because her mother never condoned self-pity or tears. A Hewitt's lot in life was to remain in the background and promote the academy, not themselves. As a result of her mother's stiff-upper-lip attitude, she wasn't used to attention of any kind.

"I'm feeling fine, honest." She placed the hat on her head, careful not to touch her sore temple.

"Your face is flushed, and that's not good. You need to get out of the sun," Gloria insisted.

Honoria knew the reason she was red, and it wasn't from the sun or the knock on her head. Granted, she'd seen stars for a second, but she'd already been coming around when Alex slid his warm, strong hands over her arms and legs. The sensation his touch created inside of her had been so intense she could still feel him stroking her skin, even though his hands now rested on his knees.

"Gloria's advice makes sense," Alex murmured in her ear. "We need to get you to the cabana. You can lie down with an ice pack while I order lunch and some tea. After you eat, I want you to take a nap and rest up for tonight."

As if on cue, the ball boy drove up in a golf cart and Leo trundled over with ice. Honoria knew she was outnumbered and didn't want to argue in front of strangers. Accepting the ice pack, she held it against the side of her head.

"Think you can make it into the cart?" asked Alex.

She raised her chin. "Of course I can."

Standing, she swayed on her feet and Alex caught her in an iron grip. "Easy there, ace. I've got you."

Her knees wobbled and she inhaled a breath. Okay, so she was a little shaky. Maybe a cup of tea and a nap would do her some good. After thanking Leo and promising Gloria she would rest, she allowed Alex to guide her to the cart. He climbed in beside her and put an arm around her shoulder, urging her to lean against him.

The ball boy steered the cart down the path carved through the tropical forest and Honoria relaxed in the safety of Alex's embrace. She thought about the accident and blew out a frustrated breath. If Faith were alive, she'd be looking down her nose with that I-told-you-so stare and reciting one of her most repeated adages: Women who play sports are unfeminine and crass, a disgrace to their gender. She'd be appalled to learn that her only daughter had been having a wonderful time until she'd been knocked on the noggin.

"How are you feeling?" Alex asked, interrupting her thoughts.

Energized. Empowered. Alive. But she certainly couldn't repeat those things to him. "Honestly?"

"Of course, honestly. If you're hurt, I need to know."

"I'm not hurt, Alex. I'm angry."

"I know what you mean. You could have fallen and broken something. The tennis court is no place for alcohol, even in fun. If you ask me, the Burnhams ought to be sent home on the next flight out of here. I should call the desk and——"

"I agree, it was stupid of them to be drinking, but that's not what has me so mad. I wanted to finish the game."

He drew back his head and stared at her. "Finish the game? You mean you actually were having fun out there?"

She removed the ice pack and set it on the seat beside her. "I was having a great time. I didn't make too big a fool of myself, did I?"

Though his expression was serious, his eyes crinkled at the corners. "You were fantastic. A natural. It was like volleying with Jennifer Capriotti and Venus Williams all at the same time."

Honoria recognized the names and knew he was joking, but the words still made her insides melt. "So how good was I, really?"

"Hmm. Definitely better than that Russian Chris Everett wanna-be—Anna somebody or other."

"Nu-uh. I read about her in *People*, and they said she can't break into the top ten to save her soul. I want to hear that I was awesome, stupendous, a contender."

"You definitely were all that."

"How about a power hitter?"

"You had a return like a cannon."

Smiling, she picked up the ice bag and set it back on her temple. "I thought so, but I wanted to be sure."

He tipped her head onto his shoulder and she nestled into his side again. A few seconds passed before she heard him chuckle. Whoever said laughter was the best medicine had been on the money, she thought, because Alex's rich, throaty rumble definitely made her feel better.

"Does that mean you'd be willing to try again tomorrow?" he asked, his voice still ripe with amusement.

"You bet I'm willing. There's just one thing."

"Wait, let me guess. You want to play doubles against the Burnhams."

The cart jerked to a stop in front of their cabana and Honoria sat upright. "I don't care if I ever set eyes on the Burnhams again, and I don't want a court next to anybody who has a drink in their hand."

"I think that can be arranged." Alex jumped down and came around to help her out.

"I just want one thing." She took his hand and stepped gingerly onto the pavement. "I want you to teach me how to serve like a pro."

Chapter Nine

"How are you feeling?"

At the sound of the deep, rumbling voice, Honoria rolled over and snuggled into the coverlet. Something cold and wet slid to her shoulder and she remembered the ice pack. Her brain felt fuzzy and her head ached, not enough to make her groan, but enough that she wished she'd taken Alex up on his offer of ibuprofen.

And speaking of Alex . . . She blinked when she saw him dressed in a white terry robe, standing at the far side of the bed. He smiled and she went soft as butter inside.

"What time is it?"

"You've been asleep for a while. It's almost seven."

"Seven!" Honoria shot to a sitting position, cringed at the pain in her head and plopped back against the pillows. "Why did you let me sleep so long? We need to get ready for the luau."

Alex walked around the bed and sat down. "We have time. Would you like that medication now?"

"No . . . yes." She sighed. "I guess I should have taken your advice earlier."

"That might have been wise." He grazed her temple with a gentle finger. "Glad to see the ice did the trick. It doesn't look too bad."

Reaching up, she touched the side of her head. "It still feels puffy."

"Barely, but it is an interesting shade of blue." He grinned. "I doubt anyone will notice in the dark."

She rolled her eyes, but even that hurt. "Great. I'm going to be the hit of the evening." She sat up again, and swung her legs over the edge of the mattress. "Do you think I could have those tablets now?"

"Coming right up."

Alex stood and she did the same. Luckily, he was there to catch her when she wobbled.

He guided her back down to the bed. "Sit right there. I'll bring everything to you."

She held her head in her hands, watching from shuttered lids as he went to the closet, took out his suitcase, and found the pain medication. Opening the bottle, he shook the pills into his hand and went to the sink, where he retrieved a glass of water and carried it to her.

"Dr. Alex says take two of these, and you'll feel good as new in no time." He handed her the water and pills. "Stay put. I'll shower first. By the time I'm through, your headache will be a distant memory."

She swallowed the tablets, set the glass on her nightstand, and collapsed against the covers. Alex was being sweet and solicitous, so different from the way Claire had talked about him at the auction. Strange how you sometimes got an idea of someone in your head that wasn't always correct. She didn't remember him as a caring kind of guy, yet he'd encouraged her to eat a light lunch, then refilled her ice pack before drawing the shades so she could rest.

She'd been so taken with his smooth moves at dinner, so drawn to him in the elevator, she now suspected his surly manner on the plane and in their soggy hotel suite was merely a façade. She just wished she knew why he hid his true self from her and the rest of the world.

A sharp knock brought Honoria to her feet. Ignoring the throbbing in her skull, she secured the belt on her robe and walked to the door.

"Good evening, Ms. Hewitt," said a smiling bellboy.

She stared at the squares of folded material in his hands. "What can I do for you?"

"I'm delivering your costumes for the evening."

"Costumes?" Confused, she accepted two pieces of fabric.

"Yes, ma'am, for you and your companion. There's an instruction slip inside each one with directions on how to wear it properly. The festivities will take place on the beach in about an hour. You can't miss it, just follow the crowd."

"Thank you." She carried the parcels to the bed. Why in the world would anyone need instructions on how to wear clothes?

She unfolded a rectangle of sturdy cotton imprinted with orange and red parrots, and found the instruction sheet labeled *for men only*. From what she could tell, the cloth was a male sarong, meant to wrap around the waist and knot at the hip.

She set it aside and unfolded the larger package, a soft fabric with a mix of pink, white, and peach-colored tropical flowers, not exactly a square or a rectangle but a combination of shapes. Honoria held the costume in front of her and checked out the longer strips of material flaring out from the edges. Okay, maybe she did need an instruction manual.

She folded the cloth over her arm and picked up the direction sheet that had fluttered to the floor. The phrase "one size fits all" was the first thing to catch her eye. Uh-huh, she thought, recalling Gloria and a few of the other women she'd met, all a size six or less. The dubious words did not fill her with optimism, but she read on.

> *Wrap the lower half of fabric around the body tightly to finish at either side. Then slide tab A through slot 1 and tie with tab B to form a knot at the waist. To wear the upper portion, raise the bodice and slip tab C through slot 2 and tie securely to tab D over a shoulder or around the neck.*

She frowned at the disjointed directions. The bathroom door opened, and Alex sauntered out, a towel draped around his slim hips much as she imagined his costume would fit.

"I thought I heard someone knock."

"We had a visitor from the hotel. According to the bellboy, these are the clothes we're expected to wear this evening." She clutched the fabric to her chest and sidled past him. "I'll try mine on in the bathroom—you can put yours on out here."

She left him inspecting his costume while she brought hers into the steamy bath and arranged it neatly over a hanger. After a quick shower, she applied a bit of mascara and blush, then tamed her hair. Sitting on the edge of the tub, she reread the instructions, hoping they would make more sense. Standing, she began to wrap the fabric around her hips. Unfortunately, by the time she slid tab A into slot 1 and found tab B, the front of the dress had disappeared.

Checking over her shoulder, she gazed in the mirror and saw the bodice hanging over her rear. Sighing, she undid the tabs, prepared to begin the job again when a knock startled her.

"You about ready in there?"

"I . . . um . . . I need a few more minutes."

"Want some help?"

"No!" *Not when I have to get into this contraption without wearing a bra.* "How about I meet you at the party?"

"I'll wait. We go as a couple, remember."

A couple. There he was, being nice again, she thought with a little sigh. But they were supposed to enjoy this vacation together.

Honoria set her lips and made a second attempt at righting the costume. This time, when she wrapped from the other direction, located the slots and tied, the bodice was in front of her. Her confidence buoyed, she lifted the top and attempted to tie a knot at her shoulder, then realized she would need a third hand. Since she wasn't about to let Alex help, she opted for the halter effect.

When finished, she admired her handiwork. The soft material conformed to her breasts, waist, and hips, hugging the line of her legs until it stopped mid-calf. Relieved, she exhaled. The outfit didn't look too bad, provided the darned thing stayed tied and her breasts didn't make a break for it and escape out the sides.

She walked into the living area and found Alex standing at the front door. His costume hung from his lean hips as if it was tailor made, showcasing his broad shoulders, muscled back, and tapered waist. He turned and she swallowed, unable to look at anything but his finely sculpted chest with its dusting of golden hair.

Alex appraised her from head to toe and back again. Then he smiled. "How's the headache?"

"Headache?" She touched her temple. "It barely hurts. Those tablets did the trick."

"That's good." He held out his hand. "I think we should get going."

She walked to his side and he clasped her palm, then led her to the porch, where they took the steps to the walkway. Just before they arrived at the beach, he pulled her off the path and into a cluster of vegetation in full bloom. Before Honoria could ask why, he plucked a bright pink blossom from a large bush and faced her.

Tucking the flower over her ear, he smoothed her hair. "There, that's perfect."

"Perfect?"

"Uh-huh. The flower completely covers that bruise."

"Oh." She fingered the creamy petals. Of course, it stood to reason Alex would want his date to look as good as he did, if that was possible. "Um . . . thanks."

Tiki torches flamed like a ribbon of fire, running the entire length of the beach. A calypso band played pounding island music on a stage under a thatch-covered roof, while couples gathered at bars set up along the shoreline. Campfires sparked at regular intervals across the sand, and colorful tablecloths set for dinner dotted the shore. Alex scoured the tables, hoping to find one that was partially deserted, when he heard a grating voice shatter the ambience of the night.

"Honey! Alex! Yoo-hoo, Honey, over here!"

Cringing, he glanced at Honoria. "Is that the annoying call of the Gloria bird I hear?" he asked jokingly, debating whether or not he could stomach the woman for an entire night.

Honoria smiled through gritted teeth. "She's coming up on your left. Be nice."

"Hey, Honey, Alex." Fancy drink in hand, Gloria planted herself at their side. "I was hoping you two would show. Leo's saving us seats right in front of the stage." Forging ahead, she called over her shoulder, "Come on, follow me."

Alex shrugged. "We don't have to go with her. I can find a less conspicuous spot, if you'd rather."

"It's all right," said Honoria. "If she and Leo get to be too much, we can always use my head injury as an excuse to leave early."

"Good thinking." He didn't add that he'd already thought the very same thing. Since the moment Honoria walked out of the bathroom, he'd longed to take her to bed. Her torso hugging costume and eager yet innocent expression made him ache to touch her. Lucky for him, she'd just given them a way out.

They caught up to Gloria at the table, and Leo smiled jovially when Honoria dropped to her knees beside him. "Hey, little lady. That was quite a wallop you took today. How are you feeling?"

Satisfaction welled inside of Alex when Honoria inched away from Leo's mountainous belly and ample thighs, and settled close beside him. From the second he'd seen her at the auction, she'd touched something inside of him. He'd spent most of his life alternately trying to protect himself from his father's barbs and hiding his disability. The longer he was in Honoria's company the more he felt a connection, an urge he couldn't name to want to see her safe.

She shouted above the racket of the crowd. "Fine, but I still feel a little achy. I'm not sure how long we'll be able to stay."

"Did you get a rest?"

"Yes, thanks to Alex. He took care of me."

Gloria sat and folded herself Indian style next to her companion. "I'll just bet he did. In fact, I'd imagine he can take care of whatever ails a woman."

Alex ignored Gloria's blatant statement and put an arm around Honoria's shoulder, hoping to make her more comfortable with the teasing. Even so, her face turned as pink as the blossom in her hair. "I'm going to order a drink. Can I get anyone anything?"

Gloria held up her Paradise Punch. "Nothing for me, thanks."

"I'll take another vodka Collins," said Leo, who already had a full drink in front of him.

"How about you?" Alex asked Honoria. "Fruit juice, or maybe a glass of white wine?"

"White wine," she answered.

Honoria admired Alex's long-limbed stride as he walked to the bar area. Several other couples took places in the sand, and she joined in the small talk, until Alex returned and passed out drinks. When he sat down, his thigh grazed hers, warming her from the inside out.

Waiters and waitresses, all wearing the same type of costume as the guests, arrived with the first course: exotic island dishes spiced with the flavor of the tropics. She inspected the table, noting the lack of silverware, and swallowed. The couples began to feed each other tidbits of fruit. The thought of taking part in such an intimate game with Alex made her fingers tingle and her stomach flutter.

He tapped her shoulder and she met his potent gaze. "I think we need to get into the swing of things," he murmured, holding out a spear of pineapple.

Mesmerized, she opened her mouth and bit the sweet, juicy fruit. Alex grinned and popped the rest of the pineapple between his laser white teeth. He chose a slice of papaya for his next offering, and Honoria succumbed to the gesture. *Live a little. Have some fun.* The limo driver's words echoed in her head. She recalled Eloise's comment: Faith was gone. No longer could she disapprove of her daughter.

Honoria smiled to herself as a weight lifted from her soul. For the first time in her life, she felt as if she were a part of something that wasn't connected to the Hewitt Academy and her rigid life back home. She was free to say, think, and do whatever she wanted. She was free to live her dream.

She gave Alex a sidelong glance. He raised a brow and took her hand, grazing the knuckles with a kiss. He touched her shoulder, her knee, her back, and she shiv-

ered at the sensation of his fingers skimming up and
down her spine or tickling her neck. He whispered in
her ear and she giggled. He entwined their fingers and
she sighed.

In the distance, a drum began to pound. A proces-
sion of torches headed toward them from the far end of
the beach. A parade of island men carrying roasted pigs
on thick wooden planks stopped at each cluster of
guests and delivered their dinner. Then a waiter holding a gleaming machete arrived and sliced the roast into
smaller chunks. When he left, the diners helped themselves to the succulent meat.

Alex chose a morsel and held it out to her. Honoria
bit it and he grinned, waiting. She leaned into the center of the table and found a tasty tidbit of her own.
Hesitantly, she raised the meat to his mouth, and he enclosed it—and her fingers—between his lips.

Slowly, she pulled away from his suggestive grasp,
and he chewed and swallowed, then took a sip of wine.
Bending forward, he licked at her lips. Then he kissed
her, and she tasted the wine on his tongue, breathed in
his essence as it seeped into her blood.

The decadent and primal actions excited her sensibilities, igniting a flame of longing deep inside of
her. Dimly, she heard a smattering of applause. When
she moved back, she realized that others at the table
were showing their approval. Gloria let loose a wolf
whistle, and Honoria covered her heated cheeks with
her palms.

Alex clasped her wrists. "I didn't mean to embarrass
you. It's just that you're so damned beautiful," he whispered.

Dumbfounded, she shook her head. He held a finger to her lips, then fed her another tidbit. Smiling, she
did the same to him. Enjoyment replaced embarrassment as they continued to play the game.

With a fanfare, their master of ceremonies from the

previous evening climbed onto the stage. Raising his hands, he called for the crowd's attention.

"Ladies and gentlemen. I have the results of last night's contest. Thanks to your votes, we're going to bring the top two couples from each seating up here for a final contest to determine the winner. Are you ready?"

The audience broke into wild applause.

"From the six-thirty seating, we have couples number twelve and forty-seven. Couples twelve and forty-seven, are you here?"

Accompanied by cheers and shouts of encouragement, two couples walked onto the stage and took a bow. The emcee let them bask in adulation for a few seconds before moving on.

"Now for the eight o'clock seating." He waggled his bushy brows and everyone laughed. "Will couples sixteen and twenty-three please come up on the stage? Couples number sixteen and twenty-three."

Alex stood and reached for her. "That's us. Come on."

Honoria rose to her feet. Their tablemates clapped with the crowd as she and Alex walked to the stage. She stood in shock as the emcee spoke to her.

"So, Honey, how are you tonight?"

"I'm . . . um . . . fine." Honoria gazed at Alex, who nodded encouragement. "Really fine."

"That's great. Ready to win the contest?"

Alex squeezed her hand and she realized she didn't have a clue what the contest was . . . nor did she care. "Uh . . . sure."

The emcee turned back to the microphone to call up the final two winners. Honoria held her breath, unable to believe she was in the spotlight. She and Alex had been voted one of the two best looking couples at their dinner seating. It had to be the dress and the contacts, she decided. She glanced up and met Alex's cool smile. And her date, of course. How could anyone resist Alex's tawny good looks and aura of confidence?

The emcee quieted the crowd. From somewhere behind the bandstand, a pair of giant island men brought out a long bamboo pole. The diners began to clap rhythmically to the calypso beat, as if they all knew what came next.

"All right, everybody!" he shouted. "This is it. Are you ready to lim-bo?"

Giggling like naughty first-graders, Honoria and Alex walked the path to their cottage hand in hand. Not only had they lost the contest—they'd been the first couple eliminated. And it hadn't even been her fault.

They'd both given the game their best shot, until the fourth round, when the bar was lowered to a height just below her breasts. Up to that point, she'd managed to execute a rumba-like, hip-swinging gyration, dancing to the beat with enthusiasm, as had Alex. They'd approached the pole at the new height, and she'd surged ahead and under before she felt Alex release his grip on her fingers. When she turned, he was flat on his back in the sand, and the audience was hooting louder than the band.

The emcee jumped off the stage to help him to his feet, and Alex limped to her side. After she led him to the far edge of the bandstand, he'd grimaced and uttered a confession. He'd injured his back in a tennis tournament a few years earlier, and his spine had never been the same. He hadn't wanted to ruin *her* good time, so he kept quiet, thinking he could handle it.

Positive he needed to visit the hotel physician, Honoria had hailed a waiter and asked for a golf cart, but after a few full-body stretches and toe touches, Alex assured her he was fine—only his pride had been damaged.

Now, standing on the darkened porch, Honoria gave him another once-over. Meeting her worried gaze, Alex answered with a little boy grin. "Sorry I screwed things up. I still think we could have won if I hadn't folded like a bad poker hand back there."

She thrust a finger into his chest. "No contest is worth the injury you almost suffered, Mr. Macho-man. You should have told me about your bad back."

Alex captured her hand and pressed it to his naked chest. The warm wall of muscle flexed beneath her palm, taking her playful gesture to a whole new level.

Shrouded in shadows thrown from the flaming torches that lined the walkway, Honoria heard the heated whispers of other couples on the path. In the distance the band continued to play. The subtle fragrance of tropical flowers permeated the air while the soft call of an island bird floated on the ocean breeze. Suspended in the heady moment, somewhere between romance and desire, she felt as if her entire life was changing.

He took a step closer and laced their fingers together. "My back hasn't bothered me for years. Besides, I was too embarrassed to mention it."

"And look where that got you. You could have been crippled or . . . or worse," she stammered. "You need to lie down."

His raised eyebrow telegraphed his thought before he replied. "I need to get horizontal, all right, the sooner the better."

Is he suggesting what I think he's suggesting?

"I can sleep on the sofa tonight, and you can have the bed," she muttered, dropping her gaze. "I don't mind."

Alex raised her chin with a finger and stared into her eyes. "I want to sleep with you, Honoria, tonight and every night we have left here."

He leaned forward and placed his lips on her brow, then feathered them over her temple and cheek, down to her mouth. Heat flared in the pit of her stomach, rising to her throat and face. Alex grazed her mouth with his, and she opened for him. He filled her with his tongue and she breathed in the taste of him, sweet and succulent like the island fruit they'd shared.

"You make me crazy," he moaned. "I've been thinking about this moment since I saw you on that stage at the academy."

"You have?"

"That dress was something else."

"It was?"

"Uh-huh." He nibbled on her lower lip. "Your friends are to be complimented for their excellent fashion sense."

Honoria sighed. She wanted Alex, too, though her desire had lain dormant for years. Back in high school, she'd dreamed of a moment like this, had remembered him on long, rainy weekends when she'd been positive there would never be anything or anyone for her in the world except the school. It didn't matter that he hadn't thought about her until the night of the auction. He was thinking of her now, in the way that counted most.

Before she could tell him how she felt, he opened the door to the cottage and guided her inside. Moonlight spilled through the window and washed over the bed, highlighting what they were about to do. His hands moved from her waist to the underside of her breasts, and she trembled. When his thumbs circled her nipples, she thought she would burst into flames. He covered her breasts with his palms, then followed the line of her sarong up to the back of her neck.

"What are you doing?" She cringed at the dopey question. "I mean, are you sure you know what you're doing?"

Slowly, his fingers pulled on tab C and tab D, peeling the fabric down from her collarbone to her waist. Cupping each breast in a palm, he raised the mounds up and continued to stare. "Oh, yeah, I know," he said, his voice a rasp. "You are incredible."

Honoria shuddered when the force of his breath

grazed her nipples. Already hard points, they ached for his mouth. As if reading her thoughts, he bent and licked one rigid bud. She leaned into him, and he enclosed the nipple with his lips. Biting down, he sent a jolt of desire straight to her womb.

She moaned and he suckled harder, until her knees turned to jelly. She ran her hands to his waist, and he stepped back. Tugging at the knot of fabric on his hip, he unwrapped himself as if giving her a present. She stared at his erection, rising from a nest of dark hair. Thick and long, his penis seemed to grow in size under her disbelieving eyes. Worrying her lower lip, she raised her gaze.

Again, he gave her that little boy grin. "One of us is wearing way too many clothes."

"I . . . um . . . guess that would be me?"

Instead of answering, he reached out and pulled the tie on her waist, drawing tab A from its slot. The fabric slid over her hips and puddled at her ankles.

Alex gazed at the scrap of lace covering the mound above Honoria's thighs. Her generous curves only reinforced his secret pleasure. Nothing about her, from her lush, full breasts and large, pink nipples, to her curving waist and womanly hips, disappointed him. He studied the length of her legs, admired the way her shapely calves led down to trim ankles and up to long, rounded thighs.

He'd bedded dozens of women, many of whom kept themselves fashionably thin. Honoria was a wonderful change of scenery. Built like a goddess come to life for him alone, he suddenly wanted to drown in her softness. And to think, if not for Cissy and that ridiculous bet, he'd be sitting at home wasting time, wasting his life, instead of being here with her.

Looking away, Honoria crossed her arms over her breasts and stomach and he immediately knew what she was thinking. "Don't hide from me, Honey."

"I'm . . . um . . . not exactly slim. I have to lose a few pounds to be considered pleasingly plump."

"That's the media hype from Hollywood talking," he told her. Stepping closer, he uncrossed her arms. "There are a lot of men who would find your figure one hell of a turn-on, myself included. Remind me sometime to repeat a few of the comments the guys sitting at my table made at the auction when you walked out in that red dress."

She flushed pink, whether from pleasure or embarrassment he wasn't sure. But he did know she had nothing to be ashamed of. Enfolding her in his arms, he sidestepped them to the bed and sat down so his eyes were level with her navel. Hooking his thumbs under the tiny straps of her thong, he slid the miniscule panties to her thighs and down her calves to her ankles. Then he gazed at her feminine curls, waiting to be explored by his fingers and his tongue.

Honoria fisted her hands in his hair and drew him to her belly. He kissed her there, then trailed his lips down to her mound. Parting the folds with his fingers, he found her warm and wet and waiting for him. She spread her legs and he pulled her over his lap. She set her hands on his shoulders and he tugged at her waist, centering her above his rigid shaft.

Bending her knees, she lowered herself in tortuous inches over his penis, until her bottom rested on his thighs, and he was sheathed to the hilt inside of her. Alex shuddered at the unbelievable sensation. She spasmed around him and he sucked in a breath.

"Don't move," he cautioned. "I want this to be good for both of us."

Chapter Ten

TO: Milton>Special-Angel-in-
             Charge>@guidingangel.god
FROM: Junior
SUBJECT: Hewitt-Vandencort assignment
Via: Heavenet

As you read this, subjects are alone and inter-
acting in a personal and very human manner.
Honoria seems to have escaped her mother's mem-
ory quite nicely, while Alex has admitted to him-
self that he feels protective. No commitment yet,
but I feel certain it is only a matter of time.

Tropical sun is wearing, as is manning a front
desk. I feel the need to swim in the ocean, so I'm go-
ing for a dip. Will contact you again, same time,
tomorrow evening. Over and out.

Junior snapped his fingers and the laptop was no more.
Standing, he pushed away from the table on Honoria
and Alex's front porch and ambled down the walkway,
whistling a happy tune. As far as he could tell, things between his charges were humming along nicely. Alex was

accepting the honorable side of his heretofore pompous and insecure personality, and Honoria was finally moving out from under her mother's stifling influence.

He crossed the grass to the nude beach. Ignoring the frantic whispers coming from the half dozen blanketed mounds spaced on the sand, he headed for the water, certain Milton would be pleased with this latest development.

He stood at the shoreline and thought about his first big accomplishment. Eloise, Nathan, and little Phoebe Marie. Even though Milton refused to give him full credit for their happiness, Junior knew it had been his advice to Eloise that had helped her see the light and make the right choice.

Putting a toe in the water, he shivered. Taking on a human body was interesting, but the emotions a flesh and blood form had to deal with were not. How he pitied Alex and Honoria, who had so messed up their lives because of their feelings of inadequacy and guilt. Honoria's mother was out of the picture, but there were still plenty of others who could meddle: Alex's father, that rude Cissy person, even Alex's sister, to name a few. As long as he could keep outside interference to a minimum, his goal would be met. He would be tending to a full roster of souls by Thanksgiving.

Junior raised his eyes to the heavens. Life was good, and the life of an angel, even better.

Alex pulled Honoria to his chest and lay back on the mattress. Rolling over so she was beneath him, he rested his weight on his arms and loomed from above. Gazing at her flushed face and moist, parted lips, he raised himself up to study her magnificent breasts, rounded belly and lower, to the place where they were joined.

Honoria adjusted her hips, contracting around his aching flesh, and he groaned. She lifted her arms, and he leaned forward until they were fused from shoulders to thighs. Capturing her mouth with his, he explored with his tongue. She clutched at his waist and he drew back, then thrust inside her. She met his movement with an encouraging moan, rising to meet him with abandon.

Her response, so eager and spontaneous, awakened something primal inside him. Stifling the urge to pound his chest like a caveman celebrating a conquest, he attributed the absurd notion to their island locale, the throbbing beat of drums, and the heat of the moment—certainly not to the prim and proper girl from his past, now writhing under him as if he was the only man in the world.

Earlier, when he'd told her he wanted to sleep with her for the rest of their time here, he hadn't lied, but he hadn't made any promises for the future. Later, he would tell her that he never made promises. But he did give the women he slept with his full attention and care . . . until the affair was over.

She sobbed, and he slowed his hips. "Am I hurting you?"

"Not at all." She rested her palms on his cheeks and met his frown with a watery smile. "I've dreamed about this moment, Alex. Please, don't stop now."

Don't stop now.

The words obliterated all coherent thought. "I want to see you happy, Honey," he answered through clenched teeth. "Tell me what I can do to make this good for you, and I'll do it."

Delighted by his thoughtful question, she wiggled beneath him, urging him to forge ahead. "This *is* what I want. You inside of me, filling me, making me whole."

Alex kissed her again, then feathered his lips over her collarbone to her breast. She moaned when he took her nipple between his teeth, arching against him as he sucked it to an aching point. Opening her legs wide, she wrapped them over his thighs. He tugged at the tip of her breast and her body milked his rigid flesh, until she felt his penis surge up high inside of her.

Holding his head in her hands, she moved beneath him, encouraging him to again take up the steady rhythm. Increasing the tempo of his thrusts, Alex drove into her, stroking until he kindled a hidden part of her she'd almost forgotten existed.

He tongued a nipple, and she shivered. He brought her to a fever pitch and she matched his quickening pace, striving to follow where he led. When his body tightened, hers vibrated in tune. Consumed with a pent-up rush of urgency, she convulsed in his arms and rode the waves of exquisite pleasure that tumbled through her body.

As if set free by her release, Alex stiffened above her. She held him to her breast, felt his passion when he climaxed and absorbed his tremors, letting them pulse through her skin and muscle, to her very bones.

Perfectly in sync, their breathing and heartbeats became as one. Seconds passed as time stilled in Honoria's mind. In a burst of striking clarity, she realized this moment with Alex was what she'd been waiting for her entire life. And now it belonged to both of them, for all eternity.

Gradually, she returned to the present. Alex lay over her, his breath a soft caress against her ear. His body conformed to hers, fitting like a second skin. She could feel him inside of her, no longer rigid and demanding, but still filling her most private space. She sighed and he stirred.

Pushing up on his elbows, he peered into her face. "I'm probably hurting you. I'll move."

Honoria pressed her hands to his back, unwilling to lose the intimate contact. "You're not."

He quirked a brow. "Then maybe we should get under the covers? It's going to get cooler as morning comes."

She smiled inside. He was right. She moved her legs from his thighs, and he placed a kiss on the tip of her nose. Sliding off the bed, he stood at the side of the mattress and helped her up with one hand while he pulled down the coverlet with the other.

Draping an arm around her waist, he nuzzled her ear. "You need anything?"

She joined her thighs together and felt the sticky wetness. "Um . . . I'd like to go to the bathroom."

He hugged her, then climbed into bed. "I'll be here waiting for you."

Honoria found her way in the dark and opened the door. A minute later, her body refreshed, she realized her mind was in turmoil. She'd had sex with only one other man, and though the time she'd spent with Richard had been physically satisfying, it had been nothing like what she'd just experienced with Alex.

Richard had been gentle, but not very solicitous of her feelings, and never had he asked if she wanted him to do anything that would make the act all she hoped it to be. Of course, once his wife returned from a sabbatical and Honoria found out he had lied about being divorced, nothing she and the English professor had done mattered. She'd hidden their affair from her mother, relegated the liaison to the furthest corner of her mind, and vowed never again to sleep with a man unless she trusted him completely.

And she did trust Alex.

As far as she could see, there was only one problem, and it needed to be rectified tomorrow if they were to continue their tryst or affair or encounter. She wasn't sure how she should refer to what they'd just done.

Alex hadn't used a condom.

The fact hit her full force, dropping her to the edge of the tub. Luckily, she was at the end of her cycle, the least likely time to conceive. The idea of being an unwed mother didn't upset her, but it did give her a lot to think about. She knew better than most how important a happy home and two loving parents were for a child. She'd grown up without a father, and always wondered if her life would have been different if she'd had one.

Over the years, she'd asked her mother about her absent dad, and each time had been told the man was out of their lives. As the months passed, she'd accepted that she would never know him, and began to think of him as more of a sperm donor than a parent. Still, she couldn't help but wonder about the way in which she'd been conceived.

Had Faith met a man she admired or was attracted to and, in a moment of glorious passion, had unprotected sex with him, as she'd just done with Alex?

No, she decided, negating the impossible idea. Her mother never would have allowed herself to be carried away by a simple biological act. More than likely, her conception had been a carefully calculated step in Faith's grand plan for the Hewitt Academy. It made more sense to believe she had interviewed prospective candidates and tallied up their IQ points before she'd consented to sleep with the man who would father her child.

Honoria sighed. Above all, she had to think of the school. Even if she found the courage to sell it, that wouldn't happen, because no one would want the academy in its present financial condition. Like it or not, the Hewitt Academy was her legacy; she had to pass it on to someone. Unfortunately, she had no prospects. She might be an innocent in the sex and relationship department, but she was smart enough to understand Alex's unspoken message. He planned to sleep with her *tonight and every night they had left together.* He hadn't said a word about tomorrows. And she wanted tomorrows for her and her children.

Of course, if the unthinkable had happened and she was pregnant, she would raise her baby differently than the way Faith had raised her. Her child would never be belittled in public, or made to feel less than worthy. Her child would have a nurturing atmosphere in which to thrive; she would encourage her son or daughter to do or be whatever they wanted.

Her child would be loved.

Suddenly, she was exhausted. Her tennis lesson and subsequent knock on the head, combined with the excitement of the luau and the rigorous bout of lovemaking she'd just shared with Alex had made her thoughts a jumble. He was waiting for her, and she wanted nothing more than to sleep beside him and enjoy what little time they had here.

She walked into the bedroom and slid under the sheet. He turned and pulled her close, snuggling her against his side, and she blew out a breath. Alex Vandencort was out of her league, in so many ways. When their time at Club Paradise was over, they would be nothing more than past classmates who had spent a week together on a wonderful vacation.

For her and Alex, that was all there could ever be.

Still, she couldn't help but wonder about her future. She had a heart full of love to give, if not to a man, then to a child. She'd decided this very night to live life to its fullest and go after what she wanted. Whatever life decided to toss her way, she would handle.

Honoria rolled to her side and nestled against a wall of smooth, warm muscle. Except for a faint square of light over the sink, the room was dark. A breeze stirred the curtains at the front windows, and she brightened at the possibilities. She was naked and so was Alex. She couldn't think of a better way to start their day.

Her gaze wandered to the sheet draped over his lower torso, tented with the evidence of his arousal. As if they had a mind of their own, her fingers combed through the crisply curling hair on his golden chest, then strayed down to dip under the covers. When he tensed beside her, she ran her hand up to his small, brown nipple and teased, imitating the way he had touched her only hours before.

He grabbed her hand and pulled her close. "It's too early for torture, Honoria, so I guess there's only one thing I can do with you."

She had a pretty good idea what he meant, but wanted him to say the words. "And what might that be?" she asked, surprising herself with her boldness.

"I'll just have to show you where this type of inventive activity leads." Growling, he rolled toward her and pressed her offending hand to his belly, then slid it below the sheet. She encircled his penis with her palm, and he sucked in a breath. Pinning her with a scorching gaze, he planted a kiss on her lips, then ducked his head and found her breast.

"Oh, Alex," she whispered.

"Oh, Alex, what?" he mumbled in response.

"Don't stop. That's . . . you're . . . it's so . . . so . . . incredible."

He bit down, and she felt the sensual pull carry her to the same heady place she'd visited last night. Fisting a hand in his hair, she urged him to take more. He moved his knee between her legs, and she opened her thighs to cradle him, then guided his erection to her waiting core.

Alex slid his rigid penis forward, then back in his own form of morning torture, each thrust bringing him a bit farther inside of her than the last. She kissed his cheek, his chin, his ear. He pumped in time with her mouth. She felt the tension build, coiling tighter and tighter throughout her body, and pressed her lips to the juncture of his neck and shoulder. Sucking his flesh, she fought back a scream, shocked that she was so ready to explode.

Clutching Alex to her breasts, she tremored when he climaxed, then followed his spiral to the stars.

Alex heard the phone ring and rolled to a sitting position on the side of the bed. Honoria was curled up beside him sound asleep. After the evening they'd shared and their erotic morning adventure, the last thing he wanted was to wake her.

"Hello," he said in a whisper, just before sanity hit. Who in the hell would be calling them here at this hour? Certainly not her friends or his. It had to be a wrong number.

"Alex, is that you?"

His gut clenched at the sound of his father's strident voice. Standing, he hissed out, "It's me. Hang on a second."

Holding the phone to his chest, he surveyed the room and saw the outfit he'd worn to the luau still on the floor. He wrapped it around his hips, then eased through the door and onto the porch.

Taking a seat at the wicker table, he huffed out a breath. He'd canceled his appointments as soon as they'd settled in their suite, but he hadn't called his father. The reasons he would have had to give to satisfy the man would have been too complicated, too personal, and too damned unbelievable. Now that he'd been found out, he would have to come up with something to explain his absence.

"Dad? Is that you?" he asked, his tone innocent.

"You know damned well it's me, and don't leave me hanging again. I'm looking for answers, and they'd better be good."

"How did you find me?" he asked, keeping his voice level.

"After the rumors started, I wheedled your where-

abouts from Rick. That boy has absolutely no respect
for authority. I had to threaten to take away his expense
account before he'd confess."

He was going to kill Rick when he returned home.
"Rumors? What rumors?"

"How about the one where you paid twenty thousand
dollars for the privilege of a date with that simpering
Hewitt woman? Or better yet, the one all Washington is
talking about—some stupid bet you made to take her to
bed?" He heard his father's derisive snort through the
phone line. "And let's not forget the most ludicrous
one. You and Ms. Hewitt eloped."

Alex groaned silently. First he was going to kill Cissy.
Then he was going to kill Rick. "That's a lie," he said,
hoping his father would center his anger on the last
statement and forget about the rest.

"Well, thank God for small favors. The woman isn't
our kind. Besides, between you and your sister, I've
given enough money to the Hewitt Academy. I'd hate to
see any more of the family fortune end up in her greedy
hands."

On rare occasions, Samuel Vandencort's ramblings
in the midst of a tirade made sense, but this wasn't one
of them. "The fortune you paid is called tuition, Father,
and it was money well spent."

"You don't know the half of it," Samuel snapped.
"But that's not important now."

"What the hell is that supposed to mean?" asked
Alex. And why did he suddenly feel as if there was a
whole other side to what was bothering his father he
knew nothing about?

"Look, son, I don't care if you screw a dozen old
maids. Just use your head, and don't let her rob you
blind, like her mother did to me. That's all."

"I don't understand what you're talking about. Honoria is nothing like her mother."

Zebra Contemporary

Whatever your taste in contemporary romance – **Romantic Suspense … Character-Driven … Light and Whimsical … Heartwarming … Humorous** – we have it at Zebra!

And now Zebra has created a Book Club for readers like yourself who enjoy fine Contemporary Romance written by today's best-selling authors.

Authors like **Lori Foster… Janet Dailey… Fern Michaels… Janelle Taylor… Kasey Michaels… Lisa Jackson… Shannon Drake… Kat Martin…** to name but a few!

These are the finest contemporary romances available anywhere today!

But don't take our word for it! Accept our gift of 3 **FREE Zebra Contemporary Romances** – and see for yourself. You only pay $1.99 for shipping and handling.

Once you've read them, we're sure you'll want to continue receiving the newest Zebra Contemporaries as soon as they're published each month! And you can by becoming a member of the Zebra Contemporary Romance Book Club!

As a member of Zebra Contemporary Romance Book Club,

- You'll receive three books every month. Each book will be by one of Zebra's best-selling authors.

- You'll have variety – you'll never receive two of the same kind of story in one month.

- You'll get your books hot off the press, usually before they appear in bookstores.

- You'll ALWAYS save up to 20% off the cover price.

SEND FOR YOUR FREE BOOKS TODAY!

To start your membership, simply complete and return the Free Book Certificate. You'll receive your Introductory Shipment of 3 FREE Zebra Contemporary Romances, you only pay $1.99 for shipping and handling. Then, each month you will receive the 3 newest Zebra Contemporary Romances. Each shipment will be yours to examine FREE for 10 days. If you decide to keep the books, you'll pay the preferred subscriber price (a savings of up to 20% off the cover price), plus shipping and handling. If you want us to stop sending books, just say the word… it's that simple.

FREE BOOK CERTIFICATE

Yes! Please send me 3 FREE Zebra Contemporary romance novels. I only pay $1.99 for shipping and handling. I understand that each month thereafter I will be able to preview 3 brand-new Contemporary Romances FREE for 10 days. Then, if I should decide to keep them, I will pay the money-saving preferred subscriber's price (that's a savings of up to 20% off the retail price), plus shipping and handling. I understand I am under no obligation to purchase any books, as explained on this card.

Name _____

Address _____ Apt. _____

City _____ State _____ Zip _____

Telephone (____) _____

Signature _____

(If under 18, parent or guardian must sign)

Offer limited to one per household and not to current subscribers. Terms, offer and prices subject to change. Orders subject to acceptance by Zebra Contemporary Book Club. Offer Valid in the U.S. only.

CN044A

Thank You!

Zebra Contemporary Romance Book Club
Zebra Home Subscription Service, Inc.
P.O. Box 5214
Clifton , NJ 07015-5214

"We'll discuss it when you get back." He cleared his throat. "When will you be home, by the way?"

Alex imagined his father pacing as he spoke, or puffing on one of his noxious cigars. "In a few more days, why?"

"Because David Ellis is coming to town. He called and asked to set up a meeting with you, personally."

"David Ellis? The television producer?"

"That's him. He did that special profile on Senator Larkin after the man was elected, and Larkin told him you were the one responsible for his new image—practically credited you with the win. Ellis is talking a big job. Seems he has a kid he needs groomed for stardom. He's looking for someone charming and savvy to teach the young man how to work a crowd, make a good impression, wear the proper clothes—the works. If he doesn't get you for the job, he's taking his business elsewhere."

Aware how difficult it was for his father to admit that his mentally challenged son was actually good for something besides window dressing, Alex smiled. He also knew his father harbored a secret ambition to hobnob with celebrities. "If I remember correctly, we have more clients than we can handle. What's so important about this one?"

"We can never have enough clients. Besides, Ellis intimated that if we were successful with this kid, there would be more. There's money to be made in Hollywood, son. Don't you forget it."

"So give the job to Rick or Chesterman. They're just as competent as I am," Alex goaded. Then he gave the knife a final twist. "Besides, they know how to write contracts."

His father waited a beat before answering. "Ellis wants you, and that's all there is to it. Rick can wrap the deal, but you have to be the one to take the initial meeting.

Now get your butt on the next plane home, so we can discuss strategy."

"I'll be home when I'm scheduled to leave, not a minute sooner. And don't call me here again."

Alex hit the disconnect button before his father could answer. He hated being treated like a mannequin, a front for the movers and shakers in the company, even if that was all his dad considered him good for. If the company had a standard contract, he'd have asked Rick to recite it into a tape recorder. Then he would have memorized it, but that idea wouldn't fly. Each of the contracts the company inked were unique to the client they pertained to. And his father charged whatever he thought the market would bear. David Ellis, Hollywood mogul and multibillionaire, was going to get soaked big time.

He furrowed his fingers through his hair. At times like this, he really wanted to tell his father what he could do with the family business, no matter the cost. If he'd been given help when his parents were first told about his problem, he might not be in this predicament. But they hadn't wanted to hear that their firstborn was less than perfect. He was an adult now, set in his ways. It was too late to find someone to help with his handicap.

And if the media got word of the fact that he'd cheated his way through high school and college—through his entire life—all hell would break lose. The company that had made a fortune on shaping and selling images would find its own tarnished to black. Not only would his father disown him, everyone in the city would know he'd been living a lie.

Mr. Perfect, Mr. Charming, Mr. Personality could do little more than write his name and address, and he sure as hell couldn't read.

"Alex?"

He softened at the sound of Honoria's sleepy voice. What would his father have said if Alex had told him he didn't want to leave Honoria? That being with her was a hell of a lot more interesting than wining and dining insecure clients in need of a makeover?

Pasting on a smile, he turned. "Sorry. I took the call out here so I wouldn't wake you."

She rubbed at her nose, then clutched the front of her white terry robe, removing from view the top of her creamy breasts. Her innocent gesture made him think of a sexy angel—virginal in public, but a wanton in his bed.

Walking to him, she touched his shoulder. "I didn't hear much, but you sounded upset. Is something wrong?"

He stood and enfolded her in his arms. "Just my father, wondering when I'd be home."

"Oh." She tipped up her head and met his eyes. "And what did you tell him?"

He grinned. "I told him I was here for another five days, and that was that."

"Then you're staying?"

"Of course I'm staying." He guided her into the cottage. "How about I take a shower while you phone in a breakfast order? And make a reservation for a tennis court. You still want to learn how to serve, right?"

She skipped away from him and picked up his racket from the coffee table. Holding it like a baseball bat, she swung it hard as she grinned.

"Venus Williams, watch out. Here I come."

After blotting her forehead with a towel, Honoria chugged ice water from the plastic bottle just delivered by a ball boy. At close to one in the afternoon, the sun was hot and she was starving. Alex had gone to the rest room, leaving her on a courtside bench. With only fifteen minutes left of their tennis time, she was anxious to finish the game and get to lunch.

"Hey, Honey!"

She recognized the too cheery voice and set the bottle down. "Gloria, hi," she said, standing. "Where's Leo?"

"Getting a massage." Gloria's apricot-tinted lower lip dipped to a pout. Her gauzy white cover-up did nothing to hide the miniscule orange bikini covering her small-but-curvy body. "I would have stayed with him, but after I found out he had a male masseuse, I figured it was okay."

"Okay?"

"Yeah, you know, a handsome guy like Leo getting oiled down by a strange woman and all. Best I can tell, he's faithful, but a girl has to be careful these days."

Honoria shuddered inwardly, shoving the idea of Leo getting *oiled down* to the darkest recesses of her brain. "Have you two been . . . together long?"

"A couple of years," Gloria answered. "He and his wife have an agreement, but I never asked for the details. How about you and Alex?"

"Alex and I went to school together, but that's about it. Until a few nights ago, we rarely saw each other. We don't exactly travel in the same social circles."

Gloria took a seat on the bench and sipped at her ever present Paradise Punch. "Is he married?"

"Alex? No!"

"That's good. It makes things so much less complicated, if you know what I mean." She raised her glass in mock salute. "Maybe he'll pop the question, and you two will get engaged."

At the woman's casual observation, Honoria plopped down beside her on the bench. How could she politely tell Gloria that her penchant for Paradise Punches had pickled her brain?

"I doubt it. Alex attends galas, goes the charity route, rubs elbows with the rich and famous. I've seen pictures of him in the society pages, and he always has a different woman on his arm. I'm definitely not his type."

"What's that got to do with love and marriage?" Gloria

asked with a grin. "I know lots of people who are happily married, and they're total opposites. As long as there's no wife in the picture, you've got a shot."

"Do you think so?" Honoria asked—just to keep the conversation moving, of course.

"I know so. I've seen the way Alex looks at you when you're not focused on him. It could happen." Gloria inclined her golden head. "Speak of the devil, here he comes now. I swear, I never saw a man fill out tennis whites better than your guy does. If I didn't think the two of you were so gone on each other, I'd be doing more than giving advice right now."

Honoria followed her gaze and zeroed in on Alex walking toward them from the clubhouse. She had to admit Gloria had a way with words, especially when it came to men.

"How are the lessons coming, by the way?" asked Gloria. "No more bops on the bean, I take it?"

Picking up both tennis rackets, Honoria stood, annoyed at the butterflies gathering in her stomach. Darn Gloria for bringing up the M word. And darn her tennis partner for looking like he'd just stepped off the pages of *GQ*. The last thing she needed to confuse her muddled thoughts was a fantasy about her and Alex and happily ever after.

He stopped at her side and kissed her cheek, then latched on to his racket. "Gloria. How are you?"

"I'm doing great, thanks," the woman said brightly. "I was just telling Honey about the salon services available in the hotel spa. Thought she might like to join me in a pedicure this afternoon."

Honoria had to hand it to her—Gloria could manipulate a conversation faster than a late night talk show host. Realizing she needed to get up to speed, she grinned. "I've never had a pedicure. I thought it might be fun."

"Go ahead," said Alex, bouncing a tennis ball on his

racket. "I can find something to amuse myself, no problem. In fact, I'll probably come back here and look for a pickup game."

"Fine. I'll go to my room and make the appointments. Check your message light after lunch for the time, Honey, and I'll meet you there."

Gloria sauntered off and Honoria smiled. "She really is a nice woman."

"I guess—once you get used to her," Alex agreed. "You ready to take a few more shots before we stop?"

"Okay, but I . . . there's . . . oh, never mind." She'd forgotten to bring up their need for condoms at breakfast. Then they'd come here and she'd done nothing but concentrate on her serve. "I'll talk to you about it . . . later," she stammered.

"Sounds serious." He glanced around the filled courts. A couple headed toward them, rackets in hand. "Looks like the next players are here a little early. How about we discuss what's bothering you while we eat?"

Honoria sighed. They had to get the topic out of the way, but she didn't think a conversation on condoms was proper for lunchtime. Removing the ball cap from her head, she spotted a bench tucked under a grove of palm trees. "How about we talk it over now?"

He followed her to the bench and sat beside her. "I'm all ears. What is it?"

"Um . . . it's . . . about condoms."

"Condoms?" His grin disappeared. "Oh."

"We didn't use any protection last night or this morning and I—"

"No, no. It's fine. I didn't think of it either. You're not—that is—there isn't any chance you could have—"

Honoria's cheeks burned with embarrassment. "It's not the right time of the month, at least I don't think so," she confided. "But we do need to take precautions, if we plan to—you know—"

He folded his arms and leaned back, his grin returning tenfold. "Have sex again?"

The heat spread downward from her cheeks to her neck and chest. "Yes."

He stood and held out his hand.

She stared, and he waggled his fingers.

He gave a sigh of infinite patience, and she rose to her feet. "What?"

Alex led her to a cluster of tall bushes covered in brilliant red flowers, and ducked inside their protective canopy. Holding her in his arms, he nuzzled her ear. His suggestive chuckle sent a tingle zinging through her system, calming her nerves and exciting her at the same time.

"I have an idea. How about we enjoy lunch, then you meet Gloria at the spa and have that pedicure. While you're there, I'll go to the gift shop and buy the biggest box of condoms they sell. We can make it a personal goal to toss out an empty box before we leave. Does that answer your question?"

Too embarrassed to speak, Honoria kept her eyes focused on the ground. Alex raised her chin with a finger and lifted a brow in question, as if waiting for her approval.

Finally, she said, "Um . . . Alex, maybe you should make it two."

Chapter Eleven

Honoria leaned back in the plush leather chair and sighed. Never had she felt so pampered or so feminine. Or so decadent. No wonder women got monthly pedicures. If she could afford it, she would do the same. But the price of this single spa treatment was more than she spent on groceries for a week. She would have to charge it to the room and put it on her credit card when she left. Once she was home, she'd figure out how to pay for it.

A manicurist had already trimmed and filed her toenails, then used a pumice stone to smooth her feet. She'd been soaking in steamy, lavender-scented water for the past ten minutes, enjoying the moment. While her chair vibrated against her lower back, she let her mind drift to all the things she had yet to experience in life.

Faith had sunk almost every penny into the school, very little into personal necessities, but none into pleasures. While growing up, Honoria had clean, neat clothing, but most of it had come from thrift stores. During college, she'd spent all her free time at the academy in preparation for running it when Faith retired. She'd never been to Europe, not only because she took to flying like a cat took to the backstroke, but because she'd never had the money. Perhaps it was time to visit France or Spain, something she'd always dreamed of doing. She also liked the idea of a cruise. Maybe she should find one that sailed the Atlantic—which would take care of her flight phobia—and visit Europe at the same time. Or she could start small, go to a carnival or a rodeo or go camping. Maybe even visit Disney World.

This vacation was the first she could remember taking, the clothes Eloise had purchased the nicest she'd ever owned. And she enjoyed and approved of it all. It was time to stop blaming her mother for the lack of excitement in her life. Honoria had no idea how much money the auction had raised for the school, but if it pulled her out of debt, she was going to make a point of realigning her priorities when she returned home. She would find the money for that trip to France or tennis lessons or maybe a long weekend at a writer's conference. She'd also make it a point to do more things for herself during the summer when the school was closed.

She often told the students that a person never knew what they could accomplish until they tried. Perhaps it was time she followed her own advice.

She gave a moan of contentment, more for the huge burden she felt had just been lifted from her shoulders than the thrill of the pedicure.

"I'll say," murmured Gloria, who was lounging beside her in an identical vibrating chair. "I think I'll talk to Leo about buying one of these babies for my apartment. I can't wait for the next act."

"You mean there's more?" asked Honoria. She couldn't imagine anything beyond the wonderful tingling in her feet. She wouldn't be surprised to find that she'd lost a shoe size.

"Honey, you don't know the half of it. I ordered us a full leg massage. When that's done, the manicurist will come back and finish the job."

"A full leg massage?"

"Yeah. It's heaven. You'll see."

Just then, Honoria noticed a woman and man heading in their direction. The man, who was buff and cute in an island sort of way, pushed a trolley holding a stack of fluffy white towels and assorted jars. The smiling, older woman reminded Honoria of a kindly grandmother.

"Ladies," said the young man. "Your key to heaven has arrived." He winked at Gloria and Honoria eased out a breath, relieved the guy wasn't here to work on her. The only male hands she wanted touching her body belonged to—

Oh, Lord, where did thought come from?

"Do a good job, big fella, and don't be gentle," cooed Gloria. "I can take anything you can dish out."

The woman, whose name tag read Lola, nodded to Honoria. "Just get comfortable, miss, and never mind Marco. He teases all the ladies 'cause he's looking for a big tip. Me, I just give a great massage."

Lola sat on a stool in front of her chair and Marco sat in front of Gloria. He opened a jar and removed a fistful of goo, then began to work on Gloria's outstretched leg while she leaned back in her chair and closed her eyes.

Continuing to grin, the woman raised Honoria's left foot and stretched it out onto a towel. After wiping it dry, she dipped into the same goo and applied the gritty mixture of oil and herbs onto Honoria's foot and calf. "Why don't you tell me what you've been doing since you got here?"

"I've had a wonderful time," Honoria answered.

"You here with your husband?" She set Honoria's left leg aside and began to slather the scented cream on her right.

"Um . . . no. I'm here with a friend."

"He's a terrific looking guy," muttered Gloria, her eyes still closed.

"Maybe he'll be more than a friend by the time you leave," Lola suggested. She went back to Honoria's left leg and, beginning with the toes, started to rub. Her strong fingers massaged from foot to ankle, continuing upward.

"I . . . don't think so." Honoria sank farther into her chair. The woman was turning her calf muscle into Jell-O. "We don't have much in common."

"Hah!" Gloria snorted out.

"Who says?" Lola's hands worked in a circular motion, up and over Honoria's knees. "You're here together, aren't you?"

"Yes."

"It's peaceful and romantic, right?"

"Definitely."

"So let yourself go, and see what happens." She moved to the right leg and started the same massage, still giving advice. "You and your friend, the moonlight, the tropical breeze, and the rolling surf . . . plenty of relationships were built on less."

Laughter bubbled up from Honoria's chest. "You sound like that tourism commercial. You know the one—New Jersey and you—perfect together."

"It's true." Lola slid her hands over Honoria's right knee. "How do you feel about him?"

"She's head over heels about the guy," commented Gloria in a sleepy sounding voice. "Only she won't admit it."

Honoria felt as if she was in a television sitcom, and she was the straight man to everyone's gags. Glancing down, she met Lola's expectant gaze. "I . . . he's . . ." She sighed. "I like him—a lot. But I doubt he thinks of me in the same way."

"Yes, he does," Gloria said through a yawn. "He just doesn't know it yet."

The older woman smiled as she continued to rub. "I think you should listen to the lady," she counseled. "You never know what can be accomplished until you try."

Honoria sat upright and stared, but Lola's eyes were downcast as she concentrated on turning her leg into a quivering mass of pliant flesh. She glanced at Gloria, but her friend was actually snoring in her chair. Amazing. Besides being an excellent masseuse, Lola was a mind reader.

She leaned back and lost herself in the massage. How could she refute such sensible advice?

Junior stood with his back to the check-in desk, filing slips and organizing guest purchases. Sometimes he thought a position managing the front desk in a busy hotel would be the perfect career for him, if he were human. He enjoyed greeting new arrivals and making nice. This job gave him something to do in between monitoring Alex and Honoria, and he got to meet all sorts of interesting people.

It also gave him time to work on a few contingency plans, on the off chance things went awry. But he couldn't imagine that would happen.

Just then, a charge notice came through from the spa under Honoria's name and he swelled with joy. Wonderful! She was taking advantage of a few of the niceties of life. She was learning to stretch her wings and have fun, as she had with the tennis thing and the limbo thing. And from the praises he'd heard sung by a few of the female souls in his care, pedicures were definitely fun.

Later tonight, he'd check in at their cabana, then e-mail Milton his report. Honoria was on the right track, and Alex was getting there, even though his thought process took a detour every once in a while. He'd handled the call from his father remarkably well. Soon he would realize he could manage his life in the same manner. Then he'd see that Honoria was the perfect woman for him, and tell her so.

After all, they were so compatible in the intimacy department, true love could be only a few steps behind.

Junior whistled along with the music playing over the hotel sound system, determined to make quick work of the filing. Things were going so well, he might even have time for another walk on the beach.

"Excuse me."

He stilled at the sound of a somewhat bossy, feminine voice. He'd heard it before, but where?

"Excuse me. We'd like to check in."

Spinning on his heels, he sucked in a breath and gave his best imitation of a smile. Cissy Westfall, in all her imperious glory, stood glowering from across the marble counter.

"Sorry, we're a bit busy this morning. How may I help you?"

"You can check us into our room. The names are Cissy Westfall and Kevin Lewiston." She glanced over her shoulder to a tall, dark-haired man who was striding across the mammoth foyer with a bellman in tow. "Here he comes now."

Completely unprepared for this little wrinkle, Junior tugged at his collar with one hand and thumbed through the reservations with the other. He swallowed when he saw Cissy's name, but refused to panic. Thinking hard, he recalled that Milton hadn't set any limitations on the amount of *divine assistance* he could use on this caper. That meant all was fair . . . to a point.

Giving a subdued blink, he smiled inwardly when Cissy's handwritten reservation disappeared. "I'm sorry, but I don't have either of those names on file. Are you certain you're booked to stay here? Perhaps you're scheduled for time at the *other* resort on the island."

Cissy dug in her designer handbag, then huffed out a breath as she slapped a sheet of paper on the marble counter. "Here's the confirmation fax I received from this hotel. Please check your records again."

Junior rolled his eyes. Where in the world was the woman's guiding angel? How dare they allow Cissy to show up and play havoc with Alex and Honoria's love life?

How could they ruin *his* chance at that promotion?

Kevin ambled to her side, his grin wide. "Let's move it along. I want to get in a set of tennis before dinner." Cissy drummed the counter with a manicured hand, and he frowned. "What's the holdup?"

"This gentleman is having difficulty locating our reservation, but I showed him the fax. It should only take another minute."

Junior quickly accessed the computerized reservation list and winked their names from the roster. Then he went to the updated rooming list that showed which suites were available for occupancy. *Presto!* There wasn't an unoccupied room in the entire resort—not even a utility closet.

"I'm so sorry, but there seems to be an error on our part. We're completely sold out. Please allow me to get you a room at the other hotel. At our expense, of course."

"I don't think so," said Cissy, her voice rising a few decibels. "Unless this resort wants to deal with a lawsuit."

Before Junior could find an appropriate comeback, the hotel manager, Mr. Mahlo, stood at his side. "Is there a problem?"

"Why no," Junior muttered. "I was just about to make arrangements for this couple at the—"

"Nonsense," said his superior, raising his chin a notch. "I know we have vacancies. Westfall and Lewiston, did you say? I remember entering those names yesterday, when Miss Westfall called in." He eyed the list with suspicion. "There must be a glitch in the system."

Oh, please, don't let their reservation be for a cottage, prayed Junior. *That will mess up everything.*

"We do have one of those romantic little bungalows on the beach, don't we?" asked Kevin. "Peace and quiet, you and me—"

"Down boy," Cissy ordered, her tone sharp. "We're on a mission, remember?"

"I remember, sure, but that doesn't mean we can't spend some time together, have a few laughs, take a walk on the beach—you know, that kind of stuff."

"Well, you thought wrong." She trained her gaze on the manager and gave a sticky-sweet smile. "If possible, we'd like a cabana near Honoria Hewitt and her roommate. We're friends and we were hoping to surprise them."

Sighing, Junior gave serious consideration to stopping everything on the spot. It would only take a second to blink Cissy and Kevin straight back to Washington, or maybe ensconce them in a hotel in Iceland. But he knew that was going beyond the simple task of changing a reservation, and would probably incur Milton's wrath.

The last thing he wanted was to anger the Special-Angel-in-Charge, not when he was so close to gaining final approval. In fact, knowing Milton, this was a stumbling block purposely set in his path, just to make sure he had the right stuff to be promoted.

Standing on tiptoe, he read over his superior's shoulder while the man flipped through the handwritten vacancy list compiled each morning by housekeeping. Several ideas came to mind. Perhaps he could stock the empty bungalows with rats or roaches. Then the manager would have to assign Cissy and Kevin a room on the opposite side of the hotel—or in the basement. Better still, he could fill their cabana with fleas, because right now, he couldn't think of a woman more deserving of waking up in a flea-infested bed than Cissy Westfall.

"Ah, yes, you're in luck. Cabin twenty, just two cottages away from Ms. Hewitt, is vacant. Let's discuss your Club Paradise passes and choose a dinner seating, shall we?"

Junior stuffed his fists in his pockets while he feigned interest in their predicament. Luckily, the only available dinner seating was the last one of the evening, not the same as Honoria and Alex's.

The manager snapped his fingers and a bellman shot to the counter. "Take Ms. Westfall and Mr. Lewiston to cabana twenty."

Cissy threw Junior a smug glare and took Kevin's arm. The manager watched them walk away, then shook a finger in Junior's face. "You need to remember, the customer is always right, young man. Now call guest services and have them send a complimentary bottle of our best champagne to cabana twenty. Then report that pesky computer glitch to the data processing department and return to work."

"Yes, sir." Deflated, Junior picked up the phone and ordered the champagne. Then he blinked the computer back to good form. Rushing around the counter, he headed out the rear of the hotel. The filing could wait. He needed to find Honoria and Alex. He had to initiate damage control.

Alex carried his latest purchase, a multipack box of prophylactics, to the cottage, where he removed it from the bag and installed it in his nightstand drawer. Twelve condoms over four days should just about do it, he figured. After another dozen encounters with Honoria, this inexplicable craving to take her to bed every time he came within ten feet of her would disappear.

Changing into a fresh shirt and tennis shorts, he noted her clothes hanging alongside his in the closet, while their shoes were aligned on the floor. He went to the bathroom to brush his teeth and found Honoria's

hairbrush and cosmetics scattered next to his shaving
gear between the two sinks.

The intimate scenario struck him hard in a spot just
left of center in his chest, and he shrugged it off. Or
tried to.

Annoyed, he paced to the main room. Why did the
idea of living with Honoria, and the memory of holding
her in his arms while she trembled beneath him, put
him in such a sentimental mood?

He'd dumped all things trite or emotionally complicated in his life years ago, when he realized he would
never live up to his father's impossible expectations. He
didn't have an addictive personality. He didn't smoke
or drink to excess, and he'd only dabbled with the occasional party drug in college. But being with Honoria,
sharing her personal space, as well as her bed, was getting to him much as he imagined a drug would take
over his system.

He'd become a master of self-control, a man who
knew how to camouflage his flaws and capitalize on his
finer points, a chameleon who could fool anyone—
classmates, college professors, even politicians.

He deplored sentimentality and feelings of need. He
didn't *need* anyone, and he certainly wasn't going to let
himself become addicted to a woman.

Walking to the mini-fridge, he removed a bottle of
water and brought it to the porch. Sitting down, he recalled their bout of bedtime activity and early morning
aerobics, dismayed when his gut tightened in response.
The thought of Honoria and how she'd changed since
their arrival overwhelmed him. It was almost like watching a lumbering, ungainly caterpillar turn into a grace-
ful butterfly.

If she were any other woman, he'd be looking forward to their having more fun, in bed and out, then giving her his usual charming brush-off once they returned
home. He'd send her one of his patent thanks-I-had-a-

great-time gifts, and that would be the end of the affair. No commitments, no strings. No further involvement.

Unfortunately for him, Honoria wasn't like any other woman.

Then he remembered that phone call from his father. He should have known better than to try and slip away without the old guy finding out about it. Not only didn't his dad have much faith in him where the company was concerned, he'd enlarged the circle of his son's learning disability to include a serious lack of common sense in Alex's private life, as well.

And what in the hell was all that mumbling about Honoria's mother robbing him of a fortune?

Alex shrugged. Probably nothing. When his dad was ticked, he often went on tangents that made no sense. His ranting was nothing more than an effort to confuse his loyal subjects without confiding the real reason for his worry.

Almost as bad, thought Alex, was the speculation his father said was making the rounds in the District. Honoria was a respected member of the community, even if she didn't run in the same elitist circle he did. Anyone who knew him wouldn't take the rumor of their elopement seriously, but they probably would believe the one about the bet.

The gossip would eventually get back to her, unless there was some way he could squelch it.

But in order to do so, he would have to shoot a few holes in his own reputation. Not only would that ruin his image, it would cost him a hundred thousand dollars to boot. Was the time he spent with her here worth the price?

Hell, he didn't know. Honoria was an adult who'd made this trip willingly. He hadn't exactly seduced her to get her into bed, so what did he owe her beyond a good time and doing his best to satisfy her between the sheets? It was too bad she was going to get caught in the crossfire, but hey, she was a big girl. She'd just have to handle it.

He flinched inwardly at that last thought, as if he'd suddenly developed a conscience where Honoria was concerned. Great, another personality change he needed to worry about.

After finishing the water in one long gulp, he picked up his tennis racket and headed for the courts. The attendant had mentioned that sometimes in the afternoon, when the female guests were at the spa or lounging at the pool, a few of the men looked to partner up for a game or two. Honoria wouldn't be finished with her pedicure for a while, so he had a couple of hours to kill.

Maybe a challenging game would ease him through the situation and help him come up with a solution to his problem. Because he certainly was going to have a problem when he got home, and not only with his father.

He arrived at the court and took stock of the players. Two couples were playing doubles, and two other courts were host to men giving a good imitation of a serious game. He was about to wheel the automatic ball return to a free court and set it on high when he heard someone call his name.

"Hey, Vandencort! Alex? Over here!"

Adjusting his sunglasses, he turned. The masculine voice sounded vaguely familiar, but he couldn't place it. Then he zeroed in on a man about his own age jogging onto the far end of the row. Still not sure of the guy's name, he folded his arms and waited until he got close.

"I thought that was you," said the man, extending his hand. "Kevin Lewiston . . . from the auction. Remember?"

With warning bells clanging in his head, Alex gave the briefest of handshakes. "Lewiston."

"This is some place, isn't it?" Kevin said, his expression jovial. "When Cissy invited me to take a few days vacation with her, I almost couldn't believe my luck. I had to pull some strings, but—"

"Cissy?" said Alex, positive he'd heard incorrectly.

"Um . . . yeah . . . Cissy Westfall. We're here together."

Disbelief joined with the warning bells, turning Alex's stomach into a churning pit of dread. "Is that so?"

"We got here about an hour ago. Cissy made all the arrangements."

"I'll just bet," said Alex. Arching a brow, he folded his arms, hoping to rein in his temper. "So, was there any particular reason she chose Club Paradise, or is that a stupid question?"

"Can't put anything over on you, can I?" Kevin's eager smile faded. "So how's it going with that Hewitt woman? Am I out twenty thousand yet?"

He resisted the urge to slam his fist into Kevin's face. The idiot had no idea Cissy was using him to perpetuate her scheme, but Alex knew better. "I had a week, remember? And I don't recall giving anyone permission to tag along and play watchdog."

"You're right, but Cissy and I got to talking, and she pointed out that no matter what happened, you could, um . . . stretch the truth, and we'd never know it. Unless, of course, someone was here to keep you on the up and up."

"So you two thought it was your duty to the rest of the crowd to come down here and keep me honest?"

"Well, yeah. Otherwise how would we know what really went on? Since the night you left, I've heard a thousand different stories about the uptight and unflappable Ms. Hewitt. Seems to me she's gonna be one tough nut to crack." Kevin locked gazes with Alex and frowned. "Hey, no offense. I only meant—"

"Are you calling me a liar?" Alex demanded.

Kevin raised his hands in the air. "Hey, not me. It's just that, well, you know—guys like to brag about their conquests. I've done it myself a time or two. And this is a big money bet. It's going to take every penny of my first bonus check to pay that twenty thousand, if you manage to win."

"*If* I manage to win?" The words came out with a swagger, exactly as Alex hoped.

"From the sound of it, you've already won," said Kevin. "Too bad. I'd earmarked that bonus for a down payment on a new Porsche."

"Don't put words in my mouth. Ask around and you'll find I never talk about my personal life. All the gossip is unsubstantiated rumor."

"Cissy called the resort and someone at the front desk said you were in a romantic little cottage on the ocean. That sounds promising to me."

"The first night we were here, we had a suite with separate bedrooms," Alex confessed. "Due to circumstances beyond our control, we were moved to one of the bungalows. And Honoria got knocked on the head with a tennis ball yesterday. What kind of gentleman would I be to seduce her when she's nursing a headache?"

The worst kind of gentleman, he silently admitted, as he lied through his teeth. He was still undecided about that stupid bet. When the time came to admit to what had happened between them, he wanted to be the one to make the decision on how it played out. Not Cissy or this jerk.

"By the way, Cissy and I are sharing one of those bungalows," Kevin remarked. "We're only two doors down from you. The bellman told me they all have just one bed."

"Each cabana also has a rollaway," he said evenly. At least that's what that guy from the front desk had told them when he'd moved them in. Only Kevin didn't need to know the cot had been missing from theirs. Or that he'd spent their first night in the cottage on the sofa.

"So where are *you* sleeping tonight?" drawled Alex,

turning the tables on Kevin. "If I know Cissy, it won't be in her bed."

Kevin's face flushed red. "She said I could have the sofa or the hammock on the porch. No one told us about the rollaway."

"Check the closet," Alex suggested. "Better yet, try the hammock. It moves with the breeze, rocks you right to sleep."

Kevin's eyes flickered in understanding. "So that's where you've been sleeping? Interesting."

"I have a few more nights, remember? And unless you plan on peeking through a window, which would be very bad form, I might add, that's about all you're going to find out until I say otherwise."

"Okay, I get it. You're working on it." Kevin scanned the courts. "How about we play a few sets. I promise to take it easy on you."

Alex bounced a ball in the center of his racket. "Sure, why not? It's been a while since I played anyone with skill."

The poor slob's grin was so hopeful Alex almost laughed out loud. When he was finished with Kevin, the guy would be lucky if he could breathe without a respirator, let alone get Cissy Westfall in the sack. He'd been hoping for a good workout. How fortuitous that his wish had been granted.

Chapter Twelve

Honoria strolled the path from the hotel to the tennis courts, her steps so light she thought she might be floating. Her leg muscles were energized and her feet felt fantastic. She stopped to sit on a bench hidden under a cluster of flower-filled bushes, and stuck out her legs to admire her peachy-pink toenails and silky smooth legs. She couldn't wait to see if Alex would notice the creamy texture of her calves and thighs when he . . . when they . . .

Sighing at the outrageous idea, she leaned against the bench. The erotic memory of Alex's hands stroking in secret places made Honoria warm all over, as if a candle burned deep inside her. If she was back in D.C. living her ordinary existence, she might convince herself a simple pedicure was the cause of her elation, but she knew better. The emotions flickering in her breast, the crazy urge to spin in circles while gazing up at the clear blue sky, even the anticipation of getting to the tennis courts, all centered on one singular thing. Alex.

And not just because of what they'd shared in bed. She truly enjoyed listening to his cryptic comments or hearing him talk about his past as a tennis pro or his bigger-than-life job. She even enjoyed sparring with him over the extravagant way he spent money.

She'd called the cabana before she left the spa and no one answered, so she assumed he was still at the courts. She'd hoped this short bit of contemplation would give her time to calm her heart and cool her head. The last thing she wanted was to overwhelm Alex or appear needy. Men, she'd often read, hated women who were needy.

But she couldn't wait to see him, even if it was to simply sit and watch him play. Earlier, when he'd given her a lesson on how to serve, he'd been caring and patient—and very complimentary of her abilities. Having Alex for a teacher made the sport fun and exciting all at once, kind of like the time they spent here at Club Paradise.

Too bad it had to end.

Unfortunately, she had responsibilities that couldn't be ignored. Even though she'd come to the freeing realization that she was no longer indentured to the Hewitt Academy, she didn't have the right to shirk her duty to the school. It was, after all, her livelihood and her legacy. Until she untangled the academy's questionable finances and got the school back on stable ground, she couldn't engage in a serious relationship.

Alex, too, had an agenda. It was obvious from the snippet of conversation she'd overheard this morning that he held an important position in his father's firm. He was a highly visible member of a company that played a big part in the political structure of D.C. People counted on him, exactly as the academy and its students counted on her. Both she and Alex had family duties that took precedence over their personal lives.

You never know what you can accomplish until you try.

The statement rang in her mind, reminding her of the tempting possibility of seeing Alex when they returned home. Yes, they had responsibilities, but so did plenty of other people, all of whom managed to make their personal lives work. Eloise had married a police detective. She was a teacher with a little girl and a baby on the way, yet she and Nathan were happier than any couple she knew. Alex's sister had three active children and ran her own business while her husband was a successful doctor. Steven was Claire's second husband, and Honoria knew from the woman's random comments that she had a wonderful marriage.

Why couldn't it be the same for her and Alex? If they both wanted to be together badly enough, why couldn't they make a relationship work?

Thinking positive thoughts, Honoria charged from her hidden bower and onto the path—where she slammed directly into a fully laden housekeeping cart and the maid who pushed it.

The cart canted to the side, wobbled on two wheels and, as if in slow motion, fell with a resounding crash, scattering towels, cleaning supplies, boxes of tissues and rolls of toilet paper in all directions. The maid, an elderly woman no bigger than a jockey, toppled with it.

Honoria stared in shock. The cleaning people were usually finished by now. Where in the world had the trolley come from? She rubbed her aching midsection. Had she really smacked the cart that hard? Flustered, she scrambled to her feet, then bent to help the woman.

"I am so sorry. Are you all right?"

Sitting with her legs splayed out in front of her, the maid seemed dazed. When she raised her wrinkled face, her towering wig, a mass of black ringlets and purple ribbons, listed jauntily to the left, giving her an oddly endearing look.

"Can you hear me? Did you break anything?" Honoria asked, assessing the maid for injuries. She looked so familiar . . .

"I'm fine," the woman answered, gazing around as if she'd forgotten where she was. Then she focused on the

upended trolley and shrieked. "My cart! My supplies!"
Struggling to her knees, she allowed Honoria to help
her up. "Oh, dear. I'm going to be fired for certain this
time."

Honoria read her name tag, which said simply: Mary.
"How do you feel? Does your head hurt? How about
your legs?"

And where have I seen that face?

Mary shook her head and the wig tipped farther over
her ear. Honoria swallowed a giggle. It was all she could
do not to reach out and right the poor woman's enormous pile of hair where it sat.

"I'm fine." She scanned the ground. "But I have to
get this mess taken care of or I'm going to be late reporting in. I'm running behind schedule today."

Honoria glanced up and down the path, which was
strangely devoid of its usual traffic of zealous hotel employees, and realized that instead of finding Alex, she
had to give Mary a hand. She'd caused the accident—it
was only fair she helped to clean it.

"First, let's get this thing back on its feet." She righted
the fallen cart, then began to gather up the dozens of
small luxury soaps that had spilled from their boxes.
Next, she attacked the little bottles of hand lotion and
shampoo. Good thing they were plastic, or the mess
would have been much worse. Mary worked alongside
her, but at a slower pace, until finally, the path was clear
and the trolley in order.

"I am so sorry," said Honoria, after she made sure
they hadn't missed anything. "What else can I do to
help?"

Mary took inventory of the supplies, then brushed off
her uniform and righted her wig. Suddenly, Honoria
realized where she'd seen the woman, or someone who
closely resembled her.

"Excuse me, but I have to ask. Are you by any chance
related to the assistant front desk manager? Junior?"

The older woman gave a megawatt grin. "Yes, I am. How nice of you to notice."

Mary looked old enough to be Junior's grandmother, but Honoria didn't want to sound rude. "Are you his mother? His aunt? A sister?"

"Why, yes."

She was about to ask which, when Mary grasped the cart handle and gave a shove. Her steps faltered, and she grabbed at her back, wincing in pain. "Oh, dear. I think I may have injured something, after all."

Too worried to press for an answer, Honoria clasped Mary by the elbow. "How about if you come over to the bench and sit down? I'll go to the tennis court and commandeer a golf cart. They always have one in case of an—"

"N-no! Not the tennis courts!" Mary sputtered. "I need to get these supplies to housekeeping as soon as possible."

"But I can find an attendant to drive you while I—"

"No, please. I'll get in trouble if I take up another employee's time. They're here to assist the guests, not the staff." Sniffling, she gave a watery smile. "Just help me get to the entrance at the rear of the hotel. I know I shouldn't take advantage, but . . ."

"Nonsense. I'm the one who ran into you," said Honoria, still wondering how'd she'd managed to do something so reckless. She placed Mary's hands on the cart handle next to her own. "Why don't you hang on and use the trolley like a walker? We'll take it nice and slow until we get to housekeeping. How does that sound?"

"Lovely," said Mary, her expression brightening.

So much for stopping at the tennis courts, Honoria thought as she, the maid, and the seriously listing cart trundled down the path. When they arrived at the split in the walkway, she gave a long, wistful look toward the pro shop and took the fork that veered away from the courts. By the time she got Mary to the hotel, Alex was sure to be back in the cabana getting dressed for dinner.

Alex stepped out of the shower and wrapped himself in a fresh terry robe. Combing his fingers through his damp hair, he stared in the vanity mirror. The man gazing back tilted his head and flashed a smile of self-confidence. The women he dated told him they found his boyish charm irresistible. In fact, if he were home right now, he might be preparing for a night on the town with one of them. But he wasn't home. Nor was he with the kind of woman he usually dated.

Instead, he was in trouble. Big trouble.

More trouble than he'd been in during college, when he'd had to bluff his way through an exam and gotten so nervous he'd actually hurled. More trouble than he'd been in when he first started to work for his father and he'd botched his one and only attempt at writing a contract to seal an important deal.

More trouble than the night of the auction, when he'd been so caught up in the sight of Honoria standing onstage like a frightened doe that he'd allowed himself to be talked into that stupid bet.

What in the hell was he supposed to do now?

He flexed a shoulder, and told himself the pain was no more than he deserved. It was worth an ache or two knowing he'd cleaned Kevin Lewiston's clock. He'd given the first set to Kevin, which had boosted the man's confidence and helped Alex to conserve his own strength. He'd let Kevin take the second set, as well, pretending to struggle. But he'd creamed the guy in the third set, and had him on his knees at the finish of the fourth. By the time they played the fifth set, Kevin was wheezing like he'd gone fifteen rounds with the current heavyweight champ.

Too bad he hadn't made the jerk a money bet, but

the mere thought of wagering had turned his blood to ice. After this week, he'd probably never make another bet as long as he lived.

The knowledge that Kevin and Cissy were here at the resort, only two bungalows away, and that they'd come specifically to spy on him and Honoria, made his skin crawl. It was bad enough they didn't trust him to be honest. Honoria was no dim bulb. The second she saw Cissy, she would know something was up.

If she got wind of the bet before he had a chance to tell her about it . . .

He huffed out a breath. He was an idiot. Over the past few days, he'd let himself get so involved in bedding Honoria he'd completely forgotten about the real world, and instead talked himself into believing he had plenty of time to explain. All along, he'd thought to be the one to tell her, because he was the only person who could outline it properly. He had to make her understand that he hadn't agreed on the wager to humiliate her. Cissy had been the one who'd suggested it, and she'd done it to get even with him.

He thought he would tell her right after they landed at Reagan National. He planned to hail a cab at the airport and escort her home, then follow her inside and, in the kindest and most careful of terms, fill her in on the particulars of what had transpired at the auction.

He would then remind her that they'd had a fantastic vacation and a great time in bed, and hand her a big fat check. How could she complain when she had a huge chunk of money for her precious school?

He could even buy her a parting gift, something expensive she could either keep or return for the cash. He'd be off the hook and she'd be out of debt. What could be more perfect?

Today, when he met Kevin, his hope for a few more days of solitude had disappeared. And knowing that Cissy was with him choked at his throat like a badly knotted Armani tie. Someone had spread rumors of their wager throughout the District, and he'd bet his trust fund it was Cissy. She was up to something. And knowing her, it was something ugly.

Funny, but he'd almost wished Honoria *had* shown up this afternoon when he'd brought Kevin to his knees. What was it about her that made him feel as if he was special, like a white knight charging to the rescue? Hell, right now the only person he wanted to rescue was himself, no matter what his newly acquired conscience was telling him.

He heard the front door open and close.

"Alex? Are you in the bathroom?"

He turned the water on in the sink to drown out Honoria's call. Her lilting voice shot straight to his gut, reminding him that she was full of surprises. This morning she'd insisted on learning how to serve like a pro, as if she truly enjoyed playing his game. Her eager expression when she set off for that pedicure made him think she'd never been inside a beauty parlor or ever done anything nice for herself.

Her breathy sighs in the throes of passion rose in his mind, stabbing like a white hot poker.

I've dreamed about this moment, Alex. Don't stop now.

She'd probably said that to other men. He'd said plenty of the same to the women he slept with, and they'd moaned identical platitudes in return. It was all a part of the act. It was the way the game was played.

Okay, so Cissy and Kevin were here looking to ruin his good time and make sure they won the wager. He could be sneaky, too. He'd already warned Lewiston to stay away and told him to pass the word to his troublemaker of a roommate. All he had to do was keep Honoria from finding out they were at the resort until he decided on the best way to clue her in on the bet.

He cinched the belt tighter around his waist and headed for the bedroom, where he stopped and propped himself in the door frame. Dressed in white shorts and a bright pink T-shirt, Honoria was bent at the waist, digging through a drawer. Damn, but she had a great ass. And fantastic legs. And centerfold perfect breasts.

Another wave of ice cold dread settled in the pit of his stomach. The urge to protect her—to keep her from finding out about that damned bet at all costs—battered his senses. Before he could say a word, she turned and jumped in place.

"Alex, you startled me. I heard the water running, so I thought you'd be in there for a while."

Her wide golden eyes crinkled, her smile so joyous he almost believed she was thrilled just to be in the same room with him. His groin tightened at the thought. Suddenly, he wanted nothing more than to take her to bed and encourage her to wrap those long legs around his waist while he thrust into her and drove them both crazy.

No Cissy or Kevin, no feelings of guilt or inadequacy, and no bet. Just the two of them making love in a world of their own.

Grinning, he ambled over and took her in his arms. "How was the pedicure?"

"Oh, my God. It was phenomenal," she chirped, still gazing into his eyes. "Do you know what those spa chairs can do? I got a back massage just sitting there. And Gloria arranged for us to have full leg massages. I thought I'd died and gone to heaven. Marco and Lola—"

"Marco? You let some guy named Marco touch your legs?" There it was again, that caveman mentality rising to the fore.

"No, silly. I would have fainted on the spot if a strange man started rubbing my legs. I had Lola, and she was wonderful." She snuggled into his chest. "I tried to get to the tennis court when I finished. I was looking forward to watching you beat the heck out of some poor unsuspecting guest."

The idea that Honoria would automatically think

him the victor of his match made his insides flip. He rested his chin on the top of her head. "What makes you think I won?"

"Oh, I don't know. Maybe because you're a terrific player. Or maybe because you deserve to win. I'm sorry I missed your game."

"Where were you?"

"I . . . um . . . had a little run-in with a housekeeping trolley."

He drew back and tipped up her chin. "Are you all right?"

"I'm fine. But you should see the cart." She giggled. "Did you know that Junior has a relative working here? A woman who's either his mother or his sister, or maybe his aunt, though she looked old enough to be his grandmother. I never did find out which."

"This is an island with an economy that depends on tourism and this resort to keep its people going. I imagine he has more than one family member on the payroll."

Honoria nestled into his chest. "You're probably right." She sighed. "I guess we'd better get dressed, or we're going to be late for dinner."

Alex ran his hands up her back and over her shoulders to cup her face in his palms. "I have a better idea."

Leaning forward, he feathered his lips against hers, then deepened the kiss, nibbling and sucking until she opened for his tongue. Honoria melted into him, molding herself to his body, rubbing her breasts against his chest and her hips along his straining erection.

"Hmm. I like your idea," she said when they finally ended the kiss.

He pulled the elastic band from her ponytail and threaded his fingers through her hair, reveling in the silky strands slipping over his hands. "You haven't heard it yet."

She stuck out her lower lip in disappointment. "You mean that wasn't it?"

"It can be, but first I thought you might like to have dinner here tonight. I can bring the table and chairs inside, light a few candles, start a fire, and order room service. How does that sound?"

"Heavenly. But I want to take a shower. Just let me have a look at the menu. I think there's one on the desk."

She turned to retrieve it and Alex pulled her back to his chest. "I don't need to read it. I'll have whatever you're having."

"If you're sure that's what you want to do, fine. But at least tell me what you're hungry for. Fish or chicken or beef. Give me a clue."

"Besides you?" he asked, automatically turning on the charm. He really didn't care what they ate, as long as he didn't have to concentrate on a menu and watch the letters swirl . . . and he kept Honoria from meeting up with Cissy and Kevin. "How about seafood? I'll order that lobster dish you had the other night for both of us."

"What else?"

"Salad, vegetables, something chocolate for dessert, and a bottle of white—Wait, how about champagne? You can drink champagne, can't you?"

"I guess a glass won't hurt."

"No problem. You go shower and I'll call the order in. By the time you're finished, everything will be ready."

Kevin Lewiston stared at his stubborn roommate, his mind boggled by her tenacity as well as her beauty. Ignoring the crush of guests making their way from the romantic cabanas to the hotel, Cissy had stopped on the walkway in front of Honoria and Alex's bungalow. Tanned to burnished gold, she wore a pristine white gown with a plunging neckline—and a frown.

Folding her arms, she glared at him as she spoke. "I just want to go onto the porch and listen at the door. What harm will it do?"

Kevin sighed. Gently cupping her elbow, he guided her off the sidewalk and onto the grass. "Didn't you tell me the desk clerk said that Honoria and Alex were scheduled for the eight o'clock seating? It's almost nine-thirty, which means they're probably still at dinner—exactly where I'd hoped to be by now."

"Yes, but they might have decided to skip out early and have dessert in the cabana," insisted Cissy, attempting to sidestep him and get back on the path. "And I don't mean the kind you eat with a spoon."

"Look, we have a couple more days to find out whether or not we've lost the bet. I say we go to dinner and start spying first thing tomorrow. Besides, you can't just stomp up to their cottage and put your ear to the door. Someone might see."

"No one saw me this afternoon, when I peeked in the window on my way to the beach," she hissed.

Kevin rolled his eyes. "Vandencort isn't stupid, Cissy. He knows—I mean he *will* know why we're here the second he sees us." He stepped in front of her. "Now come on, let's go to the restaurant. I still can't believe you didn't have any luck getting our dinner seating changed to the same as theirs. You certainly got your way with the manager when we checked in."

"When I went to the desk to change our time, I had to deal with that Junior person again, and he wouldn't budge. He insisted there were no free tables for the second seating and said we had keep what we had." She shrugged. "I'd have that little worm fired, if I ever thought we'd be back here again."

Kevin straightened his tie. He'd had the hots for

Cissy Westfall ever since the night he'd met her at that charity auction. His spirits had soared when she'd called and invited him on this surprise getaway. But the more he listened to her plans for winning the bet, the more disheartened he became. Cissy was not interested in him the way he was in her.

"The man was doing his job. He can't create a table for us if there isn't room. Now, come on. You can practice being subtle while we eat."

Cissy gazed longingly at the bungalow. "I guess you're right. The whole idea was to catch them in the act. Or not. If we announce our presence, we lose the element of surprise."

Kevin cupped her elbow and led her down the path toward the hotel, trying not to limp. Besides learning that Vandencort was a crackerjack tennis player, he'd come to a few other conclusions this afternoon while they'd played their match. Behind his charming manner, Alex was clever, with keen insights into other people's motivations. No wonder he had such a solid reputation in his chosen field.

If Cissy found out he'd already blown it with Vandencort, he'd never get her to agree to marry him or take her to bed or even go on a real date. But he'd already made up his mind that she was the woman for him. All he had to do was convince her of it.

"Uh . . . yeah. We don't want to lose our leverage, do we?"

"Did you manage to scare up a game of tennis while I was scoping out the beach and pool areas this afternoon?" asked Cissy. "I didn't see Alex or Miss Priss anywhere. Are you sure they weren't at the courts?"

"Yes, I found someone to play against," Kevin answered, carefully rearranging the truth as he steered them into the dining room. They, as in Alex *and* Honoria, hadn't been at the courts.

"Funny, I really thought Alex would be there."

"Why?" He found their table and held out her chair.

Cissy sat and picked up her menu. "It's the only other logical place for him to be. He's a fantastic player, you know."

Kevin took his seat, wincing at the ache in his knees. "Yeah, I kno—I mean, he is?"

Opening the menu, she continued to chatter. "Back in college, he broke into the pros, even beat a couple of the top ten, but he gave it up to work for his father. When a few of us asked why he didn't continue on the circuit, he said he didn't need the money or the fame, so why bother?"

"I take it the guy keeps pretty much to himself?"

Cissy concentrated on the offerings. "I wouldn't know."

"Come on," goaded Kevin. "It's obvious you have an ax to grind with the man. My guess is he never gave you the time of day in high school and you're juiced."

She raised a finely arched brow. "I'm what?"

"You know, ticked off at being ignored. Personally, I think Alex Vandencort has a screw loose."

"Thanks. I think." Cissy set the menu on the table and gave her order to the hovering waiter. "That was a compliment, right?" she asked after Kevin ordered.

He grinned. "Yes, it was a compliment." He took a sip of water. "So, tell me. Why are you so determined to get back at Vandencort? Can't you accept the fact that the guy isn't interested and leave it at that?"

Cissy drummed her fingers on the table. "Look, I don't want to talk about this anymore. As soon as dinner is over, I plan to go back to their cabana to see if anything is going on inside. End of story. If you don't want to come along, I suggest you go to our bungalow and figure out where you're going to sleep tonight."

Sighing, Kevin leaned back against his chair. Even though he considered himself a nice guy, he was still a lawyer. It wasn't his fault he was goal oriented, which sometimes gave others the impression he was a ladder-climbing snake. Now that he'd achieved his latest goal, a transfer from the New York office of Baily, Fitch and Klein, to their Washington, D.C. headquarters, he'd set his sights on Cissy Westfall.

He'd dated dozens of women, some more attractive than Cissy, and every one of them sweeter and more malleable. Unfortunately, none of them had ever captured his attention the way she did. He sensed a vulnerability about her, an insecurity he couldn't quite put his finger on, hiding beneath her snarky façade, and figured she'd been searching for the right man, just like he'd been on the hunt for the right woman. She thought Alex Vandencort was that man, but she was misguided. And he'd planned a solid case to prove it to her.

At least, he prayed he had, because if he was wrong, he was going to be one heartbroken puppy when this mess was over.

Chapter Thirteen

Junior sat on the porch of Cissy and Kevin's cabana and snapped his fingers, grinning when his laptop magically appeared on the table. He had quite a bit to report tonight and he really needed to get moving. After logging on, his cheerful expression immediately turned suspicious.

"You've got mail!" announced a chipper voice.

Mail? There was only one Heavenet member interested enough in this assignment to send him a note. And he didn't look forward to reading anything from Milton. Instead, he'd planned to do a bit of research on his own and find out what derelict guiding angel had the nerve to allow Cissy Westfall and Kevin Lewiston to show up on *his* island and play havoc with his future and that of his charges.

He inspected the header and saw that it was indeed from his superior. Glowering, he opened the e-mail.

☹ *Please remember—SEX IS NOT LOVE!* ☹
Milton

That was it? One simple sentence bracketed by those annoying little unhappy faces?

Junior huffed out a breath. Yes, yes, yes, he was well aware that sex wasn't love. But in many cases, it was an important precursor to the confounding and sometimes elusive emotion. And that was his goal with Honoria and Alex: an all-encompassing love that transcended time and space, truth and lies, right from wrong.

He planned to go in—as opposed to out—with a bang on this assignment and win that promotion, no matter the obstacles in his way. His charges were close to attaining perfect synergy, and he wasn't about to lose them now. Honoria was so near, she'd already begun thinking of happily ever after. And Alex, well, he was on his way, even though he was still fighting his miserable past and all the depressing baggage that went with it. Unfortunately, the humans with the deepest fears were always the most recalcitrant to see the light beyond the darkness that inhabited their weary heart.

Squaring his shoulders, he scratched his itchy scalp. Dressing in a maid's uniform hadn't bothered him half as much as that cursed wig. Sometimes the things he was forced to do for the well-being of his charges amazed him. But he loved his job. He would do anything short of making a deal with the *Other Side* to receive permanent guiding angel status.

His to-do list was growing by leaps and bounds. First, he'd send Milton a reassuring message to let the Special-Angel-in-Charge know he was on top of things. Then he planned to search the database and find out the names of Kevin's and Cissy's angels. If he had time, he would contact them and ask if they knew what their charges were up to.

Meanwhile, Kevin and Cissy would be here soon, which meant he would have to come up with a clever way to keep them in their cabana.

After that, he might take another walk along the beach. Since Honoria and Alex were snugly ensconced in their bungalow for the night, he could wait until tomorrow to make his next move. He thought for a moment, then began to type.

Honoria pulled back her hair, securing it with a scrunchy, then chose a bottle of gardenia-scented bath gel from the basket of assorted toiletries sitting on the floor next to the tub. Slipping into the shower, she let the warm steamy water envelope her in a cocoon of calm. She needed time to absorb Alex's surprisingly sensual greeting and his intimate suggestion for dinner alone in the bungalow.

She squirted the gel onto a washcloth, then ran the foamy cloth over her shoulders and breasts, down to her belly, thighs and calves. Would Alex notice the silky softness of her legs? Would he touch her in all the other secret places he'd explored with his lips and hands? Would he accept a massage if she offered one, knowing they would both appreciate it when she was through?

She watched the bubbles eddy at her feet as they swirled down the drain, much as her past had slipped away in just a few short days. She owed her friends a huge thank you for arranging the auction and this vacation. Through them, she'd found the courage to break free from many of her mother's constraints and take a few chances, brave new experiences, and start becoming the woman she'd always wanted to be.

Filled with thoughts of the evening ahead, she turned off the faucet and stepped from the stall. After choosing a fluffy towel from the stack on the edge of the tub, she dried off and put on a fresh robe. Then she remembered the two peignoirs folded in her dresser drawer. She'd worn the blue gown that first night, but

Alex hadn't seen her in it. One of them would be perfect for tonight.

Honoria opened the bathroom door. Scanning the room, she gave a silent gasp, too awed to speak. Burning tapers lined the nightstands and mantel, casting everything in muted, undulating shadows. The candle-filled table, set with sparkling crystal and snowy white linen, held domed warming dishes, an elegant floral arrangement, and a variety of silverware. Classical music played softly in the background, completing the romantic setting. The only thing missing was fairy dust or some other magical element that might prove the scene was a dream.

Holding a glass of champagne, Alex stood in front of the fireplace. Staring into the flames, he seemed so lost in thought it took every bit of self-control for Honoria to hold her curiosity in check and not ask what he was thinking. She cleared her throat and he started, then quickly turned. His robe gaped open, and she tried not to ogle.

"I thought I'd change into something more—" She worried her lower lip as warmth flooded her face. Well, duh! How corny did that sound?

Alex eased into a lazy grin, which brought her heated cheeks to the flash point. "Comfortable?" he said, finishing the sentence. "I wondered if I was ever going to see you in one of those gowns."

"You did?"

He ambled around the sofa. Stopping at the table, his jaw clenched as his gaze raked her from head to toe. "How about if you wear the red one?"

Dumbly, she nodded and bent to take it out of the drawer. Clutching it to her chest, she said, "I'll just be a second."

"Take all the time you need." He folded his arms, blocking the heady view of his finely muscled chest covered in curling, golden hair. "But hurry."

In the bathroom, Honoria leaned her backside against the door. Still overwhelmed by the sensual ambiance in the other room, she waited for her heart to stop pounding. Alex's hungry expression thrilled her to the soles of her feet. Just knowing he wanted her as badly as she wanted him filled her with hope for their future. She removed her robe and hung it on the wall hook, then slipped the red gown over her head. Gazing into the mirror, she let her hair down and brushed it until it swung like a velvet curtain over her shoulders.

Fine, she told herself while she brushed her teeth. Alex was waiting, and he was ready to continue their relationship. All she had to do was show him she could give as well as take. She could be just as modern and as liberated as the other women he dated.

After tonight, he would see her in a whole new light.

Alex stripped off his robe as he walked to the dresser. Opening a drawer, he found the bottom to his silk pajamas and tugged them up his legs and over his arousal. How in the hell was he supposed to sit across the table from Honoria and eat dinner while she wore that sexy red gown, when all he wanted was to devour *her* instead?

Returning to the sofa, he glanced around the room, taking in the elegant table, the glowing fireplace, and glittering candles. Could he have arranged a more obvious scene? When he'd started the fire and lighted those candles, the only thing on his mind was setting the mood. He didn't mean for her to read any more into it than what it was—sex between two single, consenting adults who were attracted to each other.

No wonder she'd gazed at him through those amber-colored eyes with such surprise. She believed all of this—the music, the champagne, the candlelight—was for real.

He liked Honoria in so many ways. She was fun, a good sport, a great conversationalist, and a fantastic bed partner. She'd even picked up the dynamics of his favorite sport. But she was way out of his league in the brains department. If his memory was accurate, she'd earned a full scholarship to Princeton, of all places. He'd been so intellectually impaired, his father had been forced to pay an exhorbitant tuition just to get him through the door.

She was a special woman with a lot to offer a man. She didn't deserve to be saddled with a charming but empty shell of a guy like him. He had to be reading her incorrectly. She had to know this was a simple week of fun in the sun. She was supposed to go home and tell her friends about the wonderful time she'd had, then go back to worrying about her precious school. Collecting that hundred grand would be icing on the cake.

The bathroom door opened and he spun on his heel. Honoria stood in the archway, a fallen angel in red silk. Her mahogany-colored hair gleamed, while her skin glowed like the finest porcelain. The sheer gown molded to her breasts, outlining her budded nipples, caressing her waist and hips as it fell to the floor. It was so transparent, he could see the dark triangle of curls at the apex of her thighs.

She walked to the table, a teasing smile on her lips, as if she knew a secret and wasn't about to share. "Sorry I kept you waiting." Her voice rippled through him, husky and smoky-sweet. "I wanted to look perfect for you."

"You are, I mean, you do look perfect," he said, stumbling over the words. She'd taken his breath away with a simple phrase. "I'm ready to eat. How about you?"

As if reeling him in with an invisible lure, she raised a hand and crooked her index finger. "I'm hungry too, but not for food."

"The lobster will get cold," he muttered, but he was unable to resist her pointed gesture and reached her side in two long strides. She smelled like a secret garden overladen with flowers and the scent of sexual desire. He swallowed, then silently cursed the adolescent gesture. Damn if she didn't have him acting like a fourteen-year-old on his first date.

"We can always order more," she said with a flirtatious grin.

She took him by the hand and led him to the bed. When she sat on the edge of the mattress, he moved between her open thighs and let her show him what she wanted. His breath hitched when she leaned forward and tongued his navel, then licked at his stomach. Moving her lips lower, she tugged at his pajama bottoms with her hands, pulling at them until they fell to the floor. When she cupped his erection and enclosed him in her mouth, he thought he would explode on the spot.

At the sound of his guttural moan, she stopped the torture and lay back on the bed. Smiling, she raised her arms above her head and waited.

Alex lost all coherent thought. Collapsing on top of her, he fused their bodies into one being, hoping to absorb her into his skin. Rolling to the side, he slid the gown up her thighs and found the sweet spot hidden inside. She arched into his hand and he captured a jutting nipple with his tongue.

"I'm wearing too many clothes again," she said on a breathy sigh. "And you need a condom."

Condom? He came to his senses and pulled away. "They're in the nightstand. Give me a second to take care of it."

She stretched out on the bed and stared through half-closed eyes as he fumbled with the box and tore open the foil packet. Then he saw the look of anticipation on her face, as if she was waiting for Christmas morning.

"Would you like to put it on?"

Licking at her lower lip, she nodded. "Please."

She sat up and he handed it to her, his every muscle rigid while she took her time rolling it down his shaft. Finally finished, she again settled back on the mattress and gazed at him with a sexy grin. Crazy with the need to sheath himself inside of her, he knelt between her legs, grabbed the neckline of her gown and pulled, tearing it to her waist. Appalled by his lack of self-control, he began to apologize—until he saw her satisfied expression.

"You, Tarzan. Me, Jane," she said with a purr.

The woman surprised him at every turn. "I'll buy you a new nightgown. Hell, I'll buy you a dozen."

"Only if you promise to remove them the same way you did this one," she said with a sassy lilt.

Alex growled deep in his throat. Then he leaned down and kissed her, long and slow and deep. Prodding at her warm, slick folds, he slid his length inside of her and began the primal rhythm that took them to the place they longed to be.

Cissy stopped at the bottom step leading up to the cabana and folded her arms in a challenging gesture. "I'm going to change, maybe put on a sweater, then head out again. You can stay inside or come with me, it's up to you."

She turned and Kevin followed her onto the porch, his gaze glued to the curve of her shapely bottom as it swayed beneath her slinky white dress. He'd listed about a hundred logical arguments as to why this was a dumb idea while they'd eaten dinner, and she hadn't listened to one of them. Her plan to sneak alongside Alex and Honoria's bungalow and peer into a window was so . . . so over the top, he couldn't believe she'd suggested it.

He watched as she kicked her high heels into the middle of the room, dug through a dresser drawer and chose fresh clothes. Without a glance in his direction, she marched into the bathroom and slammed the door.

Frowning, Kevin picked up her shoes and set them in the closet, where he did a mental count of the slingbacks, sandals, pumps, and sneakers piled in a tangle on the floor. He and Cissy were scheduled to be here three days and she'd brought a dozen pairs of shoes. Just his luck he'd fallen in love with a messy Imelda Marcos wanna-be.

Think, Kevin, think. He raised his gaze to the ceiling and paced. *There has to be something you can say or do to dissuade the woman. Turn on the charm, lie to her. Pray to a higher power. Anything.*

Then he heard it—a staccato patter on the roof that fell in a soft, hesitant cadence. He opened the front door and inhaled the invigorating scent of tropical flowers washed clean by the sudden rain. Grinning, he silently thanked whatever heavenly being had answered his prayers.

Several thoughts on how to keep her occupied for the rest of the night flashed through his mind, but he knew she'd never agree to his *first* choice. He crossed to the desk and rummaged in the drawer, found what he was looking for, and slid the box into his pants pocket.

He remembered they still had a complimentary bottle of champagne, so he walked to the mini-fridge and removed it. After peeling away the foil, he uncoiled the wire and let the cork fly. Then he filled two flutes with the sparkling liquid and set them on the table in front of the fireplace. Glancing down, he saw that whoever had taken care of their turndown service had been thoughtful enough to lay a fire.

Squatting, he struck a match and lit the newspaper under the kindling. The paper caught and the dry branches flickered to life, crackling as the flames spread to the trio of logs balanced on top. Soon, a warm, golden glow radiated into the room.

Kevin took off his jacket and tie and hung them in the closet, then undid the top button of his dress shirt and rolled up the sleeves. After slipping off his shoes and tucking them next to Cissy's untidy pile, he made himself comfortable on the sofa, noting the rain had intensified to a steady downpour.

Seconds later the bathroom door opened and Cissy sauntered out, dressed like a cat burglar in black slacks and a black sweater set. She went to the closet, found a pair of sneakers and walked barefoot to the sofa. Sitting at the far end, she said, "I hope you're cozy, because this is where you'll be spending the next few nights."

"You think so?" asked Kevin, his voice calm.

"I do. Now, are you coming or staying here?"

He picked up one of the champagne-filled flutes and offered it to her. "I'm staying, and I suggest you do the same. You're going to get drenched if you do what you planned."

"Drenched?" She cocked her head and listened, then set the drink down, raced to the front door, and flung it open. A gust of wind blew in, pelting her with a torrent of angry raindrops.

She pushed at the door until it latched. Rubbing her sopping arms, she frowned. "I suppose you're happy about this."

"Hey, don't blame me. I didn't make it rain. Nature is just telling you it's too risky to go to that bungalow and play spy." He sipped at the sparkling wine. "Don't worry, there's still plenty of time for you to make a fool of yourself."

Cissy sniffed her displeasure. "I beg your pardon? I may take risks, but I don't ever do anything foolish."

Amused by her disdainful attitude, Kevin raised an eyebrow. "Come to think of it, you might be right. It was kind of risky marrying your second husband. A man of seventy-six could make you a widow at any moment."

"Fat lot you know," she muttered, fidgeting with the buttons on her sweater. "He was seventy-three when I married him and he's healthy as a horse. I'm sure he has his next wife all picked out." Plopping on the sofa, she narrowed her gaze. "Who told you how old James is, anyway?"

"Word gets around," he said with a grin. "And since it

looks like Alex won't be husband number three, I'd like to offer for the job."

Cissy opened and closed her mouth. "You are insane."

"Maybe I am," he answered. "By the way, you'll be happy to know I've decided to sleep in the bed."

In the middle of taking a drink of champagne, she choked when she heard the statement. "I don't think so."

Kevin met her glare with his best I-dare-you expression. "I'm paying half the bill. I'm entitled to half the bed. That seems fair to me."

"You knew the rules when I invited you, and sharing a bed was never on the list," she said, her voice firm.

"True, so I thought that since you're such a risk taker maybe you'd like to play a little game. Winner gets the bed. Loser has to sleep where the winner says."

She drained her glass and set it down on the table with a thump, then sauntered to the window over the wet bar and peered into the darkness. Rain still fell, the wind rising to a gentle moan that rattled the trees and bushes surrounding the cabana. Fat drops formed on the pane and slithered down in glistening trails along the glass.

Finally, she faced him. "What's the game?" she asked, returning to the sofa.

Sliding close to her, he cupped her jaw in his hand. "First, you need to ante up." Leaning forward, he kissed her before she could argue. His lips played softly against hers, demanding but noninvasive, giving her the chance to pull away.

Instead she whimpered softly, which almost did him in. He pulled away and caught the look of wonder in her eyes. Smiling, he took the deck of cards from his pants pocket. "I believe it's called strip poker."

* * *

Honoria rolled over and snuggled closer to Alex's back, spooning herself against his thighs. She couldn't remember the last time she'd slept so soundly or felt so rested. Her stomach grumbled and she suppressed a giggle. She and Alex had been so busy last night, they'd never bothered to eat dinner. Now she was starving.

Slipping her arms around his middle, she stretched out along the length of him and rubbed her breasts against his back. She felt him inhale as he tensed under her fingers.

"You up?" he asked in a sleepy voice.

"Hm-hmm. How about you?"

He turned and enfolded her in his arms, pushing his jutting erection against her stomach. "I am now."

He kissed her, and she gasped at the way he could so quickly bring her to the melting point. Still reeling from the force of his lips, she barely caught her breath before he put on a condom and slid inside of her, filling her with his heated length.

Minutes later, still wrapped in his arms, she was panting from the force of her release. Who needed to eat, when this type of activity was so satisfying?

Alex stood and sauntered to the bathroom, and she admired the muscles flexing in his back, the taut curve of his buttocks and the symmetry of his hardened thighs. How would he look, she wondered, with a pair of tight jeans hugging his bottom, and a T-shirt molded to his broad shoulders? The idea sent a tremor dancing through her system.

She heard the shower and imagined him in the stall, his sculpted body glistening with soap and steamy water. Lost in the fantasy, she thought about how they would continue their day. Maybe they could spend a few hours on the tennis court, or just sit on the beach and read— or she could schedule both of them for a massage.

Minutes later, Alex stood at the foot of the bed, wearing a terry-cloth robe. "I was thinking we might try something different today."

"Different?"

He rubbed his hair dry with a towel. "Yeah. I thought I heard something about the hotel offering day trips into the rain forest. And yesterday I overheard someone raving about a midday picnic on top of the mountains. The guests hike up and the hotel brings them back down via helicopter."

"Both trips sound like fun," she admitted. "In fact, I think there are a few brochures on top of the desk. How about if you check them out? I have to use the bathroom."

He draped the towel over his shoulders and grabbed the ends with his hands. "Um, maybe you should read them yourself and decide what sounds best. I'd hate to reserve something that you didn't care to do."

Honoria rose nude from the bed and walked to him. "Don't be silly. It all sounds wonderful. We can do whatever you want." Sauntering into the bathroom, she called over her shoulder. "Could you order breakfast? I'm starving."

Alex watched until she disappeared into the bathroom, her body a delectable vision of sensuous curves and intoxicating dips, and got hard all over again. At the rate they were going, he'd need to buy another box of condoms before they left the resort. Honoria had become an insatiable and clever bed partner. When he was with her, he couldn't remember how it felt to be with another woman. Hell, he could barely remember any of their names.

It was the first time in forever that he'd actually given thought to living out the rest of his life with the same person, waking up to her every morning and falling asleep at her side each night. The first time he thought a relationship might work . . .

He shoved the stupid idea to the farthest recesses of

his brain. He had more to think about than forever with any single woman, Honoria included. He had a reputation to uphold, an image to convey . . .

He strode to the desk and rifled through a stack of brochures, all decorated with colorful pictures of waterfalls or mountaintops, or the lush verdant green of the rain forest. Frustrated, he scattered the brochures across the desk with one hand while he furrowed fingers through his hair with the other. He had no right to expect an educated woman like Honoria to want to live with his burden. Hell, she'd left their day up to him to decide, and he wasn't even accomplished enough to choose an activity. She deserved better, Alex knew, than what he had to offer. She was brilliant and sensitive and giving and kind, while he was suspicious of the world and all it didn't have to offer.

If he had his way, he'd just keep her in bed for the next three days. They could order food brought to their door and make love until their eyes crossed, and no one would care. But he didn't think that was fair to Honoria, even if he was trying to keep her from getting hurt—at least until he got up the courage to tell her about the bet. It would be a disaster if she ran into Cissy and Kevin before he had a chance to explain.

Gathering up the brochures, he tried to concentrate on the titles, but the letters wavered and swam into disjointed half words that made his stomach ache. Sighing, he picked up the phone and dialed the front desk.

"Junior here, Mr. Vandencort. How may I help you?"

Alex rolled his eyes. The man was everywhere. Didn't he ever take a break or have a day off? "I'd like to arrange a sight-seeing tour for today, and was hoping you could recommend something."

"How lucky that you phoned at this moment," Junior said. "We've just received a cancellation for one of our mountaintop picnics. They leave from the lobby in about ninety minutes and bring you back around six. Dress in casual clothes and wear the most comfortable shoes you have, because it will take a bit of hiking to get there. And bring towels and swimsuits if you like, because there's a lagoon for swimming. The hotel will bring you down by chopper. Shall I register you and Miss Hewitt for today?"

"Fine," said Alex. "Casual clothes, comfortable shoes, towels, and swimsuits. Ninety minutes, in the lobby."

"See you then," said Junior in his usual carefree voice.

At least that was taken care of, thought Alex as he held his head in his hands. But he was in a hole up to his eyebrows, and he hadn't a clue how to dig himself out. If he told Honoria about the bet before they left Club Paradise, her vacation would be ruined.

If he didn't keep her busy and Cissy found her, she'd make sure Honoria knew about the bet, and Honoria would think he'd played her for a fool. If he waited to tell her until they got home and she got wind of it from some well-meaning friend, she would still never forgive him.

Why, he wondered, did the thought make his gut churn and that space left of center in his chest ache like a sonofagun?

Chapter Fourteen

Junior banked to the left, piloting the chopper high into the mists that hung over the mountaintop. Surrounded by sweet pure air and glorious sky, he sighed. He loved the fluffy white mounds of cool, damp clouds. They were one of his favorite places to spend time on earth. In his current form, he realized that he'd taken their beauty for granted. Another added benefit to making the grade as a guiding angel would be the opportunity to spend more time here, enjoying all the riches the world had to offer.

He'd flown the helicopter to the pickup site early, fully aware that his humans wouldn't be ready to leave. Honoria was so entranced with the fresh water pool that she'd talked Alex into swimming in it long after the other couples opted out. All he had to do was promise the guide that someone would pick up the missing guests later, while he brought the others back now.

They didn't need to know that the regular pilot had *accidentally* overslept and missed this pickup flight. Nor did they need to know the rescue wouldn't happen until tomorrow morning. Once Alex and Honoria found the cave he'd stocked with the supplies they needed to be comfortable and safe, they would be fine.

And free from Cissy for one more day.

He made a pass over the lagoon and checked on his charges, who were bobbing serenely in the peaceful blue water. Things were going swimmingly—he chuckled at his clever pun—even though he'd been forced to make a few adjustments to his plan. Continuing on to the landing area, he spotted the small group of guests and their guide, a young island man dressed in hiking boots, a colorful flowered shirt, and khaki shorts.

Junior maneuvered the mechanical bird down with ease, set the engine to idle and hopped out. Ducking his head to avoid the spinning blades, he trotted to the waiting passengers. "Is everyone good to go?" he shouted over the roar of the chopper.

"You're early," the guide replied. "There's still one more couple swimming in the lagoon. I'll just run and get them."

"Don't bother," said Junior, raising a hand to halt him. "It's a great day for flying. Leave them a note and tell them I'll be back."

"I don't know—" the guide began.

"I'm ready to go," interrupted a woman with a flushed face. It was obvious from her red legs and even redder arms that she'd forgotten to put on sunscreen. "I need to get into a tub and soak in something for this sunburn."

"I vote we leave them a note, too," encouraged a male guest. "I'm starving and we have the early dinner seating. The wife and I would like to take a shower before we eat."

The guide gazed around the picnic area, then took stock of his eager-to-depart guests and shrugged. "Okay, I'll leave the battery operated lantern and a couple bottles of water in case it's a while before you get back. Give me a second to write and explain."

He scribbled on a piece of paper and left the note under the lantern while Junior helped the passengers climb into the helicopter. Moments later, they were soaring high into the sky.

Lost in a sea of tranquillity, Honoria floated on her back with Alex beside her. Cool fresh water lapped at her skin. The brilliant sun dipped behind a frothy billow of clouds and she smiled her contentment. The towering trees, the thunder of the falls, and the gaily feathered birds flying overhead were mesmerizing. She was truly in paradise.

The other guests had left the lagoon a while ago, but she'd pleaded with the guide for a few more minutes. She knew they should dry off and head for the pickup site, but she simply didn't want to leave. When Alex agreed to stay, it only made her decision sweeter.

The hike had been just right, not demanding enough to exhaust them, but rigorous enough to give them a healthy appetite. The hotel picnic consisted of cold poached salmon, a salad of new potatoes and capers, a tray of seasoned vegetables, crusty bread and creamy butter, and a fresh fruit tart. Chilled white wine and passion fruit iced tea had rounded out the fabulous meal.

After lunch, they'd ventured into the forest, where the guide led the hikers over a variety of pathways while he pointed out a few craters and hidden caves. They'd meandered back to the trail while he lectured on the flowers and insects that inhabited the island, then followed a different path to the lagoon and its focal point, an unbelievably beautiful waterfall. Those guests who'd worn a bathing suit under their clothes merely shed their outfits and dived in.

Honoria felt movement at her fingertips and turned to find Alex bobbing beside her. "It's getting late," he shouted over the roar of the waterfall. "Maybe we should get dressed."

She faced him and they began to tread water in tandem. "It's so beautiful, I hate to leave."

Alex swam toward her and pulled her near, his eyes a devastating color that matched the aquamarine of the water. "We can come back tomorrow or the next day, if you want."

"I wouldn't mind," she answered. "But all of this tropical splendor makes me wonder what a hike through the rain forest would be like. Maybe we could do that instead?"

Nodding in agreement, he kissed her. Honoria rested her arms on his shoulders and he grabbed her about her hips, encouraging her to wrap her legs around his waist. Tucked against his groin, she felt the proof of his arousal pressing impatiently at her core. Instead of pulling away as she might have done in her old life, she rubbed against his erection, letting him know she wanted more.

The thunder of the waterfall almost obliterated the throbbing sound of a rotor engine. Honoria raised her gaze skyward, shocked to see a huge hornet-like helicopter buzzing and dipping overhead. "Oh my gosh. Our ride's here and we're not ready. Come on."

Alex nuzzled at her neck. "Don't worry. The pilot's early. We have time."

Dizzy with the feel of his mouth on her skin, she melted into him and met his seeking lips. Long seconds passed while they explored each other in the warm, fragrant water, until she came to her senses and pulled away. "Alex, I think we really need to get going."

Together they swam for shore and climbed onto the grassy banks of the lagoon. He handed her a towel, then checked his watch. "No sweat. According to the hotel, the chopper is a good thirty minutes early. There's no need to rush."

Even so, something gnawed inside of Honoria, urging her to hurry. "I don't know. The guide said we'd take off as soon as the helicopter arrived."

"Take it easy," he said, toweling dry his hair. "They wouldn't dare leave without us."

Honoria did the same with her towel, then folded it and tucked it in her bag. After stepping into her shorts, she pulled a tangerine-colored T-shirt over her head, then twisted her hair into a knot and clamped it in place with a plastic clip she'd found at the bottom of her bag. She finished by slipping on her sneakers and resting her backside against a rock to watch Alex dress.

Her breath hitched at the well-worn, snug-fitting blue jeans sheathing his legs and butt. She hadn't even realized he'd packed normal, everyday clothes until he'd dredged the items from his suitcase and put them on in the bungalow. Strange how she'd imagined him in the same outfit this morning.

After he tugged a black T-shirt over his damp hair, he bent to tie his sneakers. Then he stuffed his towel in her bag and stood to meet her smile. "What's wrong?" He ran a hand through his sun-kissed locks. "Do I have a bug in my hair or something?"

"Nope," she said, reaching out to take his other hand. "But you certainly look different in regular clothes. Very sexy."

"I always wear regular clothes," he said, but his grin grew smug at the compliment. "Just not jeans."

"Nu-uh." She shook her head. "You wear expensive clothes. There's a difference. And how did the jeans get in your suitcase in the first place, if you don't wear them?"

Alex hoisted her carryall and led them to the edge of the trail. "Okay, I confess. I usually wear stuff like this when I sit on my roof and stargaze. As for finding them in the bag, you can blame that emcee guy—"

"Nathan Baxter."

"He's the one. He forgot almost everything I asked

him to pack when he followed me into the house, so you'll have to find out from him why he threw these castoffs in my suitcase."

"Remind me to tell Nathan thank you when I do. I think they suit you better than all that pricey, name brand stuff you bought at the hotel men's shop."

"You do?"

"Yep." She peered into the foliage and the narrow rut that led back to the pickup site. "Are you sure this is the right way to the landing area?"

"It's the way everyone else went, so I assume it will take us where we want to go. Come on."

They walked the path hand in hand, until it grew so narrow Alex took the lead. Just when Honoria was sure they were going the wrong way she heard it again—the unmistakable *thunka-thunka-thunka* of a helicopter. Alex turned to her and they took off running, but the winding trail was little more than bare earth crossed by vines and dotted with rocks and vegetation, which made it impossible to race without tripping.

They arrived at the clearing in time to see the chopper disappear over the tops of the trees.

"Hey! Hey, wait!" Honoria shouted and waved her arms, but the helicopter was gone. She turned to find Alex holding a piece of paper in his hand, his brow furrowed in what could only be described as confusion.

She walked to his side, still scanning the sky in case the pilot had seen them and was turning around, but hope dimmed as the sound of the chopper's engine died on the wind. Finally, she turned to Alex. "They left us a note? What does it say? When are they coming back?"

He stuffed his free hand in his pocked as he held the paper out to her. "Here, read it for yourself."

She skimmed the note, amazed at the instructions. "It says we should sit tight and wait—the pilot will be back later. What the heck is that supposed to mean?"

"I haven't a clue," he answered, taking stock of the area. Then he sat on the rock next to the lantern. "But I'm open to suggestions."

"Ok," Honoria paced in front of him. "How about we try to make it back to the hotel by ourselves?"

Alex set his hands on his thighs. "I'd say sure, if we had a marked trail to follow. Unfortunately, I didn't pay attention on the way up. There are at least six paths leading away from this spot, and we don't know which, if any, will take us back to Club Paradise."

"Then you're not worried about being stranded up here?"

"The note said someone would be back for us, correct? I doubt they'd leave us here overnight, so I guess all we can do is wait."

Honoria was a city girl at heart. She'd never slept anywhere but in a bed, and the uncertainty of their predicament made her nervous. She stopped in front of him and saw that his expression was calm, without a trace of panic. "But what if it gets dark and they can't find us, or we run into wild animals or—"

Alex clasped her hands and pulled her onto his lap. "I doubt any of those things will happen, but if something does goes wrong, we'll take it one step at a time, find shelter, and handle it."

"You're sure?"

Alex waggled his eyebrows. "Positive."

"This is ridiculous. We've been to the pool area three times, the tennis courts twice and the beach for half the afternoon. We even visited the spa and all the restaurants. They can't have just disappeared." Cissy flopped onto the sofa and tossed her oversized sun hat onto the coffee table. "I don't get it."

Kevin propped himself against the fireplace mantel and smiled, resisting the urge to walk over and kiss the pout off her sexy lips. Truth be told, after last night he wanted to do a whole lot more, but he doubted Cissy would cooperate. After their one kiss, she'd hidden behind another wall of bravado and shut him out.

He'd won their poker game fair and square, and she'd spent half the evening trying to wheedle her way out of their agreement. When she realized he wasn't about to budge, she'd rigged an ingenious barricade of sofa cushions and pillows to keep them separated on the mattress. In principle, they had shared the bed. Tonight would be his second opportunity to try and change her mind.

"Don't worry, they're here somewhere. The front desk said they haven't checked out yet."

"They must have taken one of those excursions to the rain forest or a hiking tour into the mountains."

"Probably. Maybe we should do the same tomorrow."

Cissy folded her arms. "Need I remind you we're not here to have fun? We're on a mission."

He sat down beside her and rested his elbows on his knees. "About this mission. Cissy, look, I really think you're making a big mistake. No matter what happens between Alex Vandencort and Honoria Hewitt, I highly doubt he'll want to go out with you."

She crossed her legs and jiggled her foot.

"Come on, you know it's true."

"I know no such thing. Alex has dated just about every single woman in the D.C. metro area. I'm on his list. I have to be."

Her plaintive words tugged at Kevin's heartstrings. He'd taken a few psychology courses to help figure out the clients he dealt with in his law practice and recognized a self-esteem issue when he heard it. "So you want to be another one of his conquests? Why?"

Slouching farther into the sofa, she sighed. "You don't understand."

He leaned closer and ran a finger upward from her

elbow to her tantalizingly bare shoulder. "Then help me to understand."

"Alex was . . . is the class golden boy. I can't remember him not succeeding at whatever he tried. Tennis, basketball, golf . . . every teacher loved him, which was odd because he never seemed to care about his grades."

"Okay, so what? He was popular and a crowd pleaser. Big deal."

"I was the class golden girl."

"Ah," said Kevin, finally getting an inkling of what she was driving at.

"Don't *ah* me. And stop with the shrink act. I'm not the crazy one in the room."

He quirked up a corner of his mouth. "If you say so."

"He took me to the prom."

"I know that, but I heard it was because you were voted king and queen and were expected to go together, not because he asked you," said Kevin, happy he'd taken the time to do some snooping into her past.

"He would have asked me—"

"Cissy," he interrupted. "Golden boys and golden girls don't always have to be together. Sometimes, it's the class bad boy and the head cheerleader, or maybe the valedictorian and the class clown. People don't belong with each other simply because of some preconceived notion of who belongs with who."

She huffed out a breath. "Oh, and since when did you become such an expert? You didn't know me or Alex until a week ago. You don't know either of us now."

He pulled at her arm until she relaxed and let him hold her hand. "What I know is that you're a grown woman living in the past. Your marriages didn't work out, so you're harboring a fantasy about going back to when your life was perfect. Accept the fact that high school and your chance with Vandencort are over and move on."

"But Alex is everything I've ever wanted in a guy.

He's got family money and a high profile career every-one envies . . ."

So much for *his* odds, thought Kevin, but he was am-bitious and bright. It was a start. "So money and prestige mean everything to you. It's the reason you married that geriatric billionaire."

"Of course not." She sniffed. "James and I fell in love. We simply fell out of it sooner than I expected."

"And you got a settlement?"

"Well, yes. Actually, I had a prenup. James was more than fair with me."

"So if you found a guy who was poor with an ordinary job, but he loved you to distraction and offered to chase the dragons away? Then what?"

"It's just as easy to fall in love with a rich man as with a—"

"Don't spout stupid adages. Just answer the ques-tion," he snapped. "Is money and position everything? Is that enough to keep you warm on a cold winter night or make you feel cherished or satisfy you in bed? Is that all you want in a life partner?"

"You make me sound cheap, as if I was a gold digger or something." She tried to jerk her hand away, but he hung on tight. "That's disgusting."

"What about children?"

"Kids?"

"Yeah, you know—miniature people with snotty noses and dirty diapers who keep you up all night and make you worry for about thirty years after you bring them into the world. Children."

"I never thought about it. I was only nineteen when I married Alan—he was my first husband. We were both kids ourselves, so when he left—when we separated—I went back to school. I worked in my father's law firm after graduation. James was a client. That's how we met."

"You worked in your father's law firm?" Kevin stifled

a grin. He'd forgotten her dad was an attorney. If she had any respect at all for her father, he might have a chance. "So do you and your dad get along?"

She seemed to relax with the question, as if on safer ground. "Sure. He's a great guy. He and my mother are both great. So are my two older sisters."

"Tell me about them," he said, settling in next to her. "What are they like?"

"I don't want to talk about them. I'd rather try and figure out where Alex and Honoria are right now."

Back to the same old song, thought Kevin. Well, he was going to have to change her tune. "Who cares? They're together. Once we find them, I don't think it will take much to figure out who won that bet."

"I know. Besides being perfect, Alex is such a persuasive guy, Honoria would be an idiot not to sleep with him."

Perfect? Well, hell, there were a few other perfect single men in the world. And he was one of them. "Cissy, I think it might be time you acknowledged that although Alex Vandencort is a wonderful guy, he isn't interested in you."

"It isn't just Alex," she said through clenched teeth. "It's Honoria, too."

"Honoria? Now I am confused."

Cissy began the foot jiggling thing again, and Kevin knew they were getting closer to the problem.

"Honoria Hewitt was the principal's daughter. She did everything right, never got into trouble, beat me out of senior class president, and made the rest of us look like idiots every chance she got."

"That's a little narrow minded, don't you think? Aside from the fact that everyone I talked to said she was a bit on the stuffy side, I never heard a bad word about her. And she's dedicated to that school of hers, to the point of having no personal life to speak of. She's trying to make a difference in the world."

"Are you implying I'm shallow?"

"Not exactly. But people change. At least the smart ones."

She raised a brow at his almost snide comment.

"You should try it—changing, I mean. It might do you a world of good." Kevin thought a second before making the next statement, because he realized it could come back to bite him on the ass. "Who knows? Alex might notice and think better of you for it."

Her baby blue eyes sparkled at the idea. "Do you think that's a possibility?"

Kevin shrugged. "It's a start."

She sighed. "Well, it's dark so it doesn't matter anymore today. We have to get dressed for dinner." Standing, she tossed him a hesitant smile. "I'm not happy with your free psychoanalysis, but I am grateful for the good idea. I'm going to take a shower and get ready."

Kevin sat back against the sofa and blew out a breath. He'd been a dope to give her that last bit of advice. In fact, he'd probably just talked himself out of a shot with her for the rest of the week. But so what? He was a resourceful guy. He'd find a way to prove to Cissy Westfall that he, not Alex Vandencort, was the right man for her.

"What was that?"

Alex grinned when Honoria pressed into his side. "A bird, I think. At least it sounded like a bird." Sitting next to her in the cave, he pulled her close. They'd waited a good hour for the helicopter to return before he decided to search for shelter. When they hadn't found a place near the pickup site, they'd headed back toward the waterfall and stumbled upon this cave. "Don't worry, we're safe in here. I doubt the island has anything more ferocious than wildcats prowling the mountains."

"Did you read that in *National Geographic?*" she asked,

her tone anxious. "Because something tells me you're not exactly an expert on the subject."

He opened his mouth, ready to confess that he didn't ever *read* anything, but thought better of it. He really wasn't in the mood to be at the receiving end of a derisive comment right now.

"You ready for something to eat?" he asked, smoothly changing the subject. It was obvious from the supplies they'd discovered in the cave that someone had been using it as a hideaway, or maybe a trysting site. They'd found two blankets, another lantern, and a knapsack loaded with bottled water and plastic-wrapped snack food. He handed her a packet of cheese and crackers. "This stuff looks okay."

"It doesn't belong to us. I wouldn't feel right eating food meant for someone else."

Her wistful tone made him suspect she was starving. Hell, he was hungry, too, but this wasn't the time to worry over proper cave etiquette. "I'll leave them some cash so they can replace it. How does that sound?"

"You brought money with you on the picnic?" She took the snack from his hand, opened it, and began to assemble their meal. "Why?"

Alex accepted her offer of a cheese-laden cracker. "I always bring money. You never know when you'll need it."

"What did you think you'd need it for out here?"

He washed down the food with water, then passed her the bottle. "I don't know. To tip the guide or the chopper pilot, though right now I'm thinking more along the lines of popping him on the nose when he shows up."

"I'm sure it was an oversight. The pilot probably got busy when he returned to the hotel, and simply forgot about us."

"We're paying guests, Honoria. That means we come first. This place is supposed to be all about service."

"Let me guess; you read that the same place you read about the wild animals, right?"

He stared at the shadows cast by the electric lanterns. "It's something I learned from my father."

"I thought you didn't want to do the things your father did?"

Frustrated, Alex removed his arm from around her shoulders and rested it on his upraised knees. He hated playing twenty questions, especially when he didn't have any answers. "I don't. But every once in a while he says something that makes sense."

"Oh." She sighed. "I'm sorry, I'm being nosy. I'll stop if you pass me a second packet of food."

He did what she asked and took another swig of water. Then he recalled the disjointed conversation he'd had with his father yesterday morning. It wouldn't hurt to ask, he thought, on the off chance Honoria knew something he didn't.

"So how about you atone for your nosiness by answering one of my questions?"

"My life's an open book. Shoot."

"Did you ever see my father have a discussion with your mother, either at the school or at your house?"

She wrinkled her forehead, as if in thought. "My mother made it a point to speak to all the students' parents at least once a year. Why do you ask?"

"Just wondering," he lied. "When he heard I was at the resort with you, my father said something that made me think he knew your mom outside of the academy."

"Did he ask about me?"

"Only in a vague sort of way," Alex said, stretching the truth until it was as thin as the skin on an onion.

"Does he do that often?"

"Do what often?"

"Ask about the girls you—the women you're involved with?"

Sensitized to her feelings, Alex guessed she was embarrassed at the thought of his father knowing they were on a vacation together. He could only imagine how upset she would be if—no, when—she learned of the rumors.

"It's been a long time since I've discussed any aspect of my personal life with my dad. And I don't intend on talking to anyone about this past week. As far as I'm concerned, what happened here stays here."

She picked up his hand from his knee and raised it so she could tuck herself under his arm. Snuggling against him, she yawned. "I didn't think you would."

It was a perfect time to tell her about the bet, he thought, or at least ease her into the idea that there might be rumors flying back home. If he told her now, maybe she wouldn't hate him. He'd only look like what he was—an uncaring and self-important jerk.

"But people are bound to talk amongst themselves. A lot of our classmates were at that auction. They heard about the trip, so there's bound to be speculation."

"Uh-huh."

"I don't want you to hold me accountable for the gossip. At least, not until I tell you why I bid on you."

When she didn't answer, he figured she was waiting for his explanation, so he plunged ahead. "It wasn't my idea to begin with, but you looked so unhappy standing on that stage . . . The people at my table got to talking and someone made a dare, and I didn't want to look stupid or embarrass you and—and things got out of hand."

He waited for her to ask him to explain, but she didn't. Unable to stand the silence, he glanced down, hoping to read the expression on her face. But all he saw in the flickering lantern light were her closed eyes and relaxed features.

Damn. She'd fallen asleep just when he'd found the courage to tell her the story.

Chapter Fifteen

Honoria and Alex awakened at the crack of dawn to the racket of a helicopter and knew immediately their ride had arrived. In a matter of seconds, they raced from the cave to the clearing and met the pilot, who assured them the hotel was willing to do anything to atone for their inconvenience.

The young man, who seemed truly apologetic, confessed he'd been the one on duty last night, but he'd fallen asleep and had no idea who had run the flight. He didn't exactly say so, but his subdued voice and hang-dog expression led Honoria to believe he'd been fired and so had the guide. Not a happy thought, since she'd been the one to insist they stay longer at the lagoon.

Now, seated next to Alex in a private office awaiting an audience with the hotel manager, she wished Junior was the one chairing this meeting. He had to be easier to deal with than the dour man she'd seen behind the front desk a time or two wearing the officious look of a VIP. Unfortunately, Junior hadn't been at the counter when they'd walked by this morning.

She longed for a hot shower, a filling breakfast, and a peaceful nap on a real mattress. Later, when she was home, she could entertain her friends with her tale of adventure. Right now, she remembered little more than falling asleep to the comforting hum of Alex's deep voice and sleeping in his arms, just as she'd been doing for the past few nights. Funny how easy it was to get used to such a simple thing.

"So what do you think they're going to have to say for themselves?" she asked Alex.

"Guess we'll find out in a minute," he replied in a serious voice. "Let me handle it."

"You're not going to yell, are you? I hate it when people shout."

Alex clasped her hand and entwined their fingers. "I promise not to shout."

The door opened and the man she expected strode in, his face set in a tight-lipped smile. "Ms. Hewitt, Mr. Vandencort, I am Mr. Mahlo." The man shook first her hand, then Alex's. "Let me begin by saying how sorry I am about your unfortunate mishap." Installing himself in the desk chair, he steepled his fingers under his chin. "I'm here to see what we can do to make up for your unfortunate situation."

She was about to say that a fruit basket and a bottle of champagne might be nice, along with making sure the guide and pilot kept their jobs, but Alex beat her to it.

"Let's start by getting something straight, Mr. Mahlo," he began in a low, even voice. "Our *mishap*, as you call it, wouldn't have occurred if your staff was more on the ball. You're lucky we found shelter, or my attorney would already be in contact with the hotel."

"Yes, well." The manager tugged at the collar of his shirt. "According to the guide, you specifically requested to spend more time at the lagoon. If you and Ms. Hewitt had been ready to leave with the rest of the guests—"

"Your pilot arrived much earlier than expected. It would have been a simple matter for the guide to have retrieved us while the others were boarding the chopper."

"I agree. Needless to say, both men have been disciplined for their poor judgment."

Honoria slid to the edge of her seat. "You didn't fire them, did you? Because—"

"Why, yes. What other course of action—"

"Excuse me, but we're here to discuss a settlement between Ms. Hewitt, myself, and Club Paradise, is that correct?"

"It is," said the manager, folding his hands on the desk blotter.

"Fine. These are our terms. Number one, Ms. Hewitt would like a full day of complimentary services at the hotel spa. Number two, we want a guaranteed week's stay here at Club Paradise—at the resort's expense and our convenience—as a show of good faith. And number three, we'd like the guide and pilot reinstated in their positions. I'm sure they now realize how careless they were and won't let it happen again."

Honoria couldn't believe her ears. Yes, Alex brokered deals for a living, but she hadn't expected such an organized assault. He didn't sound angry or threatening, just determined and professional as he outlined a list of requests she didn't even imagine they could get.

Mr. Mahlo gave a tentative smile. "If you're certain that will be satisfactory."

"We are," said Alex.

"Then I think we can carry out your wishes, provided you and Ms. Hewitt sign a release form clearing Club Paradise of any future legal action," offered Mr. Mahlo. "I'll have the papers drawn up immediately and sent to your bungalow. In the meantime, I'll contact the spa and let them know Ms. Hewitt will be calling to arrange a day of appointments, at no charge to her. We also have services for our male guests. Perhaps you'd care to join her?"

Alex stood. "I just might do that. And thanks for

being so agreeable." He led Honoria from the office and closed the door behind them.

In awe, she followed him out of the hotel and straight to their cabana. Even more than the prospect of spending a day in the spa, her mind reeled at the ease with which Alex had taken care of things.

"That was amazing," she said, once they were on the path to their bungalow. "Especially when you told him we wanted the guide and pilot to stay on the job. Thanks for making that one of the conditions, by the way."

"I thought it might be important to you."

"Where did you learn to negotiate like that?"

Alex opened the door and they went into the cabana. Grinning, he rested his backside against the wet bar counter. "I've listened to the salesmen in our firm set up deals for years. It felt great to finalize one on my own."

She stepped into his embrace and hugged him close. "But I thought you did that all the time—negotiated deals, I mean."

"It's . . . um . . . complicated. I make the initial contact, assess the customer's needs, and suggest a plan to meet their requirements, usually over a lunch or dinner. The salesman then puts the agreement on paper . . . and all that," he stammered. "The final contract is drawn up and gets passed to my father. He goes over it and sends it to the legal department, where the lawyers approve it and send it back to the salesman, who then inks the deal."

She sighed into his chest. "All that wheeling and dealing makes me dizzy. I can barely figure out how to sharpen the image of the school and attract new students. Maybe you'd agree to help me with that when we get home? You know, draw up a list of potential markets where I can go for sponsorship and such?"

"Um . . . sure . . . if you want. Now how about that shower?"

Honoria drew back and gazed into his eyes. "Could you do me a favor? Find the brochure that outlines the spa services—I think it's on the desk—and recommend a few things. I don't have a clue what some of those treatments do."

"Don't you think it would be better if you read about them yourself?"

"I could. On second thought, maybe we should walk over and decide together." She dropped a soft kiss on his chin, her golden eyes shining with pleasure. "That way, you could join me in the shower."

He ran a hand over her disheveled hair, tucking a wayward strand behind one ear. "Sounds like a plan. I'll be there in a minute."

Swallowing against the wave of nausea rising from his gut, Alex watched Honoria practically skip into the bathroom. No doubt about it, the hole he'd dug just kept getting deeper and deeper. Not only did she expect him to read the spa brochure, he'd agreed to help her draw up a list of donors for her school. The next thing he knew, she'd want him to write endowments or compose alumni letters soliciting financial support.

It wouldn't be long before she knew he was a fraud.

He walked to the phone, where he ordered breakfast and asked that it be delivered in an hour. The good thing was they'd be able to hide out in the spa for the afternoon. If they chose services that were done in a private treatment room, Cissy would never find them. Besides, it gave him one more day to try and explain that stupid bet and the rumors that were circulating back home.

And one more night to have Honoria in his bed.

"I don't understand why we have to go on this stupid nature walk," whined Cissy, "when we didn't even take the time to look for Alex and Honoria around the resort. Just because we didn't see them at breakfast doesn't mean they're not still asleep."

"I told you, it was too late to back out. Now pay attention and don't lose sight of our fellow hikers," warned Kevin. "Who knows, we still might run into them out here."

In a snit, Cissy stomped away. They were last in a line of hotel guests who had signed up for a tour through the rain forest, a trip Kevin had tricked her into taking. Besides keeping her away from Alex Vandencort, it gave him a chance to get his future wife alone.

"Why is it I get the feeling you're lying to me?" Cissy asked, interrupting his daydream.

"I never lied. I merely said Alex and Honoria *might* have decided to go on this hike. If anything, it was that assistant manager who led you to believe they'd signed up for this little junket."

"Well, he's a liar, too." Cissy tripped over a tree root and Kevin grabbed her elbow to keep her from falling. Jerking her arm away, she continued walking. "If I had any sense, I'd forget about men completely and join a convent when I get back home."

Kevin watched the delectable sway of her hips and shook his head. They were in the middle of a frickin' rain forest and she had on a hot pink, midriff-baring T-shirt, black short shorts, two-inch high-heeled sandals, and a full compliment of makeup. The idea of Cissy becoming a nun was about as ludicrous as the pope agreeing to star in a porno video.

"Don't be such a stick-in-the-mud. Try and enjoy yourself for a change." He gestured toward the colorful mounds of cascading flowers covering the brilliant green of the forest. "This is Mother Nature at her finest."

Nose in the air, Cissy ignored him and forged ahead, but she didn't go far before she stopped dead in her tracks. Hanging from an overhead branch, about a foot in front of her, was a snake. A big, ugly, beady-eyed, green-

and-red-striped snake that was staring at her with a cold and menacing glare.

"It's—it's—I—I—" she whispered in a fragmented voice. "I think it wants to eat me. Don't just stand there, Kevin. Do something."

He watched the line of hikers continue into the jungle. The snake wasn't a part of his plan, but it helped.

"Kevin, did you hear what I just said? You've got to do something."

He edged up alongside her and whistled appreciatively. "Wow, that is one mean looking mother of a snake. I wonder if it's poisonous."

"What!" She gave a shriek and jumped behind him. "I don't remember the guide saying anything about there being poisonous snakes out here."

He scanned the ground and picked up a length of fallen tree branch. "Do you really think a representative of the resort is going to tell the guests about every little venom-filled reptile and insect within spitting distance of the hotel? If he did, nobody would ever go on one of these hikes."

Leaning forward, he gently moved the snake aside with the stick, then extended his hand and invited Cissy to proceed ahead of him. If he'd known as a Boy Scout that he would one day be using his nature badge for seduction, he would have complained far less and looked forward to it more.

He turned his attention to his companion, who was now walking backward on the trail. They'd been in the jungle for close to three hours, and she looked it. Her bedraggled topknot drooped to one side and the humidity had played havoc with her war paint.

"You might want to watch where you're going," he cautioned. "Just in case there's another snake up ahead."

"The only snake I see right now is following me," she shot back, but she did come to a halt. "I wouldn't be surprised to learn you'd planted that disgusting creature on purpose just to frighten me. Besides being a liar, you're detestable."

He really needed to do something about that sassy mouth—like kiss it shut. "Hey, you want to go back there and touch that thing to make sure it wasn't made of rubber, go ahead. I'm not about to stop you."

"Why do I think that's a handwritten invitation for me to get bitten and wind up in the hospital?" She sniffed. "I say we return to the hotel and look for Alex and Honoria again. Someone has to know where they are."

Kevin glanced behind him, shocked by the amount of vegetation that had magically grown across the path. "We have to keep moving forward," he told her. "I have no idea which trail to take for the return trip. Unless, of course, you want to lead."

"Very funny." She shoved a hunk of limp blond hair off her face and turned in the direction the hikers had taken. Placing her hands on her hips, she moved in a circle, biting on her lower lip. "Where did everybody go?"

He shrugged. "They're up ahead somewhere. We'll find them." Taking her hand, he tugged her along beside him. "But I suggest we move a little faster, if we want to catch up."

Cissy went about fifty feet before she stumbled over a tangle of vines and fell flat on her face. Rolling to her back, she clutched at her foot and began to howl. "Ow! Ow! Ow!" Struggling to a stand, she hobbled off the trail and propped herself against a tree. "I think I broke something."

He knelt in front of her, propped her foot on his thigh, and removed the sandal. Probing gently, he let his fingers linger over the dainty curve of her instep and fine-boned ankle. "This wouldn't have happened if you'd dressed as instructed," he chastised. "The brochure said to wear comfortable clothes and shoes, remember?"

"These are comfortable, or at least they were until a minute ago." She swiped a hand over her face. "It's broken, isn't it?"

"I doubt it, but your ankle could be sprained." He set his knapsack on the ground and dug deep. God bless the Boy Scouts and God bless Junior. Kevin had no idea why the assistant manager had suggested he bring along this mini-survival kit, but he would be forever in the guy's debt. He pulled out an Ace bandage and carefully bound her ankle, then locked the tiny butterfly clips in place and slipped the sandal back on her foot.

Entranced by her hot-pink painted toenails, he kept his hand on her calf and used his thumb to draw small circles across her skin. "How does that feel? Not too tight, I hope, because I don't want to cut off your circulation."

He ran his hand up her thigh and over her waist as he stood. Leaning into her, he caged her between his arms and focused on her mouth, hoping to remind her of their first kiss. He smiled when he saw the dirt streaked across her cheek.

"What are you laughing at now?" she demanded.

Kevin swiped at the mud, then ran his thumb down and over her lower lip. "You have dirt on your face."

Her hand shaking, she rubbed her cheek. "Is it gone?"

"Not quite. You have some here." Slowly, he bent and brushed his mouth over her lower lip. "And here." He lingered, tasting her salty sweetness. "And here." Slanting his head, he captured her fully in a take-no-prisoners assault.

Cissy clutched at his shirt front and pulled him close. He deepened the kiss, sucking her breath like a drowning man. Filled with a sense of accomplishment, he was ready to sweep her into his arms and carry her to his lair . . . until she pushed him away. But not before he read the desire in her eyes.

"I can't—we can't—" She blinked, as if waking from

a dream, and gave him a shove. "Stop coming on to me, you pervert."

Kevin shook his head. Knowing that she wanted him was enough—for now. "Fine talk coming from a woman I've rescued twice in a matter of minutes." He feigned indifference as he assessed the trail. "Come on, let's see if we can find the others."

Honoria closed her eyes and relaxed as her muscles slowly turned to jelly. She'd had her hair cut in the beauty salon, where the stylist used aluminum foil and color to give her mud brown tresses golden highlights. After that, the woman applied some sort of heat treatment guaranteed to get rid of the frizzies. Then she'd tucked Honoria's hair into a plastic bag and secured it with a clip, wrapped a towel around the mess and sent her for a massage and wrap. She was scheduled to return to the salon for the final step in the process as soon as her body treatments were over.

Now, in a private room, she was lying on a table while Lola and her fingers of steel worked their magic, kneading Honoria's body to a pliable and sated state of bliss. And Alex was on a table next to her, getting the identical rubdown from Marco.

Honoria and Alex hadn't said much, because the tale Marco had been relating to Lola was all about them. Apparently word traveled fast at Club Paradise, especially when it had to do with lost guests.

"Where did you say they spent the night?" Lola asked Marco as she pummeled Honoria's lower back.

"In a cave near the waterfall. Someone said they found a knapsack full of supplies, so it wasn't too rustic. Still, I wouldn't want to be alone up there at night. There's spiders and snakes and all kinds of nasty stuff in that jungle."

"Hmm-hmm-hmm. I'll bet Mr. Mahlo is fit to be tied.

He's never satisfied unless this place is running like a Rolex."

"Yeah, he fired Dano and the guide, but the couple worked out a deal and got them their jobs back. Nice people."

Marco and Lola stopped gossiping when the door opened and closed. Honoria peered through one eye, watching as an attendant pushed an overladen trolley into the room and parked it between the two tables.

"There you go, folks, a double dose of seaweed for your clients."

Alex turned his head and met her gaze. Earlier, he'd taken advantage of Mr. Mahlo's offer and gotten a manicure and a haircut. Unlike her, he didn't need chemical enhancements for his naturally streaked hair.

"So, what do you think?" he asked her, grinning.

"It's fantabulous," Honoria said with an answering smile. "I've read about pampering like this, but never expected to experience it firsthand. How about you?"

He pushed up on his elbows and she did the same. In tandem, Lola and Marco began working on hers and Alex's feet, ankles and calves, covering them with a muddy-looking dark green concoction from one of the jars on the cart.

"When I have the time, I get a weekly massage at the club. Never had one of these seaweed things before, so I can't say much about them, except they smell good."

"This whole place smells good. Did you see the pool and waterfall over there in the corner, and the plants and flowers? The room is like a mini tropical lagoon." She lowered her voice to a whisper. "It reminds me of the one we swam in yesterday."

"You're right," said Alex. Glancing toward Marco and Lola, he too kept his voice low. "Only we won't have to sleep in a cave tonight."

"I didn't want to say anything in front of Mr. Mahlo,

but I really enjoyed that cave. I want to talk to you about what we discussed there."

Alex raised a brow. "Anything in particular?"

"Something you said last night jogged my memory. You asked if your father had ever talked with my mother more often than most of the other parents, correct?"

"Yes."

"Well, I do recall a few times when he came over during the day, usually when the academy was closed for spring break. At the time, I thought it was odd. I guess I forgot about it until you brought it up."

"Do you know what they talked about?"

Honoria felt a draft, and realized Lola had exposed her bottom and back to the room. She tried not to look as Marco did the same thing to Alex, but it was difficult. She cleared her throat and kept her gaze locked on his.

"I was never privy to any of the private consultations, but I think it might have involved a donation to the school."

Alex slowly closed his eyes. "What makes you think it was about money?"

"Because my mother was always very cheerful when he left. I remember that after one of the visits she phoned a contractor to come over and work up an estimate on the new track and field center, which we refurbished over the summer. Another year, right after your dad stopped in, she had the tennis courts resurfaced."

"Okay, you two," chimed Lola, "I don't mean to interrupt, but it's time to turn over."

Honoria rolled to her back and Alex did the same. Lola covered her with a sheet, then applied the seaweed mixture to Honoria's face. "No more talking, 'cause this stuff has to set. Just relax while Marco and I finish up."

The muddy mix began to tighten, and soon Honoria couldn't move her lips or crack a smile. She relaxed further as, bit by bit, Lola slathered the cool goo over her neck, shoulders, belly, and breasts, then moved on to her thighs, knees, and calves. It wasn't long before Honoria was encased in a fragrant seaweed body bag.

"We're through," Lola said. "Marco and I will be back in about thirty minutes to help you off the table and ease you into the pool. Then you'll each get a loofah sponge. Trust me when I tell you the best part of this treatment is getting it with a significant other, because you get to fool around while you scrub the seaweed off each other."

Alex barely heard the woman's instructions. Honoria's words hit him like a blow, practically taking his breath away. From the sound of it, his dad had been telling the truth. For some reason, Faith Hewitt had talked Samuel Vandencort into contributing a large amount of money to the Hewitt Academy, not once but several times.

He believed Honoria when she said she'd never been privy to the conversations. If all of it happened while she'd been a student, she'd probably been concentrating on her studies. Once she left for Princeton, there'd been little opportunity for her to keep tabs on what her mother and his father had done.

Alex was an expert on his dad's motives. The man never spent money when he didn't have to. So what was it that had made Samuel Vandencort give Faith Hewitt a pile of cash? What did his father know that he didn't? And why had both parents kept it a secret from their children?

Chapter Sixteen

TO: *Milton>Special-Angel-in-*
                Charge>@guidingangel.god
FROM: *Junior*
SUBJECT: *Hewitt-Vandencort assignment*
VIA: *Heavenet*

Mission is on course to reach final goal. On another note, have accessed Heavenet database for the whereabouts of Cissy Westfall and Kevin Lewiston's guiding angels. Came up empty on both counts. Please advise.

Junior snapped his fingers and the laptop disappeared in a glittering shower of angel dust. Realizing he'd stretched the truth a bit, he sighed. Though it was true Honoria was still on course to reach the final goal, he was beginning to worry about Alex.

He had no doubt the boy was worthy of her. What did concern him was Alex's inability to let go of the past and share what was hidden in his heart. Admitting to vulnerability was one of the most difficult things a human could do, but one of the most rewarding. For only after owning up to the fact that they needed others could they open themselves to receive the greatest gift of all.

The gift of love.

Right now it was close to midnight. Honoria and Alex were in their bungalow doing whatever it was they needed to do, but Junior still felt like a juggler in a circus, tossing Cissy and Kevin from hand to hand and hoping he didn't drop them in the process. He'd figured a way to keep them out of the picture for another night, but he sincerely wished some clever guiding angel would adopt those two meddlers and get them started on their own quest for true love.

It was obvious Kevin was an okay human who didn't want to hurt anyone, but Cissy was another story. That young woman required a serious attitude adjustment, and sooner better than later. Junior was always amazed at how the Big Boss managed to match folks up. He wouldn't have paired the two of them for a million earthly dollars. If he was their guiding angel, he'd know what had to be done and simply do it.

Consoling himself with the fact that few other humans in his charge would need as much TLC as he had to give Honoria and Alex, he walked out of the supply closet.

And straight into Mr. Mahlo.

The hotel manager glared at him, one brow raised in suspicion. "I sincerely hope you're not slacking off, Junior, because that would be the final straw."

Final straw?

"Sorry, sir, but I have no idea what you're referring to."

"No idea, eh?" Mr. Mahlo straightened his tie. "Follow me, young man, and be quick about it."

Junior thought about disappearing from sight. It would serve the pompous man right and keep him busy chasing shadows for the rest of the night. Then again, what the manager had to say could be important to this mission. Jerking into overdrive, he trotted down the hall after his earthly superior.

"Sit," said Mr. Mahlo, pointing to a chair, "and don't interrupt."

Taking a seat, Junior rested his elbows on his knees and did his best to appear humble.

"Are you aware that yesterday evening one of our guides took the inappropriate advice of an unfamiliar helicopter pilot and left a couple stranded on the mountaintop? And in doing so, opened this hotel to a lawsuit that could have irreparably damaged our reputation, thereby squelching future business?"

"Sir, I—"

Mr. Mahlo held up a hand. "And did you know that Dano, the regular pilot who *should* have made the pickup, has no memory of the event, though he does recall that the last person he spoke to before he fell into a drug-like sleep was you?"

"But—"

"And did you know that there is, at this very moment, another couple missing? A man and woman who, when they checked in, gave you a considerable amount of difficulty."

"I would never—"

"One of the other clerks saw you speaking to Mr. Lewiston this afternoon, right before he and Ms. Westfall signed up for the rain forest excursion, so don't try to deny it."

Junior hung his head. Guiding angels prided themselves on always speaking the truth, unless they absolutely had no other choice. He was usually quite adept at talking himself out of any situation without the necessity of telling a falsehood, at least not directly.

"What do you have to say for yourself?"

"I did speak to the pilot, but I never did a thing to . . . um . . . stop him from picking up Mr. Vandencort and

Ms. Hewitt." He hadn't kept the man from picking up Alex and Honoria *the next morning*, so that wasn't a lie.

"As for Mr. Lewiston, I merely cautioned him to be careful on the hike. I even gave him one of our emergency rescue kits, in case something happened that he couldn't handle."

"An emergency rescue kit? Since when does this hotel have an emergency rescue kit?"

"Um . . . since I started putting one together, sir," Junior said. "We now have a storage closet full."

"Really? And what do we pack in these kits?"

"Why, all manner of survival items, of course."

"Explain."

"A flashlight, insect repellant, antiseptic cream, an assortment of bandages, a compass, thermal blankets, bottled water and packaged food . . . the usual items for an emergency."

"I don't remember authorizing such a kit."

"I'm sorry to say, sir, that I didn't ask your permission," said Junior. A man as self-important as Mr. Mahlo was sure to appreciate a little groveling. "In hindsight, it's obvious I should have sought your approval first, but I wanted to—to surprise you."

"Well, you certainly succeeded. Where did you say these kits were stored?"

Junior waited a beat, blinking the room into existence before he answered. "In the basement, next to housekeeping," he said with innocence. "Do you want me to take you there?"

Mr. Mahlo tapped a finger to his chin. "Of course not. I know my own hotel, and I certainly don't need an escort to something as simple as a supply closet." He eyed Junior with an aura of disdain. "You're dismissed. But don't think I won't be watching you." With that he walked from the room.

Junior breathed a sigh of relief. Mr. Mahlo was one of those unfortunate humans dubbed a micromanager by his peers, and he knew the perfect way to keep the man out of his hair until this job was over. Envisioning the supply closet, he then put it on a schedule to relocate at random every fifteen minutes.

Crossing around to the desk, he sat in the plush leather chair and snapped his fingers, again calling up his laptop. Now that Mr. Mahlo was out of the picture, he could spend a little more time digging through the database. Once he found out the names of Kevin's and Cissy's guiding angels, it would take only a minute to set things to right.

He winced when he heard the obnoxious, too chipper voice announce, "You've got mail!"

Opening the missive, he stared at the short note, bracketed with those annoying smiley faces. They did not bode well.

> ☺ *Due to a serious shortage of heavenly help, the humans mentioned in your previous e-mail are on a waiting list for replacement guiding angels. Since they are in your district, and you seem to be so adept at your task, Cissy Westfall and Kevin Lewiston are now yours.* ☺
> *Milton*

Feeling blindsided, Junior shuddered in his seat. Knowing Milton, the Doughboy had been aware all along this was going to happen.

He couldn't believe it. He'd been had! And since things were already in place for the night, there was nothing he could do but wait until morning.

Kevin waited for Cissy to throw another tantrum, because he was sure she thought they were lost. She was gazing around the jungle as if she was about to burst into tears, and they hadn't seen a trace of the hiking party for the past half hour. He figured no one would realize they were missing until the group was ready to return to the hotel and the guide took a head count. By then, it would be too late and too dark to send out a search party.

"We're lost, aren't we?" she asked, confirming his suspicions. "And we'll probably die out here. I knew something like this was going to happen the second you suggested it. You're trying to kill me."

Little did she know he had a compass in his magic back-pack and directions to a cave in his head, compliments of Junior. "Stop being so dramatic. We can't be more than a mile from the hotel. But I do think we need to find shelter and wait until morning. They'll probably send out a rescue team, but we'll be able to find the way by ourselves, once the sun is up."

Cissy scanned the steadily darkening forest. A rustling noise came from the bushes to their left and she moved closer to his side. "Did you hear that?"

"I suspect it was a wild boar or a bird. Nothing to worry about."

Her eyes grew round as saucers. "A wild boar? Don't they eat people?"

"Only the sweet ones. I think that makes you safe."

Glaring, she stomped her bandaged foot. "You are truly despicable. I hate you."

Kevin held back a chuckle. Even with her wild woman hairdo and makeup, the lady was a piece of work. Once they were married, his life would never be dull. "Listen, Sylvester, I suggest you put a lid on the tantrums. And watch that ankle, because I'm not about to carry you."

"Carry me? I wouldn't let you carry me if I had a broken leg—make that two broken legs." She arched a brow. "And I do not appreciate being referred to as a cartoon character."

"Then stop acting like one. Now I'm going on ahead," he warned. Then he gave her the same choice she'd offered him that first night in the cabana, when she'd had that harebrained scheme to peek in Vandencort's window. "Come along or stay here. It makes no difference to me."

He forged up the trail, until he came to the split in the path Junior had described. When he heard the sound of hesitant footsteps from behind, he took the right fork. Ignoring Cissy's sniffles, he walked another hundred yards and spotted the mouth of the cave. With daylight fading fast, they'd made it just in time.

Ducking inside, he scanned their accommodations. It wasn't Club Paradise. Hell, it wasn't even Motel 6, but it was dry and clean and roomy, with a dark, earthy smell enhanced by the musky scent of tropical flowers.

"Please don't tell me you expect us to sleep in here . . . in the dark . . . on the ground," said Cissy, her voice a whisper.

"You can sleep wherever you want." He opened the knapsack, pulled out a flashlight, and turned it on. Digging further, he found two thin, neatly folded blankets and spread one on the packed earth. Sitting on the blanket, he propped his back against the wall and continued to scavenge. He brought out a bottle of water, three granola bars, some packaged cheese and crackers, and an apple.

"What are you going to do with all that?" she asked, still sniffling her misery.

"Have dinner." He saluted her with the bottled water. It was tough not offering her a sip, but hey—a man had to do what a man had to do.

She sat down next to him and stuck her shapely legs out in front of her. "May I have some?"

"May I have some, please."

She huffed out a breath. "May I have some, please?"

He passed her the bottle and she wiped the top with the hem of her T-shirt, then took a healthy swallow. He offered her a package of cheese and crackers.

"Thank you."

"You're welcome." Now they were getting somewhere. "How about sharing the apple?"

"Yes. Please."

He cut the apple with a pocketknife and gave her half. They ate in companionable silence. Minutes passed before Cissy said, "I . . . um . . . I have to go to the—use the—little girl's room."

He grinned. "All you have to do is walk out the same way you came in. There's a great big bathroom out there, ready and waiting for you."

She opened and closed her mouth, but he kept on smiling.

"Do you have any tissues?"

He checked the knapsack, pulled out a travel-size packet, and handed it to her.

"Don't you have to . . . um . . . go?"

Kevin thought about it for a second, then stood. "Sure, why not?" He picked up the flashlight and they walked outside. "Here, use this to find your way, then come back and I'll take my turn."

"You won't go inside, will you?" she asked with a tremor in her voice.

"I'll be right here."

Cissy heaved a breath, then headed into the forest. Kevin followed the light beam as it wavered and rose. She didn't go far, and for that he was grateful. He'd have a hell of a time getting to her if he had to crash his way through hundreds of feet of vegetation.

He imagined her searching the ground for the perfect spot, dropping those black short shorts and—Christ, he really had it bad if he was fantasizing over a woman taking a pee.

Long seconds passed, until he was ready to charge into the brush and scare the piss right out of her. Then he heard it, a whimper of sound carried across the cooling night breeze.

"K—K—Kevin?"

He squared his shoulders and headed toward the faint glimmer of the flashlight. "Hang on. I'm coming."

"H—hurry. Please."

He pushed through the foliage with his heart in his throat. She sounded scared to death. When he neared the light, he slowed his steps, just in case she was cornered by something big and hairy with four legs and fangs.

He found her backed up against a tree, her eyes wide with terror. "What? What is it?"

Cissy stared down at her stomach and that's when he saw it. It was big and hairy and it had fangs, all right, but it didn't have four legs.

In all his years of camping, Kevin had never seen a spider that big. Hell, until this moment he hadn't known spiders the size of a dessert plate even existed.

Honoria pushed away from the table. She and Alex had just finished another romantic supper in their cabana. They'd returned after their spa treatments and made love for the second time that day, then fallen asleep nestled against each other like cookies in a box. When they'd awakened, it was too late to make their dinner seating, so they'd ordered room service instead.

During the meal, Alex seemed distant, pensive, as if lost in his own world, and she couldn't help but wonder what he was thinking. "You've been kind of quiet tonight. Are you worried about something?"

He folded his arms and leaned back in his chair. "Sorry, I guess I have a lot on my mind."

"I can tell." She sipped the remains of her single glass of white wine, remembering the way Alex had acted in the limo and on the plane ride down—as if he had no idea why he'd bid on her in the first place. "If it's about this trip, I'm sure your father will understand that you didn't plan to be dragged away from your job when you went to the auction."

"It's not a big deal. The company can do without me for a few more days."

"Is it the settlement with the hotel? Because the papers from Mr. Mahlo are on the desk." Standing, she skirted the sofa and crossed the room. Picking up the envelope and a pen, she brought them to the table, removed the document, and set it in front of him. "Maybe you should read the contract and make certain it says what we want it to say."

He shoved the papers to the side. "I'm sure it's fine."

"Don't you want to go over it?"

Alex ran a hand through his hair, then picked up the papers and scanned them. Finally, he reached for the pen, scrawled his name and passed the document back to her. Standing, he walked to the window and stared into the darkness.

Working to keep her expression neutral, Honoria gave the pages a once-over, but she now knew that what she'd suspected about Alex was true. He'd given enough subtle hints on this vacation and, when she'd thought back on it, while they'd been in school, too. If she'd paid more attention, she would have figured it out sooner.

She adjusted the signature sheet and signed her name, then carried the envelope to the fireplace mantel. "I'll make sure Mr. Mahlo gets this tomorrow."

Alex moved from the window, took her hand, and led her to the sofa, then sat and pulled her onto his lap. Nuzzling her ear, he sent a jolt of desire straight to her core, only this time she didn't let it distract her. Sometime before they left, she was going to get him to talk about his problem.

"Let's just sit here for a while and think about what we're going to do tomorrow. It's our last day on the island. Before you know it, we'll be back at the daily grind."

So that was it, she thought, snuggling into his chest. Along with trying to keep his secret, he had been worried about things back home. She too had pushed the topic of their return to the back of her mind, not only because she didn't want their time here to end, but because she'd been wondering what would happen between them once they got there.

"I know what you're saying. It feels as if we just arrived."

"It does, doesn't it?"

"I've become so complacent, I haven't even called the school to check on things. Maybe I'd better do that now."

A chuckle rumbled from deep in his chest. "It's barely sunrise back home—I doubt there'll be anyone at the school."

"Oh. Right. I forgot there's no time difference." She wanted to tell him that she forgot about everything when they were together and he was holding her like this, but they had more important things to discuss. "I guess it can wait." She sighed. "I know it's late, but how about a walk on the beach?"

Alex checked his watch. At close to midnight, there was little chance they'd run into Cissy and Kevin. In truth, he was kind of surprised his evasive tactics had worked so well. Lewiston had promised he'd do his best to keep Cissy out of their way, but Alex was certain that, sooner or later, the woman would find them. When she did, the other shoe would drop, and he imagined it would be the size of one of Shaq's Air Nikes.

"If that's what you want, let's do it."

He waited while Honoria found a sweater and tossed it over her shoulders. Then he took her hand and they headed for the beach. The navy-dark sky was filled with twinkling stars, millions more than he remembered seeing from his nighttime viewings back home. He spotted a pile of towels on the service stand and spread a pair on the sand. After helping her down, he levered himself to sit beside her.

"It's really something, isn't it?" Honoria leaned back on her elbows and gazed at the heavens. "Who would have thought you could actually see so many stars at one time?"

He concentrated on the horizon, hoping to share a few of his favorite sights. "See the constellation straight ahead, the one that looks like a triangle with stars scattered inside? That one is called Hydrus, and the big, brilliant star straight below it? That's Achernar."

"You're pretty good at this. How many names do you know?"

"About seventy. It helps when you listen to Carl Sagan on tape, and I use a kid-friendly instrument back home called a Stellarscope. I just set it to the correct month, date, and time and it pinpoints their location. When the stars are spread out in front of me like a feast for the eyes, it makes me realize how small and insignificant my problems really are."

She sat up and reached for his hand. "I don't mean to pry, but do you—have problems, that is?"

He blew out a breath. "Me? Nah, what do I have to worry about?"

"I don't know, but if you did, you could confide in me. I've been told by some of the high school students I'm a good listener."

She was a good listener, Alex decided, and a good sport. In truth, he'd met very few people in his life who could measure up to her strength of character and level of compassion. While the job security of those two strangers had been Honoria's first concern, he had friends who would have been happy to learn the guide and helicopter pilot were fired, his father included.

Her offer to listen gave him the courage to bring up the bet. "Honoria—Honey, there's something I've been meaning to talk to you about, something you need to know before we get back to D.C."

Turning to face him, she grasped his hands. "I'm glad you want to confide in me, and after you tell me, we don't have to mention it again if you don't want to. But I already know what you want to say, Alex."

If she was a mind reader, she wouldn't be sitting here right now, with that I-really-care-about-you look on her face, so Alex figured whatever she *thought* she knew was speculation. "Okay, hit me with your best shot."

"I'm pretty sure I've guessed your big secret, the one you tried to keep hidden from everyone in school, and since then, I imagine. You've even tried to hide it from me on this vacation."

Perspiration dotted his forehead. His throat closed up in shock. He'd kept a few things from her on this trip, but the word school told him she could only be referring to one particular secret. He pulled his hands from her grip. "Maybe we shouldn't discuss it, after all. Because what you *think* you know isn't anyone's business but mine."

"I'm a teacher, Alex. I've been committed to helping others learn my whole life. I can't take off that hat when I see someone with a problem."

"Drop it, Honoria. It doesn't concern you."

"But it does. An inability to read is nothing to be ashamed of, especially if it isn't your fault. You can be tested. There are so many modern teaching methods in force today that can make whatever your condition is easy to overcome."

His heart slammed in his chest. The last thing he wanted was her pity or her sympathy . . . or her words of hope. Besides, Vandencorts didn't have any flaws or disabilities, at least none that were physical.

"You don't know what you're talking about."

"Don't I? Then why is it you haven't read a menu or gone over a brochure since we've been here? And how come you looked so confused when we were stuck on the mountain and you saw the guide's note? And why did you sign that settlement on the wrong line?"

"I just wanted to get it over with. I wasn't paying attention," he shot back at her.

"The pages were stapled together upside down, Alex. I watched you try to focus, recognized the absolute confusion on your face before you wrote your name. Even Mensa members find it difficult to read that way, but people who *can* read know enough to turn the page right side up. You signed your name on the line meant for me, and you signed it upside down."

Alex clenched his hands in frustration. His entire life, his father had assured him that a good front was everything in this world and more than enough to guarantee him a big score. *All you need to do is play the game, son, and you'll be safe. Be charming, be more clever than the next guy, and you'll come out on top.*

Well, the almighty Samuel Vandencort had just been proven wrong.

"You're making too much of this. It was an oversight, that's all," he bluffed. Then he played his ace. "Don't spoil one of our last nights here by hammering away at what you don't know. Don't ruin what we've had together."

Honoria closed her eyes and Alex knew he'd won. He'd been banking on what this trip meant to her, and like the player his father had raised him to be, he'd used that knowledge to his best advantage. After all, wasn't that what guys like him did? Played to win, each and every time?

Leaning toward her, he caught her chin and tipped up her face. "We're both tired and it's late. I don't want to argue. Let's go inside and hit the sheets. We can get a good night's sleep and make tomorrow a day to remember. What do you say?"

"I say okay, *for now.* But I still want to discuss it—"

Inhaling a breath, Alex kissed her open mouth, drinking in her compassion. The taste of her did little to dull his sharp words, but it didn't matter. It would all be over soon. She only suspected he had a learning disability. When she found out about the bet, she would never forgive him.

His world would go back to being as bleak and empty as it had been before he'd found Honoria again.

Before she had made him care.

Chapter Seventeen

Kevin watched daylight creep into the mouth of the cave. Stretching carefully so as not to wake his roommate, he worked out the kinks in his cramped arms and shoulders, then gazed down at Cissy, who was curled up tight against his stomach and groin.

Her long blond hair covered her face and neck like a curtain of silk. Sometime during the night, she'd managed to rub off all her makeup, probably on his shirt front. And she snored. Not loud enough to keep him awake, but loud enough to remind him she was human and therefore attainable.

She'd almost had a coronary last night, and so had he. Good thing that spider hadn't wanted her for dinner, because the bite might have killed both of them. And it could have been poisonous. She would have died before he'd ever gotten them back to civilization.

After his mental paralysis had lessened, he'd managed to pluck a big, rubbery leaf from a nearby tree and coax it under the creature's huge hairy body. Seconds later, the spider scuttled into the jungle and Cissy collapsed in his arms.

The sweetest moment of the entire trip had come

when he'd carried her into the cave and she'd snuggled next to him, still vibrating like a jackhammer. Her whispered thank you had made him feel ten feet tall. Entwined like the lovers he wished they were, they'd fallen asleep as one being.

He brushed the hair from her cheek and let his lips linger. He had one more day to make her see the light, and he wasn't about to waste a single moment.

"Hey, sleepyhead. Time to get up."

She turned and nestled closer to his groin, sending what little blood left in circulation rushing below his waist.

"Cissy, we have to head back to the hotel."

Raising one eyelid, she blinked and focused first on his chest, then his face. When her hands accidentally moved across his erection, she shot awake and scooted backward on the blanket. "Please tell me I didn't—you didn't—we didn't—"

"Unfortunately, no," he said with a grin. "I don't take advantage of terrified women."

"Oh."

His heart lightened at the disappointment in her voice.

"What time is it?"

He checked his watch. "About six. You ready to head back or do you want something to eat first?"

Wrinkling her nose, she rose to her knees and tried in vain to straighten her rumpled T-shirt and shorts. "Is there anything left?"

He sat up and pulled the backpack near. "A bottle of water and two granola bars. Want one?"

"Could I have the water first? My tongue feels like it's glued to the roof of my mouth."

He passed her the bottle and she drank greedily. Then he handed her a granola bar and tore open the last one for himself. "How do you feel?"

"Sore, mostly. I've never slept on the ground before."

"Never? Not even when you went camping?"

"I've never been camping, but it's obvious you have." She took another bite of breakfast. "You put on quite a performance yesterday. If I had to be stranded in the jungle, I was with the right person."

Heartened by the near compliment and her more pleasant attitude, he forged ahead. "I was a Boy Scout, as were my four younger brothers. My dad was our scoutmaster—still is, though he keeps threatening to quit once Brian graduates high school. Summer campouts are a ritual in our family. Even my mom came along once in a while."

"You have *four* brothers?"

"Yep. Thomas, Robert, Peter, and Brian, in descending order. Thomas is finishing up his residency at Johns Hopkins, Robert teaches history at a local junior college in North Jersey, Peter's a junior in college, and Brian is a senior in high school." He propped an elbow against his upraised knee. "What about your family? You said you had two older sisters."

She folded her legs Indian style and covered them with the blanket. "Sounds like your family is perfect."

He boomed out a laugh. "Hardly. Robert almost flunked out of med school before he got his head on straight, and Peter is on his third college, but he's going to make it this time around. The jury's still out on Brian, but he's been accepted to Bucknell, so he'll be okay."

"They sound . . . nice."

"My mother is great, very patient and understanding. Dad's a stickler for the rules. Besides being a scoutmaster, he's a grade school principal, so we all learned to tow the line. What about you?"

"My mother is a society maven, and you already know my father is a lawyer."

"And your sisters?"

Her lips puckered into a sour-lemon frown. "What about them?"

"Married? Single? Working women or stay-at-home moms? You know, the good stuff."

She continued to pout and Kevin knew he'd touched a nerve.

"Let me guess—they're convicted felons and your father is into corporate law, so they had to go to the slammer."

She giggled and he warmed all over. It was the first time she'd ever laughed at one of his goofy attempts at humor.

"Hardly. Elizabeth and Mary Grace are perfect, right down to their toenails. Married their college sweethearts, both of whom are professional men, and each has two-point-three children, a mini-mansion in the suburbs, and a Mercedes in the garage. I'm the black—um—the problem—" She reached over and stuffed her granola wrapper in the knapsack. "Isn't it time we started back? Someone is probably organizing a search party as we speak."

"No divorces in your family, I gather?"

She rubbed her nose. "Not a one, except for me. I'm the Westfall screwup. Unredeemable and bound to stay that way unless I marry their idea of the perfect—" She shrugged and began folding her blanket. "It's not important. Let's get out of here before they start beating the bushes and send a few more spiders our way."

"Cissy," said Kevin, stilling her hands. "We need to talk for a minute."

"Not a good idea." All business, she straightened her shoulders. "Talking to you is dangerous for my mental health."

"And why do you think that is?"

"For one thing, you ask too many personal questions."

"Do questions make you nervous?"

"Yours do. One minute I want to slug you and the next I want to . . ."

Her voice trailed away as she fussed with the blanket again. Unwilling to put up with anymore of her evasive tactics, he tugged it away, then rose to his knees and met her face to face. Bending forward, he held her in place and feathered his lips over hers. She sighed against his mouth, and he grinned.

"You want to—what?"

She jerked backward as if burned. "Never mind. And no more kissing."

"Why not? I got the impression you enjoyed my kisses."

She rolled her eyes and focused on the ceiling of the cave. "I hate them. They make me feel . . . unsettled . . . like I itch from the inside out and I need to—to—"

He raised a brow. "What if I said I had a cure?"

"A cure? What kind of a—" Staring at him, she struggled to get away, but it was a halfhearted effort at best. "Oh, no you don't. You stay away from me, Kevin Lewiston. I'll find a way to scratch my own itches, thank you very much. A woman has choices, and they don't always have to involve a man."

"Cissy, give me a chance here. Can't you tell that I'm crazy about you?" He tightened his grip on her arms. "Don't make me beg."

She formed an O with her mouth. "You want me that much?"

He pressed his pelvis into hers. Her features softened, as if she was gazing at a litter of newborn kittens. "No man has ever said that to me before."

"They haven't? What were they, deaf, dumb, and blind?"

She gave a mirthless chuckle. "Alan and I were teenagers and he was a little . . . fast on the trigger. I don't think he wanted me, necessarily, as much as he wanted to nail a girl with a trust fund. With James, it was once on our honeymoon and every other weekend until I asked for the divorce. He wouldn't even consider that little blue pill."

"And between Alan and James?"

She bit her lower lip and shook her head.

"How about after James?"

Cissy blinked and a fat tear rolled down her cheek.

"That's it? You've only been with two men . . . ever?"

She tried to pull away again. "I know—it's unbelievable. Modern women are expected to sleep around. But that's not the way I was raised. Mother always said men only committed to good girls, so I made it a rule not to sleep with one until I had a ring on my finger, like my sisters did." She sighed. "I even managed to screw that up."

He made a poor attempt at hiding his laughter, and she swiped away another tear. "I'm happy to know my failures are so amusing."

Kevin flattened his lips. "Sorry, it's not your . . . um . . . lack of success in the sex department that's funny. But I am laughing at my good fortune."

"Because?"

"Because you just confessed you only sleep with the men you marry. And since we're going to do the deed right here, right now, that means we're engaged."

Sitting at the porch table at dawn, Honoria faced the ocean and watched the sunrise burst over the horizon. The dunes sparkled in the morning light as the surrounding forest came awake in an explosion of color and sound. The faint rustle of lizards, the screech and flash of jungle parrots, the soft flutter of huge moths as they flew to safety before becoming breakfast for native predators, all combined to remind her of where she was.

An island paradise, far from civilization and the reality of the modern world.

She propped her chin in her hand and replayed for the hundredth time the conversation she'd had last night with Alex. He'd made a convincing argument for his error in signing the hotel's settlement papers, while neatly sidestepping the rest of her observations. She had to conclude he was in denial. What other reason could there be for his clench-jawed attitude and stiff-lipped push to change the subject after she'd persisted?

Since waking, she'd attempted to go back in time, but her head actually ached when she tried to envision Alex as he'd been in school. Twelve years had passed since graduation, and time had a way of blurring memories until they morphed into whatever a person wanted them to be. He didn't appear clearly in her mind until the third grade, when she recalled a skinny, towheaded boy with an endearing grin and sunny attitude who had, sometime during the middle grades, become quiet and reclusive.

She vaguely remembered his being rebuked by many of their teachers, mostly for his inattention, but she had a vivid recollection of one teacher in particular who seemed bent on humiliation when she accused him of not making an effort to keep up with his peers. After that, there'd been a few years of sullen rebellion as he'd suffered through what she chalked up to an adolescent male's usual bout of testosterone overload, then a year of antisocial behavior and bad boy swagger.

In high school, they hadn't been in any of the same classes, and Honoria had been given so much responsibility from Faith it was all she could do to admire Alex from afar. By the time they became juniors, he'd grown into a smooth talker and a prime athlete, which put him in good stead with the students and bought him leeway with his superiors. When she'd found the time to daydream, she'd envision herself as one of the girls he favored with a ride in his convertible or a date, or a smile of recognition, but none of her musings had ever come true.

It wasn't until senior year that she'd been forced to interact with him on a more personal level. By then, Alex had learned to charm his way out of any situation. Even she, the class brain and model student, had fallen under his spell and completed his homework assignments when she was supposed to be tutoring him— until her mother had caught her and removed her from her job.

Now she wondered how much Faith had known of Alex and his problem. The Hewitt Academy prided itself on tailoring an individual program for each child. Why hadn't her mother, who had believed herself a great educator, identified his handicap and found him help?

And what about his parents? They had enough money to hire an army of professionals. Why hadn't they done anything to rescue their son?

Last year, Eloise had come to her when she suspected that one of her kindergarten students had a reading problem. The boy's father, a foreign diplomat and truly unpleasant man, had removed his son from the academy rather than admit his child was imperfect. She and Eloise had mourned the loss and sworn they would never lose another child in their care again, at least not without a fight. Unfortunately, there was nothing they could do when parents refused assistance.

Was his father the same insensitive and uncaring type of man as that foreign diplomat? If so, no wonder Alex didn't want to emulate the man.

Sitting back in the chair, Honoria exhaled a breath. It was too much to comprehend. Coupled with her intimate feelings for Alex, it was overwhelming. The revelation had come to light slowly, creeping into her subconscious until it had a firm toehold, but now that she'd accepted the truth, it would not be halted.

Her crush had deepened to a true and everlasting love. She had lost her heart to Alex Vandencort.

Emotions dueled inside of her, warring to break free. She longed to take him in her arms and offer comfort for all he had suffered, for the wonderful books he'd missed reading and the frustration he must have felt at not being able to keep up with his peers.

She had sympathy for the bright little boy who had found a way to take control of his shortcoming and channel it into another vein, that of a proficient athlete.

And she knew love for the man who'd been so determined to succeed that he'd been able to overcome his handicap and make a life for himself he could be proud of.

But overlying the sympathy and love was a brittle sheen of anger, not only for Faith's stupidity, but for Alex's selfish and insensitive parents, a mother and a father who had refused to acknowledge an imperfect child.

At least her mother had enumerated her daughter's faults and insisted Honoria repair them. If her analysis was correct, Alex's parents simply hadn't given a damn.

The front door opened and she turned. Alex stood in the archway wearing a duplicate of her morning outfit, a terry-cloth robe. His gilded hair and sleep-sexy grin made her pulse skip a beat. He walked to her and cupped her jaw, kissing her on the cheek.

"It's barely six A.M. How long have you been out here?"

Easing her face into his palm, she reveled in his touch. "Awhile. I wanted to watch the sunrise one last time, and you were sleeping so soundly I didn't have the heart to wake you."

He took a seat next to her and clasped one of her hands. "Honoria, about last night . . ."

She gazed at him, wishing he could read all that she was thinking by simply looking in her eyes. "It doesn't matter, Alex. You were right, this is our last day and we should make the best of it. I want to play tennis with you this morning, then laze away the afternoon on the beach. And tonight, I want to make love to you a final time before we leave. I want to remember Club Paradise and the things we did here always."

"That's fine, but we're going to talk before we get home. There's a lot you don't know—so much I have to tell you. We're booked for the early flight, but we can always change to the later one, if you want to stretch out our last day."

"That sounds nice. I'll call and make the reservation. That way, we'll have all of tomorrow to talk. Until then, let's pretend we're here forever."

The clanking of a delivery trolley grated in the morning air. "I ordered breakfast," said Honoria. "My appetite's gone overboard since our plane touched down. Must be all this fresh ocean air. I'll have to go on a diet when we get home."

"How about taking up tennis? A couple of sets a week will keep you in shape." His tone was hesitant. "You could play as my guest at the club."

"I think I'd like that," she answered, overjoyed that the offer sounded like so much more.

The waiter set the table and served their meal, then they ate and discussed the day.

"Shall I call to reserve a tennis court, or do you want to do that?" Honoria asked him.

He tucked a wayward lock of hair behind her ear, his hand caressing her cheek. "I have a better idea."

She smiled and his blue eyes sparked with mischief. "What?"

"I promised you we'd go through that entire box of condoms before our stay ended, and there are a few left. How about we make sure I keep my word?"

"Now?"

"Right now." He stood and held out his hand.

Powerless to resist, Honoria followed him to the bed, her heart overflowing with hope and her mind full of ideas for their future.

Alex lobbed the ball to Honoria's side of the court, heartened that she was giving him a good workout. It was clear she had the talent and determination to become an accomplished player. He could even see her competing in and winning a few of the women's tournaments at his club, or partnering with him for mixed doubles. She needed to learn a little more finesse, but once they got in a couple of practice rounds, they'd make a great—

He returned her volley with grim resolve. Who was he kidding? It was bad enough she suspected he was dyslexic. When she found out what he'd done at the auction, she wouldn't even want to play *against* him in a match, never mind with him. She'd want nothing to do with him ever.

No matter what happened tomorrow, he was going to tell her about that stupid wager. The idea of her finding out about it from Cissy or the gossips of Washington society made his blood boil and his stomach roll. He'd been wrong to let the fiasco at the Hewitt Academy go this far. His pride and his surprise, coupled with what he had known it would do to Honoria if he reneged on the bid, had kept him from simply rescinding the offer. In hindsight, he now realized that while it might have embarrassed her at that moment, it would have been the smarter thing to do.

The ball whizzed by his face and he barely noticed. "My point," Honoria shouted, her voice ringing with excitement. "What's the matter, ace, am I too fast for you?"

Feigning a laugh, he set his hands on his hips. "Don't be so cocky, little girl," he teased, noting the score was twenty all. "I was just being courteous, letting you win one."

"One! We're tied, in case you've lost count. One more point and I win."

Pulling a ball from her pocket, she served a smash that, to a less experienced player, would have been an ace. Still, he curbed his return. Letting her feel good about her game was the least he could do—before his confession sent her crashing back to reality.

They volleyed steadily, playing in a synchronized rhythm that made Alex feel as if they'd been doing so for years. Honoria seemed to intuit his every shot, dancing to the side or coming to the net as if scripted. He found himself measuring his returns to keep the play going, to keep them moving like a well-oiled machine.

Ball after ball crossed the net. Sweat poured over his face. Honoria swiped a hand across her forehead, but still the rhythm continued.

Then she reached for a shot, her expression joyous, and a bolt of clarity struck Alex like a blow. His breath hitched in his chest as he stumbled and missed her return by inches.

Bouncing on her feet, she rushed to the net, her racket raised in the air while she did a cartoonish victory dance. "I won! I won! I can't believe it. I—" Her smile faded. "Unless you tanked the match." As she lowered her arms, her elated expression turned pleading. "Alex, please say you didn't let me win. I don't ever want you to baby me. I know you're a world-class player, so I don't mind if you stow the killer instincts, but I always expect you to give me a fair game. If I thought you'd give up just so I could feel good about myself, I'd—"

She stopped her chatter when she saw him limping. "Oh my gosh, are you okay?" Racing around to his side, she dropped her racket and grabbed hold of his arm. "Did you twist your ankle? Are you in pain?"

Raising his gaze, Alex met her golden eyes. And what he found there almost brought him to his knees. He was in pain, all right, but the ache didn't reside anywhere near his ankle. Instead, that damned spot to the left of his sternum, the one that had been bothering him ever since he'd taken her to bed, felt as if it had been struck by a runaway semi.

"I'm . . . fine. Just twisted my ankle. It's nothing."

"Here, let me help you." She nudged her shoulder under his arm and clasped him around his waist. Together, they hobbled to the bench and sat down. "Do you need ice? Should I get a golf cart and drive you back to the bungalow? Maybe I should find the hotel doctor—"

Still in shock, he bent and flexed his ankle, unwilling to chance looking her in the eye. "Nah, it's fine." He stood and took a few steps. "See."

"Yoo-hoo! Honey! Yoo-hoo!"

Alex never thought he'd be grateful to hear the sound of Gloria's nasal call, but he was. Honoria grinned at him before he could comment. "Sit here and work the kinks out until you're sure it's nothing serious. I'll just be a minute, then we can have lunch, okay?"

She leaned forward and pecked his cheek, then trotted to the far side of the courts, where she met Gloria. After a few minutes of conversation, the two women walked into the pro shop. Leaning against the bench, Alex rubbed at his chest and breathed a sigh of relief. The ache had lessened, which meant it might have been heartburn or the sun, or too much exercise—nope, scratch exercise. He'd had a physical a month ago and he was in top condition. Maybe the humid tropical air was getting to him or—

"So, Vandencort." Kevin Lewiston sat down beside him on the bench. "How're things going?"

Alex curled his upper lip and gave the man a once-over. "You and your nosy little friend still here? Since I haven't seen you around, I thought the two of you had left."

"We've been here, but I've done as promised and kept Cissy out of your hair. I just thought I'd share some good news."

As far as Alex was concerned, the only *good* news would be learning that Cissy had fallen off the edge of the mountain. "I doubt it's anything that will interest me, but I have the feeling you're going to tell me anyway, so—"

"Cissy and I are engaged."

Alex opened and closed his mouth. "You're what?"

"Engaged. Which should take care of your problem."

"You think I have a problem?" Alex folded his arms. "Brother, are you in for a surprise."

Kevin shot him a smug smile. "I know Cissy's a pain in the ass—it's one of the things I love about her. She's got a few insecurities that need to be ironed out, but I think she's worth it. I'm pretty sure I can convince her to close the book on that ridiculous bet, so you owe me one."

Relief flooded Alex's veins, causing him to go light-headed. Gathering his composure, he raised a brow. "And why would you do that?"

"Because I'm a nice guy?"

"Uh-huh, right."

The man's grin inched into the sincerity zone. "Plus, I just realized my initial suspicion about you and Honoria was correct, and I have a pretty good idea what's going on."

"Still bent on spying, I see."

"Hey, it's a good thing. Now that I know what I know, I plan to work on Cissy this afternoon, and get her to see that whatever happened between the two of you is your own business. We'll go back to D.C. and spread the word that Alex Vandencort failed to score. You may have to eat a little crow, but I figure it'll be worth it to save your and Honoria's relationship. People can believe what they want, but you're off the hook. Whether or not you write a check to the Hewitt Academy is up to you, but at least you won't look like a creep in Honoria's eyes. A smart man would make that one of his goals."

"And you're willing to do this because?"

"Let's just say it's a favor from one man in love to another."

"You're talking through your hat, Lewiston. You have no idea what I'm feeling right now."

"Oh, really? Then how about I take a guess, and you tell me if I'm wrong?" Kevin crossed his legs and struck a confident pose. "I watched the two of you play that match. I saw the way you looked at her when she won the set, ditto your expression when she thought you were injured. You've got it bad, just like me. Good thing is, it's a nice kind of pain."

Kevin shook his head. "There's an old song from the seventies, or was it the early eighties, that sums it up, and the song has your name written all over it."

Kevin stood and held out his hand. Alex found his polite gene and gave it a shake.

"By the way, we had a little hiking mix-up yesterday, so the hotel has comped our stay," said Kevin. "We'll be here a few days longer. That might give you a time to exercise damage control when you get back home."

He gave him a jaunty wave and left whistling *The Look of Love.*

Alex shook his head. The guy was either the dumbest man on the planet or the smartest, he wasn't sure which, but it looked as if Cissy had finally met her match. And how lucky was it that Kevin was willing to get him off the hook with that stupid-assed bet? If word got around that he'd failed to lure Honoria into bed, the gossip would die down fast. So what if everybody thought he'd lost his touch? At least she wouldn't be humiliated.

That meant she wouldn't have a reason to hate him. And if she didn't hate him, he could tell her—

Setting his elbows on his knees, he studied his sneakers. What *was* he going to tell her? He'd never had feelings anywhere near the kind that were spinning around in his gut right now. If this was love, it was a hell of an emotion for a guy to have to deal with.

Lost in thought, he didn't see Honoria until she plopped down next to him on the bench.

"How's your ankle?" she asked, brushing the hair from his forehead.

He took her hand and kissed her palm. That spot in his chest, the one he'd finally identified as his heart, still ached, but in a good way. "Fine. What did Gloria want?"

"To tell me good-bye. We exchanged addresses and phone numbers so we could stay in touch, but we had to go to the pro shop to find a paper and pen. She lives miles away from Washington, so I doubt we'll ever see her again, but she's been a friend."

"Uh-huh." He stood and pulled her into his arms. "You ready to eat? Suddenly, I'm famished."

"You too?" They retrieved their rackets and walked to the hotel. "Must be contagious, because I'm starving."

Chapter Eighteen

Humming the tune Kevin had begun when he'd left the tennis courts, Junior watched Alex and Honoria walk to lunch hand in hand. After climbing down from his covert position, the tippy-top of one of the palm trees that ringed the courts, he righted his uniform and headed toward the hotel. His favorite songs were the ones humans classified as golden oldies. Dusty would be so pleased to learn her music was still inspiring lovers the world over. He'd make a point of telling her so on his next visit to the Special-Angel-in-Charge.

Luckily for him, the pendulum of doom had just swung in the opposite direction. Otherwise, he'd be shopping for that new winter overcoat Milton had threatened him with only a week ago. He'd had little to do with Kevin and Cissy getting together, even though he'd orchestrated their night in the cave, but he wasn't stupid. He would happily accept the accolades for their engagement, and add it to his resume. He deserved the credit, not only because he'd been duped by Milton into taking them on, but because of the disaster that could still occur.

As he passed the outside entry to housekeeping, every

angelic instinct told him to beat a hasty retreat, but the internal warning came too late. Sighing, he turned when he heard the not-so-subtle sound of a frantic hiss.

"Psst! Junior. Get your sorry butt over here. Junior!"

He trotted to the door. He really did need to watch his back around this place. "Marco, what a surprise. Shouldn't you be in the spa right now, giving one of the guests a massage . . . or something?"

Marco shrugged, his face a near grimace. "Things are slow today. Besides, I got cornered by the big boss and he sent me on a half-assed mission. What the heck possessed you to tell Mahlo we had a closet full of emergency survival kits, bro?"

"Ah . . . don't we? I mean, we do, don't we?" Junior rolled his eyes. "We must, because I remember handing one out just the other day."

"Yeah, and it's a good thing you did. Word has it the couple you gave it to got lost in the rain forest, and used everything in it but the can of sterno and matches when they found shelter in a cave. Mahlo looked high and low for that closet you mentioned and struck out, so he gave me the job. Wants me to take a look at the darned kits and assess their contents. Problem is, I can't find the storage room either. I asked around, but no one knows what I'm talking about."

Junior feigned innocence. "Have you tried the end of the hall near the heating system?"

"Heating system?" The young man's eyebrows rose to his hairline. "Since when does this hotel have a heating system?"

Since now, thought Junior, blinking a furnace and all that went with it into existence. "Um, I'm sure we have one. Just take a left out of the elevators and follow the corridor to the end door. You'll tell Mr. Mahlo for me, won't you? There's a good man."

He scuttled away, leaving a suspicious yet hopeful Marco to handle things. Right now, he had more pressing worries, like ensuring the future of *four* charges instead of two. And protecting his own destiny in the process.

Once inside the hotel, he took the elevator to the roof and found a spot in the shade of an island palm. Cool breezes blew as he snapped his fingers and called his laptop into being. He dreaded the idea of seeing those annoying little smiley faces, but he did have to report in, because Milton needed to know about his latest success before it turned into a failure, which was still in the realm of possibility.

Locking his fingers, he stretched his arms, cracked his knuckles and held his breath. Logging on, he smiled when greeted by blessed silence. With no message from Milton, he began to type.

> TO: Milton>Special-Angel-in-
>   Charge>@guidingangel.god
> FROM: Junior
> Via: Heavenet
> SUBJECT: Hewitt-Vandencort assignment
>
> *Have begun work on Westfall-Lewiston campaign*
> *and already have achieved a modicum of success.*
> *On target with Honoria and Alex as well. Expect*
> *final result within twenty-four hours.*

Junior hit the SEND key and blinked the laptop into storage mode. No point in hanging around waiting for trouble when it was already out there stalking him. Thanks to the stubborn ineptitude of humans, wielding damage control had become his new specialty.

He only hoped Alex was brave enough and smart enough to follow his heart.

Alex gazed out over the ocean, his mind on emotional overload. Crystalline water merged seamlessly with the sapphire blue of the horizon. The golden sun beat down from overhead in a benevolent display of tropical cheer. A warm breeze redolent with the scent of salt water and exotic spices ruffled the natural border of vegetation separating the beach from the walkway that led to the cabanas.

He was going to miss Club Paradise, with its unhurried lifestyle, ideal weather, and magnificent scenery. How much of it, he wondered, had been made perfect because he'd shared it with Honoria? If they'd stayed in D.C. and had a regular date, would their relationship have gone in the same direction? In a city teeming with politicians, social climbers, and people who judged on money instead of merit, would it be possible for them to build a life?

The idea of losing Honoria forever brought a sickening pitch and roll to his gut. They hadn't talked about their feelings in detail, but he was fairly certain she wanted them to be together after they arrived home. For his part, he was damned sure going to do everything he could to make that happen.

He jammed their beach umbrella into the sand and popped open the red-and-white-striped canvas canopy, then unfolded a pair of lounge chairs and arranged them side by side. Waiting for Honoria to join him, he told himself that no matter the nature or number of promises Kevin Lewiston made, he still had to give her the facts. He had to tell her the truth.

About everything.

He owed her honesty, and that included a discussion of his handicap. He'd already brushed the topic aside once. She was an intelligent woman and, as she'd pointed out, an experienced teacher. He wouldn't be able to talk his way out of it again. All he had to do was pick his moment and plead his case.

Unfortunately, neither the time nor the opportunity had presented itself. Worse, every word, every explanation he formed in his mind sounded contrived. He found it supremely ironic that Mr. Charming, the ultimate *player* who'd had no problem bluffing his way through college and a high profile job, couldn't put together one coherent sentence when it came to telling the woman he loved the truth.

Scanning the beach, he saw Honoria sift through towels on a stand near the bar while she carried on a conversation with a waiter. Dressed in a black, backless bathing suit, she looked more lovely and alluring than any woman on the beach, many of whom wore skimpy bikinis or sunbathed topless. Granted she'd spent most of her life indoors working in solitude for the Hewitt Academy, but it still amazed him that another man hadn't found this treasure and claimed her for his own.

It was almost as if he'd been fated to attend the auction, just so he could meet her again and make that impossible bid. In a way, he owed Cissy and the rest of her moronic crew a thank you. Without their goading, he wouldn't be here with her now. He only wished he hadn't been such an arrogant jerk and allowed the bet to stand.

He exhaled a frustrated breath. Who would have guessed this love stuff would be so confusing or complicated? Not him, the top dog of D.C. society and the man who'd always thought of commitment as a dirty word. His parents and most of the people he knew reveled in playing marriage roulette. Now he was stumbling in the dark, trying to figure a way to do and say things he never believed he would. And as painful as the unfamiliar tasks were, he looked forward to every second of sharing them with Honoria.

Provided she would have him.

Finished selecting the perfect towels, she strode toward their spot in the sand, a sunny grin brightening her animated face. Once she got to his side, she praised his effort. "Thanks for securing the umbrella and taking care of the chairs. Just let me put these down . . ." She arranged a towel across first her chair, then his. "There, all set."

Sitting on her terry-cloth throne, she passed him a second towel. "You don't need to baby-sit me. I won't mind if you go for a swim."

Alex dropped onto his chair and turned to her. "I'm here to spend time with you. The ocean will always be here, but *we* won't."

"That's sweet, but I know how much you love the water. It's okay, really. I can read or take a nap. I might even get bold and order a drink if the waiter wanders over."

"How about we go in together?" He waggled his eyebrows until she giggled. "You could rescue me if I get a cramp or I'm attacked by marauding jelly fish."

"Fat lot of good I'd be. Think back to the waterfall. It was all I could do to stay afloat in that shaded lagoon." She held up an arm. "Besides, I don't have the type of skin that takes kindly to the sun."

He longed to say that her skin reminded him of an eggshell, smooth and pure and fragile looking, but the comparison sounded stupid and very unromantic. And Honoria deserved romance, not his inane analogies. He shook his head. She deserved a man who was more intelligent, more honorable . . . more of all the things he would never be.

Instead, he said, "You can use me as a life raft. And you don't need to worry about burning as long as your friends remembered to pack sunscreen."

Reaching into her tote bag, she pulled out bottled water, a paperback, a newspaper, and a magazine with the Williams sisters on the cover. The thought that she'd gone out of her way to buy a tennis magazine only compounded his guilt.

Finally, she found what she was searching for, a plastic container of sunblock. "Eloise thought of everything.

This stuff has an SPF of thirty, so I doubt I'll burn. Just give me a second to put some on."

Fisting his hands against his thighs, Alex watched as she flipped open the top and began to slather herself with the creamy liquid. He swallowed as she smoothed the goo over her shapely calves and long, milky white thighs. She was killing him. It took all of thirty seconds to elapse before he snatched the container from her hand.

"What are you doing?"

"Shamelessly using any opportunity to get my hands on your delectable body. All you have to do is sit still and let me take care of everything." He squirted lotion into his palm and gently rubbed it over her arm and shoulder, then across to her collarbone. Moving to her other side, he began the process anew. "I've kind of grown attached to your skin," he teased. "I'd hate to see it burn to a crisp. Now lean forward."

She did as he asked, and he ran his hands from the center of her back up to the nape of her neck, then reversed direction and tripped his fingers down her spine. Working in a slow circular motion, he kneaded her tender flesh while he tried to ignore the sexual pull rising from below the waistband of his swimsuit. The sound of her moan was all it took to get him hard and throbbing.

"That feels wonderful," she muttered. "Almost as good as Lola's magic fingers."

"Almost? How about I touch you in a few places she didn't? Like here." His palm dipped below her swimsuit at the curve of her back, stopping just short of the cleft in her bottom. "Or here." He quickly moved his other hand to her front and stroked the top of her breasts, skimming the tips of her nipples. "And what about here?" His fingers slid smoothly to the juncture of her thighs.

"Alex!" she squeaked out, slapping her knees together.

Pearly pink color rose in her cheeks and he smiled. He'd never been the kind of man who exchanged teasing banter with a woman. He'd stuck to dating society mavens in the making or debutantes so stuck on being seen with a wealthy and socially acceptable man, they didn't know how to have fun. And now he knew the reason why.

They had all been safe and antiseptic, more like Barbie dolls searching for their Ken. Not one of them was a real woman, one who laughed and cried and joked with passion. One he could love.

"What's wrong? Am I embarrassing you?"

She glanced at him over her shoulder. "Sort of. I've never . . . I mean no one has ever said such explicit . . . such openly suggestive things to me before."

"The question is, does it bother you so much you want me to stop?"

She shook her head. "I love it. Please don't—" She sighed as he massaged a spot at the base of her spine. "Sto-op. Hmm, don't ever stop."

By the time Alex finished his task, he was ready to drag her to the bungalow and use up the last of his condoms. Between worrying about everything he needed to tell her and the feel of her body under his palms, he was stretched as tight as the strings on a tennis racket.

Being near Honoria when she was dressed in a figure hugging swimsuit was more of a turn-on than seeing her naked. The anticipation of slipping the straps off her velvety shoulders one at a time, then peeling down the fabric to reveal her gorgeous breasts and aroused nipples was almost too much to bear. When his hands skimmed her body she would blush, and he would admire the satiny glow of her skin, then laugh at the sparkle in her honey-colored eyes—

"Earth to Alex," she said, her voice a smile as it brought him back to the present. "What are you thinking?"

"Um . . . nothing. You ready to go in?"

They stood and the caveman urge, the one that made him want to stake a claim and pound his chest while he shouted out his prowess, crept over him again. Reaching out, he scooped her up and headed for the water.

Honoria wrapped her arms around his neck and squealed out a weak protest. "What are you doing! Alex, you're going to hurt yourself. You'll throw your back out or—"

Wading into the ocean, where her weight didn't matter, he kissed away her complaints. They bobbed against each other in the pull of the surf, his chest grazing her pillowed breasts, their bodies joined as their tongues tangled in a mating dance as old as time.

Mesmerized by her childish delight and womanly desire, he decided to honor her request to make their last day here one she would always remember. He still had tonight to put his heart on the line and tell her about the bet.

"What are you reading?"

Honoria lowered her newspaper and glanced at Alex, who'd fallen asleep in his chair after their frolic in the ocean. *"The Washington Post.* I grabbed a copy when we stopped in the gift shop before lunch. It's a couple of days old, but I thought it would catch me up on what was happening in the real world." She raised a brow, hoping her next comment would pave the way to an open discussion. "Would you like a section?"

A flicker or awareness crossed his face. Then his features turned grim. Sitting upright on the lounge chair, he swung his legs over the side and rested his elbows on his knees. "Honoria, about my problem—or what you perceive my problem to be—"

Crushing the paper in her lap, she copied his pose. "Yes?"

Instead of meeting her face to face, he shuttered his

eyes and stared at his hands. "I've thought about it, and I decided you need to know the truth—about a lot of things. I want to be honest with you."

If she'd been talking with a child, Honoria thought, this would be the perfect moment for a high-five. But Alex was an adult who had lived with his disability for a lifetime. Well aware of his problem, he knew there were ways to fix it, if only he was willing to try.

"Thank you for that. Integrity was the one virtue Faith drilled into my brain while growing up. She used to say that, in the end, a person's honor was the only thing they could truly call their own."

At her statement, he heaved a breath and ran a hand through his hair. "Okay, here goes," he said, almost to himself. "I'm dyslexic, or at least I think I am. It's plagued me for so long, I've become an expert at faking it, which is why I made it sound as if you were wrong. But I don't want to ignore it anymore. I want to do what you suggested, get tested, find one of those programs you talked about and—"

"Oh, Alex." She dropped the crumpled newspaper to the sand and grabbed his free hand. "I'm so happy to hear you say that." Relief flooded through her like a warm spring rain, until a tear leaked from the corner of one eye. "It will be a challenge, but you can do it. We'll find a professional, someone who will agree to be discreet. I have connections with so many—"

"Hey, take it easy." Finally meeting her gaze, he swiped the tear away with his thumb. "I said I'd try, but that doesn't mean I'll be successful. Who knows, I might be a total flop. There's a good chance I might never learn to read."

She raised two fingers and placed them on his mouth. "Don't say such a thing. You're bright, you have a wonderful memory—"

His lips twitched into a questioning grin. "How do you know I have a good memory?"

"Isn't it obvious? You've had to keep the names of your clients, their titles, the companies they work for, and probably a ton of personal information about them in your head. You've memorized dates, times, and the places of your appointments, assimilated all kinds of things into your brain because you can't read their business cards or personal profiles. Your normal conversation could easily pass for that of a well-read person, which means you've heard the intelligent words, intuited their meaning, and remembered them. Have you ever had your IQ tested?"

He shrugged. "I don't know. Why?"

"Because they have a way of measuring intelligence these days that doesn't require reading. And even if they didn't, someone could read the question to you." Grinning at him, she dug in her bag for a tissue. "You aren't stupid, Alex. You simply have a handicap to overcome, like myopia or a lisp or being color-blind. Hundreds of thousands of average people rise above their disabilities every day, and you're far from average."

Giddy with relief, she blew her nose, then swiped at her damp cheeks. "I'll help you. Together we can do anything."

Alex took her hands and brought them to his lips, grazing her knuckles with a kiss. His blue eyes glinted wetly in the sunlight, proof of his emotional state, and she resisted the urge to pull him near and hold him in her arms. Instead, she handed him a fresh tissue and silently vowed to keep the moment close to her heart.

He sucked in a breath, his eyes never leaving hers. "When you say it, you make me believe I can do it. It gives me the hope to think that one day I might be reading that newspaper."

She snatched the scattered pages from the sand and straightened them. "Then you can find out about yourself and those important friends you spend so much time with. I've kept tabs on you for years just by perusing the society column."

"You must not have had enough going on in your life," he teased, "because I can't imagine anyone in my so-called circle of friends doing anything that would interest you or deserve your attention."

"Oh, yeah? Well listen to this." She found the section she was looking for and snapped open the page. "It's the 'About Town' column and they're reporting on the auction. Besides the positive write-up, there are lots of pictures." She bit at her lower lip, her expression one of amazement. "I still can't believe I allowed Ruth Roberts to shoehorn me into that outrageous red dress."

"Hey, I like that dress," he said, lightening the mood. "I showed off all your considerable . . . charms."

"How very *male* of you to notice," she said, secretly thrilled to know he approved of her fuller figure. "The reporter doesn't mention exact amounts, but he does talk about Mr. Belgradian being the top money winner for the men, then he moves to the women. The article mentions you and your 'impressive' bid, too. And I quote, 'The highest bid of the evening came from Alex Vandencort, one of the District's most eligible bachelors, who paid a whopping sum for a week in the sun at Club Paradise with the star of the event, Ms. Honoria Hewitt.' "

She peered at him over the top of the page. "He's talking about me, by the way, in case you've forgotten."

His mouth thinned to a line as he tried to wrest the paper from her hands. "Hey, you don't have to read about that night. We were there, remember?"

"How could I forget?"

"How about we change the subject? I hate hearing about myself and that self-absorbed crowd I'm forced to hang with."

"Then why do you? Hang out with them, I mean."

"Direct orders from my father. Bethune and Vandencort caters to the wealthiest and most politically savvy people in the country. If I'm alone, I leave early and—"

"But you're rarely alone, Alex," she reminded him. "I've seen the pictures of some of the women you date. They're all model thin, glamorous, and wealthy. And you always look as if you're having a good time."

He set his hands on his knees. "Another one of my no-talent talents. I photograph well."

"Jeez, and I thought I was down on myself. It sounds as if your father and my mother had a lot in common."

Alex gave a sad chuckle. "I'm a chip off the old block, all right, but I plan to change things. I'm thinking of quitting the company, setting a new course for my life." His expression turned hopeful. "I thought maybe you could help with that . . . if you still want to see me when we get back home."

Honoria swore if it were possible, her heart would take wing and fly out of her chest. But there were so many impediments to their relationship that had to be resolved, mainly her social standing and the school's danger of declaring bankruptcy. Things could change once they were back home in the real world.

"I think I'd like that," she answered, hoping to tell him with her smile how much she wished it was so.

Alex closed his eyes and sighed, as if a weight had been lifted from his shoulders. When he met her gaze, his expression was guarded. "Honoria, listen, there's something you need to know—"

"I know everything I need to. We can iron out the details once we're home." Life was good, she thought. The academy had received positive press, and Alex wanted to continue their relationship. For now, that was enough. "Monday morning, I'll call a friend and arrange to have you tested. We can take it from there."

She lay back against the lounge chair and looked over the paper. "Here's something interesting. There's a rather cryptic note at the bottom marked: One Final Item. 'All of Washington society is waiting to hear who will be the winner of a little side wager made the same night as the Hewitt Academy auction. Only two people will know the outcome for certain, and we doubt they'll be talking, but there's been enough speculation to convince this reporter the male will prevail.' "

She glanced at him. "Who do you think they're talking about?"

Alex reached across and grabbed the paper from her hands, tearing it down the middle in the process. Wadding it into a ball, he handed it to a passing waiter, then gave her a sheepish smile. Still sitting upright at the edge of his chair, he clasped her hand and stared with a dark intensity Honoria didn't remember ever seeing in his eyes.

"Um . . . about that talk. I don't think we should postpone it any longer. We need to have it now."

"Nu-uh. Tomorrow. I still want today to be all fun and no worries." She pulled her hand away. "Besides, now that we've discussed your problem, there isn't anything so important it can't wait."

He sighed. Then he stood. "I'm going in for a final swim. You want to join me?"

"I think I'll pack my tote bag and go back to the bungalow. How about if we meet inside? I have to call and change our reservations, remember?"

He walked backward toward the water, then turned and ran into the surf. Honoria was so pleased with their talk, she told herself Alex's worried expression was nothing more than concern over his reading disability. Well, he needn't worry, because she was going to make sure he got the best possible help. Once that happened, everything would be great.

Chapter Nineteen

Honoria and Alex walked into the dining room arm in arm. Just today, the hotel had delivered an identical blue gown to replace the one that was ruined by the exploding commode. She decided to wear it for their final night on the island. Ever the realist, she told herself that even if their sexual relationship faded, she would always love Alex; they would remain friends. The gown would be a symbol of his generosity and the special time they'd shared here.

They took their seats and received the usual expert attention from the staff. Now that she knew for certain of his handicap, Honoria was much more aware of Alex's clever ploy to cover it up. He'd told her he frequented special restaurants in and around the District where the waiters knew his preferences and read a list of specials before he chose an entree. If there were no specials, he simply asked for a recommendation from the chef. Those same restaurants stocked his favorite wines, and always had on hand a few of the desserts he enjoyed.

How sad, thought Honoria, that he'd lost all spontaneity in his life and been forced to plan each evening according to what best aided him in hiding his disability.

Alex picked up a menu and scanned it. His gaze skittered hesitantly across the pages, and she could only imagine what he saw in the letters and numbers printed there. Why hadn't she noticed his expression of uncertainty earlier, or picked up on the fact that he never really scrutinized a menu, a brochure, or a document? She placed her palm on his wrist in an attempt to tell him that she cared.

He shook his head, his smile taut. "Sorry, I keep thinking that one day the letters will magically stop swirling around and make sense to me."

"They will. Soon. You'll see."

He squeezed her fingers and glanced back at the menu.

"I can tell you what it says," Honoria began, "if you want."

He waited a beat, a muscle in his jaw tightening. Then his smile softened and reached his eyes. "I think I'd like that."

Honoria's heart jumped in place. His willingness to accept her help was proof he trusted her. It was a small step, but an important one. Opening her menu, she began to read in a low yet animated voice, adding her own comedic flair to the entrée descriptions. Laughing, he finally made his choice, as did she. The waiter arrived and took their order, while Alex continued to hold her hand, as if she were a raft on the sea of his life.

Gazing into his eyes, she sighed inwardly at the sadness she caught there. She'd always enjoyed guiding others; as an educator, it was her life's work. But helping Alex gave her so much more satisfaction than teaching, almost as if she were saving him from a world of despair.

Though they'd forged a bond, it was tenuous at best. She loved him with an intensity that sometimes frightened her, but suspected he would mistake her revelation for pity—an emotion he was sure to detest—if she told him so.

The orchestra sounded subdued as it played an older song that seemed the ideal dance number. Back to his usual confident self, Alex pushed from the table and tugged her from her chair. She stood and followed him, stepping into his arms as if she'd been born there. They held each other close while the music surrounded them, its gentle rhythm drawing them closer until they swayed as one across the floor.

"You're an excellent dancer," Honoria said, gazing into his deep blue eyes.

"Only because I have the right partner," Alex responded, smiling down at her. "By the way, did you change our flight?"

"There are two later departures; one at four and another at ten. I booked us on the four o'clock. Took care of it while you were in the shower."

"Before or after you joined me?" he asked, his voice a teasing caress.

Heat flooded her cheeks as she remembered how they'd passed the time after returning from the beach. With the condom box empty, Alex had promised he would make a stop in the hotel gift store after dinner.

"Before."

"Great. We can sleep late tomorrow and still play a round of tennis before we have to pack. We're not going back until I get a rematch."

She raised her nose in the air. "I don't see the point. I'll only beat you again."

"You think so?" He leaned in close and nuzzled her neck. "We'll see about that."

The music stopped and Alex led her from the dance floor with his palm resting possessively on her waist. They neared their table, and his hand tightened as his steps faltered.

"Um . . . maybe we have time for another dance."

"I doubt it. The waiter is opening the wine you or-dered and—" Honoria broke out in a grin as she spoke. "Oh, my gosh. It can't be—Cissy Westfall?"

Alex stopped in his tracks. What the hell were Kevin and Cissy doing at the table next to theirs? And why was that obnoxious assistant manager from the front desk fluttering around them like a demented moth?

Alex thought about steering Honoria straight out the door, but it was too late. She was already making a beeline for Cissy.

"Cissy, hello. How nice to see you here. Have you been at Club Paradise long?"

Cissy's expression seemed calm and nonthreatening. "A few days. When I heard about this place the night of the auction, I decided to check it out."

"I'm sorry I missed you, but I wasn't wearing my glasses so I didn't recognize too many people that night. I've switched to contacts, so I'm seeing things in a whole new light."

"It was obvious you were busy," Cissy said in a pleas-ant voice. "Mother and I arrived together, but I left with someone else." She threw her tablemate a sidelong glance. "Have you met Kevin Lewiston? He's just started a job with Larry's firm, Baily, Fitch and Klein." She peered up at Alex, her smile firmly in place. "Alex, how are you?"

Kevin stood and shook Honoria's hand. "I've heard a lot about you. Larry dragged me to that auction and I was impressed by what I saw of the Hewitt Academy."

Honoria and Kevin exchanged pleasantries, while Alex glared at Cissy. He felt as if he was a passenger on an ocean liner and the ship had just hit an iceberg christened with the Westfall name. He shot a frown at Kevin, then locked eyes with Junior.

"I was just explaining to Ms. Westfall and Mr. Lewiston that this is not their table, nor their seating," said the assistant manager. "I'm not at all sure they should be here."

"And I told him," began Kevin, "that the couple originally assigned here left this morning." He threw Junior a dismissive nod. "The head honcho, Mr. Mahlo, gave us this table and time, so your worries are over. Take it easy, pal."

Alex had no authority, so he had nothing to say. All he could do was cross his fingers and pray that Kevin had convinced Cissy to stay quiet. "Well then, I guess that makes it all right," he said to Junior, who was wringing his hands. "Besides, Cissy, Honoria, and I are old classmates. We have a lot in common."

One at a time, Junior gave each of them a pitying look. "I'm so sorry to have bothered you. I'll be just over there"—he waggled his fingers in the direction of the doorway—"in case anyone needs me." Throwing Alex a pointed smile, he sidled away.

Kevin shook his head. "He's a strange little guy. Gave us a hard time when we checked in, then saved our butts when he slipped me an emergency survival kit before we took that trek into the rain forest."

Honoria asked what he meant, and Kevin began to explain about the night he and Cissy spent in the cave, which gave her a reason to bring up her and Alex's night at the lagoon. While they compared notes, Alex slid his gaze to Cissy and caught her watching him through narrowed eyes. Before he could find a way to send her a signal—he wanted to get her alone and make sure she understood the deal he and Kevin had forged—the waiter served their meal.

Concentrating on her food, Honoria said, "Isn't it a coincidence that Kevin and Cissy had an adventure almost exactly like ours? I bet Mr. Mahlo was ready to expire when a second pair of guests got lost."

"Yeah, I'll bet," muttered Alex, keeping his gaze firmly on his plate.

"Is your dinner all right?" asked Honoria. "It's what you ordered, isn't it?"

He cut into his buttery soft veal with a vengeance. "It's fine. Everything is fine." Bringing the fork to his lips, he gave her a reassuring smile. "I don't plan on ordering dessert tonight, Honoria. I just want to get to the room as soon as we can. We still have to talk, remember?"

Junior dared not pop his laptop into existence. The last thing he needed was a chastising e-mail from the heavenly Doughboy, reminding him of all that was riding on the outcome of this vacation—for all four of his charges. Instead he paced the length of the entryway, lost in thought. Thanks to Mr. Mahlo, his mission was in jeopardy. He needed a brilliant idea, but his brain felt like a car with a dead battery: no juice and not a jump start in sight.

Thank goodness Alex's expression had been so determined, so unbendable, in fact, that it looked carved in stone. It was clear he was prepared to do whatever was necessary to keep Honoria from finding out the truth before she heard it from him. Honoria had a forgiving nature. She'd been averse to listening thus far, but Alex's aborted attempts should stand as a point in his favor. Her compassion for his reading problem was so all-encompassing Junior found it difficult to believe she would hold that stupid bet against him.

Still pacing, he bumped into a couple arriving late for their meal. Spinning in place, he tripped on his own feet and barely missed landing in one of the several koi ponds that decorated the magnificent foyer leading to the dining hall and restrooms. The spacious area overflowed with waterfalls, ponds, hidden alcoves, and secret niches. Each hidey-hole had its own padded bench, ideal for lovers to sit and cuddle or share an intimate moment while waiting to be seated.

Before he caught his breath, Cissy marched past him and strode into the ladies' room. Taken by surprise, Junior thought to duck into one of the alcoves and revert to Mary, his cleaning woman alter ego, so he could sneak into the lavatory and check on his charge.

But before he could take action, Alex appeared and, bold as brass, followed Cissy into the bathroom. Shocked, Junior turned invisible and popped himself into the stall next to Cissy's. Seconds passed while he heard the rustle of skirts and other usual bathroom noises, broken only by the impatient patter of Alex's wingtips beating a path on the tile floor. There was a flush, then the slide of a door clasp.

Cissy's shriek almost shattered his eardrums.

"Alex!"

Junior peered over the top of the stall door.

The young woman stared daggers at Alex. "What are you doing here?"

Alex had the good manners to look embarrassed while he spoke. "I had to talk to you privately, and this seemed to be my best shot at finding you alone."

She washed her hands and dried them on a guest towel while she spoke. "Kevin told me the two of you had words. I thought everything was taken care of?"

Without warning the door swung inward and a woman walked in. Glancing from Alex to Cissy to the sign on the door—clearly marked ladies' room—she spun on her heels and trotted out the door. Alex grabbed Cissy by an arm and dragged her into a vacant stall.

"I had to be sure." He peered through a crack in the door, then focused on Cissy. "You've never made any secret of the fact that you wanted to date me, and you've always let your dislike for Honoria show."

Junior hovered high in a corner, unable to do a thing. He thought about barring the outside door, but before he could act Honoria stepped into the room and walked quietly to the center stall.

"It's true, I've been jealous of Honoria, but Kevin helped me see the light. That's why I agreed to do as he asked and forget about the bet."

"How are you going to do that, when it was already mentioned in the *Post*?"

At the sound of Alex's voice, Honoria snapped up her head. Junior sighed. It was like watching a train wreck and being helpless to stop it.

"I plan to ignore the reporter when he calls for an update. If that doesn't work, I'll threaten to go to his editor. The Westfall name does carry a certain amount of weight in town, if you'll remember."

"And you're going to stop interfering in my life?"

"I have Kevin. There's no longer any need," Cissy said, propping herself against the side of the stall. "Do you really think you can keep that bet a secret from Honoria? All our classmates were talking about it when we left, you know. One way or another, she's going to find out you brought her here to seduce her."

Honoria's hand flew to her mouth.

"Not if I get her to listen to me. I've tried to tell her how it all came about, but for some reason she doesn't want to hear what I have to say."

Honoria hung her head. Her entire body trembled, but she didn't say a word.

"Did you ever think she might be in love with you? Oftentimes, women don't want the truth from someone they love."

"What the hell do you know about love? Kevin's going to be what, husband number three?—and you've just turned thirty."

"Don't be so glib. It took me a while to find the right man, but I'm sure he's the one. When I think back to all those years I wasted hoping it was you—"

Alex's derisive snort echoed through the washroom. "You and I never had anything in common besides money. If you can make it work with Lewiston, more power to you. Just give me the time to explain things to Honoria."

Cissy huffed out a breath. "Fine by me. Kevin and I are willing to forget about the money. I'll even call the others and tell them to do the same. If you play your cards right, she might forgive you. It's all I can do—"

"Stay out of it, Cissy. I'll send the entire hundred and twenty thousand anonymously, so that should be the end of it. But I want your word you'll tell the others I didn't get her into bed."

Tears glistened in Honoria's eyes. She fisted one hand against her mouth and pushed open the stall door with the other. Unfortunately, she ran from the bathroom without hearing the rest of their exchange.

Alex waited a beat before saying, "Do we have a deal?"

"Do you love her?"

"That's none of your business. Just make sure word gets out that she didn't sleep with me."

Cissy raised a brow. "You're telling me you're willing to throw your own reputation to the scandalmongers just to keep Honoria's standing in the community intact?"

"If that's what it takes to spare her embarrassment, yes."

"Then I guess I have the answer to my question." Her lips curved up at the corners. "We have a deal."

Junior fluttered helplessly, unable to think. Alex held open the door and Cissy walked out. He left the restroom while she fiddled with her hair and reapplied her lipstick. Torn between going after Honoria, following Alex, and staying with Cissy, he dropped to a commode and sat.

Soon he realized Cissy had left, as well.

* * *

Hands in his pockets, Alex sauntered to his table. Kevin was leaning back in his chair, sipping a glass of wine, his face wreathed in a smile.

"So did you talk to my fiancée?"

Alex held his temper in check. Kevin had kept his word. Cissy sounded sincere, first admitting she would forgive the wager, then promising she would spread the word that Honoria hadn't fallen prey to his charms. Maybe she really had lost her bitch-on-wheels attitude.

Now it was up to him to confess everything and hope for Honoria's understanding. Once she accepted that the bet was unintentional on his part, he'd give her a few days to cool off. Then he planned to begin his courtship in earnest.

"Not that it's any of your business, but I cornered her in the ladies' room. We worked things out."

Kevin raised a brow. "Must be a good-sized rest room. Are the girls still in there comparing notes?"

"Girls?" asked Alex, his stomach suddenly on a downhill slide to nowhere. "Are you talking about Honoria and Cissy?"

"What other girls are there? Honoria excused herself about five minutes after you did and said she was going to the ladies' room, too. If you and Cissy were talking inside, you should have seen her."

Cissy arrived at their table and sat down. Her expression curious, she glanced from Kevin to Alex and back again. "Why are you two so glum? I thought we'd fixed everything." She spied the empty chair across from Alex. "Where's Honoria?"

"Then you didn't run into her in the bathroom?" asked Kevin.

"Not me. Alex, did you see her?"

Standing, Alex gritted his teeth and left the building.

* * *

Honoria raced through the resort, directly to the cabana. Opening the closet, she stuffed whatever she could find of her belongings into her tote bag. She picked up a hairbrush and a lipstick, a nightgown and a pair of slacks, then tossed in the yellow sweater set she'd worn on the flight over. Tears scalded her cheeks. Her throat closed up, making it difficult to breathe, but she remembered to throw in a packet of tissues and her contact case and solution, as well as a small amount of cash and her plane ticket. Once she arrived in D.C., she would call the hotel and request they send the rest of her things.

Still dressed in her blue gown, she circled the building in order to steer clear of Alex, and followed a walkway to the front, where she asked the doorman to hail a cab. Earlier, when she'd called the airline to change their reservation, she'd been told that night's ten o'clock flight had plenty of available seats. If she hurried, she would make the plane with minutes to spare.

"To the airport, please." Honoria sniffled into a tissue as she settled in the taxi. "And hurry."

"Yes, missy," said the cabbie. Then he turned to her. "Kind of late to be flying. Where you going?"

Blinking her watery eyes, she stared at the cheerful face and wide smile. "Home. To Washington, D.C." The driver could have been Mary's twin—or Junior's. She blew her nose, then dabbed at her cheeks as the taxi pulled from the curb. "Are you related to the assistant manager at the hotel? Junior?"

"Who, me?"

The driver took a left in front of an oncoming limo and Honoria grabbed at a door handle. "Yes, you. Or maybe you know Mary, she's a cleaning woman here . . . er . . . back at Club Paradise."

"Lots of folks on this island work at the resort," the driver said with a hearty chuckle. "Is it important?"

"Not really." She gazed out the window as they whizzed

by a sign pointing the way to the airport. "Excuse me, but I think you just missed our turn."

"Who, me?"

Honoria *tsked*. The guy was starting to sound like a parrot. "I don't see anyone else driving this vehicle."

He barked out another laugh. "You're too smart for me, little missy. Now what was it you wanted to know?"

"I asked if you'd missed the turn for the airport. I thought that sign back there was our exit."

"Oh, the airport. Is that where you wanted to go?"

He grinned at her over his shoulder and she shrieked. "Look out! Watch where you're going!"

Steering the cab back into their lane, he flashed her a smile in the rearview mirror. "Sorry. My memory's a bit fuzzy these days. I'm getting too old to be driving a car."

"Then let me out, right here," she demanded, clutching the door handle again. "Because I'm too young to die."

"Hey, hey, hey. None of that now. Just give me a second to make a U-turn."

The cab bucked and jerked over the median, directly into the path of another taxi that seemed bent on slamming into them. Honoria thought her heart would stop beating before they were hit. "What are you doing!" she shouted, diving for the floor.

The dark space covered her like a comforting blanket, and she thought maybe she would stay there forever. It was certainly safer than living life in the real world, where her battered heart was exposed for all to see.

She began to cry again, softly at first, then with more fervor. She'd been such a fool, thinking a man like Alex Vandencort would ever want a date with her for real, never mind a relationship. And it figured Cissy Westfall would have a hand in the scheme. She and Cissy had never gotten along, though Honoria had no idea why.

Thanks to her mother's position in the school, she'd never fit into any group. The kids in the college prep courses thought she got good grades because of Faith, and the popular girls thought she was a geek and a snitch. She'd been as amazed as Cissy when she'd won the election for senior class president. It was the one time she felt as though she'd succeeded on her own, and Cissy had even managed to ruin that, telling everyone Faith had found a way to rig the vote count so her daughter would win.

Everything was becoming clear to her now. The glower on Alex's face when he'd arrived onstage, the surly way he'd acted when he was told they were going away for a week, his suddenly sweet and seductive attitude once he realized they would be sharing a room with a single bed.

Heck, it probably made his day when he figured out their being alone for so long would give him six additional chances to lure her into his arms. All the more time for him to con her into believing she was special. That he wanted to make love to her because he cared.

It was all a lie. A stupid bet he'd made with who knew how many of their old classmates. Another charming joke on her. But this time he hadn't tricked her into doing his assignments. He'd tricked her into falling in love.

It was then she noticed the taxi had stopped moving. Raising her head, she peered over the seat and met the driver's soulful brown eyes.

"What's the matter, little missy? You got a problem?"

She sucked down a fresh burst of tears. "N-no."

"Uh-uh-uh. Then you're just crying your heart out because you like it when your nose gets as red as Rudolph's and your face shrivels like an overripe tomato."

A smile twitched at her lips and Honoria sighed. It wasn't the driver's fault she'd allowed herself to be played for a fool. "Look, I'm in a really bad place right now, and I don't want to talk about it. If you won't take me to the airport, I'll get out and hitch a ride, so how about you just get me there and earn your fee?"

"It's man troubles, ain't it?" He shook his head as he started the cab and pulled back into traffic. "Young men these days ain't got a lick of sense when it comes to the women they love."

"Hah!" Honoria blew her nose with gusto. "Who said anything about love?"

Once again he captured her gaze in his rearview mirror. "It has to be love, otherwise I doubt you'd be carrying on so. What did the man do?"

Honoria wanted to ignore him, but she also wanted to vent. The cabbie was a stranger. Who could he tell?

"It's humiliating. He coerced me into bed so he could win a bet. Everyone back home knows what he did. I won't be able to show my face in public for months. Maybe forever."

"Hmm-hmm-hmm." He turned into the airport entrance. "And what did Al—the man say when you asked him about it?"

She gave him the name of her airline, then sidled to the other side of the cab and prepared to jump out. "He wasn't the one who told me. I overheard it when he talked with someone else."

"So you're one of them women who don't believe in everyone getting their fair say, eh? You don't think a man deserves to give his side of the story before you stomp his sorry ass?"

He stopped and she handed him his fare, plus a healthy tip. "I would never . . . Of course not."

"No need to take offense. Just think about it on your plane ride. Maybe the man has a logical explanation for what happened." He tipped his hat. "Now I suggest you hurry or you'll miss your flight."

Honoria dragged her tote out of the cab and went to the ticket counter. Thanks to sheer dumb luck, the flight still stood at the gate, waiting for passengers. She made it on board with a few minutes to spare and settled into her seat.

For the first time in her life, she wasn't in a panic about flying. She had her future to think about and decisions to make. She'd come to a crossroad in her life and wasn't about to make a mistake.

Chapter Twenty

"I don't understand exactly what it is you're showing me, Phillip," said Honoria. Her head had been swimming for a week, which was probably for the best. It had kept her mind off her aching heart. And a few other things she wasn't ready to face. But this latest find was almost too much for her to comprehend.

Phillip Cummings, the man with whom she *should* have gone to Club Paradise, shook his head. "Call it blackmail or extortion, or whatever you like, but I can only go by the evidence. I've been over it a dozen times, and if what you've told me about the school's construction and remodeling schedule is correct, there is no other conclusion."

Honoria rested her forehead in her palms. "My mother was blackmailing someone?"

"She made regular deposits for huge sums of money that match the dates and notations in her ledgers, which also match the time major improvements were done to the Hewitt Academy—none of which were paid for with tuition income or alumni donations. That money has all been accounted for under teachers' salaries, books and supplies, or taxes and utilities. The modernization of the athletic field, the resurfaced tennis courts, the re-fitted science laboratory, the new auditorium, the remodeled cafeteria, and everything else she had done took place over a ten-year period. Each upgrade happened after a sizeable entry was made in her private ledgers, and it came from someone she worked hard to protect."

The accountant walked around to her side of the desk and placed a folder on her blotter. "It was the computer wing that started the academy's present financial crisis. It was added after you received your master's degree and Faith officially hired you as vice principal. The big money had dried up six years earlier, so she emptied all her accounts to finance that improvement."

"My mother rarely socialized with people who didn't have a connection to the school. What could she have held over someone's head that would force them to give her money?"

"If you can't figure it out, we may never know, but I think the bigger question is why?" He propped a hip on the edge of her desk. "Do you have any ideas?"

Samuel Vandencort was definitely wealthy enough to have paid the exorbitant amount of money Phillip described. Alex had questioned her at Club Paradise about private meetings between her mother and his father. It was unbelievable to think Faith had been so greedy and thoughtless she would sacrifice a child's welfare for the benefit of her precious school, but it was the only answer.

Alex Vandencort had been a victim. Thanks to her selfish mother, his reading disability had been ignored and Alex had been shuffled through his education here and sent to college on the wings of the funds Faith received from Samuel Vandencort. She remembered Alex's comment about attending the same college his father had without taking the SATs. Now she knew why. Unfortunately, if she revealed her suspicions to Phillip, she'd be breaking a trust with Alex.

Even after she'd found out about that heinous wager, she wasn't able to do such a dishonorable thing. Besides, with the announcement of Cissy's engagement, everyone seemed to have forgotten about the tidbit in the *Post*. The whole affair was yesterday's news.

"What about the money we brought in from the auction? Did it help our financial situation at all?"

"It almost pulled you even. By the way, the check from the guy who topped my bid came in yesterday, but I'm still holding the anonymous bank draft for a hundred twenty thousand, like you asked. Is there some special reason you won't let me deposit it?"

When she'd first learned of the bet, Honoria told herself she would never cash the check from Alex. After she'd thought about it, she had an idea on how to spend the money but wanted to talk to him first . . . if she ever saw him again.

"Just hang on to it, Phillip. I'm aware of its source, but I can't deal with it right now. How much longer do you think it will take to get the books in order for the IRS audit?"

"I should be finished in a week, two at the outside." He stood and cleared his throat. "Um . . . Honoria. I was wondering . . . that is, if you're free . . . would you like to see a movie with me this weekend? We could have dinner first—"

She sighed as she peered at him from between her palms.

He stared at the floor. "Or not."

Of medium height, with an okay amount of wavy brown hair and kind, puppy dog eyes, Phillip wasn't overweight or skinny. He didn't have an unattractive face, or wear out of date clothes or spit while he talked, or anything else that was socially or personally unacceptable. He was a nice, average guy.

But he wasn't Alex.

Honoria had already turned down his offer of lunch

yesterday and dinner the night before. At this rate, he would simply stop asking, which might be for the best. At least until she could get her life back on track.

Phillip ignored her silence. "I realize you just returned from a fantastic vacation with a popular, wealthy guy, but give me a chance, Honoria. I'm not as boring as I look. I like to dance and go to movies. I have a few hobbies. I participate in road rallies and I enjoy sailing. Have you ever gone sailing on the Potomac?"

She muffled a laugh. Until her vacation with Alex, she hadn't done much of anything. She could never repay him for all he'd given her, and what her mother had taken away.

"I don't think so, Phillip."

His round face grew dour, but he continued to smile behind his wire-rimmed glasses. He backed toward her office door. "I understand, but if you ever change your mind . . ."

Thirty seconds later, Eloise waddled in and settled her still pregnant body into the chair across from Honoria's overladen desk. "So how does it feel to be back?"

Honoria met her turquoise blue eyes and dredged up a grin. "It feels fine. I called Rita Mae and thanked her for doing such a good job taking care of things, but you probably already knew that, huh?"

"She told me."

Honoria inhaled a breath. She'd been so caught up in dealing with the school's finances, she'd yet to say thank you for everything Eloise and her friends had done.

"I apologize if I haven't told you how grateful I am for the new clothes and the vacation . . . and everything. It was a beautiful place. You and Nathan should go there sometime soon. You deserve it."

"No, you deserved it. I'm only sorry it didn't work out exactly as planned. I take it you did have fun, at least for part of the time?"

"We—I did. And maybe when this IRS audit is sorted out, I'll tell you about it. Right now, I can't reveal what went on between Alex and me . . . to anyone."

The kindergarten teacher crossed her arms and rested them on her belly. "Have you heard from him?"

Biting her lower lip, Honoria fussed with a stack of papers Phillip had placed there for her signature. "He's tried to contact me but . . . no."

"Claire asked me if I knew why you weren't returning her brother's calls."

"I know. She phoned and quizzed me about it, too."

"So why haven't you?"

"Don't you have a class to teach?"

"In case you haven't noticed, it's lunchtime. My students are eating at their desks as we speak."

"You're not supposed to leave—"

"—them alone. It's fine, Honoria. They're with the Espinosas. Angelina is the kindergarten room mother and she's been dying to do something meaningful all year. She offered to fix the kids an authentic Mexican meal and I finally said yes. She and her husband dragged in a hot plate, frying pans, supplies—the works. I left them and fifteen five-year-olds making some kind of fancy-sounding chicken and rice dish. They're responsible for cleanup, too, so I asked Claire to bring the three of us Greek from Mr. Belgradian's deli."

"Oh, Eloise, you didn't!" Honoria looked down at her tight white blouse with its gaping buttons. She frowned. "And I'm not up to a round of questions from Claire."

"You look tired. Are you sure you didn't catch one of those rare tropical diseases?"

Picking up a pencil, she shrugged as she tapped out a nervous rhythm on the top of her desk. "About lunch today. I don't think—"

A knock on the door interrupted her. Holding up a white paper sack, Claire stuck her head around the corner. "Lunch is here."

Eloise stood. "Took you long enough. Bring it in."

"Oh, was I supposed to include Honoria? I'm sorry, I only have enough for two." She zipped out of sight, trailing laughter as she disappeared.

Grinning, Eloise hoisted herself out of the chair and stopped at the door. "Sometimes people do the right thing for the wrong reason. Whatever happens, we'll support you, Honoria, because we love you. Oh, and you're welcome to have lunch with the kindergartners."

Honoria's stomach grumbled in protest as the teacher walked out the door. Talk about cryptic comments and fair weather friends. She stood, ready to follow up on the suggestion when she heard a pair of angry male voices. Rolling her eyes, she plopped back into her seat.

Like a pair of bulls, Alex and Phillip tried to shoulder their way into her office at the same time. But Alex had three inches and about twenty pounds on the accountant and won the battle.

"I told him you were busy, but he wouldn't listen," said Phillip, his voice fraught with disapproval. "Shall I call a custodian?"

Alex tossed her a too charming smile. "Nah, don't bother. I'll take care of washing the windows and waxing the floors."

The accountant sniffed. "I meant, if Honoria wanted you thrown out."

"It's all right, Phillip. I'll handle—"

"I'm afraid it will take more than *one* janitor to remove me from the premises, fella. Unless you want to join him."

Honoria rounded the desk and walked to the door. "I'll be perfectly safe. Please go back to your job, ok?" Phillip began to babble and she closed the door in his face, then leaned her backside against it.

Dressed in a gray suit, blindingly white shirt, and red tie, Alex looked as if he'd stepped straight from the pages of *GQ*. His brilliant blue eyes and tan complexion were heightened by his little boy grin.

The sight of him put her in panic mode. She'd wished him here with her whole heart and soul every second of every day since her return. Now that her wish had been granted, she only hoped something good would happen.

Steeling herself, she raised a brow. "What do you want?"

"To talk to you." He circled her desk and sat in her chair. "You didn't answer my phone calls, you refused the flowers I sent, and the jewelry store informed me that you'd returned the bracelet I asked them to deliver. I figured the only way to get you to listen was to corner you here, in your home away from home."

Honoria sighed as she walked to the chair vacated by Eloise and sat down. She'd really liked the diamond bracelet, but she was not her mother. She had principles. "I heard everything I needed to in that ladies' room."

Leaning back, he had the nerve to smile. "Eavesdropping in a bathroom. How very unladylike of you. What would Faith say?"

The barb was a direct hit to her heart, for so many reasons. "Let's leave my mother out of this, shall we? I think she's done enough harm to last us both a lifetime."

Alex narrowed his gaze. "Then you know what she and my father did?"

"What your father did? What are you talking about?"

His expression turned serious. Resting his elbows on the desk, Alex held his head in his hands and furrowed his fingers through his hair. Then he gazed up at her. "Nothing. I don't know what I'm doing here. I shouldn't have come."

He stood and headed for the door, but Honoria got

there first, blocking his escape. "Oh, no you don't. Now that you're here, you're not leaving until you tell me why you came."

He stuffed his hands in his pockets. "I'm here because I was hoping I could convince you to forgive me. I want things to be the way they were between us at Club Paradise. I've missed you. What else do you want from me, Honoria?"

"Oh, Alex. All I ever wanted was the truth."

He rolled his eyes to the ceiling. "Whatever I say is going to sound childish."

"Let me be the judge."

He began to pace. "It started because Cissy got some ridiculous idea in her peanut-sized brain that I was a lady-killer. She was pissed because, according to her, I'd taken dozens of women to bed and none of them were her."

"Is that the truth?" she demanded.

"You think I'd have the bad taste to actually sleep with that she-witch?"

Honoria bit back a grin. "Just checking." She glided to her desk and took her rightful seat. "Continue."

"She made a bet the night of the auction. Claimed there had to be one woman in D.C. I hadn't slept with, and never could. You walked onto that stage at almost the exact moment looking like a million bucks and—"

"Thank you."

His lips twitched, as if he was thinking about smiling. "To make a long story short, you were chosen. Something about some old rhyme from high school, Honoria Hewitt, she—"

"Won't do it." Honoria grimaced. "Believe me, I'm well acquainted with the childish taunt. Go on."

"When I heard the outrageous amount of money they all agreed on, I jumped up and repeated it at the top of my lungs."

"Twenty thousand dollars." She recalled clearly her feelings of surprise and delight. "Was I worth it?"

He stopped pacing and set his hands flat on her desktop. Bending forward, he pinned her with a no-nonsense stare. "You're worth a thousand times more than the amount of the bet, Honoria, for a dozen reasons."

"Okay," she said, suddenly feeling giddy. This was going better than she'd hoped. So far.

"I thought it would just be a date or two. I'd insist I hadn't accepted the bet in the first place, and that would be the end of it. Then I found out we were leaving the country and I saw red. I was angry and thought to do the deed. I was attracted to you and got the impression you felt the same, so who would it hurt? You'd get the money for the school, Cissy would be put in her place, and it would be over. Until—"

"Until what?"

"Until I got to know you." He squared his shoulders when she raised a brow. "At first I'll admit I was afraid my reputation would be damaged if I didn't sleep with you. I'm not making excuses, but I've lived off my charm and good looks my entire life. My job, hell, the company required it. At least that's what my dad kept telling me, when he wasn't berating me for being stupid."

Her heart wept when she caught the pain flaring in his eyes. "You're not—"

"Then I discovered the real you, and I couldn't go through with it. You were different from the women I usually dated, just like you'd been different in school. Friendly, a little shy, but not afraid to speak your mind or make a joke, and a heck of a good sport. I figured I'd lie when I got home, but then I realized that wouldn't work. Cissy had already dragged Kevin Lewiston down there to spy on us; I knew she'd do anything to see this thing through. Luckily, Kevin was on our side."

"Do you know they're engaged? I got an invitation to

the party, some big blowout at a country club in Chevy Chase."

"I got one, too." He waggled his eyebrows. "Want to go together?"

"That remains to be seen. Now continue."

"God, I love it when you make like a teacher. All prim and proper on the outside, so wild and—"

Heat blossomed in her face and she held up a hand. "Stop it, right now, and finish your explanation before I toss you out of here."

"Yes, ma'am." His mouth hitched into a grin. "When you read that gossip item to me, I knew I was in trouble. I tried to tell you about the bet several times and you—"

"Wouldn't listen. I remember. And I'm sorry." She was sorry for so many things, even though she'd had nothing to do with them. "I understand about the bet, Alex."

He opened and closed his mouth. "You do?"

"I'm not happy about it, but I've given it a lot of thought. You did tell me we had to talk, and I blew you off. Besides, I know you. When I calmed down, I figured it out. Under that oh-so-charming façade there's a nice guy just waiting to be set free."

He exhaled a breath. "I was willing to use you, Honoria, to keep up the charade—"

She smiled. "Thinking isn't doing, and that leads us to our next hurdle. Your father, my mother, and a little matter of money."

"Oh, that."

"Yes, that. My mother is dead, so I can only imagine the part she played in the mess, but your father is still here. Is there some way you can ask him what went on?"

He shrugged. "I already did, this morning."

"And what did he say?"

"That he paid your mother to keep quiet about my dyslexia and make sure I passed through school. Said he did it for my own good, didn't want me to be embarrassed, but I know better. He didn't want anyone to know he had a less-than-perfect son." He swiped a hand across his eyes. "He was ashamed of me."

Honoria forced herself to stay in her chair, when all she wanted was to run to Alex and hold him in her arms. "My mother deserves half the blame. She used you to get money for the improvements she made here. According to records Phillip unearthed, Samuel Vandencort paid for the auditorium, the stadium, the cafeteria, the football field—the list is endless. I figure if we add it all up, he owns half the school by now."

"Quite a dynamic duo, our parents."

Honoria crossed mental fingers. "Any idea how we can make it right?"

His blue eyes pensive, he folded his arms. "After everything that's happened, do you think it's possible?"

Brimming with hope, she stood and met his gaze. "I've thought about it for a week now, and I'm sure we can find a way to make it right. If you want to try."

He walked to her side of the desk and enfolded her in his arms. "I was hoping you'd say that."

She turned and bumped into his chest. Before she realized it, he was sitting in her chair and she was on his lap. He kissed her, gently at first, then with intensity. Breathless, she drew back and gazed into his eyes. And what she saw there made her heart stop.

"There's something else I didn't tell you. I quit the firm today." He sounded proud and happy and strangely at peace. "I'm officially a free agent."

"You quit your job? But—but why?"

"Because I promised someone I love that I would take on her school as a client. It's going to use up most of my time."

Honoria brushed away a tear. "Say that again."

"I'm taking on a private client—"

"Not that part. The first part."

"Ah, the first part. I was wondering when we'd get

around to that." He kissed her nose. "I love you, Honoria. More than I ever thought it was possible to love another person. When you refused my peace offerings, I figured I'd better come to you on my hands and knees. If you rejected me, I'd just keep crawling back until I died or I broke you down."

She relaxed in his arms, at home for the first time in her life. "I don't need flowers of jewelry as proof of your feelings, Alex, and I didn't want you to crawl." She giggled. "Well, maybe just a little."

He chuckled deep in his chest. "Sadist."

She sighed with happiness. "I love you, too. Very much. You're not anything like the man you think you are. And for that, I love you even more."

He kissed her again and Honoria thought she could stay in his arms forever. But they had to face reality.

"What about your father?"

"My father? What does he have to do with the way we feel?"

"He must have hated my mother. And the money he spent here—"

"Went to a good cause. It didn't just help me—it helped every kid who ever walked the halls of the Hewitt Academy. What would you have done without the new auditorium, athletic field, or cafeteria? Besides, he probably figured a way to make it a tax write-off. He's a crafty sonofabitch."

"He's still your father," she said, cuddling into his side. "He's not going to be happy that you and I are together." Drawing back, she raised her head. "We are together, aren't we?"

Alex's smile stretched from ear to ear. "Definitely. I plan to make you and this school my life's work. In fact"—he fumbled in his jacket pocket and brought out a small velvet box—"I bought you something. It's the one gift I hope you don't send back."

Honoria let out a squeal of delight when she snapped

open the box and spied an oval diamond in a beautiful raised setting.

"Is this a proposal?" she asked as he slipped the ring on her finger.

"It's more of a request. I want you to be my doubles partner, now and for the rest of our lives. I can't see myself playing the game with anyone but you."

She giggled. "Why, Mr. Charming, how romantic."

He cupped her jaw in his hand. "I mean it, Honoria, you've become my whole world. When you left me alone on the island, I thought my life was over. I was sure you'd never forgive me, and I didn't want to go on. I walked to the tennis courts and returned balls until my hand bled, I was that lost and afraid."

She grabbed his hand and kissed the bandage she hadn't noticed before. "I'm sorry. When I overheard you and Cissy, I couldn't see straight. I had to leave."

"I know. Junior told me where you went."

"Junior?"

"He said he was pretty sure you'd taken a cab to the airport. He also told me you were a smart woman. Eventually you'd figure out we belong together—I just had to be patient. It only took me a few minutes to realize he was right. You understood about the dyslexia, you'd understand about the bet, once I was able to explain. I bought this ring my first day back in town, with the optimistic idea you would marry me."

"I guess we owe Junior a thank you." She relaxed against his chest. "Where do we go from here?"

"My place. There's something I want to show you." He stood and led her out the door.

Alex lay in bed with Honoria in his arms. He'd never thought his life would be as perfect as it was at this moment. She nestled closer and ran her foot down his calf, resting it over the length of his leg. Pressing his lips to her brow, he felt her softness and exhaled a sigh of contentment.

"You awake?" he asked, hoping she was rested enough for another bout of lovemaking.

"No."

Pulling her closer, he thought about his sister Claire and how eager she'd been to make that lunch date with Eloise, then check and see if Honoria was in her office. If Honoria hadn't said yes to his proposal, he would have carried her here, kicking and screaming. Even if he had to drop that accountant to his knees to do so.

The lunch he'd had catered was waiting for them, with strawberries and champagne for dessert. They'd taken the meal to the third floor master suite and eaten it after they'd made love. Then he'd given her a tour of the house and master bath, where they'd explored the many facets of his oversized tub. Honoria said she approved of his house, which was good, because he was moving her in as soon as possible.

They'd talked and laughed and planned, just as he hoped they would. He didn't want to rush her, but now that he knew what he had to do, he didn't want to waste another moment of his life stuck in his old world. A world without Honoria.

She stretched beside him and he smiled. "I hope you're ready to wake up," he warned. "Because you're missing the last item on my list of things I wanted you to see."

"You mean there's more?"

"Something special. Roll on your back and open your eyes."

Grumbling good-naturedly, she did as he asked. Focusing on the ceiling, she blinked in wonder. "Oh, Alex. It's beautiful. I can't believe I didn't notice it earlier."

"You were busy earlier," he said, staring at the skylight. "After I converted the third floor to my private quarters, it was the first thing I installed. On really cold or stormy nights, I don't have to climb onto the roof. I can lie in bed and look directly at the stars."

"It's like being outside under the open sky. I can see why you put it in." She settled into his side. "Alex, you should know that I made you an appointment with a specialist. She's coming to the academy next Tuesday to meet with the two of us."

"Us?"

"She's going to test you, if you're ready, and recommend a few avenues for taking care of your dyslexia. I'll be your tutor, and this time I'm going to do it right."

"Ok."

"There's something else."

"I figured that by the tone in your voice." He rolled to face her. "What else do I have to do?"

"It's not you, it's us. And it has to do with that one hundred twenty thousand dollars."

"Uh-huh."

"I've been doing research on a variety of reading disabilities. There are quite a few different types and a lot of ways to treat them. I want to use the money to buy some equipment and programs for the computer science center, so it can be used after school to help children who have special needs."

"Sounds good to me."

"And I want you to run it."

Alex huffed out a breath. "Aren't you forgetting something? I'm the one with the problem."

"I can't do it by myself. I want to hire an assistant, too, and I suspect Eloise's mother-in-law would be willing. Then you can handle the fund-raising and oversee the new lab, and I'll have more time for . . . other things."

"Other things?"

"You know, marriage, our home . . . a family."

"Oh, those other things." He turned on his back and gazed at the stars shining down through the skylight. "If you put it that way—"

"You do want children, don't you?"

"I never gave it much thought, my own childhood being so miserable and all, but with you, yes, I definitely want kids. I think that between us we have a pretty good idea of what *not* to do. We can work it out."

"That's good, because . . ."

"Because?"

"Oh, just because." Honoria settled beside him and watched the stars. "Tell me their names again. What's that cluster in the right corner called?"

Alex smiled, too happy to think straight. Right now, when he gazed into the heavens, he didn't see a single star. Just angels—hundreds and hundreds of angels, shining down on him and Honoria and the life they were going to build.

Together.

Epilogue

"Quite a turnout for a Christmas wedding, wouldn't you agree?" Milton turned to Junior. "You're to be commended. You took a risk allowing Honoria to fly home and leave Alex on the island by himself."

Junior beamed in silence. Coming from the Doughboy, the complimentary statement was tantamount to a human receiving an academy award or the Purple Heart. In those last few minutes when he'd been driving Honoria to the airport, he had bet everything he'd learned about his charges on the outcome. He'd counted on Honoria's strength of character and sense of honor, and Alex's determination and integrity, to bring them together and lead them to the only sensible conclusion.

Love had found the way.

He gazed down from his position in the choir loft. The church was filled to bursting. Students, parents, friends of both the bride and groom, had come to share in the glorious occasion. Alex and his best man waited at the altar, resplendent in black formal wear. Organ music sounded, and Phoebe Marie Baxter walked slowly down the aisle, dropping rose petals and grinning from ear to ear. A few seconds passed. Then a still pregnant Eloise followed her stepdaughter into the church.

"Ah, yes," Milton mumbled to himself. "Eloise and Nathan are going to be in for a big surprise tonight, when little Chloe Mae Baxter enters the world at the stroke of midnight."

"Tonight?" Junior said. "Wow. Can I be there? I've never seen the birth of a human baby."

Milton nodded as he pursed his lips. "You had better be there. Chloe is going to be the first of your legitimate charges. Not a soul you've inherited, my boy, but a soul of your very own."

Junior blinked. "You mean I've made it? I'm a true guiding angel? You're giving me my promotion?"

"Of course We are," said Milton. "I never doubted you would succeed. Did you?"

Junior thrust his thumb into his chest. "Who me? Nu-uh. I always knew I'd—"

"Ahem."

"Well, I did have a teeny tiny twinge of doubt, but only once or twice. These humans are stubborn. Hard to change their minds when they get an idea, especially if it's a negative one."

"Yes, well, I knew you'd see to things."

The organ music rose to a crescendo. Alex stood tall, his eyes shining as he watched his wife-to-be make her way to his side. Honoria passed below the choir loft, and Junior and Milton both hung upside down in order to experience the full impact of her radiance and her joy. Dressed in a form-fitting and stylish ivory gown, she walked proudly to Alex's side.

"Does Alex know yet?" asked Milton, still hanging on to the railing.

"You mean about the baby?" Junior righted himself. "Not yet. Honoria wants it to be her wedding gift to him. He is going to be one shocked fella."

"Oh, I don't know," said Milton, doing a bit of gymnastics to hoist himself upright into the loft. "He's got excellent instincts, especially where Honoria is concerned. He's noticed a few changes in her since Club Paradise, and he's been wondering. They're going to make the best parents a child could hope for."

The two angels watched in companionable silence while Honoria and Alex exchanged vows, then kissed and paraded from the church. Junior sighed at the sight of Honoria, so happy and glowing. Alex seemed to glow as well, as if imbued with newfound strength and courage.

The bridal party and guests were heading to the Hewitt-Vandencort Academy. It was a beautiful, sunny day, perfect for a reception in the auditorium, and would be over early enough for everyone to be home snug in their beds on Christmas eve. All except for Nathan and Eloise, of course.

"So," said Junior. "Is this it? Am I official?"

Milton finally broke into a grin. "There is a small but significant ceremony involved." He cleared his throat. Snapping his fingers, he brought into existence a round gold ball the size of an apple.

"Junior, angel of the most high, your polar ice cap guarding days are over. As of this moment, you are a guiding angel of the first order, and as such are charged with the care of the Lord's most important work: The caretaking of human souls."

Milton tossed the shining ball and a glitter of golden dust showered both of them. Junior rocked on his heels as he thumbed his suspenders. Milton raised his bushy eyebrows and they disappeared in the blink of an eye, leaving behind nothing but an aura of hope and peace.

About the Author

Judi McCoy has been writing romance for nine years. Her first book, *I Dream of You*, won Waldenbook's Debut Romance of 2001. Since then her novels have consistently garnered four-star reviews from *Romantic Times* and numerous online review sites. She belongs to RWA, CRW, NTRW, NJRW, RWI of Tulsa, WRW, MRW, and the Greater Dallas Writers Association. In her spare time, she judges women's gymnastics, a career she's had for over twenty five years. She currently resides on Virginia's eastern shore with her husband and two small dogs, where she is busy growing orchids and writing her next novel.